THE HORUS HERESY

James Swallow

THE FLIGHT OF THE EISENSTEIN

The heresy unfolds

*With thanks to Lindsey Priestley, Marc Gascoigne,
Alan Merrett, Steve Horvath, John Gravato, Matt Farrer and
the GW Bromley crew, and especially to Dan, Graham and
Ben for lighting the way.*

A BLACK LIBRARY PUBLICATION

First published in Great Britain in 2007 by
BL Publishing,
Games Workshop Ltd.,
Willow Road, Nottingham, NG7 2WS, UK.

10 9 8 7 6 5 4 3 2 1

Cover illustration by Neil Roberts.

First page illustration by Neil Roberts.

A CIP record for this book is available from the British Library.

ISBN 13: 978-1-84416-459-2
ISBN 10: 1-84416-459-4

Distributed in the US by Simon & Schuster
1230 Avenue of the Americas, New York, NY 10020, US.

See the Black Library on the Internet at
www.blacklibrary.com

Find out more about Games Workshop
and the world of Warhammer 40,000 at
www.games-workshop.com

THE HORUS HERESY

It is a time of legend.

Mighty heroes battle for the right to rule the galaxy.
The vast armies of the Emperor of Earth have conquered
the galaxy in a Great Crusade – the myriad alien races have
been smashed by the Emperor's elite warriors and wiped
from the face of history.

The dawn of a new age of supremacy for humanity
beckons.

Gleaming citadels of marble and gold celebrate the many
victories of the Emperor. Triumphs are raised on a million
worlds to record the epic deeds of his most powerful and
deadly warriors.

First and foremost amongst these are the primarchs,
superheroic beings who have led the Emperor's armies of
Space Marines in victory after victory. They are unstoppable
and magnificent, the pinnacle of the Emperor's genetic
experimentation. The Space Marines are the mightiest
human warriors the galaxy has ever known, each capable of
besting a hundred normal men or more in combat.

Organised into vast armies of tens of thousands called
Legions, the Space Marines and their primarch leaders
conquer the galaxy in the name of the Emperor.

Chief amongst the primarchs is Horus, called the
Glorious, the Brightest Star, favourite of the Emperor, and
like a son unto him. He is the Warmaster, the commander-
in-chief of the Emperor's military might, subjugator of a
thousand, thousand worlds and conqueror of the galaxy. He
is a warrior without peer, a diplomat supreme, and his
ambition knows no bounds.

The stage has been set.

~ DRAMATIS PERSONAE ~

The Primarchs

HORUS	Warmaster and Commander of the Sons of Horus Legion
ROGAL DORN	Primarch of the Imperial Fists
MORTARION	Primarch of the Death Guard

The Death Guard

NATHANIEL GARRO	Battle-Captain of the 7th Company
IGNATIUS GRULGOR	Commander of the 2nd Company
CALAS TYPHON	First Captain
ULLIS TEMETER	Captain of the 4th Company
ANDUS HAKUR	Veteran Sergeant, 7th Company
MERIC VOYEN	Apothecary, 7th Company
TOLLEN SENDEK	7th Company
PYR RAHL	7th Company
SOLUN DECIUS	7th Company
KALEB ARIN	Housecarl to Captain Garro

Other Space Marines

SAUL TARVITZ	First Captain of the Emperor's Children
IACTON QRUZE, 'THE HALF-HEARD'	Captain, 3rd Company, Sons of Horus
SIGISMUND	First Captain, Imperial Fists

Non-Astartes Imperials

MALOGHURST 'THE TWISTED'	Equerry to the Warmaster
AMENDERA KENDEL	Oblivion Knight, Storm Dagger Witchseeker Squad
MALCADOR	The Sigillite, Regent of Terra
KYRIL SINDERMANN	Primary iterator
MERSADIE OLITON	Remembrancer, documentarist
EUPHRATI KEELER	'The New Saint'; remembrancer
BARYK CARYA	Shipmaster of the frigate *Eisenstein*
RACEL VOUGHT	Executive officer of the frigate *Eisenstein*
TIRIN MAAS	Vox officer of the frigate *Eisenstein*

PART ONE
THE
BLINDED STAR

'If the sole trait these Astartes share in common with we mere mortal masses is their bond of brotherhood, then one must dare to ask the question – if that were lost to them, what would they become?'

   – attributed to the remembrancer Ignace Karkasy

'We are the voice and the clarion call;
 We are tyrant's ruin and rival's fall.'

   – from the battle mantra of the Dusk Raiders

'As with men so it is with silk; it is difficult to change their colours once they have been set.'

   – attributed to the ancient Terran warlord Mo Zi

ONE

Assembly
A Fine Sword
Death Lord

IN THE VOID, the vessels gathered. Shifting gently in the silent darkness, the crenellated hulls and great ornate shapes appeared as a congregation of Gothic edifices, cathedral-wrought in their complexity, drifting as if torn from the surface of worlds and carved into warships. Great sculpted bows filigreed into arrow points turned, stately and lethal, to face into the dark on a uniform heading. Torches burned on some, in apparent defiance of the airless vacuum. Plasma fires trailed white-orange streams of turbulent gas from chimneys along the kilometres of gunmetal hulls. These beacons were lit only when conflict was in the moment. The flares of wasteful, daring heat they generated were signs to the enemy.

We bring the light of illumination to you.

The craft that rode at the head of the flotilla was cut from steel the shade of a stormy sky, with a prow sheathed in dark ocean green. It moved as a slow dagger might in the hand of a patient killer, inescapable, inexorable. It bore little in the way of ornament. The ship's only decorations were martial in nature, etchings on the plough-blade bow in letters the height of a man, long lines of text that recalled an age of battles fought, worlds visited, opponents lain to wreckage. Her only adornments of any note were two-fold: a golden spread eagle with two heads across the face of the flying bridge and a great icon made of heavy nickel-iron ore, a single stone skull set inside a hollow steel ring in the shape of a star, at the very lip of the spiked blade, watchful and threatening.

More ships fell into line behind her, taking up a formation that mirrored the spear tip battle-patterns of the warriors that were her payload. In echo of the unbreakable resolve of those fighters, the warship proudly bore a name in High Gothic script across her iron hull: *Endurance*.

Behind her came more of her kind, ranging in class and size both larger and smaller: the *Indomitable Will*, *Barbarus's Sting*, *Lord of Hyrus*, *Terminus Est*, *Undying*, *Spectre of Death* and others.

This was the fleet that gathered beyond the umbra of the sun Iota Horologii, in order to bring the Great Crusade and the will of the Emperor of Man to one of the gargantuan cylinder worlds of the jorgall. Carried in their thousands aboard the ships that served their Legion, the instruments of that will were to be the Astartes of the XIV Legion, the Death Guard.

KALEB ARIN MOVED through the corridors of the *Endurance* in a swift dance of motion, holding his heavy cloth-wrapped burden to his chest. Years of indentured service had bred in him a way of walking and behaving that rendered him virtually hidden in plain sight around the towering forms of the Astartes. He was adept at remaining beneath their notice. To this day, even with so many years of duty glittering in the dull rivets fixed to his collarbone, Kaleb had not lost the keen awe at being among them that had filled him from the moment he had bent his knee to the XIV Legion. The lines on his pale face and the grey-white of his hair showed his age, but still he carried himself with the vitality of a man much younger. The strength of his conviction – and of other, more privately held ones – had carried him on in willing, unflinching servitude.

There were few men in the galaxy, he reflected, who could be as content as he was. The truth that never left him was as clear to him now as it had been decades ago, when he had stood beneath a weeping sky of toxic storm clouds and accepted his own limitations, his own failures. Those who continued to strive for what they could never reach, those who punished themselves for falling short of the dizzy heights they would never reach, they were the souls who had no peace in their lives. Kaleb was not like them. Kaleb understood his place in the scheme of things. He knew where he was supposed to be and what it was he was supposed to be doing. His place was here, now, not to question, not to strive, only to *do*.

Still, he felt pride at that. What men, he wondered, could hope to walk where he walked, among demi-gods cut from the flesh of the Emperor Himself? The housecarl never ceased to marvel at them. He kept to the edges of the corridors, skirting the broad warriors as they went about their preparations for the engagement.

The Astartes were statues come to life, great myths in stone that had stepped off their plinths to stride about him. They walked in their marble-coloured armour with green trim and gold flashing, some in the newer, smoother models of the wargear, others in the older iterations that were adorned with spiked studs and heavy-browed helms. These were impossible men, the living hands of the Imperium going to their deeds with shock and awe trailing around them like a cloak. They would never understand the manner in which mortal men looked upon them.

In his indenture, Kaleb knew that some among the Legion considered him with disrespect, as an irritant at best, worth no more than a drooling servitor at worst. This he accepted as his lot, with the same stoic character and dogged acceptance that was the way of the Death Guard. He would never fool himself into thinking that he was one of them – that chance had been offered to Kaleb and he had fallen short in the face of it – but he knew in his heart that he lived by the same code they did, and that his meagre, human frame would die for those ideals if it would serve the Imperium. Kaleb Arin, failed aspirant, housecarl and captain's equerry, was as satisfied with his life as any man could hope to be.

His load was awkward in its wrapping and he shifted it, cradling the object in a diagonal embrace across his chest. Not once had he dared to let it touch the deck or pass too close to an obstacle. It filled him with honour just to hold it, even through a thick cowl of forest green velvet. He found his way forward and up via the twisting and circuitous corridors, over the access ways that crossed the reeking, thunderous industry of the gun decks. He emerged on the upper tiers where the common naval crew were not allowed to venture, into the portions of the ship that were allotted exclusively to the Astartes. Should she wish to, even *Endurance*'s captain would need to seek the permission of the ranking Death Guard to walk these halls.

Kaleb felt a ripple of satisfaction, and unconsciously ran a hand over his robes and the skull-shaped clasp at his collar. The device was as big as his palm and made from some kind of pewter. The mechanisms within it were as good as a certified passage paper to the machine-eyes and remote scrying systems on the ship. It was, after a fashion, his badge of office. Kaleb imagined that the sigil was as old as the warship, perhaps even as old as the Legion itself. It had been used by hundreds of serfs, who had died in service to the same role he now fulfilled, and he imagined it would outlast him as well.

Or perhaps not. The old ways were fading, and there were few among the senior battle-brothers of the Death Guard who deigned to keep the careworn traditions of the Legion alive. Times, and the Astartes, were changing. Kaleb had seen things alter, thanks to the juvenat treatments that had extended his life and given him a fragment of the longevity of his masters. Forever close to the Astartes, but still held at a distance from them, he had seen the slow shifting of mood. It had begun in the months following the Emperor's decision to retire from the Great Crusade, from the time that he had bestowed the honour of Warmaster upon the noble primarch Horus. It continued still, all around him in silent motion, shifting slow and cold like glacial ice, and in his darker moments, Kaleb found himself wondering where the new and emerging way of things would take him and his beloved Legion.

The housecarl's face soured and he shook off the sudden attack of melancholy with a grimace. This was not the time to dwell on ephemeral futures and anxious worries of what might come to pass. It was the eve of a battle that would once again enforce humanity's right to stride the stars unfettered and unafraid.

As he approached the armoury chamber, he glanced out of a reinforced porthole and saw stars. Kaleb wondered which one was the jorgall colony world, and if the xenos had any inkling of the storm about to break upon them.

NATHANIEL GARRO RAISED Libertas to his eye line and sighted along the length of the blade. The heavy, dense metal of the sword shimmered in the chamber's blue light, a wave of rainbow reflections racing away from him along the edge as he tilted it down. There were no imperfections visible in the crystalline matrix of the monosteel. Garro didn't look back at his housecarl, where the man waited in a half bow. 'This is good work.' He gestured for the man to stand. 'I'm pleased.'

Kaleb gathered the velvet cloth in his hands. 'It's my understanding that the servitor who attended your weapon was a machine-smith or a blade maker in its previous life. Some elements of its original artistry must remain.'

'Just so.' Garro gave Libertas a few practice swings, moving swiftly and easily in the confines of his Mark IV power armour. He let the smallest hint of a smile creep out across his gaunt face. The nicks that the blade had suffered during the Legion's pacification of the Carinea moons had troubled him, the result of a single mis-blow on his part that cut through an iron pillar instead of flesh. It was good to have his favourite weapon in his hands once more. The substantial mass of the broadsword completed him, and the idea of venturing into combat without it had troubled Garro on some level. He would not allow himself to voice words like 'luck' and 'fate' except in mocking humour, and yet without Libertas in his scabbard he had to confess he felt somehow… less protected.

The Astartes caught sight of his own reflection in the polished metal: old eyes in a face that, despite its oft weary countenance, seemed too young for them; a head, hairless and patterned with pale scars. A patrician aspect, showing its roots from the warrior dynasties of ancient Terra, pale-skinned, but without the pallidity of his brother Death Guard who hailed from cold and lethal Barbarus. Garro brought the blade up in salute, and slid Libertas back into the scabbard on his belt.

He glanced at Kaleb. 'It predates even me, did you know that? So I have been told, some elements of the weapon were fabricated on Old Earth before the Age of Strife.'

The housecarl nodded. 'Then, master, I would say it is fitting that a Terran-born son wields it now.'

'All that matters is that it turns in the Emperor's service,' Garro replied, clasping his gauntlets together.

Kaleb opened his mouth to respond, but then a motion at the chamber door caught his eye and immediately Garro's housecarl sank again into an obeisant bow.

'Such a fine sword,' came a voice and the Astartes turned to watch the approach of a pair of his brethren. As the figures came closer, he resisted the urge to smile wryly.

'A pity,' the speaker continued, 'that it cannot be placed in the care of a younger, more vigorous warrior.'

Garro eyed the man who had spoken. In the fashion of many of the Death Guard's number, the new arrival's scalp was shaven, but unlike the majority he sported a tail of hair at the back of his head, in black and grey streaks that dangled to his shoulders. His face was craggy and broken, but the eyes set there had sardonic wit in them.

'The folly of youth,' Garro replied, without weight. 'Are you sure you could lift it, Temeter? Perhaps you might need old Hakur there to help you.' He gestured to the second man, a wiry figure with thin features and a single augmetic eye.

Rough humour emerged in a scattering of dry laughter. 'Forgive me, captain,' replied Temeter, 'I only thought to exchange it for something that would better suit you... say, a walking stick?'

Garro made an exaggerated show of thinking over the other man's proposal. 'Perhaps you are right, but how could I hand my sword to someone whose breath still smells of his mother's milk?'

The laughter echoed through the chamber and Temeter raised his hands in mock defeat. 'I have no recourse but to bow before our great battle-captain's age and venerable experience.'

Garro stepped forward and clasped the other man's armoured gauntlet in a firm grip. 'Ullis Temeter, you war dog. You only have a few years less than me on your clock!'

'Yes, but they make all the difference. Anyway, it's not about the years, it's the quality that counts.'

At Temeter's side, the other Death Guard kept a dour face. 'Then I'd venture Captain Temeter is sadly lacking.'

'Don't give him any support, Andus,' replied Temeter. 'Nathaniel has enough barbs without you helping him!'

'Merely assisting the commander of my company, as any good sergeant should,' said the veteran with a nod. Someone who did not know Andus Hakur as well as his captain did might have thought the veteran's insulting turn against Temeter to be honest, and indeed Garro heard a sharp intake of breath from his housecarl at the words; but then Hakur's manner was dry to the point of aridity.

For his part, Captain Temeter laughed off the comment. Both he and Garro had served with the older warrior in the years before they had risen to lead their respective companies. It was a point of mild dispute between them that Garro had persuaded the old Astartes to join his command squad over Temeter's.

Garro returned Hakur's nod and drew Temeter aside. 'I hadn't expected to see you until after the assembly on the *Terminus Est*. That's why I was here.' He patted the sword's pommel. 'I didn't want to step aboard Typhon's warship without this.'

Temeter flicked a questioning glance at the housecarl, then smiled slightly. 'Aye, that's not a vessel to be unprotected aboard, is it? So, then, I take it you haven't heard the news?'

Garro gave his old comrade a sideways look. 'What news, Ullis? Come on, don't play to the drama of it, speak.'

Temeter lowered his voice. 'The esteemed master of the First Great Company, Captain Calas Typhon, has stepped down from command of the jorgall assault. Someone else is going to lead us.'

'Who?' Garro insisted. 'Typhon wouldn't stand down for any Astartes. His pride would never allow it.'

'You're not wrong,' continued Temeter, 'he wouldn't stand down for any Astartes.'

The sudden realisation hit Garro like a wash of ice. 'Then, you mean…'

'The primarch is *here*, Nathaniel. Mortarion himself has decided to take part in this engagement. He's brought the timetable forward.'

'The primarch?' The words slipped out of Kaleb's mouth in a whisper, trepidation and awe in every syllable.

Temeter gave him a look, as if he were noticing Garro's helot for the first time. 'Indeed, little man. He walks the decks of *Endurance* as I speak.'

Kaleb dropped to his knees and made the sign of the aquila, his hands visibly trembling.

In spite of himself, his master's throat went dry. Until Temeter's announcement, Garro, like the majority of his Legion, had believed that the gaunt leader of the Death Guard was engaged elsewhere, on a mission of some import for the Warmaster himself. This sudden and secretive arrival left him reeling. To know that Mortarion would ride at their spear tip against the jorgall, he felt a mixture of elation and disquiet. 'When are we to assemble?' he asked, finding his voice.

Temeter smiled broadly. He was enjoying the normally stoic Garro's moment of discomfort with mild glee. 'Right now, old friend. I'm here to summon you to the conclave.' He leaned in closer, his words hushed and conspiratorial. 'And I should warn you, the primarch's brought some interesting company with him.'

THE ASSEMBLY HALL was an unremarkable space. It was nothing more than a void in the *Endurance*'s forward hull, rectangular in aspect, open at the far end to the stars through two oval panes of armoured glass holding out the killing vacuum. There were louvred shutters half-closed across the windows, casting patterns of dim white light in bars where the glow from a nearby nebula reached the vessel.

The ceiling was an arch, formed from the primary spars of the warship's iron ribcage where they met and meshed in steel riveted plate. There were no chairs or places where one might rest. There was no use for them. This was not a hall in which lengthy debate and plots would be hatched, but a place where blunt orders would be given, directives made and battle plans drawn in swift order. The only adornments were a few combat banners hanging down from the metal beams.

The room was littered with shadows. Alcoves formed from the spaces between the girder ribs went deep and ink-black. Illumination fell in pools, tuned to the same yellow-white of high sun on Barbarus. In the centre of the chamber, a hololithic tank turned on a lazy axis, a ghostly cube of blue drifting there. Mechanicum adepts ticked and skittered around the disc-shaped projector device below it, moving in orbits around each other, but never straying more than a hand's length away. Perhaps, Garro mused, they were afraid to venture out among the assembled warriors.

The battle-captain cast around, taking in the faces of ranking naval officers and designated representatives from all of the starships in the flotilla. *Endurance*'s commander, a whipcord woman with a severe face, caught his eye and gave him a respectful nod. Garro returned the greeting and moved past her. At his shoulder, Temeter whispered. 'Where's Grulgor?'

'There,' Garro indicated with the jut of his chin, 'with Typhon.'

'Ah,' Temeter said sagely, 'I should not be surprised.'

The captains of the Death Guard's First and Second Companies were in close consultation, the murmur of their words pitched low enough so that even the acute senses of another Astartes were not enough to divine their meaning. Garro saw that Grulgor had noticed their arrival, and, as was his usual manner, he ignored it, despite the lapse in protocol a failure to greet them represented.

'He's never going to be a friend to you, is he?' ventured Temeter, who saw it too. 'Not even for a moment.'

Garro gave the slightest of shrugs. 'It's not something I dwell on. We don't rise to our ranks because of how well-liked we are. This is a crusade we are winning, not a popularity contest.'

Temeter sniffed. 'Speak for yourself. I am extremely popular.'

'I have no doubt you believe that.'

Typhon and Grulgor abruptly disengaged and turned to meet their cohorts as they came closer. The First Captain of the Death Guard, master of the prime company and right hand of the primarch, was a formidable sight in his iron-hued Terminator armour. A dark tail of hair spilled over his shoulders and the man's bearded face was framed by the heavy square hood of the wargear. His helmet nestled in the crook of his arm, a single horn protruding from the brow. Whatever emotions dwelt inside him were well masked, but not so well that the lines of annoyance around his eyes could be completely hidden.

'Temeter. Garro.' Typhon gave both men a level, measuring stare, his voice a low growl.

At once the easy air that Temeter had brought with him was gone, evaporating beneath the first captain's piercing gaze. Garro could only wonder at the anger behind those dark eyes, still smarting at the slight of being usurped from leading the jorgall attack at the eleventh hour.

'Grulgor and I were discussing the changes in the engagement plan,' Typhon continued.

'Changes?' repeated Temeter. 'I was not aware–'

'You are being *made* aware,' said Grulgor, with a hint of a sneer. Despite having been born on a world on the opposite side of the galaxy, Ignatius Grulgor shared a similar bearing and physicality with Garro, even down to the hairless head and a collection of trophy scars; but where Garro was stoic and metered, Grulgor was forever on the edge of arrogance, snarling instead of speaking, judgemental instead of considering. 'The Fourth Company is to be re-tasked, to conduct boarding operations among the bottle world's picket force.'

Temeter bowed, hiding the irritation that Garro was sure his comrade felt at being denied a share of the mission's greater glories. 'As the primarch wills.' He looked up and met Grulgor's gaze. 'Thank you for preparing me, captain.'

'*Commander*,' Grulgor spat out the word. 'You will address me by my rank, Captain Temeter.'

Temeter frowned. 'My error, commander, of course. The traditions sometimes slip my mind when my thoughts are otherwise occupied.'

Garro watched Grulgor's jaw harden. Like all of the Legiones Astartes, they had quirks and customs that were unique to them. The Death Guard differed from many of their brother Legions in the manner of the command structure and ranking, for instance. Tradition had it that the XIV would never number more than seven great companies, although those divisions held far more men than those of other Astartes cohorts like the Space Wolves or the Blood Angels; and while many Legions had the tradition of giving the honorific of 'first captain' to the commander of the prime company, the Death Guard also held two more privileged titles, to be bestowed upon the leaders of the Second and Seventh Companies respectively. Thus, although they held no actual seniority over one another, Grulgor could carry the rank of 'commander' if he so wished, just as Garro was known as 'battle-captain'. It was Garro's understanding that his particular honorific dated back to the Wars of Unification, to a moment when the mark of distinction had been handed to a XIV officer by the Emperor himself. He was proud to bear it all these centuries later.

'Our traditions are what make us who we are,' Garro offered quietly. 'It's right and correct that we hold to them.'

'In moderation, perhaps,' Typhon corrected. 'We should not allow ourselves to become hidebound by rules from a past that is dust to us now.'

'Indeed,' added Grulgor.

'Ah,' said Temeter. 'So, Ignatius, you hold on to tradition with one hand and push it away with the other?

'The old ways are right and correct so long as they serve a purpose.' Grulgor threw Garro a cold look. 'That pet helot you keep is "a tradition" and yet there is no point to it. There is a custom that has no value.'

'I beg to differ, commander,' Garro replied. 'The housecarl performs flawlessly as my equerry–'

Grulgor snorted. 'Huh. I had one of those once. I think I lost it on an ice moon somewhere. It froze to death, weak little thing.' He looked away. 'It smacks to me of sentiment, Garro.'

'As ever, Grulgor, I will give your comments the due attention they deserve,' said Garro. He broke off as a figure in gold caught his eye moving through a shaft of light.

Temeter saw where Garro was looking and tapped twice on the shoulder plate of his armour. 'I told you Mortarion had brought company.'

KALEB BUSIED HIMSELF with the sword cloth, folding the green velvet mantle into a neat square. In the alcove of the arming pit, Captain Garro's weapons and battle equipment were arrayed around him on hooks and wire-frame racks. Upon one wall, resting on steel spikes, lay the heavy silver ingot of his master's bolter. It was polished to a matt sheen, the brass detail glittering under the wan light of biolume glow-globes.

The housecarl replaced the cloth and wrung his hands, thinking. It was hard for him to maintain a clear focus, with the idea gnawing at his mind that the primarch was only a few tiers above him, up on the high decks. Kaleb looked up at the steel ceiling and imagined what he might see if the *Endurance* were made of glass. Would Mortarion radiate dark and cold as some said he did? Would it be possible for a mere man such as himself to actually look the Death Lord in the eye, and not feel his heart stop in his chest? The serf took a deep breath to steady his nerve. It was a lot for him to handle, and the distraction made performing his normal tasks difficult. Mortarion was a son of the Emperor Himself, and the Emperor... the Emperor was...

'Kaleb.'

He turned to face Hakur. The seasoned veteran was one of the few Astartes who called the housecarl by his given name. 'Yes, lord?'

'Mind your work.' He nodded at the ceiling, at the place where Kaleb had been staring. 'Sees through steel, the primarch does.'

The serf managed a weak grin and bowed, gathering up a cleaning cloth and a tin of waxy polish. Under Hakur's neutral gaze he moved to the centre of the alcove and set to work on the heavy ceramite and brass cuirass that rested there. This was a ceremonial piece that Garro wore only in combat or upon formal occasions. In tandem with the honour-rank of battle-captain, the decorative over-sheath sported an eagle, wings spread and beak arched, sculpted from brass as if about to take flight from the chest plate. Similarly, the rear of the cuirass had a second eagle as a head-guard that emerged from the shoulders when worn over the backpack of Astartes armour.

What made this piece unique was that its eagles differed from the Emperor's aquila. While the symbol of the Imperium of Man had two heads, one blinded to look at the past, one sighted to see to the future, the battle-captain's eagles were singular. Kaleb fancied this meant that they only saw into the time yet to pass, that perhaps they were a kind of charm that could know the advance of a killing shot or deadly blade before it arrived. Once he had voiced that thought aloud and received derision and scorn from Garro's men. Such thoughts, Sergeant Hakur had later said, were superstitions that had no place on a ship of the Emperor's Crusade. 'Ours is a war to dispel fable and falsehood with the cold light of truth, not to propagate myth.' The veteran had tapped the eagles with a finger.

'These are inanimate brass and no more, just as we are all flesh and bone.'

Still, Kaleb's hand could not help but drift to a brass icon on a chain around his neck, hidden inside the folds of his tunic where none could see it.

THE FIGURE WAS most assuredly female, lithe and poised, clad in a shimmering snakeskin over-suit of dense chainmail and a sweep of golden armour plate that resembled a bodice. A half-mask lay open at her neck, revealing an elegant face. Garro sometimes found it hard to determine the age of non-Astartes, but he estimated she could be no more than thirty solar years. Purple-black hair rose in a topknot from a seamless scalp, bare but for a blood-red aquila tattoo. She was quite beautiful, but what locked his attention on her was the way she moved noiselessly across the iron decks of the chamber. Had he not seen her emerge from the shadows, the Astartes might have thought the woman to be a holo-ghost, some finely detailed image cast from the projector.

'Amendera Kendel,' noted Typhon, with a hint of distaste. 'A witchseeker.'

Temeter nodded. 'From the Storm Dagger cadre. She is here with a deputation of the Silent Sisterhood, apparently on the orders of the Sigillite himself.'

Grulgor's lip curled. 'There are no psykers here. What purpose could those women serve in the coming battle?'

'The Regent of Terra must have his reasons,' Typhon suggested, but his tone made it clear he thought little of what they might be.

Garro watched the witchseeker orbit the room. Her tradecraft was commendable. She moved in stealth even as she was obvious to the eye, passing around the naval officers in a way that appeared to be random, even as Garro's trained sense understood it was not.

Kendel was observing. She was cataloguing the reactions of the people in the assembly hall, filing them away for later review. It made the Astartes think of a scout, surveying the land before a battle, seeking weak points and targets. He had never encountered a Sister of Silence before, only heard of their exploits in service to the Imperium.

Their name was well deserved, he considered. Kendel *was* silent, like the wind across a grave, and in her passing, he noticed that some would shiver without being aware of it, or become distracted for a moment. It was as if the witchseeker cast an invisible aura around herself that gave mortal men pause.

Garro watched her pass by the entrance to the assembly hall and his gaze was hooked by the shine of brass and steel upon two grand figures that stood either side of the hatch. Barrel-chested in highly artificed armour, taller than Typhon, the identical sentinels blocked the steel door with crossed battle-scythes, the signature weapon of the Death Guard's elite warriors. Only the few personally favoured by the primarch were permitted to carry such artefacts. They were known as manreapers, forged in echo of the common farmer's harvesting scythe that it was said Mortarion had fought with in his youth. The first captain wielded one, but Garro recognised these twin blades immediately.

'Deathshroud,' he whispered. These two Astartes were the personal honour guards of the primarch, fated never to reveal their faces to anyone but Mortarion, even to the end of their lives. So it was said, the warriors of the Deathshroud were chosen by the primarch from the rank and file men of the Legion in secret, and then listed as killed in action. They were his nameless guardians, never allowed to venture more than forty-nine paces from their lord's side. Garro felt a chill when he realised that he hadn't even been aware that the Deathshroud had entered the chamber.

'If they are here, then where is our master?' asked Grulgor.

A cold smile of understanding flickered over Typhon's lips. 'He has been here all along.'

At the far end of the chamber, a towering shadow detached itself from the dimness beside the oval windows. Steady footsteps brought silence to the room as they crossed the deck plates. With every other footfall there came a heavy metallic report as the base of an iron shaft tapped out the distance. Garro's muscles tensed as the sound made several of the common naval officers back away from the hololith.

In the dusty Terran legends that survived from the histories of nation states like Merica, Old Ursh and Oseania there was the myth of a walker in the darkness who came to claim the freshly dead, a skeletal individual, an incarnation that threshed souls from flesh as keenly as wheat in the fields. These were just stories, though, the speculations of the superstitious and fearful, and yet, here and now, a billion light-years from the birthplace of that folklore, the very mirror of that figure rose into the half-light aboard *Endurance*, tall and gaunt beneath a cloak as grey as sea-ice.

Mortarion halted and touched the deck plates with the hilt of his manreaper, the scythe as tall as the primarch and a head again. Only the Deathshroud stayed on their feet. Every other person in the room, human or Astartes, was on his knees. Mortarion's cloak parted as he raised his free hand, palm upwards. 'Rise,' he said.

The primarch's voice was low and firm, at odds with the ashen, hairless face that emerged from the heavy collar surrounding his throat. Wisps of white gas curled from the neck brace of Mortarion's wargear, captured philtres of fumes from the air of Barbarus. Garro caught the scent of them and for an instant his sense memory took him back to the grim, clouded planet with its lethal skies.

The assemblage came to its feet, and still the primarch dominated the room. Beneath the grey cloak, he was a knight in shining brass and bare steel. The ornamental skull and star device of the Death Guard grimaced out from his breastplate and at his waist, level with the chest of a file Astartes, Garro saw the drum-shaped holster that carried the Lantern, a hand-crafted energy pistol of unique Shenlongi design.

Mortarion's only other adornments were a string of globe-shaped censers in brass. These too contained elements from the poisonous high atmosphere of the primarch's adoptive home world. Garro had heard it said that Mortarion would sometimes sample them, like a connoisseur tasting fine wines, or by turns pitch them into battle as grenades to send an enemy choking and dying.

The battle-captain realised he had been holding in his breath and released it as Mortarion's amber eyes took in the room. Silence fell as his lord commander began to speak.

'XENOS.' PYR RAHL made the word into a curse without effort, drumming his fingers across the stubby barrel of his bolter. 'I wonder what colour these will bleed. White? Purple? Green?' He glanced around and ran a hand through the close-cut hair on his head. 'Come, who'll make a wager with me?'

'No one will, Pyr,' answered Hakur, shaking his head. 'We're all tired of your trivial gambling.' He threw a glance back to the arming pit where Garro's housecarl was hard at work.

'What currency is there to wager between us, anyway?' added Voyen, joining Hakur at the blade racks. The two veterans were quite unalike in physical aspect, Voyen ample in frame where Hakur was wiry, and yet they were together on most things that affected the squad. 'We're not swabs or soldiers grubbing over scrip and coinage!'

Rahl frowned. 'It's not a game of money, Apothecary, nothing as crude as that. Those things are just a way to keep score. We play for the right to be right.'

Solun Decius, the youngest member of the command squad, came closer, rubbing a towel over his face to wipe away the sweat from his exertions in the sparring cages. He had a hard look to him that seemed out of place on a youth of his age. His eyes were alight with energy barely held in check, enthused by the sudden possibilities of glory that the arrival of the primarch had brought. 'I'll take your wager, if it will quiet you.' Decius glanced at Hakur and Voyen, but his elders gave him no support. 'I'll say red, like the orks.'

Rahl sniffed. 'White as milk, like the megarachnid.'

'You are both wrong.' From behind Rahl, his face buried in a data-slate festooned with tactical maps, Tollen Sendek's flat monotone issued out. 'The blood of the jorgall is a dark crimson.' The warrior had a heavy brow and hooded eyes that gave him a permanently sleepy expression.

'And this knowledge is yours how?' demanded Decius.

Sendek waved the data-slate in the air. 'I am well-read, Solun. While you batter your chainsword's teeth blunt in the cages, I study the foe. These dissection texts of the Magos Biologis are fascinating.'

Decius snorted. 'All I need to know is how to kill them. Does your text tell you that, Tollen?'

Sendek gave a heavy nod. 'It does.'

'Well, come, come.' Voyen beckoned the dour Astartes to his feet. 'Don't keep such information to yourself.'

Sendek sighed and stood, his perpetually morose features lit by the glow of the data-slate's display. He tapped his chest. 'The jorgall favour mechanical enhancements to improve their physical form. They have some humanoid traits – a head, neck, eyes and mouth – but it appears their brains and central nervous systems are situated not here,' and he tapped his brow, 'but here.' Tollen's hand lay flat on his chest.

'To kill would need a heart shot, then?' Rahl noted, accepting a nod in return.

'Ah,' said Decius, 'like this?' In a flash, the Astartes had spun in place and drawn his bolter. A single round exploded from the muzzle and ripped into the torso of a dormant practice dummy less than a few metres from Garro's arming pit. The captain's house-carl flinched at the sound of the shot, drawing a tut from Hakur.

Decius turned away, amused with himself. Meric Voyen threw Hakur a look. 'Arrogant whelp. I don't understand what the captain sees in him.'

'I once said the same thing about you, Meric.'

'Speed and skill are nothing without control,' the Apothecary retorted tersely. 'Displays like that are better suited to fops like the Emperor's Children.'

The other man's words drew a thin smile from Hakur. 'We're all Astartes under the skin, brothers and kindred all.'

Voyen's humour dropped away suddenly. 'That, my brother, is as much a lie as it is the truth.'

IN THE HOLOLITH cube, the shape of the jorgalli construct became visible. It was a fat cylinder several kilometres long, bulbous at one end with drive clusters, thinning at the other to a stubby prow. Huge petal-shaped vanes coated with shimmering panels emerged from the stern of the thing, catching sunlight and bouncing it through massive windows as big as inland seas.

Mortarion gestured with a finger. 'A cylinder world. This one has twice the mass of the similar constructs found and eliminated in orbits around the planets Tasak Beta and Fallon, but unlike those, our target is the first jorgall craft to be found under power in deep space.' One of the adepts tickled switches with his worm-like mechadendrites and the image receded, revealing a halo of teardrop-shaped ships in close formation nearby.

'A substantial picket fleet travels ahead of the craft. Captain Temeter will lead the engagement to disrupt these ships and break their lines of communication.'

The primarch accepted a salute from Temeter. 'Elements of the First, Second and Seventh Great Companies will stand with me as I take the spear tip into the bottle itself. This battleground is suited to our unique talents. The jorgall breathe a mixture of oxygen and nitrogen with heavy concentrations of chlorine, a weak poison that our lungs will resist with little effort.'

As if to underline the point, Mortarion sniffed at a puff of gas from his half-mask. 'First Captain Typhon will be my support. Commander Grulgor will penetrate the drive cluster and take control of the cylinder's motive power centre. Battle-Captain Garro will neutralise the construct's hatcheries.'

Garro saluted firmly, mirroring Grulgor and Typhon's gestures. He held off his disappointment at his assigned target, far down the cylinder from the primarch's attack point, and instead began to consider the first elements of his battle plan.

Mortarion hesitated a moment, and Garro could swear he heard the hint of a smile in the primarch's voice. 'As some of you have deduced, this fight will not be the Death Guard's alone. I have, on the request of Malcador the Sigillite, brought a cadre of investigators from the Divisio Astra Telepathica here, led by the Oblivion Knight Sister Amendera.' The primarch inclined his head and Garro saw the Sister of Silence bow low in return. She gestured in sign language, quick little motions of finger and wrist.

'The honoured Sisters will join us to seek out a psyker trace that has led to this bottle-world.'

Garro stiffened. *Psykers?* This was the first he had heard of such a threat on the jorgalli ship, and he noted that only Typhon did not seem surprised at such news.

'I trust that the full importance of this endeavour is impressed upon each of you,' continued the Death Lord, his low tones strong. 'These jorgall repeatedly enter our space in their generation ships, intent on spawning over worlds that belong to the Emperor. They must not be allowed to gain a foothold.' He turned away, his face disappearing into his cloak. 'In time, the Astartes will erase these creatures from humanity's skies, and today will be a step along that path.'

Garro and his battle-brothers saluted once more as Mortarion turned his back on them and moved away towards the welcoming shadows. They did not chorus in a battle cry or mark the moment with raised pronouncements. The primarch had spoken, and his was voice enough.

TWO

TWO

Assault
Brothers and Sisters
Message in a Bottle

THE THRUST OF the heavy assault boat's engines was a hammer to their bones, pressing the Astartes into the acceleration racks. Garro held his muscles tense against the powerful g-forces and let his gaze wander over the interior of the clamshell doors that formed the bow of the boarding ship. Intricate scrollwork spread across the inner face of the doors, charting the countless actions the craft had been involved in.

It was one of hundreds hurtling through the void at this moment, packed with men primed for war, each of them targeted on the jorgall world-ship with the unerring single-mindedness of a guided missile.

Through the pict-circuits laced into the lenses of his armour, Garro rapidly blink-clicked through the data available to him via his command level vox-net. There were feeds from the eye cameras of the squad leaders, quick scripts of telemetry from Voyen's medicae auspex and there, for a moment, a grainy, low

37

resolution image from outside across the boat's serrated prow.

Garro dallied on that for a few seconds, watching the motion of the vast cylinder as they approached it. The hull wall of pearlescent metal grew larger. It was so huge that the curvature of it was hardly noticeable, and the only sign that they were actually closing on it was the slow crawl of detail as surface features became clearer: here, a cluster of spikes that might be antennae, there a bulbous turret spitting yellow tracer fire.

The captain felt no fear at the jorgall guns. The assault was moving at punishing speed beneath a cloak of electronic countermeasures, heat-baffle flare bursts and glittering clouds of metal chaff that would render sensors unintelligible. He was confident in Temeter's skills, certain that the captain of the Fourth had sent the picket fleet into disarray and robbed the xenos of any usable warning.

The wall was very close, the distance vanishing in moments. Garro was aware of other boats converging at the edges of the greyed-out image. Long-range sensors had determined that this portion of the cylinder's hull was thin, and so it would be here, some half a kilometre from the cylinder's mid-line, that the Death Guard would make their ingress. Garro let the link fade and gathered himself, switching over to the general vox channel. His voice echoed in the helms of every Astartes on the boat.

'Steel in your bones, brothers. Impact is imminent. I want a clean and fast deployment. I want it so sharp the Emperor himself would applaud its perfection!' He took a breath as the standby alert began to wail. 'Today the primarch leads us, and we will make him proud to do so! For Mortarion and Terra!'

'Mortarion and Terra!' Garro heard Hakur's rough baritone through the chorus of assent.

Decius's voice cut across the channel, brimming with zeal. 'Count the Seven!' he cried, yelling out the company's call to rally. 'Count the Seven!'

Garro joined in, but his words were abruptly shaken out of him as the assault boat's thick bow rammed into the hull of the jorgall cylinder. Piercing shrieks of rendered metal and escaping atmosphere thundered around the boat's thick fuselage as it drove itself deep, clawed tracks across its flanks biting and sparking to pull it through metres of chitinous armour plate. Turning and shifting, the boat's autonomic pilot brain deployed hydraulic barbs to stop the outgassing of air from blowing back into the void.

The juddering, screeching, ear-splitting ride seemed to go on forever then abruptly it stopped. The assault ship listed. Garro heard metal scrape on metal and then the trigger rune before him on the clamshell hatch flashed on. 'Ready on release!' he snapped.

The hatch blew open on explosive bolts and Garro had his bolter loose and in his hands, ready to kill anything that dared to come in, but it was a sudden flood of brackish blue water that smashed down into the boat, not an enemy defender. The liquid was icy, swirling rapidly around his legs and up to his stomach.

'Go!' Garro roared. The battle-captain was aware of his men moving behind him as he launched himself out of the assault craft. He plunged into the cobalt murk and burst back through the surface, turning around, getting his bearings.

It was a hundred-to-one chance. The assault had penetrated through the bottom of a shallow chemical lake and the dark hulls of the boats protruded from the sluggish liquid like the tips of jagged armoured fingers. Already the waters were icing over and freezing into blue-white halos where the cold kiss of space had followed the invaders in. Through his helmet's breath screen Garro drew a rough inhalation that tasted of metallic salts. Nearby, he saw Grulgor kick angrily away from his lander and snarl out a command.

There on the shore, pointing with his manreaper, was Mortarion. The sight of the primarch was enough to send Garro's blood racing, and he stormed forward through the shallows, his bolter held high. 'Count the Seven!' called the captain, and he did not need to look behind him to see the elements of his company follow in formation.

Garro advanced from the deployment point with Hakur's veteran squad at his side, joined by Decius and Sendek for support. Around them, the chaotic crash of gunfire and blades on blades rippled over the gentle landscape of the lakeshore. Hordes of Astartes met the xenos in deadly, furious conflict.

The alien force was quickly in disarray. Even in non-humans, Garro could sense the motion and shift in the character of a battalion when they lost their nerve. Groups broke apart and reformed, milling and confused, instead of drawing out and away in any semblance of order. Butchering them would not take too much of the Death Guard's energy.

It was clear the jorgalli had understood too late that the objects on a course towards their world-ship were not massive munitions but actually manned craft. The near-suicidal manner of such a boarding operation had shocked them and they were unprepared for the brutal fury of the Death Guard incursion. Their mistake had been compounded by errors in the deployment of their combatant enhanciles. The jorgall cyborgs standing on the banks of the chlorine lagoon were massacred, their keening cries echoing over the shallow, sandy dunes surrounding the landing zone.

In the back of his mind, the battle-captain was already thinking ahead, considering how they would secure the breach point before the companies split to attend their individual objectives. Garro led his men in a thrust through a nest of spindly, whirling dervishes, fighting past sweeps of dull steel glaives and placing double-tap bolt shots through the ribs of every jorgall they saw. The Astartes expanded outward from the lake in a ring of off-white armour, the advance rolling over the defenders.

Moving and firing, Garro's troop crested a dune of crystalline granules that crunched loudly beneath their boots and found some close combat kills. A phalanx of jorgall swept and turned to them, caught in mid-flight, daring to stop and engage the Astartes. Weapons barked on both sides of the fight, the heavy roar of bolters drowning out the hissing clatter of electrostatic arc-fire from the implanted projectors of the enemy.

Decius, who favoured the blunt trauma of a power fist, slipped into the midst of the aliens and punched one to the powdery dirt, over and over, slamming its long neck and oval head into a ruin.

'Has he forgotten what I said already? I told him to aim for the torso for a quick kill,' said Sendek.

'He hasn't forgotten,' said Hakur.

With a peculiar, ululating cry, two of the larger xenos coiled and leapt directly at Garro. In mid-jump, they came open like spreading petals on a flower,

their tri-fold legs and arms wide. He saw glitters
where whole portions of limbs had been replaced
with dull metal and black curves of carbon. In one
swift motion, the captain let his bolter drop away on
its sling and drew Libertas, a blue glow of power
shimmering across the blade. In a wide, double-
handed sweep Garro cut both the creatures in half,
the sword whispering easily through their scaly tissue.

Hakur grunted his approval. 'Still sharp, then?'

'Aye,' Garro replied, shaking droplets of deep red
from the blade. He paused momentarily to examine
his work, viewing the severed limbs with the same
dispassion he had the static intelligence images on
Sendek's data-slate.

In their natural, fully fleshed state, a jorgalli adult
was perhaps four and a half metres tall, moving on
three legs with three joints that radiated from their
lower torsos like the spokes on a wheel. Apart from
the extensile neck, the upper body of the aliens
resembled the lower, but here the three limbs ended
in hands with six digits.

The egg-shaped head had deep-set, rheumy eyes
and fleshy notches for a nose and mouth. They had
skin like Terran lizards, all scales and tiny horns of
bone. However, there seemed to be no such thing as
a 'natural' jorgall. Every single example of the xenos
species yet encountered and terminated by servants of
the Imperium, from immature cubs to infirm elders,
was modified with implanted devices or cybernetic
proxy mechanisms. The slate showed oddities such as
spring piston legs, feet replaced with wheels and
rollers, knife claws, sheets of subdermal armour plating, telecameras inside optic cavities and even
ballistic needler weapons nestled within the hollows
of bones.

The similarity in intent between the alien implants and the engineered organs that he possessed as an Astartes was not lost on Garro, but these were *xenos*, and they were invaders. They were nothing like him and as the Emperor had decreed, they were to be chastised for daring to venture into human space.

Near to the sluggish waterline, a horde of clawed jorgalli, most likely some kind of hand-to-hand variant, hacked at a dreadnought from the Second Company. The venerable warrior had become bogged down in the chemical slurry at the lake's edge and Garro saw it spin on its torso axis, clubbing at them with a chainfist. A white flash fell from nowhere into the heart of the jorgall rippers and the captain heard Ignatius Grulgor bellow with wild laughter. Grulgor came to his feet surrounded by the xenos and threw back his head.

The commander of the Second had gone bare-faced; the foul air of the bottle-world did not concern him. In either hand he carried a regulation Mars-pattern bolter, and with delight, Grulgor unloaded them at point-blank range into the enemy.

The sheer velocity of the shots chopped the jorgall into reeking gobbets of flesh, giving the dreadnought valuable seconds in which to extract itself. In moments, Grulgor stood at the centre of a circle of alien carcasses, vapour coiling from the barrels of his guns. The commander saluted the primarch, and flashed a sly, daring grin at Garro before moving on in search of new targets.

'He's so artless, don't you think?' murmured Hakur. 'The esteemed Huron-Fal would have fought his own way out of that mess, but Grulgor wades in, more concerned about showing his mettle to the primarch than where best to spend his ammunition.'

'We're Death Guard. We're not supposed to be artists,' Garro retorted. 'We are craftsmen in war, nothing more, direct and brutal. We don't seek accolades and honours, only duty.'

'Of course,' said the veteran mildly.

Decius came bounding up to Garro, kicking away the corpse parts from his kill. 'Ugh. Do you smell that, sir? These things, their blood stinks.'

The battle-captain didn't answer. He hesitated, his attention drifting, watching Mortarion in the thick of his cold fury. At the primarch's side, Typhon and the twin sentinels of the Deathshroud were whirling and culling, their manreapers moving unhindered through a milling, screaming pack of jorgall. The Death Lord himself had clearly deemed these inferior strains of xenos to be unworthy of his scythe, and instead was at work putting them to the light of his Lantern.

Hard-edged white rays keened from the stub barrel of the huge brass pistol, leaving purple after-images on Garro's retina despite the enhancements of his modified eyesight. Wherever the Lantern's punishing beam struck, jorgall defenders became charcoal sketches, twisting, then turning to smoke.

Mortarion reached into a hooting scrum of aliens and ripped an injured man from their midst, batting them effortlessly away as he hauled the wounded Death Guard to safety. The primarch spared the man some unheard words and in return the bareheaded Astartes roared in assent, rejoining the fight.

'Magnificent,' breathed Decius, and Garro could sense the coiled need in the younger man, the yearning to run down the dune and press into Mortarion's company, to throw away all battlefield protocol just for the chance to fight within his master's aura. It was a difficult urge to resist. Garro felt it just as strongly, but he would not lower himself to duplicate the self-aggrandising behaviour of men like Grulgor.

Then the younger Astartes tore his gaze away and cast around. 'So this is the great creation of the xenos, eh? Not much to look at.'

'Human spacefarers once lived in cylinders such as this,' noted Sendek as he reloaded, 'in the deep past, before we mastered the force of gravity. They called them ohnyl colonies.'

Decius seemed unimpressed. 'I feel like a fly trapped in a bottle. What sort of inside-out world is this?' He gestured upward, to where the landscape curved away to meet itself kilometres over their heads. A thin bar of illuminators extended away down the axis of the cylinder, disappearing to the fore and aft in yellow clouds. Garro's eyes narrowed as he spied motes of dark green moving up there, shifting through the corridor of zero gravity at the world-ship's centre.

Hakur tensed at his side. 'I see them too, battle-captain, airborne reinforcements.'

Garro called out on the general vox channel. 'Look to the skies, Death Guard!'

On the blood-slicked sandbanks, Mortarion stabbed at the air with the blade of his scythe. 'The captain of the Seventh has keen vision! The xenos seek to distract us with easy kills, to keep our atten-tion on the ground!'

The primarch gave Garro a curt nod and strode to the top of another shallow powder dune, ignoring the scatters of enemy needle-shot that whined off his brass armour. Mortarion let his hood roll back so he could turn his face to the caged sky. 'We must correct them.'

For a long second, Nathaniel found himself rooted to the spot by his master's casual acknowledgement, despite his best intention to make little of it. The favour of his primarch, of an Emperor's son, even for an instant was a heady thing indeed, and he found some understanding as to why men like Grulgor would go so far to court it. Then Garro shook it off and slammed a fresh sickle magazine into his weapon. 'Seventh, to arms!' he cried, bringing the bolter to his shoulder and sighting upward along its length.

THE JORGALL FLYERS came in numbers that dwarfed the ragged packs of land-based fighters the Death Guard met at the lake. Clad in a flickering green armour that wound about them in strips, the airborne xenos had sacrificed two of their limbs to their mechanical surgeons. In their stead were beating wings of sharp metal feathers, each edged like a razor. Feet had become balls of curved talons, and there were more of the lethal arc-throwers and needle-guns embedded in joints where they had keen fields of fire.

They came down whistling and hooting, met a wall of bolt shell and high-energy plasma and died, but this was only the first wave and more of them, green glitters in the sky, poured out of the gauzy yellow cloud.

Garro saw one of Hakur's men wreathed in humming glints of artificial lightning and smelled the stench of crisping human meat as a flight of the xenos flyers shocked the life from him. Nearby, the dreadnought Huron-Fal deployed his missile packs and threw explosive death into the wheeling flocks, blasting dozens of them out of the air with the concussion. For his part, Garro moved carefully, low to the oxide sands, picking off the xenos in bursts of full-auto fire as they dropped in on swooping strikes. The attack pattern of the aliens was clear. They were attempting to push the Astartes back into the icy lake.

'Not today,' said the battle-captain to the air, clipping the wings of a large adult female. The creature spiralled headfirst into the sands and twitched.

He became aware that he had company. Garro glanced over his shoulder and frowned in mild surprise at the cadre of lithe golden figures coming up behind him. The Sisters of Silence moved in quick lockstep, maintaining coherent fire corridors and combat discipline with an efficiency that he had only previously seen among his brother Astartes.

It was difficult for him to tell the women apart. Their armour was polished to a glittering sheen, unadorned by any brash sigils or fluttering oath papers like the pale wargear of the Death Guard. Their faces were hidden behind hawkish gold helmets that reminded him of the barred gates to some ancient citadel, no doubt equipped with breather gear that let the unmodified Sisterhood manage the toxic air of the bottle-world. They seemed identical, as if they were forged from some mythic mould by the Emperor's hand. He wondered idly if normal men might view the Astartes in a similar way.

The Sisterhood carried swords and flamers, blades and plumes of fire licked at the jorgall flyers as they dipped into range. Some also carried bolters.

As was their vow in the Emperor's service, the women never spoke, even those speared by needle rounds or struck by arc-fire. They communicated in line of sight using a gestural language similar to Astartes battle-sign, or through a code of clicks over the vox. From the way they crossed the engagement zone, he had no doubt in his mind that they knew exactly where they were going.

As they passed, the Sister closest to him spared Garro a look, and the battle-captain felt a peculiar chill fall across him. That the Sisterhood ranged the galaxy in search of rogue psychics to capture or expunge was widely known, but what was less understood was the manner in which they did it.

Garro had heard that unlike other living beings, these unspeaking women were silent not just in the material world, but also in the ephemeral realm of the mind. There were names for them: untouchables, pariahs, blanks.

He frowned at the irrational nature of thoughts, pushing them away. In the next second, they were forgotten as warning runes blinked inside his visor. Garro caught the sound of shrieking air over razor wings.

He moved as a flight of jorgalli came down upon them. Fast as only an Astartes could be, he slammed his hand into the back of the Sister at his flank and sent her down and away as tenfold claws cut through the air towards them. Garro threw his arm up to deflect the blow and felt the talons slice gouges through his vambrace. The screeching jorgall ripped upwards and into his helmet, tearing it from his neck ring in a bone wrenching impact. He staggered and recovered, bringing his bolter to bear. Garro's gun barked and from the sand the Sister fired with him. None of the flight that had dared to attack them lived to take air again.

The battle-captain grimaced and patted his face, content to find he had gained no new scars from the encounter. Getting to her feet, the witchseeker walked to him and presented Garro with his helmet, ripped back from the jorgall claws. It was badly damaged, but the symbolic gesture was an important one. The woman looked up and inclined her head. With her free hand she touched her heart and her brow. The meaning was clear. *My thanks to you.* Unsure of the correct protocol, Garro simply nodded in return, and that seemed enough. The women moved on, leaving him behind. It was only as he saw their backs that Garro noticed the plume of dark hair issuing from the Sister's golden helm, and the red aquila etching across her shoulder blades.

He moved down to the core of the fighting, over a dunescape littered with jorgall dead and on rare occasions, fallen figures in pale grey power armour. Each brother perished here ground Garro's rage like stone on stone, for every one of them was worth a thousand of the freakish intruders.

The captain heard the slamming crack of Mortarion's Lantern once again, and looked up to see the primarch sweep it through the air like a searchlight, catching aliens afire, turning them into a rain of ashen fallout.

Typhon's harsh growl sounded on the general vox channel. 'If this is all we have to face, I question if our might will even be tested today!'

'My father sent me here.' Mortarion's words were mild, but heavy with intent. 'Do you think him wrong to do so, first captain?'

Another man might have baulked at the veiled threat, but not Typhon. 'I only chafe at such poor sport, lord commander. We dally here too long, sir.'

Garro caught a grunt of agreement. 'Perhaps we do, my friend.' When he spoke again, the primarch did it aloud, eschewing the vox to broadcast his voice. 'Sons

of Death! You know your objectives! Take your units
and prosecute the foe! Typhon, with me; Grulgor, the
drives; Garro, the hatchery. Go now!'

The elements of the Seventh Company came to him
and the battle-captain was pleased to see that there
had been few losses among them. The Apothecary,
Voyen, looked him up and down, silently comment-
ing on the state of his helmet where the headgear
hung from his belt. Decius too was unhooded and his
pale face was split with a murderous grin. The stain-
ing of viscera on his power fist was mute testament to
his kills so far.

He nodded to them, and the men of the Seventh
took up their formation. They moved, letting Grulgor's company mop up the last of the airborne jorgall.
They crossed out from the crystalline dunes at a quick
pace, and into groves of tall tree-like forms woven
from some kind of rough fibre.

Sendek ministered to his auspex. 'Tactical plot
shows heat sources comparable to jorgall hatchery
constructs in this direction.' He pointed. 'That way.
The virtual compass is having difficulty assimilating
the internal structure of the bottle-world.'

'How current is that data?' asked Hakur. 'The sense-
servitors neglected to tell us we were landing in a
chem-lake. I find myself wondering what else they
may have missed.'

Sendek frowned. 'The readings are… contradictory.'

'Best we be ready for surprises, then,' noted Rahl,
hefting the combi-bolter in his grip.

'DO NOT ALLOW yourself to be lulled into
complacency by the name of your target, captain.'
Mortarion had spoken the words without looking at
him, as Garro stared into the hololith in *Endurance*'s

assembly hall. 'This so-called hatchery is not only the crèche for the jorgalli young, but also a place of modification. You will probably find eggs filled with armed adults as well as their larvae.'

Garro recalled the primarch's words as he looked up at the towering fibrous trees. Further into the 'forest' where the stalks were planted in dense, regular rows, the tree-things were heavy with great grey orbs that hung like monstrous fruits. Some showed signs of motion inside, things shifting about in lazy thrashes. Here and there were pools of watery fluid that Sendek immediately designated as 'yolk'. Voyen agreed with the description, pointing out dripping orbs up above that hung ragged, formless and clearly empty. 'The roots of the trees drink the liquid back in to the system,' noted Sendek. 'Quite efficient.'

'I'm rapt with fascination,' Rahl said, in a tone that indicated the reverse.

Decius kept his bolter close. 'Where are the defences? Do these xenos care so little about their spawn that they leave them open to any predator that happens by?'

'Perhaps their children *are* the predators,' offered Hakur darkly.

One of the men from the veterans' squad halted and gestured ahead. 'Captain,' he asked, 'do you see this?'

'What is it?' asked Garro.

The Astartes bent and gathered up a shiny metallic object, roughly oval in shape. He turned it over in his hands. 'It's… sir, It's a helm, I think.' He held it up to show them, and Garro's blood chilled at the sight of a Silent Sister's wargear. Something shifted inside it and a severed head dropped from the helmet to the ground, trailing a plume of blonde hair.

'Clean cut,' noted the Astartes. 'Very fresh.'

Voyen's eyes narrowed. 'Where's the… the rest of her?'

Decius used his bolter to point towards different branches of the trees. 'Here, there and there. Over there as well, I think.' Wet rags of red and gold were visible on each.

'The Sisters came to the hatchery?' Hakur cast around, looking low. 'Why would witchseekers come here?'

Decius gave a dry chuckle. 'That, old man, would seem to be secondary to the question of what it was that killed her.'

From ahead of them where the trunks were thickest, there came a ripple of bolter fire. Garro spied the glitter of sporadic muzzle flashes even as a low rumble spread through the sandy dirt beneath his boots. Cracking sounds, sharp as snapping bone, reached him as trees in the middle distance shook and bent, the tops of them fluttering and falling as something large knocked them down.

'You're about to get your answer,' Rahl said, raising his bolter.

The Sisterhood came through the egg-trees, moving like dancers, harrying the jorgalli enhancile with their weapons. It was the largest of the xenos that Garro had encountered onboard the bottle-world, and of a design that had not been in Sendek's documentation. Outwardly it resembled the form of a jorgall in a basic sense, but it was perhaps ten times their mass. As high as the canopy of the trees, the thing appeared to be an agglomeration of scaled flesh and metals, a jorgall deformed by gigantism and then improved by technology to be larger still.

The battle-captain could make out fleshy matter inside a glass orb at the middle of the cyborg's mass, perhaps, he reasoned, whatever remained of the jor-gall's original form. It had no arms. Instead there were writhing clusters of grey iron tentacles sprouting from each of its upper limb sockets. Some moved like striking serpents, snapping out at the Sisters, while others knotted around an unseen burden that the thing clasped desperately to its chest.

'Some sort of guardian?' offered Voyen.

'Some sort of *target*,' retorted Decius and opened fire.

The Death Guard moved in to assist the Sisterhood, firing on the approach, adding their shots to the storm of bullets that haloed the cyborg. Garro had the fleeting impression that the machine-form was trying to escape, but then it turned around and threw any notion of fleeing aside. Perhaps it might have got away from the women, but with Garro's arrival it had no other choice but to stand and fight.

Metal feelers lashed out across the ground, keen-edged tips slicing furrows in the dirt. They flexed and moved, ripping up divots and roots. Hakur was caught off-guard as a tentacle lashed at him and threw the Astartes aside, rolling off the trunk of an egg-tree. Garro saw another rip the leg from one of the troopers and put him down in a welter of blood. The captain ducked away from the questing appendages as they hissed over his head.

A witchseeker, caught with her bolter breech open and magazine empty, met the tip of them through her breastbone. They stabbed through her torso and pinned her to a tree, then tore back out in a jet of spent vitae. Still trailing blood, the tentacles bent and whipped at the Emperor's warriors, clipping Rahl on the back swing and tearing the gold hood from another of Kendel's women. Without her helmet, a severe Null Maiden with a red topknot and portcullis faceplate choked and stumbled, the rancid atmosphere of the jorgall vessel scouring her lungs. Voyen was already moving to assist her, and Garro's face soured. The cyborg was just too fast, too wild and uncontrolled in its motions. To kill it, they would need to take a more direct approach. He thumbed the selector switch on his bolter to fully automatic fire and charged the xenos hybrid.

The battle-captain unloaded an entire clip into the legs and thorax of the cyborg, gouts of oily fluid and flashing short-circuit arcs marking where each round hit home. The jorgall thing hooted and growled, turning to focus its attention on the figure in grey-white armour. Steel-sheathed whips shot out, extending and buzzing with effort, and Garro threw himself into a roll, dodging the places where they stabbed into the soil. The tips of the lashing feelers clattered over his ceramite armour, and Garro felt a sting of pain as they raked the place where the flyer's claws had cut him on the lakeside, reopening the wounds there. A chance flexion of the tentacle, a second of delay on his part, and suddenly the captain's bolter was spinning away from him through the air, the strap hanging ragged as the gun was snapped from his grip.

Garro turned into the force of the impact, rolled again and came up with Libertas in his hand. Stabbing lines of metal came at him and he batted them away with the sword blade, flares of sparks glaring orange-white in the sullen artificial daylight of the egg-tree groves. The others were pouring their fire on to the cyborg, but its attention was still split between Garro and the object it held tight, something swaddled in thin grey muslin. The battle-captain threw himself at the jorgall mechanoid, chopping off the tips of tentacles and slashing at others. He spun as he felt iron limbs touch his legs and hacked at them, but he was close to its torso and the cyborg's appendages were thicker here, more muscular, more resilient. Powerful coils enveloped him and Garro felt the ground drop away. The machine-hybrid shook him violently, his sword-arm flailing against his side where he could not turn Libertas in his defence. His teeth rattled inside his skull and there was blood in his mouth.

He heard the splintering of flexsteel in the joints of his armour, smelled the acidic tang of spilled coolant as leaks jetted from his backpack. The Astartes hissed through his teeth as pain bit into him, compacting his implanted carapace and ribcage. It was a struggle to keep breath in his lungs, as the pressure grew greater with every moment. Garro was aware of motion as the cyborg drew him closer, up to the glassy capsule of its meat core. Hollow, predatory eyes stared at him, brimming with alien hate. The jorgall wanted to watch him die, to savour it.

The killing stress continued to increase as Garro's three lungs ran dry, his heart hammering wildly in his chest. Darkness was closing in on him. At the edges of the captain's consciousness, he glimpsed a shimmering ghost image, a figure that seemed to be his primarch, beckoning him towards oblivion.

In that moment, Garro tapped a final reserve of mad, desperate strength. *By Terra's will*, he told himself, *in the name of my home world and the Imperium of Man, I will not perish!*

New energy flooded through him, hot and raw. Garro reached deep into himself and found a wellspring of conviction, steeling himself against the

xenos's murderous embrace. The captain felt warmth
spread into his agonised muscles as he pictured
Terra's majesty in his mind's eye, and there with his
hand cupped beneath it, holding it safe, the Emperor.
In the Emperor's name, I will not fail! I dare not fail!

He unleashed a wordless, furious snarl of defiance
and fought back against the alien coils, putting every
last ounce of power he could muster into Libertas.
The power sword's blade met jorgall steel and parted
it, screeching through artificial nerves and mechanical
cabling. The cyborg faltered and stumbled as Garro
cut his way free, fragments of cracked ceramite shedding from his armour. The captain's burning lungs
drank in ragged gulps of air. He pressed forward even
as the machine-form tried to shove him away, bringing up the glowing tip of the blade.

Garro saw emotion flutter over the trembling
mouthparts of the jorgall as Libertas touched the
crown of its glass pod. Unlike the xenos, the captain
did not linger for the sake of cruelty. Instead, he
pressed his entire weight behind the sword and shattered the capsule, forcing the weapon into the fleshy
torso of the alien until it burst from the cyborg's back
in a rain of crimson.

The jorgall collapsed with a thunderous crash, tearing
down a stand of trees as it fell. Half-finished things
erupted from eggs, mewling and spitting, to be met by
the guns of the Death Guard and the witchseekers.

Taking back his sword, Garro dropped to the
ground as the cyborg's last nerve impulses fluttered
through its limbs. Its burden, the shape in grey
muslin, was released and rolled to his feet. The captain knelt and unwrapped it with the tip of his blade.

Inside there was an immature jorgall. What surprised him was not that the xenos hatchling was

completely free of any mechanical augmentation, but the freakish mutation of the tripedal being. It was conjoined, a malformation of two aliens that had somehow become merged during growth. Its skull was enormous, a bloated thing with four distinct chambers, quite unlike the ovoid heads typical of its species. Legs and arms twitched towards him, milky eyes swivelled and narrowed in Garro's direction.

Without warning, the air around him changed. The atmosphere became greasy and slick on his skin, suddenly scratchy with the sharp stench of ozone. He had felt such things before, on other battlefields, in other wars for the good of humanity. Garro's mind screamed a single word, and he understood exactly why the Sisters of Silence had come to this place.

'Psyker!' He drew up the sword in an arc, ready to take the creature's head from its shoulders.

Wait.

The word struck him like a cold flood, making his arm go rigid. The ozone stink enveloped him, clouding his thoughts and tightening on his mind just as the cyborg had coiled around his body. It reached into Garro, searching through him as easily as he might have leafed through a book.

Death Guard, it whispered, amusement in its words, *so confident of your rightness, so afraid to see the crack in your spirit.*

Garro tried to complete the killing blow, but he was locked tight, trapped in amber.

Soon the end comes. We see tomorrow. So shall you. All you worship will wither. All will–

The mutant's torso burst in a welter of blood and bone fragments as a single bolter round tore a hole through it as big as a fist. Suddenly the haze was gone and Garro blinked it away, as if waking from a deep sleep. He turned and found Sister Amendera Kendel at his shoulder, smoke curling from the muzzle of her gun. Her dark eyes studied him from the vision slits of her helmet. The captain stood carefully and duplicated her gesture from the lakeside, touching his armoured fingertips to his heart and his brow.

He became aware of a sound reaching through the wooded ranks of the hatchery, a whistling, a keening that was quickly growing in volume. The sound was atonal and harsh on his ears. It was a lament, a cry from the unhatched.

'Look!' shouted Hakur. 'In the trees! Movement, everywhere!'

Every egg-orb that Garro could see was trembling as the jorgalli things inside thrashed and tore at their confinement, frantic in their need to escape. He flicked a look to Kendel, as the Sister directed her cohorts to gather the dead mutant into a chainmail sack. She glanced up at him and nodded. Perhaps Voyen had been correct, perhaps the cyborg had been some kind of guardian protecting the psyker child, and now it was dead, its siblings were enraged.

Spatters of yolk rained down from the trunks. Kendel flicked out harsh gestures to her Sisters and the women moved off, turning their flamers on the foliage. Garro saw the merit in her action and called into his vox-link. 'Deploy grenades and explosives. Follow the Sisterhood's example. Destroy the trees.'

The fibrous matter of the egg-trees was dry and made excellent tinder. In moments, the alien woodland was burning, the grey sacs popping and boiling. Many of the enhanciles made it to the ground, mad with fury, and they were put down with detached precision.

Garro watched the blue-tinged flames sear and dance as they spread, murdering the world-ship's dormant and newborn. All across the bottle, the jorgall were perishing beneath the hand of the Death Guard, making a lie of the mutant child's final words.

'A lie,' said Garro aloud, watching the poisonous smoke turn above his head.

THREE

Aeria Gloris
A Poisoned Chalice
Put to the Question

IN THE RUINS of their enemy, the Death Guard task force regrouped and surveyed the breadth of the destruction they had wrought. The wreckage of the jorgalli picket fleet was a cloud of crystallised breathing gasses, hull fragments and the dead. Some of the teardrop-shaped xenos vessels were still relatively intact. One by one, these were being scuttled with atomic charges, reduced to sun-hot balls of radioactive plasma. In less than a standard Terran day, there would be nothing recognisable left to show the face of an enemy that the Death Guard had obliterated so utterly.

Out there in the shoal of destruction, Stormbirds on funerary details scoured the engagement area for Astartes who had been blown into the dark during boarding operations. Those found would be interred as heroes, once the progenoid glands in their corpses had been harvested. The precious flesh-matter from the dead would serve the Legion in their stead, passing on to strengthen new initiates when the next round of recruitment began. Once in a while, a lucky find would bring the recovery crews a live battle-brother, dormant inside his armour beneath the lulling pressure of his sus-an membranes, but that happened very rarely.

Beyond the zone where the Death Guard fleet gathered like carrion birds around a corpse, the jorgall bottle was executing a slow, wounded turn to sight down into the ecliptic plane of the Iota Horologii system. Drifts of wreckage and broken panels from the construct's vast solar panels floated behind it in a faint cometary tail. The main drives blinked out of sequence as the fusion motors worked the colossal mass of the world-ship about. Dissenting voices from the Mechanicum contingent aboard the warship *Spectre of Death* had petitioned Mortarion for a few days in which to loot the alien craft of technology. The primarch, as was his prerogative, refused the request. The letter of Lord Malcador's orders – and therefore, by extension, those of the Emperor himself – was that the jorgall incursion into the sector was to be *exterminated*. The master of the Death Guard clearly saw no point of confusion in those orders. There was to be nothing left of the aliens.

And yet…

Nathaniel Garro watched the play and turn of the fleet from the gallery above the *Endurance*'s main launch bay, above him a span of thick armoured glass and space beyond it, below, through skeletal brass frames and grid-cut decking, the expanse of the flight platform. Gradually, his gaze dropped.

Down among the sleek Stormbirds and heavy Thunderhawks was a single swan-like shuttlecraft, the spread wings of the ship detailed in gold and black. It stood out among the white and grey Astartes craft, a single bright game fowl nestled in a flock of pale raptors.

Aboard that vessel, a sole tangible remnant of the assault would remain after all the works of the jorgall were erased from this sector of space. He found himself wondering what other orders the Sisters of Silence had, orders that were unbound even in the face of a primarch's countermand. It was not defiance on their part to go against Mortarion's wishes if it was the Emperor's will to do otherwise, surely? This was not disobedience. This was a trivial issue, a small thing of little consequence. Garro had never known of and could barely envisage an instance when the commands of primarch and Emperor would not be in harmony.

An oiled hiss signalled the opening of the gallery's hatch and Garro looked to see who had come to interrupt his customary moment of solitude after the battle. A small smile curled at his lips as two figures entered the echoing, empty colonnade. He gave a shallow bow as Amendera Kendel approached him, a younger woman in a less ornate version of a witch-seeker's robes walking at her heels.

Kendel looked to Garro as he assumed he must have looked to her: fresh from the battlefield, fatigued, but content that the fight had gone well. 'Sister,' said Garro, 'I trust the outcome this day was satisfactory to you.'

The woman signed a few words and the girl at her side spoke. 'Battle-Captain Garro, well met. The goals of the Imperium have been ably served.'

Nathaniel raised an eyebrow and looked directly at the girl. He saw her more clearly now, noting that she had no armour or visible weapons as Kendel did. 'Forgive me, but it was my understanding that the Sisters of Silence are never to speak.'

The girl nodded, her manner changing slightly as she answered. 'That is indeed so, lord. No Sister may utter a word, unto death, once she gives the Oath of Tranquillity. I am a novice, captain. I have yet to take the vow and so I may speak to you. Sisters-in-waiting such as I serve our order when communication is needed with outsiders.'

'Indeed,' Garro nodded. 'Then may I ask your mistress what she wishes of me?'

Kendel gestured again, and the novice translated, her voice taking on a formal tone once more. 'I wished to speak with you before we departed the *Endurance*, on the matters to which you and your men were party aboard the jorgall cylinder. It is the Emperor's wish that they not be spoken of.'

The captain absorbed this. Of course, why else had Kendel killed the alien psyker with a shot to the chest instead of a round through the skull? To preserve whatever secrets it held inside that misshapen head. He nodded to himself. The Lord of Man's great works into the understanding of the ethereal realms were beyond his grasp as a mere captain, and if the Emperor required the corpse of a dead xenos mutant to further that understanding, then Nathaniel Garro had no place to contradict it. 'I shall make it so. The Emperor has his tasks and we have ours. My men would never question that.'

The Silent Sister came a little closer and watched him carefully. She signed something to the novice and the girl hesitated, questioning her mistress in return before relaying the words. 'Sister Amendera asks... She wishes to know if the child spoke to you.'

'It had no mouth,' Garro answered, quicker than he intended to.

Kendel placed a finger on her lips and shook her head. Then she moved the finger to her temple.

Nathaniel looked at his hands. There were still flecks of alien blood on them. 'I am clean of any taint,' he insisted. 'The thing did not contaminate me.'

'Did it speak to you?' repeated the novice.

The moment became long before he spoke. 'It knew what I was. It said it could see tomorrow. It told me all I worship would die.' Garro sneered. 'But I am an Astartes. I worship *nothing*. I honour no false god, only the reality of Imperial truth.'

His answer seemed to appease Sister Amendera, and she inclined her head in a bow. 'Your fealty, like that of all Death Guard, has never been in doubt, captain. Thank you for your honesty,' relayed the novice. 'It is clear the creature was attempting to cloud your intention. You did well to resist it.' The Oblivion Knight made the sign of the aquila and bowed.

The girl mirrored Kendel's gesture. 'My mistress wishes you and your company to accept the commendation and gratitude of the Sisters of Silence. Your names will be presented to the Sigillite in recognition of your service to Terra.'

'You honour us,' Garro replied. 'If I might ask, what was the fate of your comrade, the Null Maiden who was unhooded in the fighting?'

The novice nodded. 'Ah, Sister Thessaly, yes. Her injuries were serious, but she will recover. Our medicae aboard the *Aeria Gloris* will heal her in due course. I understand your Brother Voyen saved her life.'

'*Aeria Gloris*,' repeated Garro. 'I do not know of that vessel. Is it part of our flotilla?'

A smile crossed Kendel's lips and she signed to the novice. 'No, captain. It is part of mine. See for yourself.' The woman pointed out through the glass dome and Garro followed her direction.

A piece of the void moved slowly across the prow of *Endurance*, passing between the bow of the warship and the distant glow of the Iotan sun. Whereas conventional vessels of the Imperial fleets ran with pennants and signal lamps to illuminate the lengths of their hulls, this new arrival, this *Aeria Gloris*, came in darkness, arriving out of the interstellar deeps as an ocean predator might slip to the surface of a night time sea.

Garro had never laid eyes on a Black Ship before. These were the mothercraft of the Silent Sisterhood, carrying them back and forth across the galactic disc on the Emperor's witch hunting missions. It was hard to make out anything more than the most basic details of the ship's design. Framed against the solar glow of Iota Horologii, the battle cruiser was at least a match in size for the Death Guard capital ship *Indomitable Will*. It lacked the traditional plough blade prow of most Imperial vessels, ending instead in a blunt bow. A single, knife-edge sail hung below the stern and on it was an aquila cut from shimmering volcanic glass. Where *Endurance* and the ships of the Astartes flotilla were swords against the enemies of Terra, *Aeria Gloris* was a hammer of witches.

'Impressive,' rumbled Garro. There was little else he could say. He found himself wondering what it would be like to wander the decks of the vessel, at once attracted and repelled by the idea of what secrets the craft must hide.

Sister Amendera bowed again and nodded to her novice. 'We take our leave of you, honoured captain,' said the girl. 'We are to make space for Luna by day's end, and the warp grows turbulent.'

'Safe journey, sisters,' he offered, unable to tear his gaze from the dark starship.

KALEB GUIDED THE cart across the length of the armoury chamber, taking care to stay to the outer walkway around the edges of the long hall. His master's bolter lay across the trolley, the weapon's usually flawless finish marred by lines of damage from the engagement on the jorgall world-ship. As Garro's housecarl, it was Kaleb's duty to see the gun to the arming servitors and ensure that the weapon was returned to its full glory as quickly as possible. He intended not to disappoint his captain.

He passed knots of Death Guard as they debriefed and disarmed, men from Temeter's company in animated conversation about a thorny moment during the boarding of a xenos destroyer, and Astartes of Typhon's First in bellicose humour. Across the chamber he spied Hakur talking with Decius, as the younger man relayed a moment from the battle with an enthusiasm that the dour veteran clearly did not share.

The men of the XIV Legion were not given to raucous celebration in their victories – such displays, Kaleb had heard it said, were more in the character of the Space Wolves or the World Eaters – but they did, in their own fashion, salute their successes and give honour to those who fell along the way.

The Death Guard cultivated an image that other Legions were only too quick to accept: that they were brutal, ruthless and hard-hearted, but the reality had more shades to it than that. That these Astartes rarely made sport of their warfare was true, but they were not so bleak and stern as some would have believed.

Compared to the stories Kaleb had heard of stoic and dispassionate Legions like the Ultramarines or the Imperial Fists, the Death Guard could almost be considered wilful and disorderly.

Rounding a stanchion, the housecarl's train of thought stalled at the sound of harsh laughter from a figure before him. He hesitated. Commander Grulgor stood in his path, speaking in muted, amused tones to an Astartes from his Second Company. The two men clasped gauntlets in a firm, serious handshake and in spite of the dimness of the ill-lit walkway Kaleb was still able to make out the shape of a disc-shaped brass token held in Grulgor's fingers before he passed it into the other man's grip.

He understood immediately that he had intruded on a private moment, something only Astartes should share, something that a mere serf like him was not to be privy to, but there was nowhere Kaleb could hide, and if he turned around, the clatter of the cart's wheels would reveal him. In spite of himself, he coughed. It was a very small sound, but it brought with it a sudden silence as the commander broke off and noticed the housecarl for the first time.

Kaleb was looking directly at the decking, and did not see the expression of complete contempt Grulgor turned upon him

'Garro's little helot,' said the commander. 'Are you listening where you should not?' He took a step towards the housecarl and against his will, Kaleb shrank back. Grulgor's voice took on the tone of a teacher lecturing a student, making a lesson of him. 'Do you know what this is, Brother Mokyr?'

The other Astartes examined Kaleb coldly. 'It's not a servitor, commander, not enough steel and pistons for that. It resembles a man.'

Grulgor shook his head. 'No, not a man, but a *housecarl*.' The emphasis he put on the title was scornful. 'A sad bit of trivia, a dusty practice from the ancient days.' The commander spread his hands. 'Look on, Mokyr. Look at a failure.'

Kaleb found his voice. 'Lord, if it pleases you, I have duties to perform–'

He was ignored. 'Before our primarch brought new, strong blood to our Legion, there were many rituals and habits that knotted around the Astartes. Most have been cut away.' Grulgor's face soured. 'Some still remain, thanks to the dogged adherence of men who should know better.'

Mokyr nodded. 'Captain Garro.'

'Yes, Garro.' Grulgor was dismissive. 'He allows sentiment to cloud his judgement. Oh, he's a fine warrior, I will give him that, but our brother, Nathaniel, is old in his ways, too bound by his Terran roots.' The Astartes leaned closer to Kaleb, his voice dropping. 'Or, am I incorrect in my judgement? Perhaps Garro keeps you around him, not out of some misplaced sense of tradition, but as a reminder? A living example of what it means to fail the Legion?'

'Please,' said the serf, his knuckles white around the handles of the cart.

'I do not understand,' said Mokyr, genuinely confounded. 'How is this helot a failure?'

'Ah,' Grulgor said, looking away, 'but for a turn of fate, this wastrel might have walked among the Legiones Astartes. He could have stood where you do now, brother, wearing the white, bearing arms for the Imperium. Our friend here was once an aspirant to the XIV Legion, as were we all. Only he fell short of greatness during the trials of acceptance, damned by his own weakness.' The commander tapped his chin thoughtfully.

'Tell me, serf, where did your will break? Crossing the black plains? Was it in the tunnel of the venoms?'

Kaleb's voice was a whisper. 'The thorn garden, lord.' The hateful old memory emerged, fresh and undimmed despite the span of years since the event. The housecarl winced as he recalled the stabbing, poisonous barbs on his bare skin, his blood running in streaks all across his body. He remembered the pain and worse, the shame as his legs turned to water beneath him. He remembered falling into the thick, drab mud, lying there, weeping, knowing that he had lost forever the chance to become a Death Guard.

'The thorn garden, of course.' Grulgor tapped his fingers on his vambrace. 'So many have bled out their last in that ordeal. You did well to survive that far.'

Mokyr raised an eyebrow. 'Sir, do you mean to say that this... man was an aspirant? But those who fail the trials perish!'

'Most do,' corrected the commander. 'Most of them die of the wounds they suffer or the poisons they cannot resist during the seven days of trial, but there are some few who fail but live on still, and even they will largely choose the Emperor's Peace over a return in dishonour to their clans.' He gave Kaleb a cool stare. 'But not all. Some lack the strength of will even for that honour.' Grulgor looked back at Mokyr and sniffed archly. 'Some Legions make use of their throwbacks, but it is not the Death Guard way. Still, Garro chose to invoke an aged right, to save this wretch from the pit of his own inadequacy. He rescued him.' Grulgor snorted. 'How noble.'

Kaleb found a spark of defiance. 'It is my privilege to serve,' he said.

'Is it?' growled the Astartes. 'You dare to parade your own deficiencies around us, the chosen men of

Mortarion? You are an insult. You ape us, hang upon the tails of our cloaks while we fight for the future of our species, polishing guns and pretending you are worthy to be in our company?' He pressed Kaleb's cart towards the wall. 'You skulk in the shadows. You are Garro's petty spy. You are *nothing*!' Grulgor's annoyance flared in his eyes. 'If I were captain of the First, the pointless ritual that granted your existence would be ended in a second.'

'So, then,' said another voice, 'is the commander of the Second dissatisfied with his honoured role?'

'Apothecary Voyen.' Grulgor greeted the new arrival with a wary nod. 'Sadly there are many things that I find myself dissatisfied with.' He stepped away from the trembling housecarl.

'Life is always a challenge in that regard,' Voyen said with forced lightness, throwing Kaleb a sideways look.

'Indeed,' said the commander. 'Is there something you wanted, brother?'

'Only an explanation as to why you saw fit to waylay my captain's equerry during the course of his duties. The battle-captain will be returning shortly and he will wish to know why his orders have not been carried out.'

Kaleb clearly saw a nerve twitch in Grulgor's jaw in reaction to the temerity of Voyen's reply, and for a moment he expected the senior Astartes to bark out an angry retort to the junior Apothecary, but then the instant was gone as some moment of understanding he was not a party to passed between them.

With exaggerated care, Grulgor stepped out of Kaleb's path. 'The helot may go about his business,' he said, and with that, the commander dismissed them both and strode away with Mokyr at his side.

Kaleb watched them go and once again saw the glitter of the strange brass token as the Astartes tucked the coin-like object into an ammunition pouch on his belt.

He sucked in a shaky breath and bowed to Voyen. 'Thank you, lord. I must confess, I do not understand why the commander detests me so.'

Voyen walked with him as the housecarl continued on his way. 'Ignatius Grulgor hates everything with equal measure, Kaleb. You shouldn't take it personally.'

'And yet, the things he says... sometimes those thoughts are mine as well.'

'Really? Answer me this, then. Do you think that Captain Garro, the leader of the Seventh Great Company, considers you an insult? Would a man of honour like him even contemplate such a thing?'

Kaleb shook his head.

Voyen placed his huge hand on the housecarl's shoulder. 'You will never be one of us, that is true, but you still serve the Legion despite that.'

'But Grulgor was right,' Kaleb mumbled. 'At times, I *am* a spy. I go about the ship, invisible in plain sight, and I see and hear. I keep my lord captain conversant with the mood of the Legion.'

The Apothecary's expression remained neutral. 'A good commander should always be well informed. This is not plotting and scheming of which we speak. It is merely the report of talk and temper. You should feel no conflict in this.'

They arrived at the arsenal dais where the armament-servitors were waiting, and the housecarl presented them with the captain's bolter. Kaleb felt a churn of tension coming loose inside him, the need to speak pressing on his lips. Voyen seemed to sense it too, and guided him to an isolated corner near a viewport.

'It is more than that. I have seen things.' Kaleb's words were hushed and secretive. 'Sometimes in quarters of the ships, where the crewmen do not often venture. Hooded gatherings, lord. Clandestine meetings of what can only be your battle-brothers.'

Voyen was very still. 'You speak of the lodges, yes?'

Kaleb was taken aback to hear the Apothecary talk openly to him of such things. The quiet orders of men inside the Legiones Astartes were not something that was common knowledge to the outside world, and certainly they were things that a man such as Kaleb should not have been aware of. 'I have heard that name whispered.' The housecarl rubbed his hands together. The palms were sweaty. Something in the back of his mind urged him to say no more, but he couldn't help himself. He wanted to get the words out, to be free of them. 'Just now, I saw the commander give a medallion to Brother Mokyr. I have seen one before, among the personal effects of the late Sergeant Raphim after his death at the Carinea Moons.' Kaleb licked his lips. 'A brass disc embossed with the skull and star of our Legion, lord.'

'And what do you think it is?'

'A badge, sir? A token of membership for these surreptitious groupings?'

The Astartes gave him a level, unmoving stare. 'You are afraid that these meetings might threaten the Death Guard's unity, is that it? That sedition may be at their core?'

'How could they not?' hissed Kaleb. 'Secrecy is the enemy of truth. Truth is what the Emperor and his warriors stand for! If men must gather in shadows–' He broke off, blinking.

Voyen managed a small smile. 'Kaleb, you respect Captain Garro. We all comprehend the might of our primarch. Do you think such great men would stand idly by and let subversion take root in their midst?' The Apothecary put his hand on the housecarl's shoulder again and Kaleb felt the smallest amount of pressure there. He became aware of the mass and strength of the warrior's ceramite glove, enveloping his flesh and bone. 'What you have seen in sideways glances and overheard rumours is nothing that should concern you, and it is certainly not a matter with which to distract the battle-captain. Trust me when I tell you this.'

'But...' Kaleb said, his throat becoming dry, 'but how can you know that?'

The smile faded from Voyen's lips. 'I can't say.'

IN HIS INFORMAL robes, Nathaniel Garro still cut an impressive figure, even among his own men who had yet to divest themselves of their battle armour. At the far end of the wide armoury chamber, in the section of the long iron hall that was the province of the Seventh Company, he moved through the Astartes and spoke with each one, sharing a nod or a grin with those in good humour, sparing a solemn commiseration for those who had lost a close comrade in the engagement with the jorgall. He singled out Decius for mild chastisement where the younger Astartes sat at work on his power fist, cleaning the oversized gauntlet with a thick cloth.

'Our tactical approach at the bottle-world was not meant to be one of close combat, Solun,' he noted, 'you carry a bolter for good reason.'

'If it pleases my captain, I have heard this lecture already today from Brother Sendek. He informed me, at great length and in intricate detail, of exactly how I had failed to adhere to the rules of engagement.'

'I see.' Garro took a seat on the bench next to Decius. 'And what was your response?'

The young warrior smiled. 'I told him that we were both still alive, rules or no, and that victory is the only true measure of success.'

'Indeed?'

'Of course!' Decius worked at the power fist with great care. 'What matters in war above all other things is the final result. If there is no victory...' He broke off, finding his words. 'Then there is no point.'

From nearby, Andus Hakur rubbed a hand over his stubbly grey chin. 'Such tactical genius from the mouth of a whelp. I fear I may become giddy with surprise.'

Decius's eyes flashed at the old veteran's jibe, but Garro caught the moment and laughed softly, defusing it. 'You must forgive Andus, Solun. At his age, his sharp tongue is the only blade he can wield with skill any more.'

Hakur clutched at his chest in mock pain. 'Oh. An arrow to my heart, from my own captain. Such tragedy.'

Garro maintained an even smile, but in truth he could detect the weariness, the pain in his old friend's forced jocularity. Hakur had lost men from his squad on the world-ship, and the pain of it was just below the surface. 'We all fought well this day,' said the captain, the words coming of their own accord. 'Once more the Death Guard have been the tools that carve the Emperor's will into the galaxy.'

None of the other Astartes spoke. Each of them had fallen silent, faces turned over Garro's shoulder. As he cast around to learn why, as one, the men of the Seventh Company came to their knees.

'My battle-captain.'

It perturbed Garro to realise that he had not even heard the approach of his primarch. As in the assembly hall before the assault, Mortarion made issue of his presence only when it suited him to do so.

Garro bowed low to the master of the Death Guard, dimly aware of Typhon at his lord's side, and a servitor lurking behind the first captain's cloak.

'My lord,' he replied.

Mortarion's face shifted in a cool smile, visible even behind the breath collar around his throat and lips. 'The Sisterhood has taken leave of us. They spoke highly of the Seventh.'

Garro dared to raise his gaze a little. Like him, the primarch was no longer clad in his brass and steel power armour, but instead in common duty robes over a set of more utilitarian gear. Still, even in such simple garb, there was no mistaking his presence. High and gaunt, a man spun from whipcord steel muscle, he was as tall in his deck boots as Typhon was in the First Company's Terminator armour.

And of course, there was the manreaper. Sheathed across his back, the arc of the heavy black blade curved behind his head in a lightless sweep. 'Stand, Nathaniel, please. It becomes tiresome to look down upon my men.'

Garro drew himself up to his full height, looking into the primarch's deep amber eyes and steeling himself not to draw back. In turn, Mortarion's gaze burned deep into him, and the captain felt as if his heart were held in the primarch's long, slender fingers, being weighed and considered.

'You ought to watch your step, Typhon,' said the Death Lord. 'This one, he'll have your job one day.'

Typhon, ever sullen, only grimaced. Before the first captain, the primarch, and at the edges of his sight, the twin guards of the Deathshroud, Garro felt as if he was at the bottom of a well. The nerve of a common man would probably have broken beneath such scrutiny.

'Lord,' he asked, 'what service may the Seventh Company do for you?'

Mortarion beckoned him. 'Their captain may step forward, Garro. He has earned a reward.'

Nathaniel did as he was told, darting a quick look towards Hakur. His words at the lakeside echoed in his mind. *We don't seek accolades and honours.* Garro had no doubt that the veteran was keenly amused by this turn of events. 'Sir,' he began, 'I deserve no special—'

'That is not a refusal forming upon your lips, is it, captain?' warned Typhon. 'Such false modesty is unwelcome.'

'I am merely a servant of the Emperor,' Garro managed. 'That is honour enough.'

Mortarion gestured the servitor forward, and the captain saw that it carried a tray of goblets and bowls. 'Then instead, Nathaniel, might you honour me by sharing my drink?'

He stiffened, recognising the ornate cups and the liquid in them. 'Of... of course, lord.'

It was said that there was no toxin too strong, no poison so powerful and no contagion of such lethality that a Death Guard could not resist it. From their inception, the XIV Legion had always been the Emperor's warriors in the most hostile of environments, fighting through chem-clouds or acidic atmospheres that no normal human could survive in. Barbarus, the Legion's base, the adoptive home planet of Mortarion himself, moulded this characteristic. As with their primarch, so with his Astartes: the Death Guard were a resilient, invincible breed.

They hardened themselves through stringent training regimens as neophyte Astartes, willingly exposing themselves to chemical agents, contaminants, mortal viral strains and venoms of a thousand different shades. They could resist them all. It was how they had found victory amid the blight-fungus of Urssa, how they had weathered the hornet swarms on Ogre IV, the reason why they had been sent to fight the chlorine-breathing jorgall.

The servitor deftly mixed and poured dark liquids into the cups, and Garro's nostrils sensed the odour of chemicals: a distillate of the agent magenta nerve bane, some variety of sword beetle venom, and other, less identifiable compounds. No Astartes in Mortarion's service would ever have dared to call this practice a ritual. The word conjured up thoughts of primitive idolatry, anathema to the clean, impious logic of Imperial truth. This was simply their way, a Death Guard tradition that survived despite the intentions of men like Ignatius Grulgor. The cups were Mortarion's, and in each battle where the Death Lord took the field in person, he would select a warrior in the aftermath and share with that man a draught of poison. They would drink and they would live, cementing the unbreakable strength of the Legion they embodied.

The servitor presented the tray to the primarch and he took a cup for himself, then handed one to Garro and a third to Typhon. Mortarion raised his goblet in salute. 'Against death.' With a smooth tip of his wrist, the primarch drained the cup to its dregs. Typhon showed a feral half-smile and did the same, completing the toast and drinking deep.

Garro saw a flush of crimson on the first captain's face, but Typhon gave no other outward sign of distress. He sniffed at the liquid before him and his senses resisted, his implanted neuroglottis and preomnor organs rebelling at the mere smell of the poisonous brew; but to refuse the cup would be seen as weakness, and Nathaniel Garro would never allow himself to be accused of such a thing.

'Against death,' he said.

With a steady motion, the captain drank it all and placed the upturned goblet back on the tray. A ripple of approval drifted through the men of the Seventh Company, but Garro barely heard it. His blood was rumbling in his ears as punishing heat seared his throat and gullet, the powerful engines of his Astartes physiology racing to fight down the toxins he had ingested. Decius was watching him in awe, without doubt dreaming of a day when it might be *his* hand, not Garro's, holding the goblet.

Mortarion's chill smile grew wider. 'A rare and fine vintage, would you not agree?'

His chest on fire, Garro couldn't speak, so he nodded. The primarch laughed in a low chug of amusement. Mortarion's cup could have contained water for all the apparent effect it had upon him. He placed his hand on the battle-captain's back. 'Come, Nathaniel. Let's walk it off.'

As THEY CAME to the ramp that led to the balcony above the grand armoury chamber, Typhon bowed to his liege lord and made his excuses, walking away towards the alcoves where Commander Grulgor and the Second Company made their station. Garro cast back to see the Deathshroud following them in lockstep, moving with such flawless precision that they appeared to be automata and not actually men.

'Don't worry, Nathaniel,' said Mortarion, 'I have no plans to replace my guardians just yet. I am not about to recruit you into the secret dead.'

'As you wish, lord,' Garro replied, getting the use of his throat back.

'I know you frown on such things as the cups, but you must understand that honours and citations are sometimes necessary.' He nodded to himself. 'Warriors must know that they are valued. Praise... praise from one's peers must be given when the moment is right. Without it, even the most steadfast man will eventually feel unvalued.' There was an edge of melancholy that flickered through the primarch's voice so quickly that Garro decided he had imagined it.

Mortarion brought them to the edge of the balcony and they looked down at the large assemblage of men. Although *Endurance* was not large enough to hold the entire Legion, many of the Death Guard's seven companies were represented below, in whole or in part. Garro caught sight of Ullis Temeter and his comrade threw him a salute. Garro nodded back.

'You are a respected man, Nathaniel,' said the primarch. 'There's not a captain in the whole of the Legion who would not acknowledge your combat prowess.' He smiled slightly again. 'Even Commander Grulgor, although he may hate to admit it.'

'Thank you, lord.'

'And the men. The men trust you. They look to you for strength of character, for leadership, and you give it.'

'I do only what the Emperor commands of me, sir.' Garro shifted uncomfortably. As honoured as he was to have a private moment with his master, it troubled him in equal measure. This was not the direct, clear arena of warfare where Garro understood what was expected of him. He was in rarefied air here, loitering with a son of the Emperor himself.

If Mortarion sensed this, he gave no sign. 'It is important to me to have unity of purpose within my Legion. Just as it is important for my brother, Horus, to have unity across the entirety of the Astartes.'

'The Warmaster,' breathed Garro. There had been rumours aboard the *Endurance* for some time that elements of the Death Guard's flotilla would be sent on a new task after the jorgall interception. At the forefront of this talk was the possibility that they would join the 63rd Expeditionary Fleet of the Great Crusade, commanded by none other than the chosen son of the Emperor himself, Horus the Warmaster. It was clearly more than rumour, he now realised. Garro had fought side by side with the warriors of Horus's XVI Legion in the past, and had only admiration for men like Maloghurst, Garviel Loken and Tarik Torgaddon. 'I have served with the Luna Wolves in the past, lord.'

'They are the Sons of Horus now,' Mortarion corrected gently, 'just as the Death Guard were once the Dusk Raiders. My brother expects great things of our Legion, captain. A battle is coming that will test all of us, from the Warmaster to your lowly housecarl.'

'I will be ready.'

The primarch nodded. 'I have no doubt of that, but it is not enough to be ready, Nathaniel.' His fingers knitted together over the iron balustrade. 'The Death Guard must be of one mind. We must have singular purpose or we will falter.'

Garro's discomfort deepened and he wondered if the after-effects of the cup's contents were not still upon him. 'I... I am not sure I understand you, lord.'

'Our men find solace in the lines of command with their superiors and inferiors, but it is important that they also have a place in which the barriers created by rank can be ignored. They must have freedom to speak and think unfettered.'

All at once, the insight Garro had been lacking came to him in a cold rush. 'My lord refers to the lodges.'

'I have been told that you have always eschewed membership. Why, Nathaniel?'

Garro stared at the deck plates. 'Am I being ordered to join, lord?'

'I can no more command the workings of the lodge than I can the motion of the stars,' Mortarion said easily. 'No, captain, I do not order you. I only ask why. Illuminate me.'

It was a long moment before he spoke again. 'We are Astartes, sir, set on our path by the Master of Mankind, tasked to regather the lost fragments of humanity to the fold of the Imperium, to illuminate the lost, castigate the fallen and the invader. We can only do so if we have truth on our side. If we do it in the open, under the harsh light of the universe, then I have no doubt that we will eventually expunge the fallacies of gods and deities... but we cannot bring the secular truth to bear if any of it is hidden, even the smallest part. Only the Emperor can show the way forward.' He took a shuddering breath, intently aware of the primarch's unblinking stare upon him. 'These lodges, though they have their worth, are predicated on the act of concealment, and I will have no part of that.'

Mortarion accepted this with a careful nod. 'What of your battle-brothers who feel differently?'

'That is their choice, lord. I have no right to make it for them.'

The primarch drew himself up once more. 'Thank you for your candour, battle-captain. I expected nothing less.' He paused. 'I have one more request of you, Nathaniel, and this, I'm afraid, is indeed an order.'

'Sir?' Garro felt an odd flutter in his chest.

'Once we are done here, this fleet will make space for the Isstvan system to rendezvous with the Warmaster's command ship, the *Vengeful Spirit*. Horus will be holding a war council with representatives of the World Eaters and the Emperor's Children, and I will have need of an equerry to join me there. First Captain Typhon will be engaged in other duties, so I have chosen you to accompany my party.'

Garro was speechless. To extend such a privilege to a battle-captain was unprecedented, and the thought of it made his chest tighten. To stand in Mortarion's presence was heady enough, but to be close at hand before an assembly of the Emperor's sons led by the Warmaster...

It would be *glorious*.

FOUR

Two Faces
A Scream in the Darkness
Gathering of Legends

THE PICT SCREEN was a flexible thing, like cloth, and it hung from the eaves of the armoury chamber alcove in the manner of a tapestry. Cables trailed away to shining brass sockets in the walls, streams of data feeding images from the ship-to-ship vox network. The view was a live signal, attenuated by interference from the Horologii star, and although it appeared to be instantaneous, it was actually a few minutes behind the real events, the transmission slowed by relativistic physics, not that such a fact seemed to concern the Astartes gathered to watch.

The display came from remote scrying picters on the bow plane of *Barbarus's Sting*, a light frigate that had been tasked to follow the jorgall world-ship on its last journey. The images were being recorded for posterity. The better views would doubtless be worked into stirring newsreels for distribution across Imperial space.

The world ship's drives flashed red and tongues of fusion flame erupted from their nozzles, each one as long as the *Sting*. At the edges of the picture, it was possible to see the glints of smaller craft – shuttles and Thunderhawks – escaping the world-ship with the last of the Imperial forces on board. The picters rotated to follow the monolithic craft and smoked filters faded in as the Iotan sun hove into view.

The world-ship was accelerating away, gaining speed with every passing moment. The controls for the propulsion system captured by the Death Guard of the Second Company had been locked open by the adepts of the Mechanicum. *Barbarus's Sting* kept a respectful distance, drifting after the bottle-world, framing its descent towards the sun. Great loops of crackling electromagnetic energy shimmered around the pearlescent cylinder as it cut into the star's invisible chromosphere, destroying the solar panels at the aft. They crisped and burned, folding in on themselves like insect wings touched by candle flames. The world-ship fell faster and faster, dipping into the raging superheated plasma of the photospheric layer. Hull metal peeled away in curls a kilometre long, revealing ribs of metal that melted and ran. Finally, the alien vessel sank through a glowing coronal prominence and disappeared forever into the stellar furnace.

'Gone,' murmured Brother Mokyr, 'ashes and dust, as are all the enemies of the Death Guard. A fitting end for such xenos hubris.' A swell of self-congratulatory mood passed through the assembled men of the Second Company.

It was they who had made the sun dive possible, after spending their blood and fire to take the heavily defended engineering domes from the jorgall. It was fitting that they were witnesses to the alien vessel's final moments.

'I wonder how many survivors were aboard,' said a sergeant, watching the star's rippling surface.

Mokyr grunted. 'None.' He turned and grinned at his company captain. 'A fine victory, eh, commander?'

'A fine victory,' repeated Grulgor in a rancorous tone, 'but not fine enough.' He shot a hard look up at the gallery, where Garro stood in conversation with his primarch.

'Curb your choler, Ignatius. For once, try not to wear it like a badge upon your chest.' Typhon drew near, the rank-and-file Astartes parting before his approach.

'Forgive me, first captain,' Grulgor retorted, 'it is just that my choler, as you put it, is apt to suffer when I am forced to witness the unworthy rewarded.'

Typhon raised an eyebrow. 'You are questioning the primarch's decisions? Careful, commander, there is sedition in such thoughts.'

He drew close to the other man so that their conversation would be less public.

'Garro rescues women and kills newborns, and for that he is given a draught from the cup? Have the standards of the Legion fallen so low that we reward such behaviour?'

The first captain ignored the question and answered with one of his own. 'Tell me, why do you object to Nathaniel Garro with such vehemence? He is a Death Guard, is he not? He is your battle-brother, a kinsman Astartes.'

'Straight-arrow Garro!' Anger bubbled up through Grulgor's mocking reply. 'He's not fit to be a Death Guard! He is high-handed and superior, always looking down his nose! He thinks himself so much better than the rest of the Legion, too proud and too good for the rest of us!'

'Us?' asked Typhon, pushing the commander to say what he knew was there just beneath the surface.

'The sons of Barbarus, Calas. You and I, men like Ujioj and Holgoarg! The Death Guard who were born upon our blighted home world! Garro is a Terran, an Earthborn. He wears it like some sacred brand, always reminding us that he is our better because he fought for the Legion before it was given to Mortarion!' Grulgor shook his head. 'He pours scorn on my company, upon our brotherhood and comradeship of our lodge, too haughty to mix with the rest of us outside of rank and rule, and do you know why? Because his precious birthright is all he has! If he wasn't favoured by the Emperor with that damned eagle cuirass he wears, he wouldn't be allowed to ride the hem of my cloak!'

'Temeter is a Terran-born, and so is Huron-Fal, and Sorrak and countless others within our ranks,' said the captain levelly. 'Do you detest them as well, Ignatius?'

'None of them drag the old ways around like rattling chains. None of them think themselves a cut above the rest because of their birthplace!' His eyes narrowed. 'Garro acts as if he has the right to judge me. I will not tolerate such condescension from a man who grew up watered and well-fed, while my clan fought for every breath of clean air!'

'But is not Mortarion himself a Terran?' Typhon asked with a wicked smile, daring Grulgor to go further still.

'The primarch's place of birth was Barbarus,' insisted the commander, rising to the bait. 'He is, and always will be, one of us. This Legion belongs to the Death Lord first and the Emperor second. Garro should be reminded of that, not given praise he does not deserve.'

'Bold words,' noted Typhon, 'but I'm afraid you may be further disappointed. Our lord commander has not only granted Captain Garro the cups today, but will also take him as equerry to the war council at our next port of call.'

Grulgor's pale face flushed crimson. 'Did you come to mock, Typhon? Does it amuse you to parade Garro's favours in front of me?'

The line of Typhon's jaw hardened. 'Watch your tone, commander. Remember to whom you speak.' He looked away. 'You are a true Death Guard, Grulgor, a blunt instrument, lethal and relentless, and you are loyal to the primarch.'

'Never question that,' growled the Astartes, 'or I will take your head, first captain or not.'

The threat amused the other man. 'I would never dare to do such a thing, but I would ask you this – how far would your loyalty to Mortarion take you?'

'To the gates of hell and beyond, if he commanded it.' Grulgor's reply was immediate and absolute.

Typhon watched him carefully. 'Even if it was against the will of a higher authority?'

'Like the Sigillite?' snapped Grulgor, 'or those wastrels filling the Council of Terra?'

'Or higher still.'

The commander snorted with bitter laughter. 'The Death Lord first, the Emperor second. I said it and I meant it. If that makes me of lesser worth than men like Garro, then perhaps I am.'

'On the contrary,' nodded Typhon, 'it makes you all the more valuable. There are great powers soon to bloom, Ignatius, and men of your calibre will be needed when those moments come.'

He threw a dismissive glance up at the gallery. 'And what about him?'

Typhon shrugged, a peculiar gesture in the heavy plate of his armour. 'Nathaniel Garro is a good soldier and a leader of men, with the respect of many Astartes in this and other Legions. To have him at the primarch's side – as you say, a man so staunch a Terran – when a time of decision came to pass... that would carry much weight.'

Grulgor sneered. 'Garro has a steel rod up his backside. He would break before he would bend his knee to anything but the rule of Terra.'

'All the more reason for the primarch to keep a close eye on him.' Typhon's gruff voice became a rough whisper. 'I, however, see the reality in your viewpoint, Ignatius, and when the moment of choice comes and Garro does not fall in to line–'

'You might require the services of a blunt instrument, yes?'

A nod. 'Just so.'

The commander showed his teeth in a feral smile. 'Thank you, first captain,' he said, in a louder voice. 'Your counsel has been most soothing to my ill-humour.'

ENDURANCE TORE ITSELF from the mad fury of the warp and crashed into corporeal reality once more, leading the Death Guard flotilla into the wide-open diamond formation of the 63rd Expedition fleet. Garro, once again in his full battle armour and honour kit, stood behind and off to the side of his primarch as Mortarion observed the Warmaster's forces from the assembly hall. Flanked by the Deathshroud, Garro's commander stood with one hand pressed to the thick armourglass window that formed the right eye socket of the giant stone skull on the ship's bow.

'My brother seeks to impress us,' Mortarion said to the air. 'The Sons of Horus have indeed assembled a mighty force in this place.'

Garro had to admit that he had rarely seen the like, not since the days when the Emperor himself led the Great Crusade. The darkness was thick with ships of every type and tonnage, and the space between them swarmed with auxiliary craft, shuttles and fighters on perimeter patrols. The arrowhead arrangement of the green and grey liveried Death Guard ships slipped carefully into a pattern cleared for just that purpose. To the far starboard, across the bow of Typhon's flagship, the *Terminus Est*, he spied the ornate purple and gold filigree of a cruiser from the III Legion, the Emperor's Children, and high above at a different anchor, blue and red trimmed craft from the XII Legion, the World Eaters.

But what caught his attention and held it firmly was the single great battleship that orbited ahead of them all, isolated in its own halo of open space and screened by a wall of sleek Raven-class interceptors. A heavy ingot of fashioned iron, the Warmaster's *Vengeful Spirit* radiated quiet power. Even from this distance, Garro could see hundreds of gun turrets and the slender rods of massive accelerator cannons that were twice the length of the *Endurance*. Where the Death Guard ship displayed a skull and star sigil, Horus's flagship had a massive golden ring bisected by a slim ellipse. The eye of the Warmaster himself, unblinking and open to see all that transpired. Soon, Garro was to set foot aboard that vessel, carrying the honour of his company with him.

Repeater lights set into a control panel beneath the windows clicked and changed, signalling that the *Endurance* had come to her station. Garro looked up at his primarch. 'My lord, a Stormbird has been prepared in the launch bay for your egress. We are ready to answer the Warmaster's summons at your discretion.'

Mortarion nodded and remained where he was, observing silently.

After a moment, Garro felt compelled to speak again. 'Lord, are we not ordered to attend the Warmaster the moment we arrive?'

The primarch grinned in a flash of rictus. 'Ah, captain, we move from the battlefield to the arena of politics. It would be impolite of us to arrive too soon. We are the XIV Legion, and so we must respect the numbering of our brethren. The Emperor's Children and the World Eaters must be allowed to arrive first, or else I would earn the ire of my brothers.'

'We are Death Guard,' Garro blurted. 'We are second to none!'

Mortarion's smile widened. 'Of course,' he agreed, 'but you must understand that it is sometimes tactful to let our comrades think that is not so.'

'I… I do not see the merit in it, lord,' Garro admitted.

The primarch turned away from the viewport. 'Then watch and learn, Nathaniel.'

IN THE CONFINES of the Stormbird's spartan crew compartment, Garro once again felt dwarfed by his commander. Mortarion sat across the gangway from him, hunched forward so that his head was only a hand's span from the battle-captain's. The Death Lord spoke in a fatherly tone. Garro listened intently, absorbing every word as the small ship crossed the void between the *Endurance* and the *Vengeful Spirit*.

'Our role at this war council is an important one,' Mortarion said. 'The data you hold in your hand is the lit taper for the inferno that is about to engulf the Isstvan system.' At this, Garro opened his palm and studied the thick spool of memory-wire there. 'We bear the responsibility of bringing the news of this perfidy to the Warmaster's ears, as it was our battle-brothers who came across the warning that Isstvan has turned from the Emperor.'

Garro examined the coil. It was so innocuous an object to contain so volatile a potential. The little device hardly seemed capable of representing the death warrant of entire worlds. Before they had departed the *Endurance*, the primarch had shown Nathaniel the pict record contained on the spool, and the images left him with a chill that he found difficult to shake off.

He saw it again, the recall fresh and close to the surface. Garro had watched the terrified face of a woman loom in the assembly hall's hololithic tank, a shape of haze and shade like some mythical spirit bent on haunting the living. She was a minor officer of the army, a major. At least, she was somebody wearing the uniform of one. Garro saw glimpses of a stone stockade's walls among the jumping shadows, the dance of orange light from a chemical candle. Perspiration made her sallow face gleam, and the slender tongue of flame reflected from her anxious green eyes. When she spoke, it was with the voice of a person broken by horrors that no mortal should ever have lived to witness.

'It's revolution,' she began, pushing the words from her lips like a desperate curse. She rambled on, speaking of 'rejection' and of 'superstition', of things a line soldier like her had never believed could be real. 'Praal has gone mad,' she growled, 'and the Warsingers are with him.'

Garro's brow furrowed at the names and his master halted the replay, providing an explanation. 'The noble Baron Vardus Praal is the Emperor's Designate Imperialis on the capital world of the system, Isstvan III.'

'He… She means to say the governor of an entire world broke with the rule of Terra to throw in with some pagan idolaters?' Nathaniel blinked, the idea unconscionable from a man of such significant rank within the Imperium. 'Why? What madness could compel such a thing?'

'That is what my brother, Horus, will have us learn,' intoned the primarch.

The Astartes studied the woman's face, blurred in mid-motion as she turned to look at something out of view of her picter's lens. 'The other word, "Warsinger", my lord, I am unfamiliar with it.' He wondered if it were some kind of colloquial name, perhaps some sort of honorific.

'They were a local myth, according to the records of the 27th Expedition that enforced compliance here over a decade ago, a cadre of fantastical shaman warriors. Nothing but anecdotal evidence of their existence was ever found.' Garro's master was circumspect, and he tapped the hololith controls with a slender finger, letting the recording run on.

With abrupt violence, the woman drew a heavy stub pistol, and shot and killed something indistinct at the margins of the image pick-up. She hove back into view, filling the screen, her unchained panic leaching out through the hologram. 'Send someone, anyone,' she pleaded. 'Just make this stop–'

Then there was the scream.

The sheer wrongness of the noise, the utterly alien nature of it made Garro's gut knot, and his fingers tightened reflexively around a bolter trigger that was not there. The impact of the sound beat the woman down and shredded the picter's image control, shifting the replay into a stuttering series of blink fast flash frames. Nathaniel saw blood, stone, torn skin, and then silent darkness.

'No word from the Isstvan system followed this,' said Mortarion quietly, allowing Garro to measure and understand what he had just viewed. 'No vox transmissions, no picter relays, no astropathic broadcasts.'

The battle-captain gave a stiff nod. The scream had cut though him like a knife-edge, the echo of it a weapon turning to pierce his heart. Garro shook off the eerie sensation and turned back to his liege lord. Mortarion explained that by pure chance, the distress signal had been picked up by the crew of the *Valley of Haloes*, a supply hauler in service to the XIV Legion. Suffering a dangerous Geller Field fluctuation while in transit to the Death Guard's Sixth Company flotilla at Arcturan, the *Valley* had emerged from the immaterium to effect emergency repairs.

There, as the ship drifted in space at the edge of the Isstvanian ecliptic plane, the desperate message had found purchase. Data addressing the rate of energy decay, pattern attenuation and the like were scrutinised by tech-adepts, revealing that the transmission had been flung into the ether more than two years previously. Garro considered the frightened officer he had seen on the hololith and wondered about her fate. Her last, awful moments of life were frozen and preserved forever while her bones lay out there somewhere, forgotten and decaying.

'Did the crewmen of the *Valley* detect anything else of import, master?' he asked. 'Perhaps if the men aboard the transport were fully debriefed–'

Mortarion glanced away, then back. 'The *Valley of Haloes* was a casualty at the Arcturan engagement. It was lost with all hands. Fortunately, this recording of the Isstvan signal was conveyed to the *Terminus Est* before that regrettable event.' The primarch spoke with a leaden finality on the matter that Garro felt compelled to accept.

The Death Lord placed the spool in the battle-captain's hand. 'Carry this burden for me, Nathaniel. And remember, watch and learn.'

INSIDE, THE VENGEFUL *Spirit* was no less impressive than it had been from a distance, the vast open space of the landing bay so wide and long that Garro imagined it would be possible to dock a starship the size of a small cutter in here with room to spare. An honour guard slammed their fists to attention in the old martial manner, saluting with hand to breast instead of the usual crossed palms of the aquila.

The battle-captain kept pace behind the Deathshroud and Mortarion, while Garro in turn was followed by a contingent of warriors from Typhon's First Company, their lockstep footfalls pulsing like ready thunder as the XIV Legion's contingent marched on to the Warmaster's flagship. Garro could not help but glance around, taking in as much as he could of Horus's vessel, committing everything he saw to memory. He noticed other Stormbirds on landing cradles in the process of refuelling for return flights, one adorned with the snarling fanged mouth of the World Eaters and another trimmed in regal purple with the golden wings of the Emperor's Children.

'My brother, Fulgrim, has not graced us with his presence,' murmured Mortarion, casually dismissing the purple Stormbird with thinly veiled sarcasm. 'How like him.' Garro peered closer and saw that the ship did not fly the pennants associated with the carriage of a primarch. Indeed, he recalled that there had been no sign of the *Firebird*, Fulgrim's assault ship, among the war fleet.

He found himself wondering if this was some element of the politics that his master had spoken of before. Garro frowned. He had always fancied that the primarchs were an inviolate fraternity, comrades of such exalted status that they were beyond any petty emotions like rivalry or contention, but suddenly such thoughts seemed naïve. Astartes warriors like Garro and Grulgor were raised above normal men, and yet they still disagreed in their manners, more often than Nathaniel would have liked. Would it be surprising then to learn that the primarchs, who stood above the Astartes as much as the Astartes stood above mortal men, were also prey to the same differences?

Perhaps it was a good thing, Garro decided. If the primarchs were elevated too far towards godhood, they might lose sight of the fact that this was the Imperium of Man, and it was for the good of the common people of the galaxy that they served the Emperor.

With a silent member of the Sons of Horus leading their party, the Death Guard contingent moved across the cavernous bay to where a pneu-train carriage awaited to speed Mortarion to the bow decks of the *Vengeful Spirit* and the Lupercal's Court. Garro let his gaze turn upward, to the maze of skeletal gantries and walkways overhead, some heavy with cranes and weapons pallets, others ringed with catwalks for servitors and crewmen. It seemed oddly static up there for a working starship in preparation for a major combat operation. The battle-captain had expected dozens of figures clustering in the metal galleries to observe the arrival of the primarchs. Even aboard so illustrious a ship as the Warmaster's personal barge, it would have been a rare occurrence for parties from not two, but three other Legions to be aboard at one time. He looked hard, expecting to see men from Horus's Legion watching the proceedings, but saw only a handful, a scattering of deckhands and nothing else. Garro shook his head. Had the circumstances been reversed and the war council been taking place on *Endurance*, he would warrant that every Astartes on the ship would have come to see. It seemed as if something were missing.

'What troubles you, Nathaniel?' The primarch had halted at the pneu-train and was studying him.

Garro took a breath and the nagging thoughts in his mind abruptly crystallised. 'I had been told, lord, that the 63rd Fleet carried a substantial contingent of remembrancers with it. Considering the import of this day's meeting, it seems strange to me that I see not a single one of them hereabouts to record it.' He cast around with open hands.

Mortarion raised a pale eyebrow. 'Are you concerned that your heroic profile will be rendered incorrectly in some poet's doggerel, captain? That your name might be misspelled, or some other indignity?'

'No, my lord, but I had expected that they might mark such an uncommon moment as this gathering. Is that not their function?'

The primarch frowned. The Emperor's edict to introduce the army of artists, sculptors, composers, poets, authors and other sundry creatives to the fleets of the Great Crusade had not met with positive response from his sons, and despite the insistence from Terra that the endeavours of the Astartes were to be documented for posterity there were only a few in the Legions that were willing to tolerate the presence of civilians. Garro himself was largely indifferent to the idea, but he understood in an abstract way the value that future generations of humanity might gain from true accounts of their mission. For his part, the master of the Death Guard had been careful to ensure that the ships of the XIV were always engaged elsewhere, somewhere beyond the reach of the remembrancer delegations that were part of the larger expeditionary fleets.

Mortarion's character, like that of his Legion, was inward-looking, private and guarded in the face of those he did not regard. The Death Lord considered the remembrancers to be little more than unwanted intruders.

'Garro,' he replied, 'those gangs of ink-fingered scribblers and salon intelligentsia are here, but they do not have the run of the fleet. The Warmaster informed me that there was... an incident in recent days. Some remembrancers lost their lives because they ventured into areas that were unsafe for them. As such, tighter controls have been placed on their movements, for their own safety, of course.'

'I see,' replied the captain. 'For the best, then.'

'Indeed.' Mortarion entered the carriage. 'After all, what we discuss today will be its own record. There will be no need for scribes or stonecutters to immortalise it. History will do that for us.'

Garro took one last look around the bay as he ascended the boarding ramp, and from the corner of his eye a swift movement drew his attention. He glimpsed the figure only for a moment, but his occulobe optic implant allowed Nathaniel's brain to process every facet of the moment with pin-sharp clarity. It was an elderly man in the robes of an iterator of some senior rank, quite out of place in among the steel stanchions and rail tracks of the landing bay. He was quick and furtive in motion, keeping to the shadowed places, intent on some destination that he seemed fearful of ever reaching. In one of the iterator's hands was a fold of paper, perhaps a certificate or a permission of some kind. The old man was puffing with effort, and almost as soon as Garro registered him, he was gone, ducking into a companionway that disappeared within the depths of the warship.

The Death Guard grimaced and boarded the tram, the curious moment adding more definition to the sense of ill-ease he had felt from the moment he had arrived on the *Spirit*.

WHAT SHOULD ONE think of a place that was named the Lupercal's Court? The title had great vanity to it. It seemed to come with a sneer on the lips of the Sons of Horus, as if the chamber were in some manner a pretender to the grand court of the Emperor on distant Terra. Garro marched in at his rightful place, his chest stiff inside his ornamental cuirass from expectant tension. He did not know what to anticipate before him. The battle-captain had seen the Warmaster in the flesh only once and that was in passing, as he led the Seventh Company in review by the stands during the great parade after Ullanor.

But there he was, seated on a black throne upon a raised dais, beneath gales of sullen, uncommon banners. There were other people in the room, he was sure of it, but they were dim reflections of light and colour off the blaze of presence that was Horus. Garro felt a curious twinge in his legs, as if almost by muscle memory he felt the urge to kneel.

The Warmaster. He was indeed every iota of that, a perfect sculpture of the Astartes ideal on the stone chair, handsome and potent, radiating chained power. Robes laced with cords of white gold and copper pooled around him, cascading over the basalt frame of the throne. He wore armour of a kind Garro had only seen before in artworks, intricately worked plates of emerald-tinted flexsteel with vambraces made of black carbon.

Pieces of Horus's battle gear resembled elements of the older Mark III Iron Armour and the current Mark IV Maximus type, while some parts were more advanced than anything used by the Death Guard. An exotic pistol that appeared to be fashioned from glass nestled at the Warmaster's hip in the folds of an animal-skin holster. If anything, Horus seemed barely restrained by the bonds of ceramite and metal he wore, as if one mighty flex of his shoulders might split and throw them off.

Even at rest, the Lord of all Legions was a supernova made flesh, ready to detonate into action in an instant. The gleam of the slit-pupil Eye of Horus glared from his chest, catching the brooding glow from drifting glow-globes. With a near-physical effort, Nathaniel tore his gaze away from the being before him and pressed down the churn of emotion he felt. Now was not the time to be awestruck and unfocused, addled like some neophyte noviciate. *Watch and learn*, Mortarion had ordered. Garro would do just that.

His eye line crossed that of another Astartes on the dais in the new green livery of Horus's renamed

Legion, and he nodded in brief greeting to Garviel Loken. Garro had once shared a bunker with Loken and some of his men, during the prosecution of the ork invasion of Krypt. The Death Guard and the Luna Wolves had fought together for a week across the frozen plains, turning the blue ice dark with xenos blood.

Loken gave him a tight smile and the simple gesture served to ease Nathaniel's tension a little. Nearby he saw the other members of Horus's inner circle, the Mournival – the warriors Torgaddon, Aximand and Abbadon – and an odd thought struck him. The body language of the four captains was subtle, but not so understated that Garro could not read it. There were lines of stress drawn here, Loken and Torgaddon on one side, Aximand and Abbadon on the other. He could see it in the way that they did not meet each other's eyes, the lack of the easy camaraderie that Garro had come to think of as a key characteristic of the Warmaster's Legion. Was there some concealed enmity at large within the Sons of Horus? The Astartes filed the information away for later consideration.

His primarch had correctly surmised that the lord of the Emperor's Children was not at the gathering. In his stead was a ranking officer whom Garro knew of through first-hand experiences, from crossings in battle that underlined the man's less than complimentary reputation. Lord Commander Eidolon and his troops were clad in wargear so elegant it made the Death Guard in their grey and green trim seem utterly featureless in comparison. The Legion had a reputation as dandies, preening over their armour and decorating themselves when other warriors looked to battle, and yet the wicked hammer carried by Eidolon and the swords of his men spoke to obvious martial skill on their part. Still, Garro could not help but think that the Emperor's Children were overdressed for the occasion.

The other presence in the room was almost as imposing as Horus, and the battle-captain found himself measuring the primarch of the World Eaters against his own liege lord as the two leaders exchanged a neutral look. Where Mortarion was tall and wolf-lean, the primarch Angron was thickset and heavy. The Death Lord's pale aspect was at the far end of the spectrum from the Red Angel's clenched fist of a face, eyes deep-set among an orchard of scars. Angron's mere presence leaked the coiled potential for feral violence into the chamber.

As Mortarion embodied the dogged, silent promise of death, so his brother primarch was the personification of raw and murderous aggression. The Lord of the World Eaters stood broad and deadly in bronze armour and a heaped cloak of tarnished chainmail that trailed the smell of old blood in the air. A cadre of his chosen men were at his side, led by an Astartes that Garro knew by reputation alone, Khârn, master of the Eighth Company. Unlike Eidolon, who was known for braggadocio, Khârn's name was synonymous with brutality in battle. There were rumours of slaughters Khârn had caused that even the most ruthless of the Death Guard found difficult to stomach.

Garro halted as Horus spoke, the voice commanding his total attention. 'With our brother, Mortarion, we are complete.' The Warmaster stood and once again Garro fought off the urge to kneel. From a shadowed niche near where Nathaniel stood, a lipless servitor operated a control and the court's lamps dimmed as a hololith bloomed before them. He recognised Isstvan III from the pict slates he had seen at Mortarion's hands, orbital shots taken by long range imagers, some hazed by the bright shape of the planet's largest satellite, the White Moon. This, then, was the world where the vile seed of Vardus Praal's treachery had taken root.

Horus spoke with keen urgency, each word sounding across the chamber as he repeated the details that Mortarion had given to Garro on the Stormbird, describing how years earlier the Primarch Corax and his Raven Guard had left Isstvan in good order to be turned to the Imperial way.

'Are we to assume that the truth didn't take?' Eidolon interrupted, his tone arch and sardonic, and Garro shot him a disdainful look. It seemed the lord commander's poor manners had not improved since last he had seen him. Horus ignored the outspoken Astartes and instead gestured to Mortarion, who took up the thread of the briefing, moving on to the matter of the distress signal. Nathaniel knew his cue and proffered the memory spool to the waiting servitor, which dutifully loaded it into the hololith console.

The message unwound and played to the assembled warriors. Instead of watching the recording again, Garro slowly let his gaze cross over the faces of his brother Astartes, searching for some measure of their reaction to the dead woman's panic and terror. Khârn mirrored his master Angron in his impassive mien, the very faintest twitch of a sneer pulling at the corner of his lips. Eidolon's haughty expression remained in place, apparently dismissive of the dishevelled and unkempt condition of the messenger. Horus was unreadable, his face as calm as that of a statue.

Garro looked away and found the men of the Mournival. Only Torgaddon and Loken seemed affected, and of them Garviel looked to feel it the most. When the horrific killing scream came, Garro had steeled himself against it but still felt a churn of revulsion. He was watching Loken at that moment and saw the Son of Horus flinch, just as he himself had aboard the *Endurance*. Garro openly shared his comrade's discomfort. The dark message the distress signal carried was not just a call for help, a cry for the Astartes to leap to the defence of innocents. It was something much deeper, much more sinister than that. The Isstvan recording spoke of duplicity of the most base and foul kind, where men of the Imperium had turned back to the black path of ignorance, and done it willingly.

The mere thought of such a thing made the Death Guard feel sick with revulsion. At Isstvan, it would not be xenos or criminals, or foolish men blind to the Imperial truth that they were to face in combat. This foe had once been their comrades in the Emperor's service. They would be fighting tainted men, turncoats and deserters: *traitors*. The disgust churning in him turned hot and became ready anger.

Garro's mind snapped back to the moment, as the Warmaster showed them the Choral City, the seat of government on the third planet of the system and the source of the signal. The attack was to be huge, with elements of all four Legions, platoons of common soldiery and Titan war machines converging on Vardus Praal's base of operations in the Precentor's Palace. Nathaniel absorbed every detail, committing each element to his memory. The mention of his primarch's name caught his attention once more.

'Your objective will be to engage the main force of the Choral City's army,' said Horus, directing his words to Mortarion.

The battle-captain could not help but feel a swell of
pride when his master spoke up after the supreme
commander had laid out his orders. 'I welcome this
challenge, Warmaster. This is my Legion's natural battlefield.'

There would be one objective to complete before
the assault on the Choral City began, and that was a
raid to silence the monitors on Isstvan Extremis, the
outermost world of the system and home to the
nexus of its sensor web network. Once blinded, the
defenders of Isstvan III would only know that retri-
bution was on its way. They would not know where or
when it would strike.

'Aye,' whispered Garro to himself, staring into the
depths of the hololith and the sprawl of urban complexity it presented. The Choral City would make a
demanding theatre of combat, but it was one that
Nathaniel was already eager to explore.

The rest of the order of battle was swiftly laid down.
The Emperor's Children and the World Eaters would
target the Palace and the Warmaster's own Legion
would attack an important religious shrine to the
east, a vast cathedral complex called the Sirenhold.
The name resonated in his mind and once again
Garro turned the strange words over and over in his
thoughts.

Sirenhold… Warsinger…

Unbidden, the alien phrases brought back the
creeping sense of unease, and a cold foreboding that
would not release him.

FIVE

Choices Made
Omens
In Extremis

OVER THE RUMBLE and clatter of docking gear, Nathaniel heard a voice call his name and turned in place to see an Astartes in shining purple armour throw a salute. Garro hesitated, glancing back to see if he hadn't broken some minor protocol by stepping out of the formation. Beneath the spread wings of the Stormbird launch cradles, he saw his primarch and the master of the World Eaters leaning close together, speaking in a careful and measured fashion. He concluded that he had a moment or two before his lord commander would require him.

The warrior of the Emperor's Children was approaching and Garro's eyes narrowed. During the briefing neither Commander Eidolon nor the men of his honour guard had even deigned to acknowledge the battle-captain's presence, yet here was one of them calling out for his attention. He didn't recognise the pennants on the man's armour, but he was sure that this Astartes hadn't been present in the Lupercal's Court.

'Ho, Death Guard,' said a wry voice from behind the blunt-snouted breath mask of the helmet. 'Are you so slow-witted that you ignore your betters?' The figure reached up and removed his headgear, and Garro felt a warm grin cross his lips for what felt like the first time in days.

'Blood's oath! Saul Tarvitz, aren't you dead yet? I hardly recognised you underneath all that finery.'

The other man gave a slight nod, shoulder-length hair falling across a patrician face marred only by a brass plate across his brow. '*First Captain* Tarvitz, I'll have you note, Nathaniel. I've moved up in the world since last we spoke.' The two Astartes clasped each others wrists and their vambraces clattered together. Each had a small eagle carved there by knifepoint, a sign of the battle debt they owed one another.

'So I see.' Garro saw it now, the etching and the filigree on the shoulder plates that designated Tarvitz's new rank. 'You deserve it, brother.'

There were few men outside the Death Guard that Garro would ever have given the distinction of that address, but Tarvitz was one of them. He had earned Nathaniel's amity during the Preaixor Campaign and proven to him that for all the reputation of Fulgrim's Astartes as overconfident peacocks, there were men among the ranks of the Emperor's Children that embodied the ideals of the Imperium. 'I had wondered if we might cross paths here.'

Tarvitz nodded. 'We'll do more than that, my friend. Our companies are to form part of the spear tip to silence the monitor station.'

'Yes, of course.' Garro was aware that the First Company of the III Legion would be fighting alongside his

Seventh Company, but now that he knew Saul Tarvitz would be there, he felt a greater confidence. 'Eidolon has given you this one, then?'

Tarvitz hid a grin. 'No, he'll be there at my shoulder. He's not one to miss even a sniff of glory. I imagine he will goad me on to ensure the Death Guard don't take the lion's share of the kills.'

Garro's smile turned brittle. 'It cheers me to see you, honour brother,' he said, his emotions suddenly raw, there and then gone.

Tarvitz caught the moment too. 'I know that look, Nathaniel. What's troubling you?'

He shook his head. 'Nothing. It's nothing. I am fatigued, that is all, and perhaps a bit overawed by all… all this.' He gestured around.

The other officer glanced at the primarchs, still intent on their conversation. 'Aye, I share that with you.' He smirked. 'Is it true what they say? That the Warmaster can stop your heart as soon as look at you?'

'He's impressive, of that you can have no doubt,' agreed Garro, 'but then would you expect any less of an Emperor's chosen?' He hesitated. 'I'm surprised you weren't part of the honour guard. Doesn't your rank entitle you to that?'

'Eidolon has favour over me,' Tarvitz replied, 'and he would never share his moment in Horus's spotlight with another officer.'

Garro grunted. 'If he preens about the moment too much, you might ask him to recount how Angron shouted him down for his impudence and the Warmaster gave his approval to it.'

Tarvitz laughed. 'I doubt that part of the story will ever be told!'

'No.' Garro looked back at Mortarion and saw the Death Lord give a shallow bow to the World Eater. 'I think we'll be leaving now. Until the battlefield then, Saul?'

'Until the battlefield, Nathaniel.'

'Tell Eidolon we'll try to leave a little glory for him. If he asks us politely.' The battle-captain saluted and followed his master aboard the Stormbird.

'Do you REALLY think you can take him?' asked Rahl, tapping a quizzical finger on his chin.

Decius did not look up. 'This is a battle, like any other, and I intend to win it.'

Rahl glanced at Sendek, who waited, poised and ready. 'He's going to beat you to a standstill.' The Astartes leaned in closer, over the arena of combat. 'Look here, your magister is under threat from his castellan. Your dragonar is pinned by his cannonades, and–'

'If you want a game, you can wait until after I have dispatched Sendek,' snapped Decius. 'Until then, if you must watch, be silent. I need to think.'

'That's why you'll lose,' Rahl retorted.

'Let them play, Pyr,' said Hakur, the veteran pulling Rahl away from the regicide board as ill-temper flared in the younger Astartes's eyes. 'Stop distracting him.'

Rahl allowed the older warrior to draw him back. 'Care to make a bet on the outcome?'

'I'd hate to embarrass you, again.'

He smiled. 'Solun's going to lose, Andus, that's as plain as your face.'

Hakur returned the smile. 'Really? Well, although I may not be as handsome as you, I have the benefit of wisdom, and I'll tell you this. Solun Decius isn't the fool you think he is.'

'I never said he was a fool.' Rahl was defensive. 'But Sendek is the thinker, and regicide is a game of the mind. I've seen the mess Solun makes of the practice cages. *That's* where the lad's strength lies, in his fists.'

Andus smirked. 'You shouldn't underestimate him. He wouldn't be part of the battle-captain's cadre if he was a dim candle.'

The veteran cast a look over at the table, where Decius had just moved a soldat to take one of Sendek's iterators. 'He's young, that's true, but he has a lot of potential. I've seen his kind before. Let him grow unguided, he'll turn down the wrong path and wind up a corpse. But mould a man like him with care and intention, and at the end you'll have a brother fit to be a captain himself one day.'

Rahl blinked. 'I thought you didn't like him.'

'Why, because I make sport of the lad? I do that to everyone. It's part of my charm.' Andus leaned closer and lowered his voice. 'Of course, if you tell him I said any of those things, I'll deny it to the hilt, and then I'll break your legs.'

There was a decisive clack of wood on wood, and Rahl glanced around to see Sendek pressing his empress to the board, surrendering the game to Decius with a grudging smile on his face. 'Well played, brother. You are a singular opponent.'

'You see?' prodded Hakur.

'Ah, he must have let him win,' Rahl said lamely, 'as a small mercy.'

'Mercy is for the irresolute,' broke in Voyen as he entered the exercise enclosure, intoning the battle axiom with insincere solemnity. 'Who asks for it?' He shrugged back the hood of his off-duty robes.

Andus nodded to the other Astartes. 'Brother Rahl does. He has once again been proven wrong and it no doubt chafes upon him.'

Rahl finally bared his teeth in mild annoyance. 'Don't make me hurt you, old man.'

Hakur rolled his eyes. 'And what of you, Meric? Where have you been?'

The question was a mild one, but Rahl saw a fractional flicker of tension in the Apothecary's eyes. 'At my business, Andus, little more than that.' Voyen quickly turned the conversation away from him. 'So, Pyr, I trust you are ready for the coming fight? I think the score is in my favour still, yes?'

He nodded. Rahl and Voyen had a casual competition between them as to which man would take a kill first on any given mission. 'Only combatants count, remember? That last one was only a servitor.'

'*Gun*-servitor,' corrected Voyen. 'It would have killed me if I had let it.' He looked around. 'I believe we will have ample chance to test the mettle of these defectors on Isstvan. There's to be a multi-stage offensive, first a landing to deny the monitor stations on the outermost world. Then on to the inner planets for an assault in full.'

Hakur's lip curled. 'You're very well informed. Captain Garro has not returned from the Warmaster's barge and yet already you know the details of the mission.'

Voyen hesitated. 'It's common enough knowledge.' His tone shifted, becoming more guarded.

'Is it?' Rahl sensed something amiss. 'Who told you, brother?'

'Does it matter?' the Apothecary said defensively. 'The information came to me. I thought you would wish to know, but if you would rather remain unapprised–'

'That is not what he said,' Andus noted. 'Come, Meric, where did you learn these things? Someone in the infirmary babbling under the influence of pain nullifiers, perhaps, or a talkative astropath?'

Rahl became aware that the rest of the men in the room had fallen silent and were watching the exchange. Even Garro's housecarl was there, observing. Voyen saw Kaleb too and shot him a frosty glare.

'I asked you a question, brother,' said Hakur, and this time it was in the tone of voice he used on the battlefield, one accustomed to giving orders and having them obeyed.

Voyen's jaw hardened. 'I can't say.' He stepped around the veteran and took a few paces towards his arming alcove.

Hakur caught his arm and stopped him. 'What is it you have in your hand?'

'Nothing of your concern, sergeant.'

The elder Astartes was easily twice the Apothecary's age, yet for all those decades Hakur's martial skills were deft and undimmed. He easily took Voyen's wrist and applied pressure to a nerve cluster, trapping his hand. Meric's fingers uncurled of their own accord and there in his palm was a mottled brass coin.

'What is this?' Hakur demanded in a low voice.

'You know what it is!' Voyen snapped back. 'Don't play me for a fool.'

The dull disc bore the imprint of the Legion's sigil. 'A lodge medal,' breathed Rahl. 'You're in the lodges? Since when?'

'I can't say!' Voyen retorted, shaking off Hakur's grip and walking to the alcove where his sparse collection of personal effects were kept. 'Don't ask me anything else.'

'You know the battle-captain's feelings on this matter,' said Andus. 'He refutes any clandestine gatherings–'

'*He* refutes,' Meric interrupted. 'He does, not I. If Captain Garro wishes to stay beyond the fraternity of the lodges, then that is his choice, and yours too if you wish to follow him. But I do not. I am a member.' He blew out a breath. 'There. It is said.'

Decius was on his feet. 'We are all part of the Seventh,' he growled, 'and the company's command cadre at that! Garro sets the example we should follow, without question!'

'If he would take the time to listen, he would understand.' Meric shook his head and gestured with the medal. 'You would understand that this is not some kind of secret society, it's just a place where men can meet and talk freely.'

'That seems so,' noted Sendek. 'From what you have implied, in this lodge it appears that even the most sensitive of military information is bandied about without restraint.'

Voyen shook his head angrily. 'It's not like that at all. Don't twist my meaning!'

'You must end your membership, Meric,' said Hakur. 'Swear it now and we'll speak no more of this conversation.'

'I won't.' He gripped the coin tightly. 'You all know me. We are battle-brothers! I've healed every one of you, saved the lives of some, even! I am Meric Voyen, your friend and comrade in arms. Do you really think that I would take part in something seditious?' He snorted. 'Trust me, if you saw the faces of the men who were there, you'd understand that it's you and Garro who are in the minority!'

'What Grulgor and Typhon do with their companies is their own lookout,' added Decius.

'And the rest!' Voyen replied. 'I am far from the only soldier of the Seventh in the association!'

'No,' insisted Hakur.

'I would never lie to you, and if holding this token makes you think any less of me, then…' After a long moment he bowed his head, deflated. 'Then perhaps you are not the kinsmen I thought you were.'

When Voyen looked up again someone else had joined the other men in the chamber.

Rahl heard a razor-edge of anger in Captain Garro's voice as he spoke a single command. 'Give me the room.'

WHEN THEY WERE alone and Kaleb sealed the door behind him, Garro turned a hard stare on his subordinate. His mailed fingers tensed into fists.

'I never heard you enter,' Voyen muttered. 'How much did you hear?'

'You do not refute,' he replied. 'I stood outside in the corridor a while before I entered.'

'Huh,' the Apothecary gave a dry laugh. 'I thought your housecarl was the spy.'

'What Kaleb speaks of to me is guided only by his conscience. I do not task him.'

'Then he and I are alike.'

Garro looked away. 'You say then that it is your principles that made you join the lodge, is that it?'

'Aye. I am the senior healer for the Seventh Company. It's my duty to know the true feelings of the men who are part of it. Sometimes there are things a man will tell his lodge-mate that he would not tell his Apothecary.' Voyen stared down at the deck. 'Am I to assume that you will have me posted to another company in light of this disclosure?'

Some part of Garro expected himself to explode with fury, but all he felt now was disappointment. 'I eschew the lodge and then I learn a most trusted friend within my inner circle is a part of it. Such a thing might make me seem weak or short-sighted to others.'

'No,' insisted the Astartes, 'Lord, please know, I did not choose this in order to undermine you! It was only... the right choice for Meric Voyen.'

Garro was silent for a few moments. 'We have been brothers in warfare for decades, over thousands of battlefields. You are a fine warrior, and a better healer. I would not have had you join my cadre otherwise. But this... you kept this from us all, and made our comradeship cheap. If you stay under my command, Meric, you will not find it easy to earn back the trust that you have lost today.' He met the other man's gaze. 'Go or stay. Make the choice that is right for Meric Voyen.'

'If I wish to remain, will my departure from the lodge be a condition of that, lord?'

The captain shook his head. 'I won't force you to disassociate yourself. You're still my battle-brother, even if your decisions are sometimes not in line with mine.' Garro stepped forward and offered Voyen his hand. 'But I will have a pledge from you. Promise me, here and now, that if the lodge ever compels you to turn from the face of the Emperor of Man, you will destroy that medal and reject them.'

The Apothecary took Garro's hand. 'I swear it, lord. On Terra itself, I swear it.'

THE MATTER DEALT with for the moment, Garro gathered his men back together and briefed them on the battle plans the Warmaster had outlined. By his example, not a single harsh word was said to Voyen, but the Apothecary kept silent and to the edge of things. No voice was raised in question as to why

Voyen still stood with them, but Garro saw reservations in the eyes of Decius, Rahl and the others.

When it was done, Garro left his dress wargear to Kaleb's attention and took his own council. So many things had come and gone in so short a time. It seemed like only moments ago that he had been looking over attack simulations for the raid on the jorgall world-ship, now the Legiones Astartes massed for the first hammer-blow strike on Isstvan Extremis, and Garro saw conflict in the heart of his own company.

Had he made the wrong choice in letting Voyen remain? His mind moved back to the conversation with Mortarion before the war council, where questions of the lodges had risen as well. It troubled the captain that he could not determine an easy path through these thoughts. At times he wondered if he were at fault, holding firmly to a conservative course, keeping the tradition and heart of the Legion alive while time moved on and things changed.

Yes, things *were* changing. The shift of mood here on *Endurance* was slight, but visible to his trained senses, and aboard the Warmaster's ship, it was more obvious still. Bleak emotions gathered at the edges of his thoughts like distant storm clouds. He could not shake the sensation that something malign was waiting out there, gathering strength and biding its time.

And so Garro did what he had made into a quiet personal habit, in order to clear his mind and find focus for the coming battle. High up atop the *Endurance*'s dorsal hull lay the oval dome of the ship's observatorium, a space put aside so that naval crew might be able to take emergency star fix sightings should the vessel's cogitators become inoperative. It also served a purely ornamental function, although there were few among the Death Guard who ever used it for so trivial a purpose.

Garro dimmed all the glow-globes in the chamber and seated himself at the control console. The operator chair shifted back and reclined on quiet hydraulics. Presently, the battle-captain was tilted so he could take in the unfettered sweep of the starscape.

Isstvan's blue-white sun was a bright glow off in the lower quadrant, attenuated by a localised polarisation in the augmented armourglass. He looked away from it and let the blackness surround him. Gradually, tension eased from the knots in his muscles. Garro felt adrift in the ocean of stars, cupped in the bubble of atmosphere. He saw past the silver flashes of ship hulls, out into the deep void, and not for the first time, he looked and wondered where home was.

Officially, the home world of the XIV Legion was Barbarus, a cloud-wreathed sphere near the edge of the Gothic Sector. It was from that troubled world that most of the Death Guard's number originated, men like Grulgor and Typhon, Decius and Sendek, even Kaleb. Garro had learned to have deference and respect for the planet and its testing nature, but it would never be home to him.

Garro had been born on Terra and drawn up into the Legiones Astartes before men had even known the name of Barbarus. In those years the XIV Legion had gone by a different title, and they had no primarch but the Emperor himself. Garro swelled with pride to remember that time. They had been the Dusk Raiders, so known because of their signature tactic of attacking a foe at nightfall. Then, they had worn armour without the green trim of the current Legion. The wargear of the Dusk Raiders was the dull white of old marble, but with their right arm and shoulders coloured in a deep, glistening crimson. The symbology of the armour showed their foes what they truly were – the Emperor's red right hand, the relentless and unstoppable. Many enemies had thrown down their weapons the moment the sun dipped beneath the horizon, rather than dare to fight them.

But that too had changed. When the Emperor's clone-sons, the great primarchs, had been sundered from his side and scattered across the galaxy, the Dusk Raiders joined their brother Legions and their master in the Great Crusade that began the Age of the Imperium. Garro had been there, centuries past.

It did not seem so long ago, and yet there were countless years of time measured by Terran clocks that he had lost in the confusion of the warp, in cryogenic stasis and through the strange physics of near-light speed travel. Garro had been there as the Emperor crossed the galaxy in search of his star-lost children – Sanguinius, Ferrus, Guilliman, Magnus and the rest. With each reuniting, the Lord of Mankind had gifted his sons with command of the forces that had been created in their image. When at last the Emperor came to Barbarus and discovered the gaunt warrior foundling leading its oppressed people, he had located the avatar of the XIV Legion.

On Barbarus, where Mortarion had come to rest after falling through the chaotic turmoil of a warp storm, the boy-primarch found a planet where the human colonists were ground beneath the heel of a clan of mutant warlords. He grew up to fight them and liberate the commoners, creating his own army of steadfast warriors to lead the way into the poisonous heights where the warlords hid. These men Mortarion named the Death Guard.

So it was written, that when at last the Emperor and Mortarion met and defeated the dark master of the warlords, Barbarus was free and the primarch accepted a place in his father's Crusade at the head of the XIV Legion. Mortarion's first words to his army were carved in a granite arch over the airlock gate of the battle barge *Reaper's Scythe* in memory of the moment. He had come at the Emperor's bidding with the elite of his Barbarun cohort at his side and hundreds more on the way. Garro had been there, as nothing more than a line Astartes, when he heard his new primarch speak.

'You are my unbroken blades,' he told them. 'You are the Death Guard.' And with those words the Dusk Raiders were no more. Things changed.

On the day of Mortarion's coronation as primarch, a good majority of the XIV Legion had been of Garro's stock, men born on Terra or within the confines of the Sol system, but slowly that number had dwindled, and as new recruits joined the Death Guard fold they came only from Barbarus. Now, as the Thirty-First Millennium turned about its axis, there was only a comparative handful of Terrans in the Legion. In his blackest moments Nathaniel imagined a time when there would be none of his kinsmen left among the XIV, and with their deaths the traditions of the old Dusk Raiders would finally fade away. He feared that moment, for when it came to pass something of the Legion's noble character would die as well.

Memory was a curious companion. In some instances, Garro's fragmentary reminiscences of his deep past were clearer than those of battles some months old, by a peculiarity of the Astartes implants in his cerebrum. He recalled a moment as a boy growing up in Albia, in front of a memorial to warriors that dated back beyond the Tenth Millennium, a great arch of white stone and figures made of black metal, the surfaces worn smooth but protected by a layer of synthetic diamond. And he remembered a night on Barbarus, atop one of the highest crags, peering into the sky. The clouds parted for the rarest of moments and Nathaniel's eyes had found, as they did now beneath the glass dome, a lone dot of light in the great darkness.

Now, as then, he looked to the distant star and wondered again if it were home. Could the Emperor, in his matchless capacity, be turning some small scrap of his towering mind towards him? Or was it vanity on Garro's part to think he would even merit the notice of the Lord of Mankind?

With the next heartbeat the captain's breath caught in his throat as the light he watched glittered brightly, and then faded to nothing, dying before him. The blinded star vanished, leaving a dark pall over Nathaniel's spirit.

DECIUS TURNED HIS hand over and held up his palm to the air, catching some of the fat, lazy flakes of snow drifting down around him. In the low gravity of Isstvan Extremis, the powdered shavings of nitrogen ice floated in slow motion towards the monochrome grey of the mottled surface. He smiled at the moment in self-amusement and turned the open palm into a ball. It was the match of his right hand, but nowhere near as large as the monstrous power fist lined with green enamel and patient little ticks of lightning. He flexed the heavy fingers experimentally. Decius's control over the glove was so deft that he could pick a flower or crush a skull with equal ease.

Not that there was flora of any kind on this dead ball of ice and stone. But there were plenty of heads to break. That was certain. The thought made Decius's smile widen into a cocky grin. He glanced back over his shoulder, across the rippling, crater-pocked plain of the western approaches. Death Guard waited in every shadowed lee, behind every rock and outcropping, silent and ready. The dull colour of their armour was nearly a match for the grey landscape, and it was only the lines of jade trim around their shoulders and breast plates that broke up the camouflage.

They were quiet, like their namesake, and prepared for the moment. Decius saw a glint of gold. Captain Garro was speaking into the helmet of Sergeant Hakur. In turn old Hakur moved and passed the order on to Rahl, then to another man, on and on, the command spreading in a whispering ripple.

The Seventh Company had observed vox discipline since the Thunderhawks had set them down over the horizon of the planetoid, out of sight of the monitor station's sensor towers. They communicated by hushed words or by battle-sign, advancing with stealth towards the shield wall protecting the west face of the enemy dome complex. This had been done to ensure that all the attention of the Isstvanians would be turned elsewhere, out to where the brightly armoured and very visible Emperor's Children advanced. Now they were close, and all the waiting – hours, so it seemed to Decius – was done. The attack was at hand.

Sendek leaned close and spoke into Decius's audio pick-up. 'Be ready for the word.'

He nodded in acknowledgement and passed the command on to the Astartes at his side, a warrior with the cobra-head shape of a missile launcher on his shoulder. The thin atmosphere of Isstvan Extremis did not carry sound well, but such was the cacophony coming from the far side of the rebel complex that it still reached them. Decius could pick out the strained rattle of combi-bolters, the smack-thud of krak grenade detonations. The noise made his palms itch with anticipation.

Then, over the general vox-channel, he heard Garro break radio silence. 'Seventh. In position.'

The battle-captain's voice was grim and heavy. Decius's commander had not been himself since he returned from the *Vengeful Spirit*, and once more Solun found himself thinking about what might have gone on aboard the Warmaster's barge. And then this business with Voyen... He shuttered the thoughts away.

Decius watched the battlements of the west wall through the magnifiers of his optics, studying the motion of the black figures patrolling up there. They were milling around, unsure of where they were meant to be. The attack by the Emperor's Children was doing its job, drawing the concentration of the defenders. 'They're good for something, at least,' he murmured to himself. Decius had always thought the III Legion to be more self-indulgent than the rest of the Astartes.

A voice came back over the general channel, a single word loaded with the ready glee of battle. 'Execute!' shouted Eidolon, and as one the Death Guard surged up from their concealment in a heavy wave of storm-grey armour.

'Count the Seven!' cried a voice, and Decius repeated the call, hearing it over and over down the line of advance. The men of the XIV Legion were done being quiet.

The guards on the battlements were already red ruins, falling from their perches to shatter on the rock floor, cored by bolt shells sniped from the middle distance. Small-gauge missiles from man-portable launchers lanced out in a wave over Decius's head, converging on points in the wall where auspex scans had discovered weaknesses. The Astartes saw motion at the foot of the barrier. There were self-contained bunker pods strung out there, each equipped with pintle-mounted lasers. Thread-thin lines of crimson blinked, joining the ovoid pods to running men. Burns scored across ceramite and a few unlucky ones caught a charge in the face, blinded by the beams.

The defence did nothing to slow the Death Guard advance. Once their blood was up, it was simply impossible to halt them, the crushing infantry charge boiling over stone and broken sheets of gas-ice, guns crashing out into the thin air. Decius gave a full clip of bolter rounds to the closest pod and reloaded on the run, his pace never faltering. He heard a strangled cry issue out from the gun slit.

The battle-brother with the missile launcher was still with him, sporting the ugly singe mark from a glancing shot on his torso, but otherwise untouched. He saw the Astartes drop to one knee, and then with the ammunition carousel chattering, the missileer released a four-shot salvo at the bunker. The rockets hit in a perfect cluster and tore the pod open, the roof peeling back as a fireball forced its way out. Incredi-bly, figures in black stumbled from the smoking ruin, some of them on fire, all of them brandishing weapons.

Decius fired from the hip, killing a handful, and stormed in to take the last survivor by hand. Decius punched the Isstvanian squarely in the chest and the power fist cannoned him back into the bricks of the shield wall. The enemy soldier fell from a ragged impact crater and dropped at Decius's feet, a boneless rag-doll.

A hissing sound reached his ears and the Astartes crouched to investigate. The man had lost a vox head-set in the impact and it lay on the dirt next to him. Decius gathered it up and listened. Strident noise came from it, a disharmony of raw screeching tones that clawed up and down the chords. He tossed it away and stood up again.

Decius glanced around, seeing the other bunker pods all burning or shattered, then nudged the corpse with his boot. A face bloated with new death looked back up at him, one eye peering through the shat-tered red lens of an aiming reticule. 'You won't be my last today,' he told the dead man.

'Fall back to a safe distance,' Garro's voice shouted. 'Charges to detonate!'

The Astartes with the launcher tapped him on the shoulder. 'Brother, come. They're going to blow the wall.'

Decius sprinted back a few hundred metres to where the Death Guard was massing in good order. He saw Tollen Sendek at his heels, a sapper-command signum unit in his grip. 'Ready!' snapped Sendek.

Garro's helmet bobbed. 'Do it.'

Sendek stabbed at a glowing key and Decius heard a sharp, fizzing report from the stone fortification. Then, in the next second, tortured air molecules

screamed aloud and a great length of the stone wall
became rubble and powder.

'Take the dome!' Garro drew his power sword and
cut the air with it. 'For Terra and Mortarion!'

Decius ran at the battle-captain's flank and plunged
into the roiling clouds of rock dust, his helmet optics
automatically rendering the terrain before him in
grainy wire-frames over the standard visual spectrum
display. Sendek had, in defiance of conventional battlefield doctrine, used powerful hull-cutter charges
designed for starship boarding actions instead of
standard krak munitions. The resultant overpressure
from detonation in an atmosphere – even one as thin
as that of Isstvan Extremis – had blown down a large
part of the west wall and gone on to cut a bite from
the central dome beyond it. Decius didn't need to
look up to remember the form of the target facility.
He had committed it to memory on the journey from
the *Endurance*, fixing in his subconscious the shape of
the oblate hemisphere and its forest of odd, pipe-like
towers.

His boots crunched on the bodies of dead men
pulped by the breaching charges. Lines of twisted
metal rebar crowded in around the Astartes, with
bits of dangling ferrocrete strung along them like
dusty pearls. Garro drew back his sword arm to cut
through them, but Decius stepped in before him.
'No, lord, allow me.' Decius struck out with the
power fist and hammered it four times against the
stone, the final blow clearing the last of the block-
age before them. He grinned to himself. It wasn't
every battle where a man would find himself
punching a building.

The Death Guard spilled through the breach and
into the dome proper, figures in off-white armour

filling up the space inside. Decius saw hooded figures in black swarming like maddened ants through the smoke and dust, and beyond them...
He blinked, drinking in the sight of the peculiar structure that dominated the dome. The briefing had told the Astartes to expect a standard Imperial sensor platform, perhaps with some recent modifications, but nothing more. Decius imagined they would penetrate the dome and find banks of cogitators, wave-monitors and the like. He could not have been more wrong.

Every tier of the dome's inner levels had been removed, making the entire space wide open. In the middle of the smoke-wreathed chamber there was a construct that seemed to be made of stone, but not the local variety of grey rock shot with mica. It was a rough-sided ziggurat hewn from different slabs of minerals in a panoply of colours. The stones could only have come from other worlds, that was obvious, but why? What possible reason could there have been for something like this, in a place this remote, where no one but a few hundred traitors would ever see it?

On the inside face of the dome there were patterns of lines and discs that seemed to go on forever, baffling the eye with illusions of depth and movement where there was none. Then there was the light and the sound, the same discordant noise he had heard on the headset. It was coming from the apex of the construction, rolling down the steep sides of the pyramid in slow, punishing waves. There was a figure up there, floating–

Red lasers stitched the air around Decius's head, tearing his attention away from the ziggurat and back to the battle at hand. The Death Guard force was large, but they had underestimated the number of turncoats clustering inside the main dome. He heard Rahl's voice on the vox, furious with tension. 'Encountering heavy resistance at objective!'

Decius slammed an enemy trooper to death, the blow sending the dead man into a ring of his comrades and in turn taking them off their feet. Captain Garro sliced through the Isstvanian lines with Libertas shining with gore, the bolter in his other hand banging with each kill-shot it released. Solun kept pace with his commander, gathering Rahl and Sendek to him. Hakur and his squad had the flanks as they pushed in towards the foot of the arcane construction. Decius laughed, the rush of the battle coursing through him, making a dozen more close-range kills with his bolter, blood flicking off his wargear. They were at the base of the ziggurat when a dull concussion rumbled through the dome and a set of blast doors caved in with an agonised creak. Muscled giants in purple and gold punched through the entrance and laid into the black hoods.

'Fulgrim's boys have decided to grace us with their presence,' said Garro, baring his teeth. 'Let's not let Eidolon say he made the peak before the Death Guard!' The moment of confusion in the defenders caused by the new arrivals was enough to give the men of the Seventh the opening they needed, and swiftly the battle-captain led the squad up the rough-hewn face of the pyramid.

Decius's gaze ranged up the steep, peculiar little mountain and found the apex again. Yes, he saw it clearly now. A woman was up there, and by some means she hovered, suspended in a cowl of glitter. Light popped and writhed around her shimmering form, each tiny sun-bright flash accompanied by more sound, more shrieking, lethal noise that pounded into his eardrums.

'Blood's oath!' he shouted, barely loud enough for his words to carry over the horrific dissonance. 'What in the name of Terra is she?'

Garro threw a look over his shoulder and spat out a name. 'Warsinger.'

SIX

SIX

To the Brink
Triad of Skulls
New Orders

GARRO STOLE A glance down the sheer slope of the ziggurat and saw the wild play of the battle spread out beneath him. All around the interior of the dome there was a churning sea of men engaged in the business of killing one another. Figures in black hoods swarmed at the white and purple shapes of the Astartes, laser fire flashing in chains of red lightning among the flares of yellow flame from bolter muzzles. Emperor's Children were scaling the pyramid beneath them, following the path his men were forging with every heavy boot step. Dust and stone fragments crackled with each footfall, the peculiar patchwork construct resonating with each tortured stanza of the Warsinger's song.

Garro pressed on, using the thick fingers of his gauntlets to dig handholds from the stonework and haul himself upward. He saw red granite, crumbly limestone and strange chunks of bifurcated statuary as he climbed. The mess of bricks seemed to have no regularity in its design or purpose. They were close to the woman now, and the Astartes could vaguely sense voices on his vox, but the deafening operatic screams of the enemy champion flattened them under an indecipherable roar. The Warsinger was steady and unmoving, and strange etches of colour and light drifted around her, just as the lazy snowflakes had drifted out on the plains. She had her hands to her chest, her head back, throwing a keening dirge to the roof. The song was endless, without pause for breath or meter, each note locking to the next, cutting through Garro's attempts to think clearly. It was unearthly. No human throat should have been able to voice it, no human lungs able to give it breath. Some force about the razored melody was ripping and picking at the very air, cutting into the flesh of the real. The top of the dome rippled like water, warping.

Indolently, as if it were something done out of boredom rather than directed cruelty, the woman flicked her wrist and sent coils of shimmering aural force humming away down the lines of the pyramid. The waveforms caught around Pyr Rahl and hoisted him off the stone, flipping him over in mid-air. Ash came off him in wreaths, his armour puckering and bending in the wrong places. He released a strangled cry that ended in a crackle of bone as he imploded. The Death Guard's crushed remnants bounced away into the melee below. Garro snarled in anger at the casual manner of his battle-brother's death, charging upward.

Then, almost unexpectedly, he made the top, letting his bolter fall away around his hip on its sling. The battle-captain brought up Libertas in a firm, two-handed grip, and laid into the Warsinger. At his flank, he was aware of Decius giving him covering fire, grimacing as the bolt rounds whined away in ricochets from the sheer energy of the wall of music.

The Warsinger turned her notice to Garro, resentment forming on her face as his attacks invaded her sensorium. He saw her shift and turn, the long streamers of her hair drifting past her screaming face. Holding on to the fury from the cold murder of his subordinate, his sword swept across and connected with her songshield, the noise of the impact like a knife point drawn down a sheet of glass. Effortlessly, the enemy champion drew the sound in and threaded it into her cacophony, weaving it into the mad chorus.

In a flash of understanding, the nature of his foe was revealed to him. The Warsinger could not be brought down by the energy of light and heat. Only raw sound would be enough to kill her.

From the terrible mantra filling the dome space, the Warsinger teased out a single line of screaming clamour and spun it into a fist of glowing resonance. Garro saw the blow coming and shoved Decius aside, dodging away from her. She moved at the speed of sound, and with a sonic boom shocking the air into white rings of vapour, the Warsinger hit Garro with a hammer made of hymnals.

DEAFENED. FALLING. PAIN.

Decius's mind reeled with the edges of the impact, clinging to the simplest of reactions, barely able to process the sudden violence wrought upon him. The dome spun around and he felt the rough surface of the ziggurat rise up and strike him as he fell back along the slope of it. Decius's power fist slapped down flat and open palmed on a jutting piece of aged gargoyle and the fingers closed around it with a snap.

The stone statuary chipped and cracked, but held, halting his ignominious descent. His head tolled like a struck bell, a strange fuzzy pressure crowding in on his eyes. Decius swore a guttural Barbarun oath under his breath and righted himself. His hyperaware senses told him of contusions and minor breaks in some of his bones, but nothing that would warrant more than passing notice. Garro... Captain Garro had saved his life up there, pushing him out to the edge of the Warsinger's attack.

Something sparked inside, an anxious flare of emotion that was as close to panic as an Astartes might ever get. Where was he? Where was the battle-captain? Decius came to his feet, pleased to find his bolter still at hand, the strap wrapped about his wrist guard, and batted away an Isstvanian's clumsy attack. He swept the flank of the pyramid and found his commander. Garro's marble-grey armour was stained with the rich red of Astartes blood. A warrior of the Emperor's Children was standing over him, *Tarvitz*, he remembered. Garro had spoken well of this man in the past. Still, a dart of offended pride rose in Decius's chest at the idea of a man from the III Legion coming to the aid of a Death Guard, honour brother or not.

Ignoring the grinding pain of bone on bone in his legs, Decius sprinted back up the ziggurat, regaining some of the ground he had lost in his headlong tumble. He caught a snatch of conversation between the two captains as he came closer.

'Hold on, brother,' Tarvitz was saying.

'Just kill it,' Garro coughed, blood on his lips, his head bare where the Warsinger's blow had sundered his battle helmet.

'I have him,' said Decius, stepping up. 'He'll be safe with me.'

THE FLIGHT OF THE EISENSTEIN

Tarvitz threw him a nod and then began his ascent.

The Astartes turned back to his commander and his gut knotted as the stink of fresh blood filled his nostrils. The smell was familiar and hateful to him. There were patterns of crushing damage to Garro's torso and his arm, and somewhere up there he had lost his bolter. But in his other hand, his good hand, the battle-captain still gripped the hilt of Libertas with grim fury, clutching the sword like a talisman. Thin blades of shattered granite and obsidian punctured him, shock-gel pooling around the places where they had punched through the captain's ceramite weave like bullets, but the worst of the wounds was the leg.

Decius's face soured behind his breath mask and he was grateful that his commander could not see his expression. Less than a hand's span down Garro's thigh his right leg simply ended in a wet red scrap of fleshy rags, burnt bone and charred meat. It could only be the potent flood of coagulants, neuro-chemical agents and counter-shock drugs from his gland implants that were keeping the captain conscious.

Contemplating the sheer agony of the wound took Decius's breath away. The Warsinger hadn't simply torn Garro's leg from its socket. She had sheared it off with a serrated blade of pure sound.

'How do I look, lad?' asked the captain. 'Not so pretty as the Emperor's Children?'

'It's not that bad.'

Garro spat out a pain-wracked chuckle. 'You're such a poor liar, boy.' He waved the Astartes forward. 'Help me up. Saul will finish what we started.'

'You're in no condition to fight, lord,' retorted Decius.

Garro dragged himself up to use the Astartes as a crutch. 'Damn you, Decius! As long as a Death Guard draws breath, he's in a condition to fight!' He cast around, unsteady with the pain. 'Where's my bloody bolter?'

'Lost, sir,' Decius noted, guiding him downward.

The battle-captain spat. 'Terra curse it! Then help me into sword range and I'll cut these fools down instead!'

Together, leaving a trail of blood down the flank of the ragged pyramid, Decius and Garro hobbled to the floor of the dome and back into the thronging melee. Decius was aware that above them the Warsinger's song was shifting and changing, but his mind was narrowing to the controlled murder of the close battle at hand. He became his captain's rock, feet spread and standing firm in the roil of combat, gunning down black hoods with his bolter in one hand and punishing those who strayed closer with his mailed fist encasing the other. Garro stood to his back, holding himself up with his damaged arm and cutting shimmering arcs of death with his racing sword. Blood pooled at their feet, the captain's mingling with that of the Isstvan turncoats.

Decius yelled into his vox pick up for a medicae, but only scratches of static returned to him. The impact from the fall had probably damaged his communications gear, and even at the top of his lungs, his shouts could barely match the screaming of the Warsinger. Finally, Garro slumped, the Herculean effort and blood loss too much for even his Astartes physiology. Decius helped the battle-captain to the ground and propped him against the ziggurat wall. 'Sir, take this.' He slammed a full clip of ammunition into his bolter and laid it on Garro's lap.

'Where are you going?' his commander asked thickly. Garro was having trouble keeping focus.

'I'll be back, captain.' Decius turned and charged into the maelstrom, using the power fist to punch his way through the enemy ranks. Isstvanian fighters were thrown and gored as he barrelled through them, cutting a channel across the dome through the figures in dark cowls. They moved like water, churning around him and pooling back into the path he made.

At last Decius found what he sought and roared as loud as he could. 'Voyen! Hear me!'

The Death Guard Apothecary's head snapped up from the body of a brother who had been cut apart by laser fire. 'I can do no more for this one,' he said grimly.

'The Emperor knows his name,' shouted Decius, 'and the captain will join that roll of honour as well, unless you come with me now!'

'Garro?' Voyen sprang to his feet. 'Show me, boy, quickly! The captain of the Seventh won't perish if I can help it.'

They waded back into the morass, fighting and moving. 'This way!'

'He's still my commander,' grated Voyen, 'do you understand that? No matter what is said and done, that will never change. Do you understand, Decius?'

'Who are you trying to convince, Voyen? Me, or yourself?' Decius threw him a hard look. 'At this moment I don't care a damn for you and your blasted lodge. Just save—'

The rest of the Death Guard's words were lost in a final, shrieking exultation of noise from the top of the pyramid. Every man who could clapped his hands to his ears in blind reflex as the Warsinger sang her last, desperate attack, and died. Decius looked up and saw two figures in shimmering purple at the peak, saw a torn shape in diaphanous robes fall away and tumble unceremoniously down the steep face.

'Eidolon!' cried an Astartes at their side. 'Eidolon made the kill! The bitch is dead!'

An oval object arced though the air trailing white streamers and Decius grabbed it before it could impact on the ground. He turned it over in his hand and found it was a human head. 'The Warsinger,' he pronounced, holding it up by the woman's long pale tresses. The neck had been severed by a single clean blow. With a grimace, he tossed it to the warrior of the Emperor's Children and pushed on, ignoring the cries of victory. As one, the surviving black hoods stopped fighting. Some had fallen to their knees and were weeping, rocking back and forth, or cradling their headsets in their hands, mewing over the sudden loss of their precious song. Most of them just stood there, milling around like lost children, choking the dome with their numbers.

'Out of my way, out of my way, you turncoat cattle!' bellowed Decius, fighting against the moaning crowd. He began punching them down where they stood, cutting the Isstvanians like wheat before the scythe. Other Astartes joined in, and soon it became a wholesale cull. The Warmaster's orders had not spoken of prisoners.

By the time they forced their way back to the foot of the ziggurat, Garro lay before them deathly pale and silent. An Apothecary from the III Legion knelt at his side, frowning.

Voyen, his face tight with distress, shot a hard look at the other medicae. 'Stand aside. You're not to touch him!'

'I saved his life, Death Guard,' came the terse reply. 'You should be thanking me. I did your job for you.'

Voyen cocked his fist in anger, but Decius stopped him halfway. 'Brother,' he began, turning to the other man, 'thank you. Will he survive?'

'Get him to an infirmary within the hour and he may live to fight another day.'

'Then he will.' The young Astartes saluted in the old martial fashion. 'I am Decius of the Seventh. My company is in your debt.'

The Apothecary gave a slight smile to Voyen and made to leave. 'Fabius, Apothecary to the Emperor's Children. Consider my care of your captain a gift among comrades.'

Voyen's words dripped venom as the Astartes left. 'Arrogant whelp. How dare he–'

'*Voyen*,' snapped Decius, silencing the other man. 'Help me carry him.'

GARRO WAS FALLING forever.

The warm void around him was thick and heavy. It was an ocean of thin, clear oil, as deep as memory, and beyond his ability to know its edge. He sank into it, the warmth wrapping around him in gossamer threads, in through his mouth and nostrils, filling his lungs and gullet, weighing him down. Down and down, deeper. Falling. Still falling.

He was aware of his injuries in a vague, disconnected way. Parts of his body were blacked out in his sensorium, nerve clusters dark and silent while the patient engines of his Astartes physiology went to work on keeping him alive. 'My wounds will never heal,' he said aloud, and the words bubbled past him, solidifying. Why had he said that? Where had that come from? Garro wondered with elephantine slowness and pushed at the thoughts in his mind, but they were impossible to shift, large as glaciers and ice-cold to the touch.

The trance. Part of his brain eventually provided him with this small fragment of data. Yes, of course.

His body had closed its borders and sealed him inside it, all other concerns and outside interests forgotten as his implants worked in concert to stop an encroaching death. The Astartes was in stasis, of a kind: Not the artificially generated fashion, where flesh was chilled down and chemical anti-crystallisation agents were pumped into the bloodstream for long-duration, low-consumable starflight. This was the semi-death of the wounded man and the near killed.

Odd how he could be at once so aware of it and yet so unaware as well. This was the function of the catalepsean node implanted in his brain, switching off sections of his cerebellum as a servitor might douse lamps in the unused rooms of a house. Garro had been here before, during the Pasiphae Uprising, after a suicide attack on the *Stalwart*'s pod decks had ripped the flank of the battle-barge open and tossed a hundred unprotected men into space. He had survived that, awaking with new scars and months of missing time.

Would he live through this? Garro tried to probe his thoughts for an exact recall of his last conscious moments, and found rough, broken perceptions and spikes of brutal pain. *Tarvitz*. Yes, Saul Tarvitz had been there, and the lad Decius as well. And before that... Before that there was only the humming echo of white noise and heart-shrinking pain. He let himself drop away, let the agony shadow fade. Would he live through this? Garro would only know when it happened. Otherwise, he would fall and fall, sink and sink, and the captain of the Seventh would become another soul lost, a steel skull-shaped stud the size of his thumbnail hammered into the iron Wall of Memory on Barbarus.

He found he did not have a will to fight. Here, in this non-place, coiled inside himself, he only *was*. Marking time, waiting, healing; that was how it had been after Pasiphae, and so that was how it should be now.

How it *should* be.

But he knew something was different even as the thought drifted through him. That shattering pain down in the dome, that had been like nothing he had ever experienced before. Hundreds of years of warfare had not prepared him for the Warsinger's brutal kiss. Garro knew now, too late, after the fact, that she had been an enemy of a kind he had never before encountered. Where her power sprang from, what form it took... These were things new to him in a universe where the Astartes had thought himself incapable of being surprised. That would teach him not to be complacent.

In his own way, the battle-captain marvelled at the play of events. It was incredible that he had survived to fall into a healing trance after challenging the Warsinger. Other Death Guard, other Emperor's Children, had also met her might and died of it. He thought of poor Rahl, crushed like a spent ration can. There would be no more wagers or games for him. As those brothers lay dead, Garro lived still, clinging to the raw edge of life. 'Why?' he demanded. 'Why me and not them? Why Nathaniel Garro and not Pyr Rahl?'

Who made the choice? What scales were balanced by a man's death or his life? The questions hooked into him and pulled the Astartes back and forth, burrowing deep. It was such foolishness to ask these pointless things of an uncaring universe. What scales? There were no scales, no great arbiter of fates! It was pagan idolatry to consider such notions, to insist that the lives of men ran in some kind of clockwork beneath the winding fingers of a deity. *No:* here was truth, Imperial truth. The stars turned and men died without a creator's plan for them. There were no gods, no here-fores and hereafters, no futures but those we made for ourselves. Garro and his kinsmen simply *were*.

And yet...

In this place of death sleep, where things were at once murky and clearer, there seemed instances where Nathaniel Garro felt a pressure upon him that came from a place far distant, beyond himself. At the corners of his sensorium, he might perceive a small fragment of brilliance thrown across countless light-years, the merest suggestion of interest from an intellect that towered over his. Cold logic told him that this was wishful, desperate thinking dredged up from the crude animal core of his hindbrain. But Garro could not quite let go of the feeling, of the raw hope that the will of something greater than he was acting upon him. If he was not dead, then perhaps he had been *spared*. It was a giddy, perilous thought.

'His hand lies upon all of us, and every one of us owes Him our devotion.'

Who spoke those words? Was it Garro or someone else? They seemed strange and new, echoing from a distance.

'He guides us, teaches us, exhorts us to become more than we are,' said the colourless voice, 'but most of all, the Emperor protects.'

The words disturbed Nathaniel. They made him turn and shift in the thick sea, his comfort fading. He sensed the pressure of dark storms brewing out in the impossible spaces around him, the visions of them coming to his mind through someone else's eyes;

through a soul not far from his, yes, bright like the distant watcher, but only a single candle against the greater light's burning sun; black clouds of churning emotion, seething and pushing at the warp and weft of space, looking for a weak point through which they could flow. The storm front was coming, inexorable, unstoppable. Garro wanted to turn away but there was no place in the drifting fall where he did not find them. He wanted to rise up and fight it, but he had no hands, no face, no flesh.

There were shapes in the gloomy shifting coils that rose and fell, some resembling the spirals of symbols he had seen inside the dome on Isstvan Extremis, others he had glimpsed on the uncommon banners of the Lupercal's Court, and repeating, over and over, a three-fold icon that seemed to be seeking him out wherever his attention moved: a triad of skulls, a pyramid of screaming faces, three black discs, a trio of bleeding bullet wounds, and other variations, but always the same arrangement of shapes.

'The Emperor protects,' said a woman, and Garro felt her hands upon his cheek, the salt tang of her fallen tears on her lips. The sensations came to him from far, far away, drawing him to them and out of the haze of the threatening storms.

Nathaniel was rising now, faster and faster, the warmth turning chill upon him, the pain coiling around his legs and stomach. There was… there was a woman, a head of short hair framed in a penitent's hood and…

And agony, awakening.

'Eyes of Terra!' gasped Kaleb, 'he's alive! The captain lives!'

✠ ✠ ✠

'I WOULD LIKE to see him,' said Temeter stiffly.

Sergeant Hakur frowned. 'Lord, my captain is in no state to–'

Temeter silenced him with an upraised hand. 'Hakur, old blade, out of respect to you for your service and record, I won't consider your obstreperous manner to be discourteous to my rank, but do not mistake what I just said for a request. Get out of my way, sergeant.'

Hakur gave a shallow bow. 'Of course, captain. I forget myself.'

Temeter stepped around the veteran and strode purposefully into the *Endurance*'s tertiary infirmary, throwing nods to men from his own company who were still healing from wounds taken on the jorgall world-ship. Most would not return to combat status, but would suffer the comparative ignominy of becoming permanently stationed as ship crew, or else return to Barbarus to live out their days as commandant-instructors to the noviciates. Ullis Temeter hoped that Garro would not share such a fate. The day that the battle-captain was forced to step off the battle line would be the day the man's spirit perished.

He entered a cordoned-off medicae cell and found his comrade there in a support throne, surrounded by brass technologies and glass jars of fluids piping gently into the sockets of Garro's implanted carapace. The battle-captain's housecarl jumped as Temeter swept in and came to his feet in a jerk of shocked motion. Kaleb clutched a fist of inky papers to his chest and blinked with watery eyes. Temeter immediately had the sense that he had caught the serf doing something wrong, but he decided not to press the matter.

'Has he said anything?'

Kaleb nodded, tucking the papers into an inner pocket in his tunic. 'Yes, sir. While the captain was healing, he spoke several times. I couldn't divine the meaning of it all, but I heard him speak names, the Emperor's chief among them.' The housecarl was anxious. 'He has not been in contact with anyone else beyond the medicae staff and myself since his healing coma concluded.'

Temeter looked at Garro and leaned closer. 'Nathaniel? Nathaniel, you old fool. If you're done sleeping, there's a crusade on, or haven't you noticed?' He kept a note of good humour, masking his own concern. His smile became genuine when Garro's eyes fluttered open and fixed on him.

'Ullis, can't you handle a fight without me?'

'Ha,' said Temeter. 'Your wounds haven't dulled that wit of yours, then.' He laid a hand on Garro's shoulder. 'Word from that peacock Saul Tarvitz. He's back on the *Andronius*, but he wanted to thank you for softening up the Warsinger for him.'

The captain grunted in amusement, but said nothing.

'Your lads were concerned,' Temeter continued. 'I hear Hakur was afraid he might have to step up and take the eagle cuirass.'

'I can still carry it, if only these sawbones would let me go.' Garro winced as a wave of pain shocked through him. 'I heal better standing up.'

Temeter shot a look out into the infirmary proper where Voyen hovered silently. He took a breath. 'How's the leg, Nathaniel?'

Garro's face went a little grey as he looked down the chair. His right limb was misshapen and out of place. Instead of a form of strong, firm muscle and sinew, there was a skeletal construct of dense steel and plates made of polished brass that mimicked the planes of a thigh and calf. The augmetic leg was of excellent quality, but it was no less shocking to see it there. Conflicting thoughts warred over Garro's expression. 'It will suffice. The chirurgeons tell me that the nerve bonding went without incident. According to Brother Voyen, in time I will not even be aware of it.'

Temeter heard the thinly veiled disbelief in his comrade's voice, but chose not to respond to it. 'That's the battle-captain I know. What other man can leave a good cut of himself on the field and still come back for a rematch with teeth bared?'

Garro gave a wan smile, his voice strengthening. 'I hope that will be soon. Tell me, brother, what have I missed while I was healing? Did I sleep through Isstvan's pacification and the rest of the Great Crusade?'

'Hardly.' Temeter worked at keeping a light tone, even as he saw where Nathaniel was taking the conversation. 'Orders from the Warmaster have come down from Lord Mortarion. The fleet's at high anchor over Isstvan III as we speak. All the turncoat's local orbitals have been taken down by the Raven squadrons and what system ships we encountered are wreckage. The skies belong to Horus.'

'And the attack on the Choral City? If you are here then I assume it's still to come.'

'Soon, brother. The Warmaster himself has chosen the men who will form the speartip against Vardus Praal's forces.'

Garro frowned slightly. 'Horus is picking the units? That is… atypical. That's usually a task for the Legion Master.'

'He is the Warmaster,' Temeter replied with a hint of pride. 'Atypical is his prerogative.'

Garro nodded. 'He chose your unit, didn't he? No wonder you're so happy about it.' The captain smiled. 'I look forward to fighting alongside you again so soon after the jorgall assault.'

And there it was. As much as Temeter didn't want to show a reaction, he knew he did, and he saw that Nathaniel caught it.

The ends of Garro's smile tightened. 'Or not?'

'Nathaniel,' he sighed, 'I thought I should be the one to tell you, before that dolt Grulgor made sport of it. The Apothecaries have not declared you fully healed and therefore you are deemed unfit for battle-field operations. Your command remains at a limited duty standing.'

'Limited.' Garro bit out the word and shot a savage, angry glare at Voyen, who hurriedly turned and walked away. 'Is that how I am considered, as *limited*?'

'Don't be petulant,' snapped Temeter, heading off his friend's anger as quickly as he could, 'and don't take it out on Voyen. He's only doing his duty to the Legion, and to you. If you tried to lead the Seventh Company now, you'd risk failing them and that's a chance the Death Guard can't take. You're not going down to Isstvan III, Nathaniel. Those orders come direct from First Captain Typhon.'

'Calas Typhon can kiss my sword-hilt,' growled Garro, and Temeter saw his housecarl blink in shock at the normally stoic captain's insult. 'Get this cage of ornaments off me,' he continued, forcing away the medicae monitors and philtre vials.

'Nathaniel, wait.'

With a grunt of effort, Garro shoved himself off the support throne and on to his flesh and metal feet. He took a few firm steps forward. 'If I can move then I can fight. I'll go to Typhon and tell him that in person.' Garro pushed away and paced out of the cell, fighting off a hobble in his walk with each angry step.

KALEB WATCHED HIS master rise from his sickbed and stride away, the steel and brass of his new limb as much a part of him as his iron will to survive. Alone again for a moment in the small chamber, he pulled out the sheaf of papers tucked in his pocket and spread them smooth on the rough matting of the support throne. With furtive care, from a chain around his neck the housecarl drew a small metal fetish carved out of a bolt shell case. It was a rudimentary thing, rough in form but cut with the sort of care that only devotion could bring. Held to the light, thin lines of etching and patterns of pinholes showed the outline of a towering figure haloed by rays from a sun. Kaleb put the small icon down on the top of the papers and ran his palms over one another.

Now he was convinced, as ridiculous as the idea was that he might have required further proof for his faith. As his honoured master had dallied between death and life there before him, Kaleb had stood sentinel over Captain Garro and read in hushed whispers the words that traced across the dog-eared leaflets. 'His hand lies upon all of us, and every one of us owes Him our devotion. He guides us, teaches us and exhorts us to become more than we are, but most of all, the Emperor protects.'

Indeed, the Emperor had protected Nathaniel Garro. He had answered Kaleb's entreaty to save the life of his master, and shown the Death Guard the way back from the brink. Now the housecarl fully understood what he had only suspected before. *Garro is of purpose.* The Astartes lived, not through chance or caprice of action, but because the Lord of Mankind wished it to be so. There would come a moment, and the housecarl instinctively knew it would be soon, when Garro would be set to a task that only he could fulfil. When that time came, Kaleb's role would be to light the man's way.

Kaleb knew that to speak of this to his master would be wrong. He had kept his quiet beliefs to himself for this long, and the moment was not yet right to speak openly of them. But he could see it. He was sure that Garro was gradually turning to the same path that he already walked, a path that led to Terra and to the only truly divine being in the cosmos, the God-Emperor Himself.

When he was sure he was not being observed, the housecarl began to pray, his hands spread wide across the pages of the *Lectitio Divinitatus*, the words of the Church of the Holy Emperor.

GARRO'S FACE WAS hard with chained anger, and he felt it surge each time the new leg made him limp. The minute gyroscopic mechanisms in the limb would take time to learn the motions and kinetics of his body movement, and until they did, he would be forced to walk as if lame. Still, he reflected, at least he *could* walk. The ignominy of relying on a cane or some other support would have been difficult to bear.

Temeter kept pace with him. The captain of the Fourth had given up trying to convince him to return to the infirmary, and followed warily at his side. The uncertainty on Temeter's face was clear. Garro's battle-brother had not seen him in such a foul humour before.

They reached the *Endurance*'s commandery, the nexus of private chambers and sanctorum their primarch took as his own while he was aboard, crossing

the small atrium to the entrance. Garro saw another
Death Guard walking in front of him, intent on the
same destination, and to his concern he realised it
was Ignatius Grulgor. The commander of the Second
Company turned at the sound of a steel foot on the
marble tiles of the floor and gave Garro a disdainful,
appraising look.

'Not dead, then.' Grulgor folded his arms and
looked down his nose. He was still wearing his
wargear, where Garro had only simple duty robes.

'I hope that's not too great a disappointment to
you,' Garro retorted.

'Nothing could be further from the truth,' lied the
commander, 'but tell me, in your invalid state, would
it not be safer for you to keep to your sickbed? In such
a weakened condition–'

'Oh, for once in your life be silent,' snapped Temeter.

Grulgor's face darkened. 'Watch your mouth, captain.'

Garro waved the other Astartes away. 'I don't have
time to spar with you, Grulgor. I will have the primarch's ear.' He continued on towards the doors.

'You're too late for that,' came the reply, 'not that
the Death Lord would have deigned to spare his
attention to a cripple. Mortarion is no longer aboard
the *Endurance*. He's with the Warmaster once again, in
conference on matters of the Crusade.'

'Then I'll talk to Typhon.'

Grulgor sneered. 'You can wait your turn. He summoned me here only moments ago.'

'We'll see who waits,' snapped Garro, and slammed
the commandery doors wide open.

Inside, First Captain Typhon's head jerked up from
the battle maps laid out on the chart table before

him. Typhon's hulking armoured form was framed by a tall stained-glass window that looked out over the length of the warship's dorsal hull. 'Garro?' He seemed genuinely surprised to see the battle-captain up and walking.

'Sir,' replied Nathaniel, 'Captain Temeter informs me that my combatant status has not been restored.'

Typhon gave Grulgor a slight sign with his hand, a command to wait. 'This is so. The Apothecaries say–'

'I care little for that at this moment,' Garro broke in, ignoring protocol. 'I request my command squad be immediately tasked to the Isstvan III assault!'

A quick, almost imperceptible look passed between Typhon and Grulgor before the first captain spoke again. 'Captain Temeter, why are you here?'

Temeter hesitated, wrong-footed by the question. 'Lord, I came with Captain Garro, in, uh, support.'

Typhon gestured to Garro with a wave of his hand. 'Does he need support, Temeter? He can stand on his own two feet.' He gave a sharp nod at the commandery doors. 'You are dismissed. Attend to your company and the preparations for the drop.'

The captain of the Fourth frowned and saluted, giving Garro a last look before he exited the chamber. When the doors banged shut, Nathaniel met Typhon's gaze again. 'I'll have an answer from you, first captain.'

'Your request is denied.'

'Why?' Garro demanded. 'I am fit to lead! Damn it, I stood and fought on Isstvan Extremis with a leg torn from me, and yet I cannot prosecute the Emperor's enemies with this tin prosthesis bolted to my torso?'

Typhon's hard amber eyes narrowed. 'If it were up to me, I would let you do this, Garro. I would be willing to let you stumble into that war zone and live or die on your own stock of bravado, but the word comes from his lordship. Mortarion makes this command, captain. Would you oppose the will of our primarch?'

'If he were here in this chamber, aye, I would.'

'Then you would hear the same words from his lips. If time enough had passed and your injury was fully healed, then perhaps, but not here and now.'

Grulgor couldn't resist the opportunity to twist the knife. 'I'll bring a little glory back for you, Terran.'

Garro's ire rose in a hot surge, but Typhon's gruff voice snapped out again before he could speak.

'No, Captain Grulgor, you will not. It is my decision that you will also remain with the orbital flotilla during the Isstvan III operation.'

The commander's arrogant bluster died in his throat. 'What? Why, lord? Garro, he is injured, but I am at battle-ready strength and–'

Typhon spoke over him. 'I called you here to give you this order personally, before I departed to board the *Terminus Est*. I was going to send a runner to Captain Garro with his orders, but as he has presented himself here before me, I see no reason why I shouldn't inform both of you together.'

The first captain stepped around the chart table towards them and took on a formal, commanding tone. 'Based on the battle plans of his excellence the Warmaster Horus and our liege the Death Lord Mortarion, it has been determined that you will both be assigned to duty stations with your command squads aboard an Imperial warship. This will be a supervisory posting. The rest of your great companies will remain in reserve. During the assault on Isstvan III and the Choral City, you will provide standby tactical support for the drop-pod deployment operation, and remain on alert to perform rapid-reaction interdict duties.'

A servitor approached Garro and handed him a data-slate containing the details of the official battle edict.

'Interdiction against what?' demanded Grulgor. 'Praal's army has nothing that flies, we destroyed it all!'

'Which of us will have operational command?' asked Garro in a low, resigned voice, paging through the content of the slate.

'That responsibility will be shared jointly,' Typhon replied.

On some level, Garro felt defeated and empty, but at least he could draw small consolation from the fact that he would not have to face Grulgor lording his superiority over the men of his command squad. In an instant, the burning discontentment that had flooded through him cooled and faded. Garro's old, usual manner of dogged endurance came easily back to the fore. If Mortarion said it was to be so, then in all truth what right did he have to say otherwise? He hid a sigh. 'Thank you, first captain, for illuminating me. At your discretion, I wish to assemble my men and brief them on this new task.'

Typhon nodded. 'You are dismissed, Captain Garro.'

Nathaniel Garro turned and walked away, the clicking of the steel foot a ticking metronome for his discontent.

GRULGOR MADE TO leave as well, but Typhon shook his head. 'Ignatius, a moment.' When Garro had left the chamber, he stepped closer to the commander. 'I know you feel that I have slighted you, brother, but believe me, the reverse is so.'

'Indeed?' Grulgor was unconvinced. 'The key battle of this campaign and you tell me I must watch it from orbit, corralled in a tin can with a gang of swabs, and Garro playing the wounded martyr? Please, my esteemed first captain, tell me how this thing does me such great honour!'

Typhon ignored the sarcasm. 'I spoke to you before of our master's desire to bring Garro to the Warmaster's banner over Terra's, but we both know that Garro will not change. He's too much the Emperor's dutiful warrior.'

Grulgor's brow furrowed. 'Isstvan III... Could this be the turning point?' Typhon said nothing, watching him. 'Perhaps...' He nodded slowly, forming his thoughts. 'I think I see an intention emerging: the unusual pattern of mission assignments to specific units from the Legions, instead of complete companies. One could imagine that the Lord Horus seeks to isolate the elements that do not share his convictions.'

Typhon nodded. 'When the turning point, as you call it, arrives there are certain duties Horus would have you perform.' His voice dropped. 'Despite Mortarion's munificence and lenience towards him, I know Garro will attempt to betray our liege lord and the Warmaster.'

Grulgor nodded in return, for the first time exactly aware of his position in the scheme of things. 'I will not allow that to transpire.'

GARRO STOOD IN the centre of the armoury chamber and repeated Typhon's words. He forced away the chill impression of storm clouds and building threat, the sense of vast and silent machinations thundering unseen above him. Garro put these things aside and spoke to his men as their brother and commander, preparing them for the battle to come. There were grumblings of dissension, but Hakur stamped on them immediately, and in good order the assembled squads of Astartes began their arming procedures prior to embarkation to their new posting.

'This ship, sir,' said Sendek, 'the vessel where we're to be sent. Do you know anything of it?'

'A frigate,' replied Garro. 'It's called the *Eisenstein*.'

SEVEN

Hard Landing
Life-Eater
Decision

IT WAS THE honour of the Death Guard that they be the first Astartes to set foot on the surface of Isstvan III, in the mission to restore the world to compliance. Ullis Temeter's heart swelled with martial pride to know that he and the men of his company would form the very point of the spear tip. The captain's drop-pod hammered into the compacted mudflats adjoining the Choral City's trench lines with a solid thunder of torn earth. The concussion of the landing echoed over and over as hundreds more pods rained from the sky in burning red-orange streaks, half-burying themselves in the dirt.

The invasion force numbered in the thousands, with warriors of every rank and stripe coming in hard, cold fury to the surface. In the minds of each Astartes there was anger and censure for the rebels, and the Death Guard were but a part of the multiple brigades of warriors and war machines turned to that purpose.

The flanks of Temeter's pod flew open, propelled by explosive bolts, and he took his first breath of Isstvanian air to call out to his men.

'For Terra and Mortarion!' The captain led his command squad out of the shallow crater their landing had created and opened fire, laying down a chattering fan of tracer against a group of turncoat soldiers who had ventured close to observe.

Vardus Praal had prepared his defences well, gutting the forest that had previously stood in this place and making the flat landscape into a sparse killing ground of trenches, tunnels and low bunkers. Beyond it, a few kilometres distant, were the outskirts of the Choral City itself. The cool blue-white sunlight of the day made it glitter and shine. Temeter saw more streaks of fire descending on the city proper, towards the striking shapes of the Precentor's palace and the Sirenhold: the drop-pod assault elements of the World Eaters, Emperor's Children and the Sons of Horus.

He smiled. The Death Guard would meet them soon enough, but first he had a punishment to mete out. The traitor Praal's men had fashioned these earthworks in defiance of the Emperor's call to obedience, and it was Captain Temeter's duty to show them the error of their ways. It would have been a simple matter for the Astartes invasion force to bypass the trench lines and land behind them, but to do that would have sent the wrong message. It would have implied that the fortifications were somehow a challenge to Imperial might, when clearly they were nothing more than a minor impediment. So, Temeter and the Death Guard would walk into the fire corridors of the Isstvanian lines. They would rend and destroy them, and march on to the Choral City to show these deluded fools the truth. Nothing could stand in the way of the Emperor's will.

The Astartes moved across the dull mud in a thick line of marble-grey and green armour, a heavy wave of ceramite and flexsteel fording snarls of razor wire and barriers made of rough-cut tree trunks. They strode through kill points and shrugged off hails of stubber bullets. Some of Temeter's troops paused here and there as they found concealed pop-up hatches and closed them permanently with melta bombs.

The captain glanced back and saw the venerable dreadnought Huron-Fal moving to his right flank, the spread clawed feet of the hulking warrior churning up the mud. Sprays of fire from the twin-mounted cannons on Huron's right arm lanced out and blew huge divots of clotted earth from the enemy lines, sending traitor soldiers scattering.

The defenders of the Choral City wore drab fatigues that matched the colour of the dull mud, but such pitiful attempts at camouflage were rendered useless by the image intensification lenses and infra-red prey sight functions of an Astartes helm. He gave the command in battle-sign for the line to split into skirmish parties and watched as the warriors broke into packs.

Temeter knew most of the men in this detachment by name or reputation, although there were some Death Guard here today that he had never fought with. The Warmaster's deployment plan for the assault, while sound, was not one that Temeter himself would have constructed. Rather than follow the traditional lines of unit by company division, Horus had combed the Legions for individual squad-level elements and assembled a force that drew men from dozens of different companies.

It was the captain's understanding that this had happened not only with the Death Guard, but also in the World Eaters, the Emperor's Children and Horus's own Legion. He had to admit, the strategic thinking behind such a selective deployment was beyond him, but if the Warmaster had ordered it to be so, then he had no doubt there was a reason for it; privately, the captain of the Fourth was pleased to have a battlefield to himself for a change, able to fight without taking a back seat to Grulgor's grandstanding or Typhon's brutal tactics.

The foe was regrouping, recovering from the shock of the initial landing to the point where their fire was no longer random. Over the flat blares of ballistic shot, Temeter's keen hearing captured scratchy, atonal sounds that sounded like singing. He had read the after-action chronicles from Isstvan Extremis and knew of these so-called 'Warsingers' and their strange choral witchery. It seems that here on the third planet, the arcane power of their peculiar music also held sway. Temeter raised his combi-bolter and began a symphony of his own.

THE EISENSTEIN WAS an unremarkable vessel, an older pattern of ship in the frigate tonnage grade, just over two kilometres in length from bow to stern. It bore some resemblance to the newer Sword-class craft, but only inasmuch as most Imperial ships shared a similar design philosophy. Almost every line vessel in service to the Lord of Terra was constructed of congruent elements: the dagger prow, the massive block of sub-light and warp drives, and forged between them amidships of crenellations and complex sheaves of steel.

'It doesn't look like much,' Voyen remarked quietly, peering through the Stormbird's viewport as they crossed from the *Endurance*. He was still wary around Garro and it showed in his voice.

'It's just a ship,' replied the battle-captain. 'There or elsewhere, we do our duty no differently.'

In the frigate's landing bay, which seemed cramped and narrow in comparison to the *Endurance*, the ship's master was waiting to greet the Death Guard with a formal bridge party.

'Baryk Carya,' he said, with a clipped accent and a brisk salute. 'Commander Grulgor, Battle-Captain Garro. As the primarch has ordered, this ship is yours until death or new duty.'

Carya was thickset and tawny, with a matting of stubbly grey hair around his head and chin. Garro noticed the shine of a carbon-plated augmetic at his cheek and saw the stud-plug cords dangling in a queue from the back of his skull. He was terse in manner, but just on the right side of obedient.

As ship's master, Carya would be de facto captain when a ranking Astartes was not on board, and he didn't doubt the man had some resentment about stepping out of that role for this assignment. The ship-master glanced at the lean, thin-faced woman at his side. Garro recognised the status pins on her epaulets as those of executive rank. 'My deck officer, Racel Vought.' She bowed and made the sign of the aquila.

Grulgor took this opportunity to sniff in slight disdain. 'You may carry on, shipmaster. When Captain Garro or I require you attention, you will be made aware of it.'

Carya and Vought saluted and left. Garro watched them go, aware that Grulgor was already attempting to place himself in a position of superiority less than a minute after they had stepped on to *Eisenstein*'s decks.

He looked back towards the aura-field holding out the vacuum of space as the last of the Stormbirds drifted into the landing bay on darts of blue thrust, angling to land next to the transports assigned to the elements from the Second and Seventh Companies. A momentary crease of uncertainty crossed Garro's face. He counted the Stormbirds. Surely the new arrival was one too many for their needs? It wasn't as if the entirety of their commands had come with the two unit leaders.

The ship settled and folded its raptor wings to its fuselage. The captain watched it from the corner of his eye, waiting for the embarkation hatch to drop open to release more of Grulgor's men, but it remained static. There were no passengers aboard, then? Perhaps the ship only carried inanimate cargo.

Grulgor crossed his line of sight and showed Garro a thin, humourless smile. 'I intend to make an inspection of this vessel to ensure it is fully prepared for the battle.'

'Very well.'

The commander signalled to a handful of his men and strode away without looking back. Garro sighed and turned to Kaleb, where the housecarl stood, bowed. 'Supervise the *Eisenstein*'s servitors to unload our wargear and equipment.' He paused. 'And report to me any information about the payload from that last Stormbird.'

'Aye, lord. I'll have the crew install the gear on the frigate's arming racks.'

Garro looked at Sergeant Hakur. 'Andus, take the men and find us a good billet before Grulgor's men take the choice spaces.' Off the veteran's salute, the battle-captain turned to his command squad. 'I'm going to the bridge. Decius, Sendek, you'll join me.'

Voyen gave him a look. 'While Grulgor stalks the lower decks? Forgive me, lord, but I find something about his manner unsettling.'

'Who doesn't?' offered Sendek.

'He's your superior, Apothecary,' Garro said, more bluntly than he had intended. 'He has the authority to do as he wishes, within reason.' Nathaniel waved Voyen away. 'Go with Hakur. I'm in no mood for idle speculation at this moment.'

With his warriors following him, Garro walked to the elevator platform that would take them up to the frigate's central tiers. He kept his face neutral, but Voyen had struck a sore point. It would be divisive and unseemly for the battle-captain to have spoken openly in front of line Astartes, but the truth was Garro too suspected an ulterior motive on Grulgor's part.

Have we come to this? His thoughts echoed in his mind. *When men of the same Legion cannot look upon one another without a bloom of distrust? There is rivalry between warriors and then there is enmity... And this... What am I sensing?*

'CAPTAIN!' TEMETER LOOKED up into the face of one of his junior officers. 'Sir, our approach on the northern flank is being forced into a bottleneck. The defenders have a twinned quad-barrel cannon sweeping the area. It is emplaced in a ferrocrete bunker. Shall I give the command to go around?'

Temeter snorted. 'We are Death Guard, lad. When we encounter a boulder in our path, we do not slink and flow around it like water. We strike and shatter it!' He rose and beckoned his command squad with him. 'Show me this impediment.'

They moved low over undulating ground, leaping over shallow trench works clogged with Isstvanian dead and shell casings. The crack and screech of shots whizzed around them, and still Temeter heard the doleful droning dirges of the enemy. Crossing a shallow incline, the captain deliberately stepped out of line and stomped on a fallen speaker horn where it had fallen from a support pole. The device sparked and fell silent.

'There, lord,' said the officer.

It was a flat hexagon set deep in the grey mud, the clean shade of ferrocrete not more than a few years old. Pits were being dug in the facia of it from bolt rounds as Death Guard sharpshooters sniped from cover. As the young Astartes had said, the wicked barrels of the quad-guns were spitting an endless stream of tracer out over the approaches. A handful of broken bodies in the killing zone showed where battle-brothers had advanced and died in the attempt. Temeter frowned. 'Shot and shell won't do the deed. Bring up the men with flamers and plasma weapons.'

The order was relayed and a troop of Death Guard carrying inferno guns came forward. Temeter tossed his combi-bolter to the young officer and beckoned another man closer. 'Your torch, give it to me.' The captain took the warrior's flamer and shook it, hearing the satisfying slosh of a near-full tank of liquid promethium. 'Bolters, draw their attention. Flamers, give them the heat.'

The Astartes opened fire and as Temeter expected, the heavy quad-guns inched around to track on them. His men understood the plan without the need for him to lay it out in detail. The moment the quads were depressed, the Death Guard with flamer and plasma weapons crested their cover and sent jets of superheated gas and burning fluid washing over the sides of the bunker and into the interior. The defenders couldn't range the guns back fast enough, and within moments, Temeter had led his men to the very wall of the low blockhouse. For good measure he had a sergeant toss a fist of krak grenades through the aiming slot and then projected himself up and over the bunker roof.

Temeter ran and dropped down into the S-shaped entry tunnel, smashing a hooded trooper into the ferrocrete with an ugly crack of bone. He heard the confusion inside the dugout and waded into it. Within, black smoke and licks of guttering fire clung to the walls and the heat radiating from the thrumming quad-guns was thick. The captain triggered the borrowed flamer and hosed it across the space before him, a hissing red whip of flame carving through the air at chest height. Men became torches and boxes of unspent ammunition in compartments below cooked off in blaring detonations. One of the Isstvanian soldiers ran at him, shrieking and aflame, and pulled Temeter into an embrace. The captain let the flamer drop from his grip and ripped the man in two, tearing him apart. He beat out the flames and grimaced as the rest of his troop waded in and finished the task.

The bunker silenced, Temeter glanced into the tunnel mouths that branched downward from it. 'Seal all of these,' he ordered. 'We don't want rats popping up behind us after our line advances past this point.' Without the roar of the cannons, once again the captain became aware of the reedy caterwauling issuing from a vox-speaker. He punched it into pieces with his fist. 'Destroy those repeaters wherever you see them,' Temeter continued. 'That oath-forsaken noise is damaging my calm.'

'Sir!' called one of the men, pointing out through the gun slit.

Temeter saw a huge shadow dropping towards the horizon on pillars of retro-rocket fire, and then felt the earth tremble like a struck bell. Every Astartes in the bunker left the floor for a split second, and he heard the ferrocrete roof crack with the shockwave. The captain peered out and saw a massive cylinder standing upright in a shroud of steam, some distance beyond the zone where the drop-pods had put down. It was easily the size of a hive-city habitat block, guidance fins still glowing cherry-red with the heat of re-entry. There came a mighty moan of stressed metals and the sides of the cylinder fell away, trailing flexible pipes and streams of white vapour. From inside the monstrous drop-capsule came the hooting call of a battle-horn, and then planes of steel and iron emerged from the smoke to become a colossus bristling with armour and guns. The ground resonated with each thunderous footfall as the Imperator-class Titan strode out towards the Choral City.

'*Dies Irae,*' said Temeter, naming the massive war machine. 'Our cousins from the Legion Mortis have decided to join our outing.' He allowed himself to marvel at the huge battle construct, then shook it off. 'Signals,' he called, 'contact the *Irae*'s princeps and update him on the battle situation.'

The young Astartes officer handed Temeter back his combi-bolter and frowned. 'Lord, there is a concern with the vox.'

'Explain,' he demanded.

'We're having difficulty making contact on some channels, including the feed to the Titan and our ships in orbit.'

Temeter glanced up. 'Are the locals jamming us?'

The Astartes shook his head. 'I don't believe so, captain. The drop-out is too selective for that. It's as if…

Well, it's as if certain vox frequencies have just been switched off.'

He accepted this with a brisk nod. 'We'll work around it, then. If the problem gets worse, then inform me. Otherwise, we proceed with the attack plan as determined.' Temeter bounded out of the cloying air of the dead bunker and strode forward. 'On to the Choral City,' he called. A vast shadow hove above him and the captain looked up to see the underside of the *Dies Irae*'s foot as it passed over him, descending to fall upon another bunker some distance ahead. The heavy impacts of artillery were starting to converge, coming down in twists of smoke. 'Death Guard!' he called, shouldering his bolter, 'we'll let the giant take the brunt of the big guns. Into the trenches, brothers. Sweep the ground clean of these rebellious scum!'

CARYA LOOKED UP as the brass leaves of the bridge iris whispered open to admit Garro and his two warriors. The man shot a quick, nervous look across at the woman Vought and then put up the mask of sullen authority that he had worn in the landing bay. 'Battle-captain on the bridge,' he intoned, and saluted.

Garro accepted the honour with a nod. 'Ceremony was appeased down below, Master Carya. Let's not overburden ourselves with it here, and stick to the necessities instead, yes?'

'As you wish, captain. Are you going to take the conn?'

He shook his head. 'Not without good reason.' Garro took in the layout of the ship's command chamber. It was unornamented, as was fitting to the lean and spare intentions of a vessel in the service of the Death Guard. Unlike some starships, where decorative panels of wood or metal covered the walls, the *Eisenstein*'s conduits and workings were bare to the eye. Twisted snarls of cables and piping ranged around the bridge space, clustering around cogitator consoles and viewports. They reminded Garro of the gnarled roots of ancient trees.

Vought seemed to catch on to Garro's train of thought. 'This vessel may not be pretty, but it has a strong heart, captain. It's been an unswerving servant of the Emperor since the day it left the Luna ship-yards, before I was born.' He noticed how she was careful not to look directly at his injured leg. Even under his power armour, the stiffness in his gait made the aftermath of his recent injury obvious.

Garro put a hand on the central navitrix podium, studying the etheric compass enclosed in a sphere of glass and suspensor fields. A discreet gunmetal plaque fixed to the podium's base showed the ship's name, class and details of the frigate's launching. Nathaniel read it to himself and felt amusement tug at his lips. 'Fascinating. It seems the *Eisenstein* took to space in the same year I became an Astartes.' He glanced at Vought. 'I have a kinship with her already.'

The deck officer returned his smile, and for the first time Garro felt a moment of genuine connection with a member of the crew.

'*Eisenstein*,' ventured Sendek, rolling the word over his lips. 'It is a word from an old Terran dialect, of the Jermani. It means "iron-stone". It is fitting.'

Carya nodded. 'Your warrior is correct, Captain Garro. It also shares its name with two noted men from the Age of Terra, one a remembrancer, the other a scientist.'

'Such history for a mere frigate,' Decius opined.

The shipmaster's eyes flashed for an instant. 'With respect, lord, in the Warmaster's military there is no such thing as a *mere* frigate.'

'Forgive my battle-brother,' said Garro mildly, 'he has grown too comfortable in the spacious bunks aboard the *Endurance*.'

'A fine ship,' Carya replied. 'We'll do well to match the battle record of so illustrious a vessel.'

Garro smiled slightly. 'We're not here to win accolades, shipmaster, just to do our duty.' He approached the front of the bridge, where rows of consoles and operator pulpits glowed with the actinic blue of pict-screens. 'What is our status?'

'At station-keeping,' said Vought. 'The Warmaster's orders were to hold at these co-ordinates until all Astartes were aboard, then await further commands.'

The battle-captain nodded. 'I am afraid that we may not be making much history today. Our primarch has ordered that we maintain orbit here at high anchor and watch for enemy ships that may attempt to escape Isstvan III under cover of the ground assault.'

Garro had barely finished speaking when a bell chime sounded from a shadowed nook off to the starboard side of the bridge. A heavy sound-curtain was bunched up to one side of the dim recess, held open by a thick silver cord. It was a vox hide, an alcove where important communications could be received in relative privacy during combat operations. A gangly young officer wearing a complex signalling collar and holding a data-slate in his hand stepped out into the light and snapped to attention. 'Machine-call message, prioris cipher, expedite immediate.' He wavered, looking between Garro and Carya, unsure of who to address. 'Sir?'

The shipmaster offered an open hand. 'Let me have it, Mister Maas.' He glanced at Garro. 'Captain, if you will permit me?'

Nathaniel nodded and watched Carya page quickly through the data. 'Ah,' he said, after a moment. 'It seems Lord Mortarion has decided to make a different use of us. Vought, bring manoeuvring thrusters to standby.'

Garro took the slate as the deck officer carried out her directions. 'Is there a problem?'

'No, sir. New orders.' The shipmaster bent over the helm servitor and began giving out a string of clipped commands.

The data-slate was curt and to the point. Directly from the vox dispatch nexus aboard the *Vengeful Spirit*, marked with the signet runes of the Death Lord and Horus's equerry Maloghurst, the fresh directives were for *Eisenstein* to depart from the current navigation point and drop into a lower orbital path.

Like all Astartes of senior rank, Garro had training and experience in starship operations and he fell back into the learning drilled into his mind by hypno-conditioning as he read, figuring the status of the frigate once the new co-ordinates were reached.

He frowned. Typhon had told him that *Eisenstein* was to act as an interceptor for Isstvanian absconders, but once settled at this new posting, the ship would be too close to the edge of the third planet's atmosphere to react quickly enough. To function correctly in their assigned role, the frigate had to stay high, giving the gunnery crews time to spot, target and destroy enemy ships. The drop in altitude only narrowed their field of fire. Then he studied the corresponding planetary co-ordinates and his concern deepened. The orbital shift would put the *Eisenstein* directly over the Choral City, and Garro was certain that no void-capable craft had been left intact down there.

He handed the slate back to Maas, his frown deepening. Had they been carrying drop-pods and Astartes for a second assault wave, then the reasoning behind the orders would have been clear, but the frigate was not configured for those sorts of operations. It was, in the most basic sense, only a gun carriage. Decked with weapons batteries that emerged from her flanks in spiky profusion, *Eisenstein*'s only function when ranged so close to a world was one of stand-off planetary bombardment, but such an action seemed unthinkable. After all, Horus had already eschewed Angron's demands to blast the Choral City into ashes at the war council. The Warmaster would surely not change his mind so quickly, and even if he had, there were hundreds of loyal men down there.

Garro became aware that Carya was looking at him. 'Captain? If you have nothing to add, I'm going to execute the orders.'

Garro nodded distantly, feeling an ill-defined chill wash through him. 'Proceed, Master Carya.' The Death Guard stepped closer to the main viewport and stared out through the armourglass. Beneath him, the cloud-swirled sphere of Isstvan III began to drift nearer.

'Something wrong, lord?' Decius spoke in a sub-vocal whisper, below the hearing of the crewmen.

'Yes,' said the battle-captain, and the sudden honesty of the admission surprised him. 'But by Terra, I don't know what it is.'

KALEB SHRANK DEEP inside the folds of the ship-robes and moved with care along the edges of the service gantry. Over the years he had become quite adept at being unseen in plain sight and to an outside observer the housecarl would have resembled nothing but a common serf. His badge of fealty to the Death Guard and the Seventh Company was swaddled beneath the grey material. There was a part of his thoughts that cycled an endless loop of anxious warnings against what he was doing, but Kaleb found himself moving forward despite it, going onward.

How had he changed so? What he was doing had to be some sort a criminal act, masquerading as an *Eisenstein* crewman instead of openly walking with his real identity visible, and yet, he felt filled with the rightness of his actions. Ever since the Emperor had answered Kaleb's prayers in the infirmary and saved his master Garro, the housecarl had become emboldened. His orders were coming from a higher power. Perhaps they always had, but only now was he sure of it. The battle-captain had told him to follow the Stormbird's cargo, and he was about it. If it was Garro's wish, then this was the Emperor's work, and Kaleb would be right in doing it.

After the men of the Seventh had left the landing bay, Kaleb had placed himself where he could give directions to the frigate's servitors but also observe the last Stormbird. It had only been a few minutes before one of Grulgor's men had returned to the bay – the boorish one, Mokyr – and drawn off a work gang of serfs to unload the shuttle's cargo. Kaleb watched the heavy steel cubes roll out of the vessel, and then watched the serfs bind them to chain carriages and shift them towards the aft. The containers were identical: blocks of dull metal scarred and pitted from use, detailed with the Imperial aquila and stencilled warning runes in brilliant yellow paint. They could hold anything. From this distance, Kaleb could not read the lading scrolls fixed to the flanks.

He watched with interest as one of the helot teams fumbled and a crate slipped on its moorings, falling a metre before the men caught the slack and stopped it slamming into the deck. Mokyr stormed over to the foreman and backhanded him to the floor. Over the constant noise of the bay, Kaleb could not fathom the words he spoke, but the tone of the Death Guard's ill-temper was obvious.

In a steady train, the crates shifted up and away. Kaleb watched them, hesitating. He had orders to supervise the equipment transfer, yes, but Garro had also demanded information on the nature of the Stormbird's cargo. Kaleb convinced himself that the latter was the more important command.

So, keeping his distance, the housecarl threaded his way through the *Eisenstein*, keeping the convoy of containers in sight, careful to stay out of Mokyr's eye-line. The crates were halted in the service gantries that ran down the spine of the frigate. On either side of the open steel tunnel were loading gears and hopper mechanisms for the ship's primary weapons batteries. Large open gun breeches lined the walkway, ready to accept war shots from the ammunition magazines that towered above them. The crates were being shifted to the staging areas near the portside guns. Kaleb's face showed confusion and he let his gaze follow the length of one huge cannon out beyond the hull through the armoured slits of the sighting port. He saw the dim reflection of a planetary surface out there, drifting in the dark.

The work gangs had some of the crates open and he shifted forward to get a better look, slipping over the lip of seal plates where wide emergency barrier partitions would drop into place in the event of a munitions discharge or misfire. Kaleb's dismay grew stronger when he

recognised the tall, broad shapes of Death Guard standing watch over the serfs while they worked. Bareheaded
and intent, Commander Grulgor was at their forefront,
shouting out orders and giving directions with sharp
jerks of his hand. The crate closest to him gave out an
oiled hiss and unfolded like a gift box. Inside there were
hexagonal frames, and racked upon them were a dozen
glass spheres. Each one was at least a metre in diameter,
and all of them were filled with a thick chemical slurry
of vomitous green fluids.

A black symbol made up of interlocking broken
rings decorated each capsule, and some basic animal
reaction made Kaleb's hands clench around the rail-
ing he hid behind. A quick mental calculation told
him that if all the crates were identical, then there
were over a hundred of the spheres in Grulgor's cargo.
Things added up: Mokyr's abrupt anger, the commander's presence at the unloading, the exaggerated
delicacy with which the crewmen moved the capsules. Whatever the liquid was inside them, the glass
pods represented something utterly lethal.

The thought crystallised in Kaleb's mind with such an
impact that it pushed him back up to his feet. Suddenly,
all the bravery he had felt at his clever little disguise
evaporated, and stabs of fear shot through him. The
housecarl spun about to run and slammed into an
ambling servitor with a tray of tools. The piston-legged
machine slave tipped over and collapsed, sending its
gear flying. The tool-parts sent up a cacophony of
sound, drawing the attention of Grulgor's Astartes.
Kaleb saw Mokyr start towards his hiding place and the
housecarl fled into the deeper shadows.

Fear enveloped him as readily as the thick material
of the ship-robes. It was only as his eyes adjusted to
the dark that the housecarl realised he had backed

into a wide alcove with no other exits. The dead-end
stopped with a sheer wall of hull metal and hanging
catwalks overhead that he couldn't hope to reach. He
would be found. He would be found and they would
know who he was and who had sent him. Nerves in
the servant's legs twitched. Grulgor would end his
life, he was certain of it. He remembered the look in
the commander's eyes back aboard the *Endurance*, the
loathing. But that death would be nothing compared
to the crushing failure it represented. Kaleb Arin
would die and he would perish having failed both his
master and the Master of Mankind.

Mokyr gave the servitor a sideways look and kept
coming, straight towards Kaleb, one hand resting on
the hilt of his combat blade. The housecarl prayed
silently. *Emperor, Lord of Man, protect me and hold me
safe against the enemies of Your Divine Will–*

In the next second he was yanked from his feet and
felt strong hands pull him off the deck, up and away.
Kaleb thrashed, coming to face a serious aspect there
in the dimness.

'Voyen?' he whispered.

The Apothecary put a finger to his lips and held
Kaleb tightly. The housecarl looked down from the
catwalk and watched Mokyr run a cursory glance over
the alcove below them, then snort and stride back to
Grulgor. After a moment, Voyen relaxed his grip and
let Kaleb settle on to the scaffold.

'Lord?' whispered the servant. 'What are you doing
here?'

Voyen's voice was a low rumble. 'Like you, my sus-
picions were piqued. Unlike you, my skills in stealth
are of a decent standard.'

'Thank you for saving me, sir. If Mokyr had found
me there–'

'It would not have gone well.' It was clear the Apothecary was deeply troubled.

Kaleb looked back at the loaders and the glass spheres.

'Those orbs, what are they?' The work gangs were busy detaching the warhead cowlings from thruster-guided glide bombs, exchanging the explosive charges inside for the globes of liquid.

Voyen tried to speak, and it was as if the words caught in his throat, too distasteful for him to even bring to bear. 'Those are Life-Eater capsules,' he managed. 'It is an engineered viral strain of such complete lethality that it can only be deployed in the most extreme cir-cumstances, usually against the most foul xenos.'

He looked away and Kaleb felt a chill at the war-rior's mien. If an Astartes could be fearful of these things...

'It is a bane-weapon of the highest order, a world-killer. Only the largest capital ships are permitted to carry it in their armouries.'

'They brought it from the *Endurance*?' Kaleb blinked. 'Why, lord? Why are they loading it to fire on the planet?'

Voyen gave him a hard look. 'Kaleb, listen to me. Go to the captain and tell him what we have seen. As fast as you can, little man. Go. Go now!'

And so Kaleb ran.

'What's this?' Decius heard the warning tone in Carya's voice and looked up from the hololithic dis-play and across the frigate's bridge. The shipmaster was speaking to Maas, the vox-tender. 'There aren't any scheduled movements in this battle sector. Did the deployment pattern get altered without my knowledge?'

'Negative,' said Maas. 'No recorded changes, sir. Nevertheless, this signal from the *Lord of Hyrus* is clear. A craft from the *Andronius* is on our scopes and it does not register a mission flight plan.'

'The *Andronius* is Eidolon's ship,' said Sendek. 'Has he suddenly become eager to join our battle-brothers down on the surface?'

'Perhaps the scent of all that glory was too much to resist,' added Decius.

Captain Garro walked back from the far end of the chamber, grimacing a little as he limped. 'Are you sure?' he asked, addressing his demand to the communications officer.

Maas nodded and brandished a data-slate. 'Very sure, captain. An Emperor's Children Thunderhawk is passing through our engagement zone.'

'A fine way to get yourself shot down,' murmured Sendek, drawing a wry nod from Decius. The Astartes toggled the hololith to show the data from Maas's report and his eyes widened. Not only was there a Thunderhawk arrowing through *Eisenstein*'s patch of space, but behind it was a cluster of Raven interceptors and they were in an attack delta.

Garro was speaking to the woman, Vought. 'Smells like trouble. Put us on an intercept course.'

Decius looked to his commander as the deck officer relayed Garro's orders. 'Lord, is this some sort of test? First we are taken off our assigned duty station and now our own ships are launching without authorisation?'

'I have no answer for you.'

'Captain!' Sendek called out urgently. 'The fighters trailing the Thunderhawk... They have just opened fire on it.' The shock was clear in his voice.

'A warning shot,' suggested Carya.

Vought shook her head. 'No. Cogitators are detecting energy blooms on the vessel's hull. The drop-ship is taking hits.'

The familiar bell chime sounded once more, and Maas emerged from the alcove again. 'Battle-Captain Garro, I have a message sent in the clear on the general vox channel.'

'Quickly,' Garro ordered.

'From Lord Commander Eidolon, starship *Andronius*. Message reads: Fugitive Thunderhawk is acting against the Warmaster's commands and is to be considered a renegade. All fleet elements are ordered to destroy the ship on sight.'

'Shoot down one of our own vessels?' Sendek was clearly aghast at the mere thought of such an idea. 'Has he taken leave of his senses?'

'The Thunderhawk is turning,' reported the deck officer, 'he's seen our approach. Confirm, the Thunderhawk is closing in on us.' She looked up at Garro. 'He's well within lascannon range, lord.'

Carya's face was stony, and a hard silence fell across the bridge. 'What are your orders, Captain Garro?'

Decius's commander threw him a look, and then turned to Maas. 'Can you get me a ship-to-ship link with that Thunderhawk?'

'Aye, sir.'

'Then do it now.'

'But, lord, the orders–' began Decius.

Garro shot the warrior a sharp glare. 'Eidolon can give all the orders he wants. I will not fire on a fellow Astartes without first knowing why.' The battle-captain strode to the mouth of the vox hide and snatched a hand communicator from Maas. 'Thunderhawk on a closing course with the *Eisenstein*,' he barked, 'identify yourself!'

Through the crackle of interference came an anxious reply. 'Nathaniel?' Decius saw the colour drain from Garro's face in recognition. 'It's Saul. It's good to hear your voice, my brother!'

'Saul Tarvitz,' whispered Sendek, 'First Captain of the Emperor's Children. Impossible! He's a man of honour! If he's turned traitor, then the galaxy has gone insane!'

Decius found he couldn't look away from Garro's shocked expression. 'Perhaps it has.' It was a long moment before Decius realised the words had been his.

PART TWO

A
SUNDERED VOW

EIGHT

Point of no Return
Sacrifice
Oath of Moment

TOLLEN SENDEK PRIDED himself on his orderly mind and his controlled, regimented will. It was a point of honour for him to be logical and intent in his service to the XIV Legion and to the Emperor. He eschewed irrationality and the incautious nature that some of his brethren embraced. Rahl had often made fun of him about it, joking that Sendek took the word 'stoic' to new extremes, but he thought of his dead comrade now and wondered what Pyr would have made of the look on his face, the purely emotional surprise that gripped him.

It had taken only a moment to bring him to this state. The rogue Thunderhawk, the signal from Eidolon, the incredible command to terminate the fleeing vessel and the ranking Astartes officer aboard it... Sendek shook his head, trying to fight off the confusion. Had Decius been correct, was it a test? Some bizarre sort of battle drill to assess the mettle of the

Eisenstein's command crew? Or could it be true that Saul Tarvitz had indeed turned renegade and was fit only for execution? If it was possible for an Imperial governor like Vardus Praal to go against the Emperor, then perhaps an Astartes might do the same.

Captain Garro gripped a vox microphone in his hand and was speaking urgently into it, his knuckles white around the device. 'Tarvitz? What in the name of the Emperor is going on? Are those fighters trying to shoot you down?'

Sendek flashed a look at the *Eisenstein*'s hololith. The answer to Garro's question was self-evident, as the frigate's sensors showed flickers of beam fire dashing from the flight of Ravens, snapping at the Thunderhawk's stern. As he watched, the raptor-like interceptors adopted an attack posture. They were lining up to make a final strike.

He heard Garro shout into the vox, demanding some explanation, *any* explanation. 'Be quick, Saul. They almost have you!'

Tarvitz's next words made Sendek's guts knot. 'This is treachery!' bellowed the captain of the Emperor's Children, desperation filling his voice. 'All of this! We are betrayed! The fleet is going to bombard the planet's surface with virus bombs.'

At once, everyone on the bridge in earshot of the vox speaker was shocked rigid. 'What? No!' said Vought, shaking her head. Officers at other deck stations looked up from the command pit in disbelief.

'That cannot be,' began the shipmaster, taking a wary step forward.

Decius's face was tense. 'He's mistaken. Our brothers are down there–'

Their voices overlapped one another in loud profusion, and Sendek heard only snatches of Garro's conversation with Tarvitz. 'On my life, I swear I do not lie to you,' cried the captain. Sendek's commander sagged, as if the weight of the man's claim was pressing down on him. He caught Tarvitz's final, frustrated words. 'Every Astartes on Isstvan III is going to die!'

He looked back at the hololith. Tarvitz's life was measured only in ticks of the clock. The Thunderhawk was wallowing badly, bleeding fuel as the Ravens moved in for the kill.

Captain Garro shoved himself away from the vox alcove and stormed across the bridge. 'Weapons!' he shouted. 'I want lascannon command, this very second!'

Vought's fingers danced over her console. 'Closequarters batteries are active, sir,' she reported, 'cogitators are computing a firing solution.' The woman blinked. 'Sir, are... are you going to shoot him down?'

'Give me manual control.' Garro waved her away from the panel. 'If anyone is to pull this trigger, it will be me.' The battle-captain gripped the side of the pulpit and then stabbed at an activation rune.

'Firing,' reported one of the toneless servitors.

ON THE EISENSTEIN'S dorsal hull, a cluster of highenergy laser cannons swivelled and shifted in unison, tracking to face the Thunderhawk and the Ravens. The guns discharged silently through the void, for a single instant filling the dark with a storm of flickering energy. Spears of collimated, coherent light reached out and found their target, tearing through armoured hull metal, ceramite and plastic. Fusion cores detonated in a flashing cascade, a thick cloud of radioactive debris riding out in a perfect sphere behind a wall of electromagnetic radiation.

SENDEK'S EYES NARROWED as light flared in through the bridge's viewing slits and the hololith bloomed with a sudden globe of crackling, impenetrable static. The Astartes looked to Garro as his captain stepped down from Vought's console and limped back to Maas's station at the vox hide. 'He killed him.' Tollen's voice was barely audible. 'Blood's oath, he killed Tarvitz.'

Decius eyed him, conflict visible on his face. 'Those were the orders.'

'Those were Eidolon's orders!' Sendek snapped, his usual calm disintegrating. 'You see that eagle carved upon the captain's vambrace? Tarvitz has one just like it, Hakur told me of it! Garro and Tarvitz are honour brothers! He wouldn't just murder him in cold blood!'

'But if Tarvitz had turned...'

The battle-captain gave the communications officer Maas a hard shove and pushed him out of the vox hide. Garro bent to allow his armoured form into the alcove and yanked the sound curtain across the entrance with a savage swipe of his hand, cutting himself off from the bridge.

Sendek heard Vought's question to Carya. 'What is he doing in there?'

'Reporting back to Eidolon,' suggested the shipmaster.

The Astartes leaned down, almost with his face in the edges of the hololith cube. Flickering storms of energy and colour made it impossible to read. The power of the explosion out there reflecting off the planet's upper atmosphere would fog the ship's sensors for several minutes.

'Tollen,' began Decius, 'whatever bond the battle-captain had with Tarvitz, that cannot rise above the duty of the service. Eidolon is a lord commander. He outranks Garro.'

'No.' Sendek shook his head, working the controls on the hololith's projector podium, spooling back the time index record. 'I refuse to accept he would do such a thing. You know him as well as I do, Solun. "Straight-Arrow Garro", the men call him. He is an archetype for the nobility of the Legiones Astartes! Can you ever imagine our commander agreeing to slay a battle-brother on the whim of one of the Emperor's Children?'

'Then, what happened out there?' demanded Decius. 'You saw the Thunderhawk explode!'

'I saw *an explosion*,' countered Sendek. He toyed with the controls and then let the hololith run the brief engagement again in slow motion. Indicators showed the *Eisenstein* turn and fire, the bolts sweep towards the other craft, and then the stormy aftermath. The Astartes nodded slowly. 'He didn't target the Thunderhawk at all. The shots must have struck the lead Raven. The other interceptors were in close formation. The detonation would have caught them all in the shockwave.'

'Then, where is Tarvitz?'

Sendek pointed at the deck. 'He was close to Isstvan III's atmosphere. I'll warrant he's using the sensor disruption to slip away.'

Decius glanced around to be sure that the rest of the frigate crew were not aware of what they were discussing. 'So Tarvitz escapes and five pilots are killed in his stead?'

'They were only crew-serfs, not Astartes. I doubt Eidolon will weep over their loss.' Sendek looked across to the vox hide. 'He's not talking to the *Andronius* in there,' he said, with grim certainty.

'If you are correct, then we have just witnessed our commanding officer disobey a direct order from his superior. That is dereliction of duty, grounds for severe chastisement at the very least!' Decius frowned. 'You know I have no love for Fulgrim's fops, but if the Warmaster learns of this, it will taint all of us, the entire Death Guard!'

Sendek grimaced. 'How can you be so quick to set your colours? Our captain would never act without conscience! If he has done this thing, then there is no doubt in my mind that he has a credible motive. Will you not at least learn what that is before you begin lamenting for your reputation?'

Decius's eyes flashed. 'Very well, brother. I shall ask him, now.'

Before Sendek could stop him, Decius rounded the hololith and strode quickly to the vox hide and grabbed the sound-deadening drape. As he wrenched it back, both Astartes heard the battle-captain speaking into the vox.

'Luck of Terra be with you,' he said. Only static answered him.

Garro looked up from his crouch by the communications pulpit and met their gazes. The hollow, broken look upon his face cut Decius to the very core. Even when he had seen the captain in his healing trance after falling on Isstvan Extremis, he had not seemed so empty and ill as he did at this moment.

'Lord?' he asked. 'What is it?'

'The storm is coming, Solun,' the battle-captain said in a dead voice.

✠ ✠ ✠

IT TOOK GREAT effort for Garro to propel himself out
of the vox hide, as Tarvitz's revelations churned in his
mind, sapping the will and strength from his muscles
like some strange malaise. The things he had said...
The import of them was staggering. He took heavy
steps away, ignoring the loaded stares of the *Eisenstein*'s crew and the visible distrust radiating from
Maas as the comms officer made for his alcove once
again.

Garro threw a command at Maas over his shoulder.
'Contact *Andronius*. Tell them that the rogue was
destroyed, and the explosion claimed their pursuit
ships as well. No survivors.'

'Is that what really happened?' asked Decius accus-
ingly.

'Tarvitz brought me... brought *us* a warning. You
heard what he said on the vox.'

'Lord, all I heard was some wild shouting about
betrayal and virus bombs. On that alone you have
gone against orders?'

Sendek and his brethren moved to the rear of the
compartment, instinctively keeping their voices
pitched low.

'If Tarvitz spoke of it, then it was no falsehood,'
insisted Garro softly.

Decius sneered. 'With respect, captain, I did not
know the man and I do not hold that hearsay is
enough to let a direct command be ignored—'

Garro's temper came back in a hot rush, and he
grabbed Decius by the gorget and pulled him off balance. 'I *do* know Saul Tarvitz, you whelp, and his word
is worth a thousand of Eidolon's!' He thrust his vambrace up before Decius's face. 'You see this, the
etching there? That mark is all the guarantee I need!
When you have fought for as long as I have, you will

learn that some things transcend even the commands of your masters!' Furious, he released the other warrior and his fists tightened.

Sendek's face was pale with shock. 'If what he said was true, if there are ships in the fleet preparing to drop blight warheads on the planet, it would mean the wholesale slaughter of thousands of our kinsmen.' He shook his head. 'Oath's sake, there is no need to sacrifice men to wipe out the Choral City. Why would Horus allow such a thing to happen? It makes no sense!'

'Exactly,' said Decius, recovering his composure. 'What possible reason could the Warmaster have for doing this?'

Garro opened his mouth to speak, to actually say the words aloud to his battle-brothers for the very first time, and found that he could not. The sheer horror of it, the ripping, echoing void inside his thoughts stopped him dead. *Betrayal.* He couldn't make the word, couldn't force it from his throat. That Horus himself, great Horus, the beautiful and magnificent Warmaster, had done this... The idea of it made him go weak. And with that realisation there came another. If Horus had prepared this treachery, then he had not done it alone, it was too big, too monumental an endeavour even for the Warmaster to have managed by himself. Yes, Horus's brothers would be a part of it too: Angron, ever ready to take any path that led him to more bloodshed. Fulgrim, convinced of his own superiority and perfection over all, and the Death Lord himself, in secret conspiracy with the Warmaster.

'Mortarion...' Garro saw those hard amber eyes once again, remembered the questions and the intent of his primarch. *It is important for my brother Horus to have unity across the entirety of the Astartes.* He had said those words. *We must have singular purpose or we will falter.*

Was this duplicity the purpose Mortarion had alluded to? Garro turned away, pressing the heel of his palm to his forehead, fighting down the conflict inside him. He saw a frantic, shuddering figure come rushing in through the iris hatch of the bridge, face tight with fear. 'Kaleb?'

The housecarl bowed shakily. 'My lord, you must come quickly! Brother Voyen and I... In the ship's gunnery racks, we discovered...' He struggled, sucking in gasping breaths of air. 'Grulgor and his men are loading the main guns... loading them with Life-Eater globes!'

'Virus bombs,' said Sendek, in a cold, distant voice.

'Aye, lord. I saw it with my own eyes.'

Garro pressed down the turmoil within and drew himself up. 'Show me.'

VOYEN LOOKED ON, aghast. With each new sphere that emerged on the back of the loader crews, he felt his horror plunge deeper. As a trained Apothecary, it was his duty to be knowledgeable in the patterns and pathologies of many types of biological warfare agents, and the Life-Eater was known to him. He wished it was not. He flashed on a moment of memory, a day during his advanced training with the Magos Biologis when the mentors had given live demonstrations on condemned criminals of the effects of various toxins upon unprotected flesh. He had seen the damage a single droplet of the voracious virus could do, watching it eat into a screaming heretic from behind impenetrable armourglass. Out there, in those globes, there were gallons of the thick green transmitter medium, every cupful swarming with countless trillions of the killer microbes. He estimated that the war shots aboard the *Eisenstein* alone would be enough to wipe out a large city.

Commander Grulgor walked carefully among the loaders and his own men, showing no fear, directing the arming process personally. He was taking responsibility for it, Voyen realised, doing it himself to put his own stamp of perverse pride on the deed.

He turned as soft footfalls across the maintenance gantry caught his attention. Garro, his face like thunder, arrived with Sendek in tow and Kaleb panting at the rear.

The battle-captain spoke without preamble. 'Is it true?'

'It is.' Voyen pointed. 'Look there. The sigil on the spheres is unmistakeable. It is the rot-bane, lord, a weapon even the Emperor is loath to use.' He shook his head. 'Why has Grulgor done this? What madness has possessed him?'

Garro's eyes were hard and flinty. 'It is not madness, brother. It is treason.'

'No,' insisted Voyen, desperately tying to rationalise the situation as he had been since he sent Kaleb running. 'Perhaps, if I spoke to Grulgor, I could discern the truth. I could approach him, as a lodge brother. He would listen–'

The captain shook his head. 'He will not. Mark me, this will end only one way.' Garro stood up, coming out of the shadows of the gantry, and walked slowly and deliberately down the ramp to the main level of the loading bay. He ducked beneath the hanging lip of a blast hatch and called out. 'Ignatius Grulgor! Come here and explain yourself!' The captain's voice boomed off the tall, wide corridor above the gun carriages.

Voyen and the others followed warily, and the Apothecary saw Grulgor's expression stiffen at the new arrivals.

'Garro,' he sneered. 'It would be best for you to take your men, turn about and leave. What occurs here is not of your concern.' All around him, the work gangers and the Astartes from the Second Company became still.

Garro's hand was on the hilt of Libertas. 'That will not happen.'

Grulgor nodded, a smile of amusement on his lips. It was clear he had expected no less.

'Answer me,' commanded Garro. 'In the Emperor's name, you will answer me!'

The commander's face twisted in a grimace. 'The Emperor,' he said in a mocking tone. 'Where is he now? What coin does his name carry in this moment?'

'Blasphemer!' spat Kaleb beneath his breath.

'Why should we answer to him?' Grulgor snarled. 'He abandoned us! When we needed him the most, he cut away, left us behind out here and fled back to your precious Terra! What has he done since that day, eh?' The commander spread his hands, taking in his men. 'He has sold off our birthright to a council of fools and politicians, taken civilians who have never known hardships or the kiss of war and made them lords and lawmakers in our stead! The Emperor? He has no authority over us!'

Voyen blinked back his surprise at such a raw, seditious pronouncement, and gasped when he heard a chorus of angry assent among the men of the Second.

'Only the Warmaster and the Death Lord can command us!' Grulgor continued. 'What we do here, we do by the will of Horus and Mortarion!'

Garro advanced menacingly, and with his thumb he flicked the hilt of Libertas so that a length of the blade emerged from its scabbard. 'You and your men will stand down and quit this insanity.'

Grulgor chuckled. 'You are three Astartes and a housecarl. I have my entire command squad and a handful of naval crew. The odds do not favour you.'

'I have right on my side,' Garro said, 'and this will be the last time I ask you.'

The commander studied the battle-captain. 'Very well, then. Go ahead.' He tipped back his head and showed his bare throat. 'Kill me, if you will.' When Garro wavered, Grulgor's rough laugh cut through the tense air. 'You can't! I can see it in your eyes. The thought that you might have to take the life of another Astartes, it horrifies you!' He looked away. 'You're as crippled in spirit as you are in the flesh! That is why you fail to see, Garro. Beneath that rigid exterior you are weak. You are too afraid to do what must be done.'

GARRO'S MAILED FINGERS were clasped around the sword's hilt, but it seemed cemented in the scabbard, unwilling to be drawn. Curse Grulgor, but Garro knew that on some level, the braggart was right. For a brief instant, the words of the jorgall psyker were there in his mind again, pressing at his will. *Death Guard, so confident of your rightness, so afraid to see the crack in your spirit.*

He gasped, and Grulgor saw the hesitation. Suddenly the commander was tearing the stubby frame of a bolt pistol from his belt and shouting. Garro saw it coming up and Libertas leapt into his hand, the metal flashing. Time skipped and there was gunfire in the chamber, shouts and the crashing of metal on metal.

'Check your fire!' Grulgor bellowed, drawing a battle knife with his free hand.

Garro was aware of Voyen and Sendek slipping away into battle stances and he saw Kaleb duck out of the line of fire. He thought of Decius, up on the bridge where he had left him. The youth's close combat skills would have been a useful asset, had he been here. Grulgor had not lied. The odds were indeed stacked against them, but the clutter of machinery and equipment across the gunnery decks and the presence of the volatile warhead globes made it awkward for his men to move in and engage. On a level battlefield, the fight would already have been over.

Not here. Garro surged forward and advanced at the commander, but two of his men blocked his path, each armed with heavy combat hammers. He moved swiftly, parrying a blow from the left with the sword and striking out to the right with a punch that staggered the second opponent. Garro spun in place and used Libertas to cleave the haft of one hammer and send the owner falling backward with a sword gouge down the torso of his armour. Following through, Garro struck the second man again, this time with the heavy pommel of the blade. The Astartes dropped, his face a red ruin of smashed bones.

This was not the first time Nathaniel had shed the blood of his battle-brothers in combat. On many occasions he had fought to a standstill against live opponents in the practice cages, but those incidents were always under controlled circumstances and never with fatal intent. Inwardly he cursed Grulgor for forcing him into this situation. Off to the edges of his sight, he saw Voyen and Sendek had their own battles to fight. Garro sensed another aggressor coming to his rear and shifted just as a fractal-edged steel knife blade scraped at his shoulder. Reacting without conscious thought, the battle-captain reversed his grip on Libertas and thrust it backwards under his armpit. The sword ran through his attacker and he turned to draw it back out. Garro's heart tightened in his chest as he watched his kill fall away to the deck plates with a crash. A Death Guard was dead, and it was by his hand.

THE SCRUM OF crewmen swarmed over Kaleb, kicking and punching him to the floor. Not one of them had the courage or stupidity to take on an Astartes, and so en masse they had sought the next best target. The house-carl railed at them for taking Grulgor's side over Garro's, but he wasted his breath. The swabs saw only which captain had the greater numbers and gave their loyalty to him. Kaleb fought as well as he could, but it was wild and mad, clothes and skin tearing, hair ripping away.

He felt sharp-nailed fingers rend his tunic and snatch at his neck. His collar pulled tight against him and he felt a surge of anger. Kaleb head-butted his attacker and swore, finding new rage to fuel him. 'Emperor curse you filthy whoresons!'

A blocky metal shape rose up before him and clubbed his temple. Kaleb shook off the blow and grabbed at it. He smelled the odour of gun oil. It was a stub-pistol. The housecarl shoved against the men trying to hold him and snatched at the small weapon. It went off with a spitting crack of sound and someone screamed. Kaleb rolled free of the mob and came up still gripping the hot metal ingot. His fingers easily found the trigger and grip, and he blasted the next man to come at him through the eye. The gun was his salvation, a gift from his divinity. 'The God-Emperor protects!' he snarled. 'I am His servant and His subject!'

He staggered away, breathing hard. Kaleb blinked and saw a figure before him in the marble-white and green trim of a Death Guard captain. The Astartes was aiming a bolt pistol into the melee with great care. Instinctively, the housecarl looked to see who the target was.

Garro was oblivious to the imminent kill-shot, grimly fighting hand-to-hand with another warrior.

No! He cannot die! The thought burned like fire across the serf's mind. *I will not permit it. The God-Emperor has chosen him!* Kaleb raised the tiny gun and spoke a prayer aloud. 'Divine One, guide my hand.'

He fired. The shot was released an instant before Grulgor's finger tightened on his trigger. The stub-bullet from the handgun was of such small gauge that all it did was nick the metal of the bolt pistol where it struck the frame, but even that was enough to deflect the commander's aim. The bolt shell from Grulgor's pistol went wide, keening off a girder near Garro's head and arcing away in a ricochet.

Grulgor reacted with preternatural speed and turned, throwing his battle knife at the housecarl. The Astartes blade buried itself in Kaleb's chest, the impact throwing him down to collide with one of the gunnery bay's control lecterns. It all happened in an instant, barely a second from the report of the stub-gun.

Blood filled Kaleb's mouth, his throat and his lungs as a new sound crossed the room, a brittle, fierce noise, eggs breaking, ice cracking, glass shattering. Through his fogged vision Kaleb saw a thin line of dark haze issuing from one of the warhead spheres, hissing with virulent potency.

✠ ✠ ✠

'The globe!' shouted Voyen, kicking away from the thick of the fight. Grulgor's deflected bolt round struck a glancing hit, webbing the frangible glass ball with a spreading fan of fractures. 'Get away!' He yanked at Sendek's arm, pulling him backward.

Black gas was forming into a slow, malevolent haze, buzzing like a swarm of gnats. Work gangers close to the mist were already vomiting and clawing at their exposed skin. In moments, it would fill the width of the gunnery chamber.

Garro's line of sight swept the room and he found Kaleb staring fixedly at him, pink froth leaking from his lips. 'Lord!' he cried, blood bubbling in his throat. 'You are of purpose! The God-Emperor wills it!' The house-carl lurched up on to the control lectern, wheezing. 'His hand lies upon all of us! The Emperor protects!' Garro reached out a hand in a warding gesture as Kaleb threw himself forward, using the last of his strength to press down on an emergency release switch.

Sirens blared and in the steel ceiling overhead, huge cogwheels disengaged, letting walls of thick iron drop down towards seal wells in the deck. Garro flung himself under the falling blade of metal, landing hard and rolling out to where Voyen and Sendek were crouched in the next compartment. One of Grulgor's men, the warrior named Mokyr, threw himself after Garro, clutching at his heels. Mokyr landed short, with only his upper body across the well. The iron wall slammed shut across him, the massive guillotine severing the body of the Astartes with a sickening crunch of bone and ceramite.

Garro's heart hammered against the inside of his ribcage, matching the pounding of fists from the inside of the thick gate. A phantom ache hummed through his augmetic leg.

'Blast shields,' gasped Sendek. He swallowed hard.

Voyen nodded. 'He saved our lives. The hatch is proof against the bane. The little man gave himself up to save us, and the ship.'

The banging on the metal doors grew softer and softer, until finally it ceased altogether. Garro got to his feet and crossed to the shield, placing his palm against it. It felt blood-warm, probably from the virulent chemical reactions of the rot taking place inside. He tried to block out thoughts of the carnage contained in there, the bodies bursting with liquefied organs and organic decay. He tried and he failed.

Kaleb's words echoed in his mind. It was clear now that the voice that had spoken to him of the Emperor and divinity through the fog of his healing coma must have been Kaleb's. And now, the loyal servant had given his life in trade for his master's.

'I am of purpose,' Garro mumbled. 'What purpose?'

'Sir?' Sendek came to him, calling out to be heard over the hooting roar of the klaxons. 'What did you say?'

He turned away from the shield. 'Purge that compartment! Tell Carya to vent the air in there to space! The Life-Eater reaction will spread to every one of the container spheres and release the entire war load, but it can't exist without an atmosphere. I want it off this ship!'

Voyen nodded. 'And the bodies in there, captain? They will be decaying and–'

'Leave them,' he snapped, fighting off the dark mood settling upon him. 'We must move swiftly, unless we wish to join them in death.' Garro frowned and slammed Libertas back into its sheath. 'The die has been cast.'

LIKE THE ENDURANCE, the *Eisenstein* had her own observatorium on the dorsal hull, situated just forward of the frigate's command tower. It was nowhere near as large, however, and with the broad and tall figures of several Astartes crammed into it, the open chamber seemed smaller still. Decius's face set in a grimace as the hatch opened and another two Death Guard entered. The Apothecary Voyen stepped into the chamber with Sendek at his side and the expression upon both of their faces was enough to give him pause. Decius looked across to where Sergeant Hakur was standing with men from his squad, and he saw that old Andus shared the black disposition of the new arrivals.

'Meric, what is going on?' demanded the veteran. 'I'm suddenly ordered to drop everything and come up here, tell no one… and I hear distant sirens and snatches of scuttlebutt from the swabs about gunfire and explosions?'

'There were no explosions,' said Sendek grimly.

'Where is the captain?' asked Decius.

'He'll be here in a moment,' Voyen replied. 'He's gone to fetch some others.'

Decius wasn't content with another evasive answer. 'When I was on the bridge there was a fire alert from the gunnery decks. An entire compartment amidships was sealed off. That's four weapon carriages disabled, according to the control servitor. Then I hear you on the vox shouting for an emergency decompression down there?' He pointed at the Apothecary. 'First the lodges, then Tarvitz, and now this? I want an explanation!'

'The captain will give it to you,' the other man retorted.

'Saul Tarvitz?' Hakur broke in. 'What about him? The last I heard he was on the *Andronius*.'

'By now he'll be in the Choral City, if he didn't burn up on the way down,' Sendek said grimly. 'He broke protocol, stole a Thunderhawk and made for the surface of Isstvan III. Lord Commander Eidolon ordered that he was to be shot down.'

Hakur's disbelief was palpable. 'That's ludicrous. You must be mistaken.'

Decius shook his head. 'We were all there. We heard the order, but Garro disobeyed it. He let Tarvitz escape.' The younger Astartes was still smarting over what had taken place, his loyalties pulling him in different directions over his commander's actions. 'It is sedition.'

'Yes, it is.' Garro's voice issued from the hatch as he entered, with the Shipmaster Carya and the deck officer Vought following behind. The woman closed the seal behind them at Garro's nod and it was only then that Decius noticed the housecarl wasn't with them.

The battle-captain moved into the centre of the room and placed a folded cloth packet on the observatorium's control dais. He took in all of them with a heavy, calculating stare. Decius had the impression that Garro was reticent to move on, to say the words that were pressing at his lips. Eventually, he sighed and nodded to himself, as if he had made a choice. 'When we leave this room, we will be rebels,' he began. 'The guns of our brothers will be turned against us. I will call upon you to do questionable things, but there is no other path now. There is no choice. We alone may be the only souls capable of carrying the warning.'

'What warning is this, lord?' One of Hakur's men asked, scowling deeply.

Garro looked at Decius. 'A warning of sedition.'

Carya cleared his throat. Unlike his second-in-command, the shipmaster did not seem ill at ease being outnumbered by so many Death Guard in so close a proximity. 'Honoured battle-captain, with all due respect, this is my ship and I will have you explain what has gone on aboard her before we go any further.'

'Indeed, as is right,' nodded Garro. He looked down at his mailed hands and took a deep breath. In a solemn, metered voice, Decius's mentor relayed the events of his confrontation with Grulgor. Shock took hold as he spoke of the virus bombs, turning into a grim, loaded silence as Garro went on to convey the commander's declaration against the Emperor and the horrifying result of the meleé on the gunnery decks. Decius felt his head swim with the import of these things. It was as if the floor was turning to mud beneath his boots, dragging him down into disarray and confusion.

Vought was pale as paper. 'The Life-Eater... it will not spread?'

Sendek shook his head. 'It was contained in time. The viral strain burns out very quickly.'

'I would recommend the compartment not be opened for the next six hours,' added Voyen, 'to be certain. The war load will have dissipated harmlessly into space after the atmosphere vents were opened, but dormant clades might linger in the bodies of the dead.'

'Our own men.' Hakur shook his head. 'I can barely believe it. I knew Grulgor was a braggart and a glory seeker, but *this*... Why would he do something so outrageous?' The veteran looked to Garro, an almost naïve imploring in his eyes. 'My lord?'

GARRO WANTED TO explain Grulgor's actions away. Like Voyen, some secret part of him had hoped that perhaps this was all some strange dream, or a temporary madness that had taken hold of his rival, but the moment he had looked Ignatius in the eye, he had known it was not so. Grulgor would never ally himself to a cause if he thought it might have a risk of failure. The certainty, the complete assurance on the other Death Guard's face, that sealed the truth of it for Garro. Grulgor was the proof of Tarvitz's warning, the damning reality snapping hard into place like a magazine into the breach of a bolter.

All the small things, the little asides and the moments of doubt, the dark feeling of ominous import, the mood aboard *Endurance* and the *Vengeful Spirit*, every element that had troubled Nathaniel these past days turned in place and became a part of the same whole.

'Saul Tarvitz, my honour brother and friend, brought me a forewarning. In risk to his own life, he fled the ships of the Emperor's Children to the planet below in order to tell our kinsmen down there that a viral attack is imminent. For this, Eidolon attempted to have him killed before he could succeed.' Garro nodded again. 'I chose not to follow that command. As a result, Saul is on Isstvan III as we speak, doubtless rallying men of the Legiones Astartes to find cover before the attack begins. My faith in what he told me is ironclad, as strong to me as my bond is to you.' He extended a hand and tapped Hakur on the shoulder, then began to walk around the room. Garro met the gaze of each person there as he did so, impressing his own truth upon them. 'Here is the horrific truth. Grulgor and Eidolon are not two errant souls pursuing some personal agenda, but soldiers in a war of betrayal that is about to unfold. What they have done is not of their own volition, but under the orders of the Warmaster himself.' He ignored the scattering of gasps that the statement brought forth. 'Horus, with the support of Angron, Fulgrim, and though it sickens me to say it, our master Mortarion, has done this.'

Across the chamber, Carya almost collapsed into an observation chair. He was struggling to make sense of Garro's words. Vought stood beside him, her face twisted as if she were ready to be physically ill. 'Why?' asked the shipmaster. 'Terra take me if I can see the logic and truth in all this, but why would he do it? What would Horus have to gain by turning against the Emperor?'

'Everything,' muttered Decius.

Voyen's head bobbed in a rueful nod. 'There has been talk of the Warmaster at second- and third-hand in the lodges. Talk of how far away the Emperor is, and of discontent over the commands of the Council of Terra. The tone of things has been strained ever since Horus was injured at Davin, after he returned from his healing.'

'The very tip of treason's blade, glimpsed in hidden places,' said Sendek.

Garro pressed on. 'Horus personally chose all the units for the assault on the Choral City. He picked only the men he knew would not turn if he called them to his banner. The bombing will rid him of the only obstacle to open insurrection.'

'If this is so,' demanded Decius, 'then why are we not down there as well? Your staunch loyalty to the Emperor and Terra is hardly a secret, sir!'

Garro gave a cold smile and tapped on the thigh plate of his armour. 'If the Warsinger on Isstvan Extremis had not forced this piece of pig-iron on me, I have no doubt we would be alongside Temeter and his troops, unaware that a sword is poised at our necks, but the turn of events has played in our favour, and we must seize our opportunity.'

'Tarvitz's escape will not remain undiscovered forever,' said Vought. 'When the Warmaster learns of what you did, *Eisenstein* will be under the guns of the entire fleet.'

'I have no doubt of that,' Garro agreed. 'We have a few hours, at most.'

'What do you propose?' asked Sendek. 'This frigate is only one ship. We cannot hope to assist the ground forces by intercepting the bombardments or attempting to engage the Warmaster.'

Garro shook his head. 'If Saul succeeds, we'll have no need to stop the bombing. If not...' He swallowed hard. 'There is nothing we can do to help those men.'

Decius saw it first. 'You plan to flee.'

'Watch your tone!' snapped Hakur.

Decius ignored the veteran. 'You want us to run.'

'We have no choice. If we remain, we will perish, but if we can get this ship out of the system, there is a chance we can still stem the tide of this treachery. We must finish the mission that Saul Tarvitz began. We must carry the warning of this perfidy to Terra and the Emperor.' He looked at the dark-skinned man. 'Master Carya, can the *Eisenstein* make space for the Sol system, or at the very least a star close to the Imperial core?'

He shook his head slowly. 'On any other day I would say it could, but today, I cannot be certain.'

'The warp has become increasingly clouded in recent weeks, full of storms and turbulence,' Vought broke in. 'Interstellar travel has become very difficult. If we attempted to translate now, our Navigators would be virtually sightless.'

'But you could still make the jump,' Hakur noted. 'We could still get away, even if we went into the warp blind.'

Carya snorted. 'The ship would be cast to the etheric currents! We could find ourselves light-years off the charts... anywhere!'

'Anywhere but *here*,' said Garro with finality. 'I want preparations made. Baryk, Racel.' He fixed them with a hard eye, using their given names for the first time. 'Will you resist me on this?'

The two naval officers exchanged glances, and he saw that they were with him. 'No,' said the shipmaster, 'many of my men are faithful Terrans and they won't falter, but there are some who will baulk. I imagine I have men who follow Horus among my crew.'

'There's also the matter of Grulgor's other Astartes on board,' added Sendek. 'They will be asking questions very soon.'

Garro looked to Hakur. 'Hakur, take what you need and secure the ship. Apply whatever force is required, understood?'

There was a moment of silence as the reality of Garro's command became clear. Then the veteran saluted. 'Aye, lord.'

Garro bent over the control dais and unwrapped the cloth bundle he had brought with him. In it were a dozen thin slips of paper dense with writing in a quick, forceful hand. The battle-captain handed one to everybody in the observatorium, including Carya and Vought.

The woman frowned at the piece of parchment. 'What is this?'

'An oath of moment,' said Decius. 'We will swear our duty upon it.'

Garro opened his mouth to speak, but the clang of the hatch stilled his tongue. The communications officer blundered headlong into the observatorium and skidded to a halt, mouth agape at the clandestine meeting he had interrupted.

'Maas!' bellowed Carya. 'For Terra's sake, man! Knock before you enter!'

'Your pardon, sir,' puffed the vox operator, 'but this priority signal came in for Commander Grulgor's eyes only. He doesn't answer–'

Carya snatched a data-slate from him and paled as he scanned it. He read aloud. 'It's from Typhon on the *Terminus Est*. Message reads: Weapons free, bombardment to commence imminently. Permission granted to terminate any and all impediments to operation.'

All eyes turned to Garro. The subtext of the message was clear. Typhon was handing Grulgor the authority to kill Garro and his men. He held up the paper. 'The oath, then,' he rumbled, pausing to take a breath. 'Do you accept your role in this? Will you dedicate yourself to the safe carriage of the warning to Terra, no matter what forces are ranged against us? Do you pledge to do honour to the XIV Legion and the Emperor?' The captain drew Libertas and held the sword point down.

Hakur was the first to place his hand upon the blade. 'By this matter and this weapon, I so swear.' One by one, the Astartes followed suit, with Decius the last. Then Carya and Vought gave the vow as well, as Maas looked on wide-eyed.

As they filed from the chamber, Decius caught his commander's arm. 'Fine words,' he said, 'but who was there to act as witness to them?'

Garro pointed out at the stars. 'The Emperor.'

NINE

A Prayer
Rain of Death
Refugees

HE WAS ALONE in the barracks compartment. Hakur and the others were out about the ship, executing his orders to take *Eisenstein* under their complete control. Distantly, Garro thought he heard the faint echoes of bolter reports, and his lips thinned. There was only a handful of Grulgor's men still at large on board the frigate. Like his Seventh Company, the majority of the late commander's Second was scattered elsewhere about the fleet, with only a few squads here to oppose Garro's plans. Carya's willing agreement to take the oath of moment had cemented his trust in the shipmaster, and through him he had control of the bridge officers. He had no doubt there would be malcontents among the naval ratings, but they would quickly fall into line when the Astartes gave them orders, and if they refused, they would not live for long.

By rights he should have been out there doing the job of securing the ship himself, but the thundering

churn of emotion inside him was making it hard for
Garro to concentrate. He needed a moment with his
own counsel, to centre himself in the face of the
events that had been set in motion.

Over and over he thought of the men he had fought
alongside in the hosts of the Death Guard and wondered how and why they could turn their faces from
the Emperor. For the most part, his brothers were
good and honourable men, and Garro thought he
knew the colour of their hearts, but now he doubted
that certainty. The awful realisation of it was, not that
his kinsmen were ready to shake off the Emperor's
commands and embrace treachery, but that most of
them were merely *weapons*. They would not pause
when orders came to them, even if those orders were
beyond their comprehension.

It was the lot of an Astartes simply to *do*, not to
question, and he felt damned by the understanding
that Horus would play that unswerving allegiance to
his bitter ends. He had considered briefly the idea of
opening up all of *Eisenstein*'s vox transmitters to maximum power and broadcasting the truth of the
treachery across the entire 63rd Fleet. There were
noble men out there, he was sure of it, warriors like
Loken and Torgaddon in the Warmaster's own
Legion, and Varren of the World Eaters... If only he
could contact them, save their lives; but to do so
would have meant suicide for everyone on the frigate.

Every minute they kept their silence was a minute
more for Garro to plan an escape with the warning.
Kinsmen like Loken and the others would have to
find their own path through this nightmare. The message was far more important than the lives of a
handful of Astartes. Garro only hoped that once his
mission had been fulfilled he might see them again,

either back on Terra at the end of their own escape or here once more with a reprisal fleet at his back. For now, those men were on their own, as were Garro and his warriors.

The battle-captain crossed to the arming alcove that Kaleb had set aside for him, seeing the eagle cuirass mounted there on a stand. It was polished and perfect, as if the armour had come from a museum and not been battered in combat less than a week ago. He laid a hand on the cool ceramite and allowed himself to feel his full regret at the housecarl's death. 'You died well, Kaleb Arin,' he told the air, 'you did honour to the Death Guard and to the Seventh.' Garro wished that he could promise the man's memory some form of tribute. He wanted to place the serf's name upon the Wall of Memory on Barbarus, give him the credit as if he had been a full-fledged battle-brother, but that would not happen, not now. Garro doubted that he would ever see the dank skies of the Death Guard's home world again, not after the events at Isstvan. Kaleb's spirit would have to be content with the esteem of his master.

Garro's lip curled. 'Here I am, thinking of spirits, talking to myself in an empty room.' He shook his head. 'What is happening to me?'

Next to the cuirass, a bolter lay upon a folded green cloth, and like the armour it too was pristine and unblemished, fresh from the Legion artificers. Garro took off a gauntlet and ran his fingers over the slab-sided breach. The weapon was deep with etchings in High Gothic script, combat honours and battle records listed along the length of it. There were names imprinted here and there, lined in dark emerald ink, each the name of a battle-brother who had carried the gun into war, and perished with it on them. Garro's

weapon had been lost to him on Isstvan Extremis,
destroyed by the brutal sonic attack of the Warsinger.
Nothing but shattered, brittle metal had been left.
This bolter, then, was to be his new sidearm, and it
was with bittersweet pride he took it up and held it to
parade ready. A new name glittered on the frame: *Pyr
Rahl*. 'Thank you, brother,' whispered Garro, 'I will
take a dozen foes with it in your name.'

As was the way of the Astartes, Rahl's wargear was
salvaged and what could remain in use to the XIV
Legion did so. In this manner, the Astartes kept the
memories of their dead kinsmen alive long after they
had perished. Garro's eyes fell to find a carry-sack
made of roughly woven fabric, lying forgotten in the
corner of the alcove. He dropped into a crouch and
took it up.

Kaleb's belongings. He sighed. When an Astartes
died, there was always a brother ready to gather up
the meagre possessions he might have left behind
and see to them, but there were no provisions for a
simple housecarl. Garro felt an unfamiliar kind of
sorrow over Kaleb's passing. It wasn't the hard fury he
had for the death of Rahl or the hundreds of others he
had witnessed. Only now that Kaleb was gone, did
Garro understand how much he had valued the little
man, as a sounding board, as a servant, as a comrade.
For a moment the captain considered ditching the
sack in the nearest ejector chute and making an end
of it, but that would have been ignoble. Instead, with
a gentleness belied by his large, heavy hands, Garro
traced through Kaleb's effects: utility blades and
armoury tools, some changes of clothing, a trinket
made from a bolter shell…

He turned the object between his fingers and held it
up to the lamplight. A matrix-etching of the Emperor

stared back at him, beneficent and all-knowing. He pocketed the icon in a belt pouch. With it there were dog-eared papers held together by a worn strap. In places they had been taped where they had become ripped. Some of the pages were on different kinds of paper, some handwritten, some from a crude mimeograph with words smudged and blurry from hundreds of reproductions. Garro found sketchy illustrations that made little sense to him, although he could pick out recognisable elements, iconography of the Emperor, of Terra, repeated again and again. '*Lectitio Divinitatus*,' he read aloud. 'Is this what you kept from me, Kaleb?'

Garro knew of the sect. They were common people who, despite the constant light of the secular Imperial truth, had come to believe that the Emperor of Mankind was himself a divine being. Who else, they argued, had the right to crush all other belief in gods, than the one true deity himself? Was not the Emperor a singular, god-like entity?

Despite his open rejection of such beliefs, the Emperor instilled such dedication and devotion. Immortal and all-seeing, possessed of the greatest intellect and psychic potential of any living human, in the eyes of the *Lectitio Divinitatus*, what else could he be but a divinity?

Yes, now Garro saw it, he realised Kaleb's connection to the Cult of the God-Emperor had been there all along, simmering beneath the surface. A hundred tiny words and deeds suddenly took on new meaning in the light of this discovery. He had decried Grulgor on the gunnery deck for speaking blasphemy against the Emperor, and before in the murk of his healing coma, Garro had heard the invocation from Kaleb's lips, the entreaty for protection. 'You are of purpose,'

he intoned flatly, the housecarl's final words returning once again. 'The God-Emperor wills it. His hand
lies upon all of us. The Emperor… the Emperor protects.'

He knew that it was wrong to go any further, that it
went against the letter of the Imperial truth he had
dedicated his life to, but still Nathaniel Garro read
on, absorbing the words of the tracts, page by tattered
page.

Although he would never have showed it openly,
the passing hours had shaken him to his core. He had
always imagined himself as a blade in the Emperor's
hand, or as an arrow in mankind's quiver to be
nocked and sent tearing into the heart of humanity's
foes, but what was he now? All the blades were
blunted and twisted upon one another, the arrows
broken about their shafts.

The firm ground Garro's beliefs stood upon was
turning to quicksand beneath them. It was almost too
much to contain within his mind! His brothers, his
battle lord, his very Warmaster all ranged against him;
the blood of a Death Guard on his sword and much
more to come; the foreboding pall at the boundary of
his thoughts; the omen of the blinded star, the smug
prophecy of the dead xenos child and Kaleb's dying
plea.

'It's too much!' Garro shouted, and sank to his
knees, the papers tight in his hand. The horrible taint
of this knowledge was a poison that threatened to
shrivel his soul. Never in centuries of service had the
Astartes felt himself to be so totally, so utterly vulnerable, and in that moment, he understood there was
only one to whom he could reach out.

'Help me,' he cried, offering his entreaty to the darkness, 'I am lost.' Of their own accord, Garro's hands

found the shape of the aquila, palms open across his chest. 'Emperor,' he choked, 'give me faith.'

Behind his eyes, Garro felt something break loose inside him and leap, a sudden release, a flood of energy. It was beyond his ability to describe it, and there in the gloom of the half-lit alcove, he felt the ghost of a voice brush over the edges of his psyche. A crying woman, pale and elfin, strong and delicate all at once, was calling him: the voice from his dream.

Save us, Nathaniel.

Garro cried out and stumbled backwards, fighting to recover his balance. The words had been so clear and close, it was as if she had been in the chamber with him, standing at his ear. The Death Guard recovered his composure, panting hard, and got back to his feet. He sensed a peculiar, greasy tang in the air, fading even as he noticed it. The stroke upon his thoughts had been like the jorgalli's intrusion into his mind, but different. It shocked him in its intimacy, and yet it did not feel wrong like the telepathic touch of the alien. Garro took a shuddering breath. As quickly as it had happened, the moment vanished like vapour.

He was still staring at the bundle of pages in his hand when Decius stormed into the chamber, anger tight on the younger man's face.

SOLUN DECIUS WATCHED his commander stuff a fold of papers into a belt pouch and turn away, as if he wasn't ready to look the Astartes in the eye. 'Decius,' he managed. 'Report.'

'Resistance was encountered,' he growled. 'I... We dealt with the remainder of Grulgor's men. They made an attempt to reach the landing bay. We suffered some casualties as they were repelled.' Decius's face became a grimace. 'It was a slaughter.'

Garro eyed him. 'They would have done the same to us, if we had given them the opportunity. Why else do you think that Typhon placed both Grulgor and me aboard this ship, if not to have my command terminated when the moment came?'

Decius wanted to snap out the angry reply boiling in his thoughts, to say that maybe that was true, but perhaps it was only Garro who had been on the target list. He stared angrily at the deck. What exasperated him more than anything was that he had not been given the choice! His fate was tied to the battle-captain's now, whatever happened. Yes, perhaps this might have been what Decius would have chosen had he been given the opportunity, but the sheer fact he had not made him rebel against it!

His mentor read the emotion on his face. 'Speak plainly, lad.'

'What would you have me say?' Decius retorted hotly.

'The truth. If not here and now, then you may never get another chance,' Garro replied, keeping his tone level. 'I would have you speak your mind, Solun.'

There was a long pause as Decius worked to frame his resentment. 'I put down three men wearing my own colours back there,' he said, jerking his head at the corridor and the ship beyond, 'not xenos or mutants, but Death Guard, my brother Astartes!'

'Those men ceased to be our brethren the instant they chose Horus's path over the Emperor's.' Garro sighed. 'I share the pain of this, Solun, more than you can know, but they have become traitors–'

'Traitors?' The curse exploded from him. 'Who are you to decide that, Battle-Captain Garro? What authority do you have to make such a determination, sir? You are not Warmaster, not a primarch, not even

a first captain! Yet you make this choice for all of us!'
Garro watched without responding. Decius knew that
daring to take such a tone with a senior officer was
worth punishment and censure, but still he raged on.
'What… what if it is *we* who are the traitors, captain?
Horus will no doubt paint us as such when he learns
of what you have done.'

'You have seen what I have seen,' said his commander evenly. 'Tarvitz, Grulgor, the kill orders from
Eidolon and Typhon… If there is an explanation that
would undo all of that, that would make this all go
away, I would give much to know it.'

Decius advanced a step. 'There is something you fail
to consider. Ask yourself this, my lord: What if Horus
is right?'

He had barely uttered the question when the combat alert sirens began to wail.

'SAY THAT AGAIN!' snapped Temeter, pulling the
Astartes holding the long-range vox towards him.

With the constant drumming of shellfire back and
forth between the Death Guard assault force and the
Isstvanian defenders, it was difficult to hear the man's
words. Another blistering salvo of vulcan bolter fire
from the *Dies Irae* roared over their heads, blotting
out everything else as the Titan continued its slow
advance.

'Lord, I have fragmentary signals! I can't make head
nor tail of them!'

'Just give me what you have,' Temeter said, crouch-
ing down behind a broken ferrocrete emplacement,
ignoring the whine of needler rounds and the snap-
crack of crimson laser beams.

'Still nothing from the orbital elements,' continued
the Death Guard, 'I caught an intercept to the Sons of

Horus, Squad Lachost, from Lucius of the Emperor's
Children.'

'Lucius? What did he say?'

'It was very garbled, sir, but I distinctly heard the
words "bio-weapon".'

Temeter's eyes narrowed. 'Are you certain? There
was nothing in the mission briefing to indicate the
Isstvanians have that capability. This is their holy city,
after all. Why would they deploy something like
that–'

Temeter suddenly broke off and looked up. The
overlapping sounds of the battle had become background noise to him, a constant rush of shot and
shell, but suddenly something had changed.

It was the Titan. The *Dies Irae* was only a few
hundred metres from where Temeter crouched, and he
had quickly become accustomed to the ground-
shaking impacts it made with every footfall,
anticipating the rhythm of them, but the massive
humanoid machine had stilled and now it stood there,
a vast iron citadel, joints hissing and ticking. Mortar
shells arced past them and impacted harmlessly on
Dies Irae's torso hull, drawing no reaction from the
crew. The Titan's mighty guns were still pointed
directly at the enemy lines, but they were silent.

'What in Terra's name is that fool up to?' Temeter
snarled. 'Raise the Titan! Get Princeps Turnet on the
vox and have him explain himself!'

The captain of the Fourth Company scanned the
hull of the machine with his optics. There was no visible damage of such scale that would cause a Titan to
shut down, no possible reason that Temeter could see
for it to just *stop*. His line of sight passed over the
access hatches in the hull and he saw all of them were
shut fast. Temeter searched for and found power shaft

vents in the thigh armour of the mechanism. Normally they would be puffing with the release of spent coolant gasses, but instead they were sealed. Chill knives of apprehension stabbed into him.

'I can't raise the *Dies Irae*,' said the other man. 'Why don't they answer? They must be able to hear us!'

'A bio-weapon.' Temeter reached up and checked the seals at his neck, a creeping sensation of trepidation coming over him. The captain's head tipped back, his gaze moving to take in the yellowish sky over the Titan's huge iron shoulders. He saw twinkling glitters up there, streaks cutting through the upper atmosphere with trails of white vapour behind them. The sight shocked him into action. 'Squad-wide comms, now!' he shouted. 'All Death Guard disengage and seek cover! Bio-war alert! Make for the bunker complex to the west.'

The other Astartes relayed his orders into the vox even as he and Temeter broke from their meagre cover.

Temeter saw the dreadnought Huron-Fal turning in place. 'Ullis Temeter!' The venerable warrior's synthetic machine-voder was loud and scratchy. 'Who has done this?'

'No time, old friend,' he said on the run. 'Just get the men inside, *now*!' With every pounding step he took, a part of Temeter's mind was reeling with the import of what was taking place. The bombs were falling, and there was only one person who could have sent them.

GARRO AND DECIUS made it up the ramp to the windowed gallery overlooking the barracks chamber in time to witness the ships of the Warmaster's fleet open fire on Isstvan III. A myriad of silver streaks, almost too fast to see with the naked eye, streamed over and around the *Eisenstein* and the other smaller ships at low anchor above the Choral City. Although they were just blurs, Garro didn't need to see them clearly to know what they were: Atlas-class heavy warheads converted for space-to-surface functions, servitor-guided missile bombs and multiple impact penetrator munitions. It seemed as if only *Eisenstein*'s guns remained silent, as if every capital ship in the 63rd Fleet were taking some part in the brutality. The bombs came in a solid rain of murder, falling fast, turning and converging towards pre-designated target points all across the planet. From this terrible god's-eye view of the onslaught, the distant grey-white patch upon the main continent that was the Choral City was easily visible.

Garro watched in abject horror as the instruments of Horus's betrayal flared red as they punched through the atmosphere and fell upon his battle-brothers. At his side, Decius's face was rapt with a peculiar, grotesque fascination as he struggled to comprehend the magnitude of the destruction.

TEMETER AND HURON-FAL were at the shallow ridge before the bunker's steel hatch, shouting at their kinsmen to run and run, to run and not look back. Temeter felt a pang of fear, not for himself, but for his men. They had responded perfectly to his command, falling back in good order and surging away from the enemy along the trench lines they had already cleared. Hundreds of them were already in the bunkers, sealing themselves in to weather the imminent bombardment, but there were many more he knew would not live to make it to the doors. He looked up again at the sickly sky and Temeter became torn inside. *Who betrayed us,* he asked himself, echoing the aged dreadnought's question? *Why, in Terra's name, why?*

'Ullis!' barked the old warrior, stomping to his side. 'Get in there! We have only a few seconds!'

'No!' he retorted. 'My men first!'

'Idiot!' growled Huron-Fal, throwing protocol to the wind. 'I will stay! Nothing will be able to crack my hide. You go, now!' He shoved Temeter with his colossal manipulator claw. 'Go inside, damn you!'

Ullis Temeter stumbled back a step, but his gaze was still on the sky. 'No,' he said, just as flickers of brilliant light turned the day a glittering white.

At high altitudes overhead, the first wave of the virus warheads detonated in series, a wall of airbursts instantly unleashing a black rain of destruction. The viral clades, capable of hyper-fast mutational change and near-exponential growth rates, feasted on native airborne bacteria. The thin, dark bloom of the death cloud rolled out over the Choral City, just as the second wave fell. The shells did not explode until they hit the ground, bursting to smother city districts, open fields and trench lines with tides of destructive haze.

The Life-Eater did as it had been engineered to do. Where a molecule of it touched an organic form, it spread instant, putrefying death. The Choral City, every living thing, every human, animal, plant, every organism down to the level of microbes was torn apart by the virus. It leapt boundaries of species in a second, burning out the life of the planet. Flesh rotted and blood became ooze. Bones shredded and turned brittle. Isstvanians and Astartes alike died screaming, united in death by the unstoppable germs.

Temeter saw the warriors running towards him, dying on their feet. Figures fell to the mud as their corpses turned to a red broth of fleshy slurry, viscous fluids seeping from the chinks in their power armour. He knew that he had dallied too long, and he shouted with all his might. 'Close the hatch. Close it!' The men in the bunker did as he told them, even as he tasted blood in his mouth and felt his skin prickling with budding lesions. The metal door slammed shut and hissed with a pressure seal, locking him out. Temeter hoped they had been quick enough. With luck, they would not have taken any of the virus inside with them. He managed two stumbling steps before he fell, the muscles in his legs singing with agony.

Huron-Fal caught him. 'I told you to run, you fool.'

The captain flung off his helmet with a final, agonised gesture of defiance. It was useless now, the virus having moved effortlessly through the breather grille and into his lungs. His hand flailed at the metal flank of the dreadnought and traced a runnel of dark fluid. Even through the pain, Temeter understood. There was a small fracture in the old warrior's ceramite casing, not enough to have slowed him on the battlefield, but more than the virus needed to reach inside the dreadnought's hull and savage the remnants of flesh inside. 'You… lied.'

'Veteran's prerogative,' came the reply. 'We'll go together then, shall we?' Huron-Fal asked, embracing Temeter's body to him, moving swiftly away from the bunker.

It took every last effort from Temeter to nod. Blinded now, he could feel the tissues of his eyes burning and shrivelling in his head, the soft meat of his lips and tongue dissolving.

Huron-Fal's systems were on the verge of shut-down as he stumbled to a safe distance, skidding to a halt. 'This death,' rasped the voder, 'this death is ours. We choose it. We deny you your victory.'

With a single burning nerve impulse, the mind of the warrior at the heart of the dreadnought uncoupled the governor controls on his compact fusion generator and let it overload. For a moment there was a tiny star on the battered plains outside the Choral City, marking two more lives lost within a maelstrom of murder.

GARRO TURNED AWAY from the blossom of darkness across the dying world and glared at his protégé. 'Now do you believe it? With a planet scoured of life before your eyes, do you have proof enough of this madness?'

Decius spoke in an awed whisper. 'It... it is incredible. The power of such destruction...'

Garro felt unsteady and held out a hand, placing it on the thick armourglass of the gallery window. 'It is not over yet. There is one more strike to come before this killing is complete.'

'But the virus, it is consuming the whole planet... all life, everywhere! What other devastation can the Warmaster turn upon it?'

Garro's words were weary and hollow. 'With so many dead, so fast, the Life-Eater burns out quickly, but the mass of corpses it leaves behind moulder and rot.' His face soured. 'The... remains turn to gaseous putrefaction and decay. Imagine it, Solun, a whole world turned into a gigantic charnel house, the very atmosphere stinking and choked with the stench of new death.'

Out in the fleet, the ships were shifting, the formation parting so that a single vessel could move into a pre-determined firing position. It was the Warmaster's flagship, the bright sword-blade shape of the *Vengeful Spirit*.

'Of course,' Garro said bitterly, 'Horus. He comes to make the killing shot himself. I should have expected no less.' Garro wanted to close his eyes, to look away, but everywhere he turned his gaze he was haunted by the faces of the men that he had left alone down there. He saw Temeter and Tarvitz, imagined them dying in the onslaught, hoping, even *praying* that they might have survived the first wave. 'Now they must survive the final blow.'

The *Vengeful Spirit* drifted to a halt and turned with stately menace to point her bow down at Isstvan III. In the silence, there was a flicker of light from the maws of the warship's twin lance cannons along the flanks of the hull. The bolts of blinding fire touched the atmospheric envelope of the planet and a new colour bloomed among the blackened clouds: the searing orange of a firestorm.

'A match to tinder,' breathed Decius. 'The fumes from the decayed dead are lit. The flames will burn across the world.'

'All by the hand of Horus,' said Garro, fighting off the sickness in his heart.

They stood there for what seemed like hours, watching the fires cross continents and raze cities as the Warmaster's flagship orbited above it all, the lone arbiter of Isstvan III's destruction. Time fell away as the two Astartes stood witness to the distant slaughter.

At last, a loud chime sounded through the chamber over the frigate's inter-craft vox net and shattered the silence. 'Captain Garro to the bridge.' It was Carya's voice, low and toneless. 'We have a problem.'

Nathaniel finally turned from the windows and walked away. Decius remained a few moments, his eyes glittering, before he followed suit, running to keep up with his commander.

BARYK CARYA COULDN'T bring himself to look out of the bridge's forward viewports. The slow death of the planet below was abhorrent to him, a brutal act that went against every fibre of his being. He had not taken an oath of fealty to be part of such horror. He scanned the chamber and found Maas glaring at him from the vox alcove, still gripping the message slip the shipmaster had given him. He advanced towards the junior officer, working to maintain his outward mask of authority. 'Is it done?' he demanded.

'I…' Maas grimaced. 'I have sent the signal you ordered me to send, sir.'

The young man's displeasure was clear on his face, although Carya could have cared less for his unwillingness to broadcast what was an outright lie. The master snatched the paper from his grip and shredded it between his fingers. The message had gone to *Terminus Est* with Grulgor's command rune carefully forged by Vought. In terse phrases that he hoped would emulate the speech of an Astartes, Carya had informed First Captain Typhon that *Eisenstein* had suffered a weapons malfunction that prevented it firing on Isstvan III. It was a poor ruse, as thin as the paper he had scribbled it on, but it would buy them time.

'What you have done will cost you your rank,' hissed Maas in a sullen voice. 'You are upon the verge of open mutiny against the Warmaster's command!'

'Get your terms straight, boy,' retorted Carya. 'Mutiny is when the enlisted men take over a vessel. When the ship's master does it, it's called barratry.'

'Whatever name you give it, it is wrong!'

'Wrong?' Carya's anger went white-hot in an instant, and he grabbed Maas by the scruff of the neck, dragging him from the alcove and across the bridge. 'Do you want to see wrong, boy? Look at that!' He forced the vox officer's face towards the viewports and the distant carnage. He gave him a half-hearted shove. 'Get back to your damn station, and keep your thoughts to yourself!'

Vought came to his side. 'Sir, your pardon? The other ship, I have confirmed it. It's on an approach vector at full military thrust.'

'Within gun range?'

She nodded. 'I've taken the liberty of getting a firing solution, although that earlier trick won't work this time. If we kill it, the whole fleet will see.'

The bridge hatch irised open and the commander of the Seventh Company entered with one of his men, his eyes hollow. 'Shipmaster,' said Garro gravely, 'is there a matter of urgency?'

He nodded. 'There is. Racel, show him.'

Vought manipulated the controls on the hololith to display a close-range globe of space around the frigate. A red arrowhead was moving steadily towards the vessel. 'Another Thunderhawk,' she explained, 'on an intercept vector.'

'Tarvitz?' asked the other Astartes, the one called Decius. 'Has he been in orbit all this time, or returned from the surface?'

Racel shook her head. 'No, this ship's ident codes are different. The designation is Nine Delta. It belongs to the Sons of Horus, assigned aboard the *Vengeful Spirit*.'

'He knows,' said the vox officer. 'Horus knows what happened here. He's coming to–'

'Shut up, Maas!' snapped Carya.

'He could be right,' said Decius.

Garro ignored the hololith and went to the viewport, searching for the transport with his own eyes. After a moment he pointed. 'There, I see it.'

'Captain, what are your orders?' The shipmaster shifted uncomfortably, perturbed by the strange sensation of events repeating themselves. This was how it had all begun, with a lone Thunderhawk, with Tarvitz and his warning.

Some emotion Carya couldn't identify crossed Garro's face like a cloud passing before the sun. Then he turned on his heel and marched to the communications panel. Without preamble he snatched up the vox pickup and spoke into it. 'Thunderhawk gunship, identify yourself.' Garro glanced back at Vought and threw her a look that said *be ready*.

A throaty voice thick with a Cthonian accent growled from the speaker. 'My name is Iacton Qruze, formerly of the Sons of Horus.'

'Formerly?' repeated Garro.

'Yes, formerly.'

Decius nodded to his commander. 'I know of this one, sir, an old campaigner, past his time, the third captain under Horus. They call him "the Half-Heard".'

Garro took this without comment. 'Explain yourself,' he demanded. Carya found that his hands were tight, his knuckles bloodless with the tension.

He heard the agony beneath the veteran's next words, even through the crackling hiss of the vox channel. 'I am no longer part of the Legion. I can no longer be a party to what the Warmaster is doing.'

The battle-captain held the vox away and rubbed at his face.

'It could be a ruse,' insisted Vought. 'That transport could be packed with Astartes from Horus's ship!'

'Let them come,' growled Decius. 'I would prefer honest battle to all this subterfuge.'

'Or perhaps a bomb…'

'No.' Garro's voice brought silence. 'She is aboard. He does not lie.'

She? Carya's brow furrowed. *Who is he talking about?*

'There are refugees on that vessel, I am certain of it. Open the landing bay and prepare to take the Thunderhawk aboard,' he ordered.

THE BLOCKY SHIP manoeuvred uneasily into the capture cradle and the thrusters flared out. With grinding hisses, the deck servitors worked the manipulator arms to bring the Thunderhawk forward and down on to the same grating where Garro and his men had arrived less than a day ago. Hakur and his squad were ready with their combi-bolters cocked and aimed, but Garro refused to draw a weapon. He saw Voyen and the others watching him carefully, the question clear on their faces. They thought him mad to do this, he realised. He would have said the same in their place.

He did not blame them, but then they did not see as he did. Even Garro himself found it hard to articulate the compulsion he felt in his heart. He had knowledge. That was it. Although he could not explain it, he knew with absolute certainty that the ship before him carried a cargo as precious as the warning he had dedicated himself to delivering. The dream… It all came back to the dream.

The Thunderhawk's forward hatch spat atmospheric gasses and yawned open, allowing four figures to disembark. At the head was a craggy, aged warrior in the power armour of the Sons of Horus. He walked with the same stiff pride Garro had seen in a hundred other Cthonian Astartes, but his expression was one of sorrow, of a soldier who had seen too much. He bore the signs of recent combat, new wounds still wet with freshly clotted blood, but he paid them no mind.

'So you are Garro,' he said. 'Young Garviel spoke of you once or twice. He said you were a good man.'

'And you are Iacton Qruze. I would like to say well met, captain, but that is as far from the truth as it could be.'

Qruze nodded heavily. 'Aye.' He paused for a moment and then met Garro's gaze. 'You'll want this, then, I suppose.' The old warrior held out his bolter and the other Astartes tensed at the motion. 'Take it, lad. If you mean to end us, then do it with this, if that is to be the way of things. We can run no further.'

Garro took the gun and handed it away to Sendek. 'I'll have it cleaned and returned to you,' he said. 'I fear I will need every able man in the coming hours.' The captain stepped forward and offered Qruze his hand. 'I have a mission to take warning of Horus's perfidy to Terra and the Emperor. Will you join me in this?'

'I will at that,' Qruze said, accepting the gesture. 'I pledge my command to your mission, such as it is. I'm afraid all I have to offer from the Third Company is a single Luna Wolf, getting along in his years.'

'Luna Wolf?' repeated Decius. 'Your Legion–'

The old soldier's eyes flashed with anger. 'I'll not be known as a Son of Horus again, mark that well, lad.'

Garro gave a small smile. 'Just so, Captain Qruze. I welcome you to the motley company of the starship *Eisenstein*. We number less than a hundred battle-brothers.'

'Enough, if the fates smile kindly.'

Garro nodded at Qruze's injuries. 'Do you require a medicae?'

The Luna Wolf waved the question away, instead turning to gestured to the other passengers from the shuttle. 'I am remiss. Loken asked me to keep these people safe and that I've done by bringing them here. You should greet them too.'

Nathaniel looked down at an elderly fellow and recognised him instantly. 'You, I know you.'

The old man wore the robes of a highly-ranked iterator, now somewhat the worse for wear, but still with the manner of his esteemed office beneath his troubled expression. He managed a weak smile. 'If it pleases the battle-captain, I am Kyril Sindermann, primary iterator of the Imperial truth.' The words trickled out of his mouth by rote, but the pat response crumbled as he said it. 'Or, at least I was. I fear that in recent days I have come to a moment of transition.'

'As have we all,' agreed Garro, musing for a moment. 'I remember, I saw you on board the *Vengeful Spirit*, passing through the landing bay. You were going somewhere. You seemed disturbed.'

'Ah, yes,' Sindermann threw a look back at the other two passengers. 'Such is my vanity that I hoped you might have known me from my speeches, but no matter.' He composed himself. Clearly the escape from Horus's ship had taken its toll on the man. Sindermann placed a wary hand on Nathaniel's vambrace. 'Thank you for the sanctuary you have granted us, Captain Garro. Please, allow me to present my companions. The lady Mersadie Oliton, one of the Emperor's documentarists...'

'A remembrancer?' Nathaniel watched with interest as the ebon-skinned woman's head emerged from beneath a roughly woven travelling hood. She had a peculiar skull that extended beyond the back of her neck far more than that of a normal human, and it shimmered like glass. He instantly thought of the jor-gall psyker, but where that xenos child had been a thing of haphazard, ugly mutation, the documentarist was dainty and brimming with grace, even under these trying circumstances. Garro caught himself staring and nodded. 'My lady. Forgive me, I have never met a storyteller before.' She was quite different from what he had expected. Oliton seemed as if she was made of spun glass and he was afraid to touch her for fear she might break.

'You remind me of Loken,' she blurted suddenly, the outburst seeming to surprise her. 'You have the same eyes.'

Garro nodded again. 'Thank you for the compliment. If it was Captain Loken's desire to see you kept safe, then it is mine as well. Do not fear.'

Sindermann saw the brittleness in her and gently guided the remembrancer to one side. 'One other refugee, captain—'

Nathaniel saw the last figure and his throat tightened. It was a woman in simple robes. He blinked, unsure if what he saw before him was real or some kind of strange vision. 'You,' he managed. Garro knew her even though they had never met. He had felt the salt tang of her tears on his face, the ghost of her voice in the depth of his healing trance, and again in the barracks.

'My name is Euphrati Keeler,' she said. The woman laid her hand flat upon his chest plate and smiled warmly. 'Save us, Nathaniel Garro.'

'I will,' he said distantly, for long moments losing himself in her steady, shimmering gaze. With effort, he tore himself away and gestured to his men to stand down. Garro took a breath and beckoned Voyen. 'Get these civilians to the inner decks where they will be safer. See to their wellbeing and report back to me.'

Qruze hovered at his side. 'Do you have a plan of action, lad?'

'We fight our way out,' said Hakur as he approached. 'Punch through and go to the warp.'

'Huh, blunt and direct. How very like a Death Guard.'

Hakur eyed the Luna Wolf. 'I've often heard the same said of your Legion.'

The old Astartes nodded. 'That's true enough. The humours of our brotherhoods do find themselves in lockstep.' He looked at Nathaniel. 'To battle, then?'

Garro watched Keeler and the others walk away, his thoughts conflicted. 'To battle,' he replied.

TEN

Terminus Est
The Gauntlet
Into the Maelstrom

As ISSTVAN III revolved beneath them, the ships of the 63rd Expeditionary Fleet moved with it, following the planet as it turned from the watery sunlight of day and into the leaden darkness of twilight. The ships remained in geostationary orbits, the swarm curled around the world in a loose, iron-fingered grip. As night fell, the burning cities still smouldering from the passage of the firestorm were visible, the glow of the massive pyres sullen and shimmering through the murky cloud. So much ash and fumes had been thrown into the planet's atmosphere that the skies were turning into a shroud of chemical haze. In time, the climate would start to shift, becoming colder as the warmth from the Isstvan star was blotted out. If there had been any native flora or fauna remaining, this would have been the death sentence for them, but everything that had evolved to life on Isstvan III was already dust and cinders.

233

The fleet kept watch, sensors to the surface in search
of any who might have survived the virus bombardment, and with the attention of the other ships
elsewhere, it had become possible for the *Eisenstein* to
shift slowly out of formation. Carya and his crew
allowed the frigate to come up from the high anchor
station, fading into the press of the other warships,
but now they had gone as far as they could without
courting suspicion. If *Eisenstein* were to escape the
Isstvan system, it would not be by stealth.

MASTER CARYA PEERED into the hololith tank, looking
through the glowing symbols to Garro, the Luna Wolf
Qruze and the other Death Guard warriors. The fingers of Carya's left hand were mechanical augments,
replacements from an accident years earlier when a
plasma holdout gun had overloaded in his grip.
Inside them were delicate slivers of circuitry that,
among other things, allowed him to manipulate the
virtual shapes in the tank as if they were real objects.

The hololith showed a basic representation of the
Isstvan system, distorted to present the close orbital
space around the third planet in greater detail. Carya
pointed to a stylised cross drifting high up over the star
system's ecliptic plane. 'Vought has computed a mini-
mum distance vector for us, using the ship's cogitator
chorus. If we can reach this point, we will be beyond
the c-limit and free to make a warp translation.'

'Naval terminology was never my strong point,'
grumbled Qruze. 'Indulge an old war dog and explain
it to me in terms a soldier might grasp.'

'We can't go to the warp while we're still inside the
gravity shadow of the sun,' said Sendek briskly, indi-
cating the Isstvan star. 'That is the threshold the
shipmaster speaks of.'

Carya nodded, a little surprised to find a line Astartes with a basic grasp of astrogation. 'Indeed, the footprint of the solar energy interferes with the warp transition. We must go beyond it and reach the jump point in order to enter the immaterium with any degree of safety.'

'It's a long distance,' mused Garro. 'We'll have to travel several light-seconds at maximum burn to get there, and with the drives at full, it will light a torch to show Horus where we're heading.'

Qruze leaned into the hololith. 'There are capital ships all around. It would only take a couple of them to lay their lances on us and we'd be finished. Somehow I don't think the Warmaster will be willing to let us leave unchallenged, eh?'

'Our void shields are at full capacity,' continued Carya. 'We can weather a few indirect hits and we have agility on our side.'

Decius gave a humourless chuckle. 'While it heartens me to see that the good master here has confidence in his ship and his crew, if must be said that only a fool would not think the odds are stacked high against us!'

'I don't deny it,' retorted the naval officer. 'Given the circumstances, I rate our chances of survival at one in ten, and in that, I am being more than generous.'

Vought spoke up cautiously. 'At this time, *Eisenstein* is close to the rear edge of the fleet pattern. I took the liberty of informing the fleet master's office that we were suffering a malfunction in one of our tertiary fusion generators. It is standard naval procedure for a ship under those circumstances to drop back from the main formation, to prevent other vessels being damaged in case of a cascade failure and core implosion.'

'How long will that lie last us?' asked Garro.

'Until the moment we fire our main engines,' replied the woman.

Qruze made a *tsk* noise under his breath. 'We can't fight our way out on this little scow, and we can barely run. We may be able to duck and dive, but how far do you think we'll get before one of those monsters...' he stabbed a finger at the large warships flanking them, 'before one of them gets its fangs into our throat?'

'Not far enough,' said Sendek grimly.

Carya tapped his metal fingers on the control console. 'It is true that the *Eisenstein* lacks the velocity to make it to the jump point clear of any pursuit. That is, *if* we follow the most direct course.' He traced a straight line from the ship's orbital location to the cross icon. The shipmaster pulled at the course indicator and stretched it in another direction. 'Vought has come up with an alternative solution. It is not without risk, but if we succeed, we will be able to outrun the Warmaster's guns.'

Garro studied the new course plot and smiled at the daring of it. 'I concur. This is so ordered.'

'A bold action,' countered Decius, 'but I must highlight the single large impediment to it.' The Astartes leaned in and pointed at a massive vessel floating off to the port. 'That course takes us right across the arc of this ship's engagement zone.'

'Typhon's command,' said Garro, 'the *Terminus Est.*'

CALAS TYPHON FINGERED the cutting edge of his manreaper with bare fingers, letting the keen blade pull at the hardened skin there, drawing faint lines of dark Astartes blood. His mood was a mixture of conflicting, polar emotions. On one level, he felt a simmering elation at the unfolding events around him, an anticipation of what great things were coming to pass. Typhon felt liberation, if an Astartes could know such a thing, a cold and cruel joy to know that after so long, after so many years of nurturing and hiding his secret wisdom, he would soon be free to walk openly with it. The things he knew, the words he had read in the books shown to him by his kinsman Erebus... The enlightenment the Word Bearers chaplain had brought to Calas Typhon had changed him forever. But Typhon was angry with it. Oh, he knew that his master Mortarion was slowly coming to the same path as he was, thanks to the direction of Horus, but both the primarch and the Warmaster were only just starting down that road. Typhon and Erebus and the others... they were the ones who had been truly illuminated, and it chafed at him that he was forced to play the role of dutiful first captain when in fact it was his knowledge that outstripped theirs.

The time would come, Typhon promised himself, and it would be soon, when he would cut loose from Mortarion's shadow and stand alone. With the patronage of darker powers, Typhon would become a herald before which whole worlds would tremble. From his command throne, the Death Guard's gaze ranged across the bridge of the *Terminus Est* to take in the servants and Astartes toiling in his service. Their loyalty was to him, and it was emboldening.

With that, Typhon's thoughts turned to Grulgor. He frowned and rubbed the black stubble of his beard. In the hours since he had sent Ignatius the command to remove Garro and join the attack on Isstvan III, the braggart commander had been uncommonly quiet. Now the bombardment was over and Horus's plan was in a moment of ellipsis, he had pause to reflect.

Grulgor was not a man to stay silent about his victories, and Typhon knew that Ignatius would relish the chance to relay the story of how he had murdered Nathaniel Garro. The commander's powerful dislike for the battle-captain had grown into full-fledged hate over the years, as Grulgor used Garro as a target for his every ill-humour and odium. Typhon had no idea where the roots of the enmity had been born, and he did not care. It was Typhon's nature to seek and exploit weakness. The rivalry had become a thing that fuelled itself, and Typhon had taken advantage of it. It was easy to use the poison in Grulgor's heart to make him his attack dog, and through Grulgor the first captain had been able to touch the lodges hidden inside the XIV Legion and guide them as well.

He gestured to a Chapter serf. 'You, check the communications logs. Have there been any machine-calls from the frigate *Eisenstein*?'

The servile was back in a moment. 'Lord captain, we show a signal to the fleet command, a message regarding a weapons malfunction, and then another, with reference to an ongoing issue with the ship's power system. The former bears Commander Grulgor's authorisation.'

'Nothing else?'

The serf bowed low. 'No, lord.'

Typhon rose and placed his battle scythe across his bridge throne. 'Where is the *Eisenstein* now?'

'Moving on a transition vector, captain,' answered a deck officer. 'Port high quadrant.'

'Where is he going?' A creeping discontent pushed at Typhon's thoughts. 'Vox! Hail the *Eisenstein* and get me a voice link. I want to talk to Grulgor, *now*.'

MAAS LISTENED CAREFULLY to the tinny voice in his headset, his opposite number on board the *Terminus*

Est repeating the orders of Captain Typhon with flat, emotionless precision. He had the vox pickup in his fingers, holding tightly to it, trembling slightly. Maas hazarded a sideways look at Carya, Vought and the other Astartes. They were all engaged in conversation, watching as the frigate made its way along the path that the deck officer had set.

Maas licked his lips, the tension making him thirsty. It was still difficult for him to fully grasp the chain of events that had led him to this point. His assignment to the *Eisenstein* had been recent, and in his eyes, it had not come soon enough.

Years of dogged service aboard armed transports and system boats had finally been rewarded with a promotion to an actual expeditionary fleet, and while the Death Guard's exploits were not as glamorous or renowned as those of other Legions, it was a step up for Maas's ambitions. He coveted command, and there wasn't a day that passed when he didn't think of a future where it would be Shipmaster Tirin Maas at the throne of a cruiser, running a vessel like his own private kingdom.

Now, all of that was in danger of crumbling away. The posting he had been so euphoric to be granted was turning into a millstone around his neck. First this high-handed Garro had taken command and set things awry, and now Carya himself was following the fool's insane orders! If what he had gleaned was true, this Death Guard had already murdered several of his own, allowed another turncoat to escape destruction and wilfully destroyed a dozen fighters! Maas felt as if he was the only sighted man in a room full of blind people.

He looked around the bridge for any glimmer of expression on the faces of the other officers, anything at all that might have shown him they felt as he did, but there was nothing. Carya and his arrogant executive had them all playing along! It was inconceivable. The shipmaster had defied the decrees of Horus himself, and then Vought had compounded things with her falsification of signals. Maas had tried to reason with Carya, and what had he got in return? Censure and violent reproach!

He shook his head. The vox officer felt soiled by the willing piracy unfolding before him. They had sworn an oath to the fleet, and Horus was at the head of that fleet. What did it matter if the orders the Warmaster gave were distasteful? A good captain did not question, he served! But Tirin Maas would never get to do that now, not after Carya's rebellion. Should he survive, Maas would be tarred with the same brush as the shipmaster, labelled disloyal and doubtless executed.

The young man stared at the vox unit. He had to take steps. Already, he had broken protocol and secretly disabled the enunciator circuits so that the bridge would not be alerted to incoming signals unless he wished it. That alone was a flogging offence, but Maas saw it was necessary. It was clear that he could only trust himself, and that meant he alone bore the responsibility to warn the rest of the fleet of the duplicity brewing aboard the *Eisenstein*. He raised the communicator to his lips and drew back into the vox alcove. Maas was afraid, that was undeniable, but as he began to speak in a careful whisper, a sense of purpose and strength came to him. When this was done he would have the gratitude of Horus himself. Perhaps, if *Eisenstein* wasn't destroyed as an object lesson after the rebellion had been put down, he might even solicit the Warmaster for command of the ship as his reward.

'REPEAT YOURSELF,' DEMANDED Typhon. He loomed over the Chapter serf at the vox console, the broad form of his armour dark and menacing.

The helot bowed. 'Lord, the message comes from a person claiming to be *Eisenstein*'s communications officer. He says that Grulgor is missing, and that the ship's command crew are in revolt. He claims treachery, sir.'

The first captain rocked back, and in his mind the pieces of an unwelcome picture fell into place. 'The bellicose idiot failed me! He tipped our hand to Garro.' Typhon spun in place and barked out orders to the ship's crew. 'Sound general quarters! Power to the drives and the prow lances! I want an intercept course to *Eisenstein*, and I want it now!'

'Captain, the vox officer,' said the serf, 'what shall I tell him?'

Typhon smiled grimly. 'Send him my gratitude and the commiserations of the Warmaster. Then get me a link to Maloghurst aboard the *Vengeful Spirit*.'

GARRO SAW THE brief flicker of fear on Carya's face as the sing-song siren call blared from the forward command console. Vought was already at the station, punching control strings into the keyboard.

'Report!' said the shipmaster.

Vought paled. 'Sense-servitors are registering a distinct thermal bloom emanating from the drive blocks of *Terminus Est*, sir. In addition, there are readings of possible bow configuration changes in line with lance battery deployment.'

'He knows,' snapped Qruze. 'Warp curse him, Typhon knows!'

'Aye,' agreed Garro, facing Carya. 'It's time. Give the order.'

The naval officer swallowed hard and threw a nod to Vought. 'You heard the battle-captain. All decks to combat stations, release drive interlocks and make for maximum military speed.' He gestured to a junior rating. 'Get below and alert the esteemed Severnaya to prepare himself for the jump. I want him ready to go.' Carya saw the question in Garro's look. 'Severnaya, the Navigator,' he explained, pointing at the deck. 'Two tiers below us. Spends his days meditating inside a null-gee sphere. I'll warrant he doesn't have the slightest idea what's going on up here. He lives only for the thrill of the jump, you see.'

Garro accepted this. 'The warp is stormy. Do you think he will baulk to enter it when your order comes?'

'Oh, he'll go all right,' said Carya, 'but what I fear is whether he will survive the leap.'

Vought broke in to the conversation. 'What about the gun batteries, sir?' she asked, her voice taut with tension.

Carya shook his head. 'Make them ready, but I want all available power to be on hand for the void shields and the engine clusters. What we need is strength and speed, not firepower.'

'Aye sir, all ahead full,' she replied, and went to work implementing the orders.

Garro felt a faint shudder through the soles of his boots as the frigate's decking trembled with the abrupt application of velocity. Chimes and bells from the enginarium relays sounded as *Eisenstein* went instantly from a stately drifting course to a full battle pace.

'*Terminus Est* is moving from her orbital station,' said Sendek, reading the data from a pict-screen repeater. 'Turning now, swinging guns to our bearing.'

'Any other ships following suit?' asked Garro.

'I don't see them, lord,' he replied, 'only Typhon.'

'Captain Garro,' Vought called, 'we have no records of the warship's capabilities. What can Typhon field against us?'

'Sir, if I may?' broke in Sendek. '*Terminus Est* is a unique craft, not of a standard template construct pattern, well armoured but ponderous with it and very burdensome on the turns.'

Carya nodded. 'That we can play to our advantage.'

'Indeed, her forward armament is formidable, however. Typhon has an array of bow-mounted lances, and more in turrets that prey abeam and ahead. If he pulls alongside us, we're finished,' he concluded grimly.

'We'll keep the behemoth out of our baffles, then,' said the shipmaster. 'Watch the reactor temperatures!'

'How did he guess?' Decius snarled at his commander. 'Could it not be a coincidence? Perhaps he is only taking the ship to another orbit?'

'He knows,' Garro repeated Sendek's words. 'This was inevitable.'

'But how?' demanded the younger Astartes. 'Did he have a seer pluck your intentions from the ether?'

Garro's eyes strayed to the vox alcove and met those of the man cowering there, his face pale and sweaty. 'Nothing so arcane,' said the battle-captain, reading the truth in the naval officer's expression. In three swift steps he was across the bridge chamber and dragging Maas to his feet. The vox officer appeared to have been crying. 'You,' growled Garro, his eyes turning flinty. 'You alerted Typhon.'

Hanging there in his grip, Maas suddenly jerked and flailed at Garro, weak blows rebounding off his power armour. 'Traitor bastard!' he shouted. 'You're all conspirators! You've killed us with your duplicity!'

'Fool!' Carya retorted. 'These are the Emperor's men. It's *you* that's the traitor, you arrogant dolt!'

'My oath is to the fleet. I serve the Warmaster Horus!' Maas bellowed as he started to weep. 'Until death!'

'Yes,' agreed Garro, and with a savage twist of his wrist, the Death Guard broke the vox officer's neck and let him drop to the floor.

There was only a breath of silence after the killing before Vought's voice called out across the bridge. 'Lance discharge, port rear quadrant! We're under attack!'

The crew turned their faces away from the viewports as a dazzling sword of white light crossed over the frigate's bow. The shot was a miss, but the edges of the lance's energy nimbus crackled over the exterior hull. On the bridge a handful of stations flickered and popped as the backwash raced through the control systems.

'I think he wants us to heave to,' muttered Qruze.

'A request so politely phrased as well,' said Sendek. 'We'll show him our exhausts by way of reply.'

'Look sharp!' snapped Garro, turning away from the man he had just executed. 'Warn Hakur and the others to be ready for impacts and decompression! I want those civilians kept alive–'

The next shot was a hit.

At the periphery of its range, the lance fire from the *Terminus Est* was at its weakest, and yet the collimated beams of energy were still enough to inflict serious damage on a ship with the tonnage of *Eisenstein*. The bolts cut through the void shields and sent them flickering. They raked over the dorsal hull at an oblique angle that tore decks open to space and ripped several portside gun turrets from their mountings.

Puffs of gas and flame popped and faded. Cascade discharges vaulted down the corridors of the frigate, blowing out relays and setting combustion. In a single secondary explosion, an entire compartment on one of the tertiary tiers became a brief, murderous firestorm as stored breathing gas canisters ignited.

A handful of Garro's men left there to stand guard died first as the air in their lungs turned to flames. The backdraft flooded over their bodies, torching the living quarters and sanctum of *Eisenstein*'s small astropathic choir. Safety hatches slammed shut, but the damage was done, and with no more air to burn, the chambers became dead voids of blackened metal and ruined flesh.

Some of the impact transferred into kinetic energy that staggered the ship and made it list, but Carya's officers were battle-hardened and they did not let it turn them from their course. *Terminus Est* was moving upon them, the massive battleship filling the rearward pict screens with its deadly bulk.

'AN EXPLANATION, TYPHON,' growled Maloghurst over the crackling vox link, 'I await an explanation as to why you saw fit to draw me from my duties during this most important of operations.'

The first captain grimaced, glad he did not have to look the Warmaster's equerry in the eye. There was no great esteem held between the Son of Horus and the Death Guard, a holdover from an incident years

earlier when they had disagreed fiercely over a matter
of battlefield protocol. Typhon disliked the man's
insouciant manner and his barely restrained
arrogance. That Maloghurst was known by the epithet
'The Twisted' was, in Typhon's opinion, an all too
accurate description. 'Forgive me, equerry,' he
retorted, 'but I thought it important you be informed
that your primarch's grand plans are in danger of
faltering!'

'Don't test my patience, Death Guard! Shall I call
your primarch to the vox to have him chastise you
instead? Your ship has left the formation. What are
you doing?'

'Attempting to excise an irritant. I have received
warning that one of my battle-brothers, the lamenta-
bly conservative Captain Garro, has taken control of
a frigate called the *Eisenstein* and even now attempts
to flee the Isstvan system.' He leaned back in his command throne. 'Is that matter enough for your
attention, or should I address myself directly to
Horus instead?'

'Garro?' repeated Maloghurst. 'It was my understanding that Mortarion had dealt with him.'

Typhon snorted. 'The Death Lord has been too
lenient. Garro should have been allowed to die of his
wounds after the battle on Isstvan Extremis. Instead
Mortarion hoped to turn him, and now we may pay
for that folly.'

Maloghurst was silent for a moment. Typhon could
imagine his unpleasant face creased in thought.
'Where is he now?'

'I am pursuing the *Eisenstein*. I will destroy the ship
if I can.'

The equerry sniffed archly. 'Where does Garro think
he can go? The storms in the warp have grown fiercer

with every passing hour. A small vessel like that cannot hope to weather a journey through the immaterium. He'll be torn apart!'

'Perhaps,' admitted Typhon, 'but I would like to make sure.'

'I have your course on my data-slate,' said the other Astartes. 'You'll never catch him in that cumbersome barge of yours, he has too much distance on you.'

'I don't need to catch him, Maloghurst. I just need to wound him.'

'Then do it, Typhon,' came the reply. 'If I am forced to inform Horus that word of his plans has been spread unchecked, it will be you who feels his displeasure soon after I do!'

The first captain made a throat-cutting gesture and his vox attendant severed the connection. He glanced down from his command throne to where the shipmaster of the *Terminus Est* was bowed and waiting.

The man spoke. 'Lord Typhon, the *Eisenstein* has altered her course. It's travelling at full burn towards Istvaan III's satellite, the White Moon.'

'Come to new heading,' snapped Typhon, rising once more. 'Match *Eisenstein*'s course and get me a firing solution.'

The shipmaster faltered. 'Lord, the moon's gravity well—'

'That was not a request,' he growled.

'STILL WITH US.' Vought read the distance vectors from a pict-screen. 'Aspect change confirmed. *Terminus Est* is following, no other signs of pursuit.'

'Just so,' said Carya. 'Continue on a zigzag heading. Don't make it easy for Typhon's gunners to get a firing angle.'

Garro stood directly behind the shipmaster, looking over his head and out of the viewports. The stark, chalk-coloured surface of Isstvan III's largest moon steadily grew larger as he watched it, craters and mountains taking shape on the airless surface. To an untrained observer, it might have seemed like the frigate was on a collision course. 'Be honest with me.' Garro spoke quietly, so only Carya could hear him. 'What chance is there that Vought's computations will be in error?'

The dark-skinned man glanced up at him. 'She's very good, captain. The only reason she hasn't been given a ship of her own is because she has a few issues with fleet authority. I have faith in her.'

Garro looked back at the moon. 'My faith is in the strength of a starship's hull and the power of gravity,' he replied, but even as he said the words, they seemed hollow and incomplete.

Carya eyed him curiously. Perhaps he sensed the captain's disquiet. 'The universe is vast, sir. One can find faith in many places.'

'Coming up to first course correction,' called the deck officer. 'Stand by for emergency manoeuvres.'

'Mark,' said a servitor in a toneless voice. 'Executing manoeuvre.'

The frigate's deck yawed and Garro felt the motion in the pit of his stomach. With all the available energy channelling into the drives, the ship's gravitational compensators were lagging behind and he felt the turn more distinctly than usual. He gripped a support stanchion with one hand and put his weight on his organic leg.

'Thermal bloom from their bow,' warned Sendek, having taken it upon himself to assist the bridge crew at the sensor pulpit. '*Discharge*! Incoming fire, multiple lance bolts!'

'Push the turn!' shouted Carya. He said something else, but the words were drowned out as heavy rods of tuned energy struck the aft of the *Eisenstein* and pitched her forward like a ship cresting a wave. The compensators were slow again, and Garro's arm shot out and grabbed the shipmaster, halting his fall towards a console. The battle-captain felt something in Carya's wrist dislocate.

'Engine three power levels dropping!' shouted Vought. 'Coolant leaks on decks nine and seven!'

Carya recovered and nodded to Garro. 'Increase thrust from the other nozzles to compensate! We can't let them gain any ground!'

The ship was trembling, the throbbing vibration of a machine pushed to the edge of its operating limit. Sendek called out from his station. 'We're entering the White Moon's gravity well, captain, accelerating.'

Carya gasped as he snapped his augmetic hand back into place. 'Ah, the point of no return, Garro,' he said. 'Now we'll see if Racel is as good as I said she was.'

'If her calculations are off by more than a few degrees, we will be nothing but a new crater and a scattering of metal shavings,' Decius said darkly.

The moon filled the forward viewport. 'Have faith,' Garro replied.

'LORD, WE HAVE been captured by the lunar gravitational pull,' reported Typhon's shipmaster. 'Our velocity is increasing. I would humbly suggest we attempt to evade, and–'

'If we break contact now, the *Eisenstein* escapes,' the first captain said flatly. 'This vessel has power enough to pull free, yes? You'll use it when I order you to and not before.'

'By your command.'

Typhon glared at the gunnery officer. 'You! Where are my kills? I want that frigate obliterated! Get it done!'

'Lord, the ship is agile and our cannons are largely fixed emplacements.'

'Results, not excuses!' came the growling retort. 'Do your duty or I'll find a man who can!'

On the giant pict screen over his command throne, Typhon watched the trails of fumes and wreckage spilling from *Eisenstein* and smiled coldly.

RACEL VOUGHT BLINKED sweat out of her eyes and pressed her hands on the flat panel of the control console. The reflected ivory starlight from the White Moon's surface illuminated the bridge with stark edges and hard lines. It was a funerary glow, devoid of any life, and it seemed to draw her energy from her. She took a shuddering breath. The lives of every person aboard the frigate were squarely in her hands at this moment, gambled on a string of numbers she had hastily computed while Isstvan III had died before her eyes. She was afraid to look at them again for fear that she might find she had made some horrible mistake. Better that she not know, better she hang on to the fragile thread of confidence that had propelled her to this daring course in the first place. If Vought had made any miscalculations, she would not live to regret it.

The theory was sound, she could be sure of that. The gravity of the dense, iron-heavy White Moon was already enveloping the *Eisenstein*, dragging it down towards the satellite's craggy surface. If she did not intervene, it would do exactly that, and like the dour Death Guard had said, the frigate would become a grave marker.

Vought's plan was built on the mathematics of orbits and the physics of gravitation, a school of learning that extended back to the very first steps of mankind into space, when thrust and fuel were precious commodities. In the Thirty-first Millennium, with brute force engines capable of throwing starships wherever they needed to go, it wasn't often such knowledge was required, but today it might save their lives.

Racel glanced over her shoulder and found both Baryk and the Death Guard battle-captain looking back at her. She expected judgemental, commanding stares from both men, but instead there was silent assurance in their eyes. They were trusting her to fulfil her promise. She gave them an answering nod and went back to her task.

Klaxons warned of new salvos of incoming fire. She tuned them out of her thoughts, concentrating instead on the complex plots of trajectory and flight path before her. There was no margin for error. As *Eisenstein* fell towards the planetoid, the drives would shift and ease her through the White Moon's gravitational envelope, using the energy of the satellite to throw the frigate about in a slingshot arc, boosting the vessel's sub-light speed, projecting her away towards the jump point. The *Terminus Est* would never be able to catch them.

The frigate's shuddering grew as the craft entered the final vector of the slingshot course. 'Prepare for course correction,' Vought shouted over the rumbling. '*Mark!*'

STREAKS OF FIRE jetted from the *Eisenstein*'s port flank as the autonomic trim controls slewed the ship away from the moon. The bow veered as if wrenched by an invisible hand, shifting the axis with brutal force. The extremes of tension between the lunar gravity and the artificial g-forces generated inside the vessel knotted and turned. Hull plates popped and warped as rivets as big as a man sheared off and broke. Conduits stressed beyond their tolerances ruptured and spewed toxic fumes. Forced past her limits, *Eisenstein* howled like a wounded animal under the punishment, but it turned, metre by agonising metre, falling into the small corridor of orbital space that would propel the frigate away from Isstvan III.

'TYPHON!' SHOUTED THE shipmaster, throwing procedure aside by daring to address the first captain without the prefix of his rank. 'We must evade! We cannot follow the frigate's course, we'll be drawn down on to the moon! Our mass is too great–'

Furious, the Death Guard struck the naval officer with a sudden backhand, battering the man to the decking with his cheekbones shattered and blood streaming from cuts. 'Evade, then!' he spat, 'but warp curse you, I want everything thrown at that bloody ship before we let him go!'

The rest of the bridge crew scrambled to carry out his orders, leaving the mewling shipmaster to tend to himself. Typhon snatched up his manreaper and held it tightly, his anger hot and deadly. He cursed Garro as the *Eisenstein* slipped out of his grasp.

THE TERMINUS EST bore down, the warship's drives casting a halo of crackling red light, a shark snapping at a minnow. The craft groaned as the monstrous thrust of her drives tore the ship out of the White Moon's gravity well, the blade-sharp prow crossing the path of the frigate. As it did so, every lance cannon

on Typhon's battle cruiser erupted as one in a screaming concert of power, tearing across the dark towards
the fleeing vessel.

'INCOMING FIRE!' BARKED Sendek. 'Brace for impact!'

Garro heard the words and then suddenly he was
airborne, the deck dropping away from him. The
Death Guard spun and tumbled across the bridge,
rebounding off stanchions and clipping the ceiling
before the energy of the slamming impact dissipated
and he collided with a control console.

Nathaniel shook off a daze and dragged himself
back to his feet. Small fires were burning here and
there as servitors struggled to bring the bridge back to
any semblance of order. He saw Carya sprawled over
the command throne, with Vought at his side. The
woman had a severe cut across her scalp, but she
seemed to be unaware of the streaks of blood down
her cheek. Dimly, he heard Iacton Qruze swear in
Cthonian as he climbed off the deck.

'Report,' Garro commanded, the rough metallic
smoke that hazed the air tasting acrid on his tongue.

Sendek called out from the other side of the chamber. '*Terminus Est* has broken off pursuit, but that last
salvo hit us hard. Several decks vented to space. Drive
reactors are in flux, engines are verging on critical
shutdown.' He paused. 'Slingshot manoeuvre was suc-
cessful. On course for intercept with jump point.'

Decius grunted as he pushed aside a fallen section
of panelling and stepped over the lifeless body of a
naval rating. 'What good is that if we explode before
we get there?'

Garro ignored him and moved to Carya's side. 'Is he
alive?'

Vought nodded. 'Just stunned, I think.'

The shipmaster waved them off. 'I can stand on my own. Get away.'

Garro disregarded the man's complaints and pulled him to his feet. 'Decius, call the Apothecary to the bridge.'

Carya shook his head. 'No, not yet. We're not finished here, not by a long shot.' He staggered forward. 'Racel, what's the Navigator's status?'

Vought cringed as she listened to a vox headset. Even at a distance, Garro could hear yelling and shouting from the tinny speaker. 'Severnaya's still alive, but his adjutants are panicking. They're climbing the walls down there. They are weeping about the warp. I can hear them screaming about darkness and storms.'

'If he's not dead, then he can still do his job,' Carya said grimly, chewing down his pain. 'That goes for all of us.'

'Aye,' said Garro. 'Order the crew to make the preparations for warp translation. We will not have a second chance at this.'

'We may not have the *first* chance,' grumbled Decius beneath his breath.

Garro turned on him and his face hardened. 'Brother, I have reached my bounds with your doleful conduct! If you have nothing else to volunteer but that, I will have you go below and join the damage control parties.'

'I call it as I see it,' retorted Decius. 'You said you wanted the truth from me, captain!'

'I would have you keep your comments to yourself until we are away, Decius!'

Nathaniel expected the younger Astartes to back down, but instead Decius stepped closer, moderating his tone so that it would not carry further. 'I will not.

This course you have set us upon is suicide, sir, as surely as if you had bared our throats to Typhon's scythe.' He stabbed a finger at Vought. 'You heard the woman. The Navigator is barely sane with the terror of what you ask of him. I know you have not been deaf to the reports of the turbulence in the warp in recent days. A dozen ships were displaced just on the voyage to Isstvan–'

'That is rumour and hearsay,' Qruze snapped, coming closer.

'Are you sure?' Decius pressed. 'They say the warp has turned black with tempests and the freakish things that lurk within them! And here we sit, on a ship held together by rust and hope, with intent to dive into that ocean of madness.'

Garro hesitated. There was truth in Decius's words. He *was* aware of the talk circulating about the fleet before the attack on the Choral City, that there had been isolated incidents of Navigators and astropaths going wild with panic when their minds stroked the immaterium. The sea of warp space was always a chaotic and dangerous realm through which to travel, but so the reports had hinted, it was rapidly becoming impassable.

'We have already tested ourselves and this ship beyond all rational margins,' hissed Decius. 'If we touch the warp, it will be a step too far. We will not endure a blind voyage into the empyrean.'

The skin on the back of Garro's neck prickled. The innate danger sense that was second nature to an Astartes sounded in him and he turned towards the bridge's main hatch. Standing in the doorway, wreathed in thin grey smoke, the woman Keeler was watching him. The battle-captain blinked, for one moment afraid that reason had fled from him and she was some kind of ephemeral vision, but then he realised that Decius saw her too.

Keeler picked her way through the wreckage and came to stand directly in front of him. 'Nathaniel Garro, I came because I know you need help. Will you accept it?'

'You're just a remembrancer,' said Decius, but even his bluster was waning before her quiet, potent presence. 'What help can you offer?'

'You'd be surprised,' murmured Qruze.

'The survival of this ship is measured in moments,' she continued, 'and if we remain in this place we will surely die. We must all take a leap of faith, Nathaniel. If we trust in the will of the Emperor, we will find salvation.'

'What you ask of him is blind belief in phantoms,' Decius argued. 'You cannot know we will survive!'

'I can.' Keeler's reply was quiet, but filled with such complete certainty that the Astartes were given pause by it.

From the forward consoles, Vought called out. 'Captain, the ship's Geller Field will not stabilise. Perhaps we should abort the warp jump. If we enter the immaterium, it may fail completely and the ship will be unprotected.'

'You have only one choice, Nathaniel,' said Keeler softly.

'There will be no abort, deck officer.' Garro watched the shock unfold on Decius's face as he spoke. 'Take us in.'

ELEVEN

Chaos
Visions
The Resurrected

THE EISENSTEIN FELL.

The warp gate opened, a ragged-edged wound cut through the matrix of space, and it drew the damaged frigate inside. Unreal energies collided and annihilated one another. With a brilliant flicker of radiation, the ship left reality behind.

It was impossible for a person possessed of an unaltered mind to comprehend the nature of warp space. The seething, churning ocean of raw non-matter was psychoactive. It was as much a product of the psyches of those that looked upon it, as it was a shifting, wilful landscape of its own. On Ancient Earth there had once been a philosopher who warned that if a man were to look into an abyss, then he should know that the abyss would also look into the man. In no other place was this as true as it was in the immaterium. The warp was a mirror for the emotions of every living thing, a sea of turbulent thought echoes, the dark

257

dregs of every hidden desire and broken id mixed together into a raw mass of disorder. If one could apply a single word to describe the nature of the warp, that word would be *chaos*.

The Navigators and the astropaths knew the immaterium as well as any human could, but even they understood that their knowledge stood only in the shallows of this mad ocean. Description of the warp was not something they could easily relay to the limited minds of lesser beings. Some saw the realm as if it were made of taste and smell, some as a fractal backcloth woven from mathematical theorems and lines of dense equations. Others conceived it as song, with turning symphonies to represent worlds, bold strings for thought patterns, great brass reveilles for suns, and woodwinds and timpani for the ships that crossed the aurascape. But its very existence defied comprehension. The warp was change. It was the absence of reason unleashed and teeming, sometimes mill-pond calm, sometimes towering in titanic, stormy rages. It was the Medusa, the mythic beast that could kill an unwary man who dared to look upon it unguarded.

Into this the wounded starship *Eisenstein* had been thrown, the shimmering and unsteady bubble of her protective Geller Field writhing as the insanity tried to claw inside.

THE BLAST BAFFLES slammed shut over the bridge viewports the instant the ship began its transition. Garro was grateful for it. The familiar lurching sensation in his chest that a warp jump forced upon him made the Death Guard grimace. There was something that disturbed him on the deepest, most primal level about the hellish light of warp space, and he was glad not to be bathed in it as the frigate translated.

'We're through,' gasped Vought. 'We're away!'

Qruze patted her on the shoulder as a rough-throated cheer sounded from the crewmen, all except the shipmaster, who gave Garro a grim-faced look. 'We shouldn't take our glories too soon, lads,' he said, addressing his men, but facing the Death Guard. 'As of now we have only traded one set of dangers for another.'

The shaking, rolling gait of the *Eisenstein* showed no sign of easing. If anything, the smooth voyage through normal space was a distant memory, and the rattling swell it rode through had become the norm. 'How long will it take us to reach safety?' Garro asked.

Carya sighed heavily, the fatigue he had been holding at bay brimming over to flood him. 'It's the warp, sir,' he said, as if that would explain everything. 'We could be in Terra's shade in a day or we might find ourselves clear across the galaxy a hundred years hence. There are no maps for these territories. We simply hold on and let our Navigator guide us as best he can.'

The ship rocked and a moaning shudder rippled the length of the bridge chamber. 'This is a tough old boat,' Carya added grimly. 'It won't go easily.'

Garro caught sight of Decius, listening intently to his helmet vox. 'Lord,' he called, any signs of their earlier disagreement gone. 'Message from Hakur below decks. He says there are... there are intruders on board.'

Nathaniel's hand went for the hilt of his sword. 'How can that be? We detected no craft launched from Typhon's ship!'

'I don't know, sir, I'm only relaying what the sergeant says.'

Garro toggled the vox link on his armour's collar and caught fragmentary barks of noise over the general channel. He heard the harsh snarls of bolter fire and screaming that clawed to inhuman heights. For an instant he thought of the Warsinger and her alien chorus.

'Alarm triggers sounding on the lower tiers,' reported Vought. 'It's Severnaya's adjutants again, at the navis sanctorum.'

'Hakur is there,' added Decius.

'Decius, with me. Sendek, you will remain here,' said Garro. 'Tell Hakur we're coming to him, and send to all the men to be on alert.'

'Aye, sir,' Sendek nodded his assent.

Garro turned to the older Luna Wolf. 'Captain Qruze, I would have you take my post here, if you will.'

Iacton saluted briskly. 'This is your ship, lad. I'll do as you order me. My experience may be of some use to these youths.'

Garro made to leave and found Keeler still there, standing before him. 'You will be tested,' she said, without preamble.

He pushed past her. 'Of that, I have never been in doubt.'

ANDUS HAKUR HAD killed many times in his life. The countless adversaries that had fallen before his guns, his blades, his fists, they were a blur of swift and purposeful death. In service to the XIV Legion, the veteran had fought ork and eldar, jorgall and hykosi, he had fought beasts and he had fought men, but the enemies that he fought today were a kind that he had never seen the like of.

The first warning came when Severnaya's navis adjutant threw herself screaming from the door of the sanctum, weeping and shouting incoherently. The woman collapsed in a heap of thin limbs and knotted cloak. Her hands jerked and pointed to the corners of the corridor, as if she could see things up there that Hakur and the other Astartes were blind to. He stepped to her and felt his skin go cold, as if he had entered a refrigerated chamber. Then he saw it, just at the edges of his vision, the merest flicker of oddly coloured light, like fireflies shimmering in the dark. It came and went so fast for a moment he thought it might have been a trick of his brain, an after-effect of stress and battle fatigue.

He was still processing this when the first of the things emerged out of the smoky air and killed the Death Guard standing with his back to him. Hakur had the impression of a spinning disc, a wide purple blade trailing stinging cilia from its edges, and then the Astartes was being ripped open, blood and gore issuing out in runnels. Hakur fired reflexively, aware that his battle-brother was already beyond rescue, snapping off a three-round burst at the diaphanous shape. It died with a shriek, but the sound became a clarion call and suddenly new and different forms were emerging from the walls and floor. They brought a stench of such potency with them that Hakur's gorge rose and he tasted acid bile. The adjutant was already on her knees and puking violently.

'Blood's oath!' cursed one of the men in his squad. 'Rot and death!'

It was that, and a hundred times worse. The slices through which the creatures emerged allowed draughts of foetid plague-house stink to coil into the corridor. Patches of fungus and rusty discolouration fingered along crevices in the iron decking where the stench crawled forth, but this was only precursor to the diseased horrors of the invaders themselves.

They sickened Hakur to such a degree that he attacked instantly, so abhorrent were these things that the thought of their continued existence revolted him. The shape of the creatures was vaguely that of a man, but only in the grossest, most basic sense. Ropey limbs that shook with palsy flicked and clawed with black, decayed talons. Distended, malformed hooves scraped across the decking, leaving lines of acid slime and excrement. Each one was naked, and bloated around the torso and belly with gaseous buboes and grotesque sores that wept thick pus. Heads were shrunken balls of flaking skin over rictus-grinning skulls. All of them had trains of buzzing insects following behind them, tiny bottle-green flies that dived in and out of the invaders' open wounds.

Where bolter rounds struck them, gobbets of flesh were torn off and rolled away in bloody hanks of stinking meat. They took a lot of killing, the skittering, burbling things coming at the Death Guard in hooting profusion. Hakur watched them take a second brother, and two more, even as he poured shot after shot into them.

Then Garro hove into view at the opposite end of the corridor, Decius and a handful of reinforcements with him. Caught between two packs of Astartes, the advance of the creatures was staggered, and the battle-captain waded into the mass of them. Libertas shone as it rose and fell. Decius had liberated a flamer and torched the things with jets of promethium. Hakur used the distraction to recover the adjutant and pull her out of the line of battle.

She screamed and flailed at him, beating her hands on his chest plate. He could see now where her hands were bloody with self-inflicted scratch marks. 'Eyes and blood!' she wailed. 'But inside the pestilence!'

Garro stamped the last of the creatures to death and scraped the remains from his boot with a grimace. 'Silence her,' he snapped.

Decius's palm went to the breath grille of his helmet. 'In Terra's name, that rancid smell!'

Hakur handed off the woman to one of his men and made his report to the battle-captain. Garro listened intently. 'Word is coming in from all over the ship, the same thing: mutant freaks materialising and leaving decay in their wake.'

'It's the warp,' said Decius grimly. 'We all know the tales, of predators that prey on ships lost or weak.' He gestured at the walls. 'If the Geller Field fails, those things will overrun us.'

'I'll trust Master Carya's crew to keep that from happening,' Garro replied. 'In the meantime, we will destroy these unclean filth wherever we find them.'

'Unclean, unclean!' chorused the adjutant, ripping herself from the grip of Hakur's trooper. 'I have seen it! Inside the eyes!' She tore wildly at her face, ripping the skin and drawing blood. 'You see it too!'

The woman threw herself at Garro with furious speed, and before he could deflect her, the adjutant impaled herself upon the hissing blade of his power sword.

Garro jerked back, but it was too late. The adjutant, a Navigator tertius in service to the senioris Severnaya, pressed into him and raked bloody fingers over his torso. 'You see!' she gasped. 'Soon the end comes! All will wither.'

The end comes. Once more, the words of the jorgalli child fluttered through his thoughts like a dying raptor, falling and screaming. Garro's skin went hot with the flush of blood through his veins, his throat tightening in just the manner it had when he had taken the draught from the cups with Mortarion. He trembled, suddenly unable to speak. The woman's upturned face became paper, aged and crumbling. She slid away from him, off the tip of Libertas, turning into rags of meat and dead flesh, ash and then nothing.

'My lord?' Hakur's words were slow and thick, as if they were echoing through liquid. Garro turned to face his trusted sergeant and recoiled. Creeping decomposition was washing over Hakur and the other men, and none of them seemed to be aware of it. The resplendent marble-white of their armour bled away to become discoloured by a feeble, sickly green the shade of new death. The ceramite warped and became rippled, merging with their flesh until it strained and throbbed. Parasites and bloated organs pulsed within, and in some places wounds opened like new mouths, red-lipped with tongues of distended bowel and duct.

Pus, thick and pasty, leaked from every joint and orifice with streaks of brown rust and black ooze. Flies floated in halos around the misshapen heads of the plagued Astartes. Garro's disgust rooted him to the spot. The malformed shapes of his warriors crowded in, words falling from their crackled, lisping maws. Upon their shoulders, Garro saw the skull and star of the Death Guard gone, replaced with three dark discs. His attention was drawn up and away. Beyond the men he saw a ghostly form towering above them, too tall to fit in the cramped corridor yet there before him, beckoning with skeletal claws.

'Mortarion?' he asked.

The twisted image of his primarch nodded, the figure's blackened hood dipping in sluggish acknowledgement. What Garro could see of his primarch's armour was no longer shining with steel and brass, but discoloured and corroded like old copper, wound with soiled bandages and scored with rust. The Death Lord was no more and in his place stood a creature of pure corruption.

'Come, Nathaniel.' The voice was a whisper of wind through dead trees, a breath from a sepulchre. 'Soon we will all know the embrace of the Lord of Decay.'

The end comes. The words tolled in his mind like a bell and Garro looked down at his hands. His gauntlets were powder, flesh was sloughing off his fingers, bones emerging and turning into blackened twigs. 'No!' he forced the denial from his throat. 'This will not be!'

'My lord?' Hakur tapped him on the shoulder, concern on his face. 'Are you all right?'

Garro blinked and saw the dead woman lying on the deck, her body still intact. He cast around. The horrific vision was gone, burst like a bubble. Decius and the others eyed him with obvious concern.

'You… seemed to leave us for a moment, captain,' said Hakur.

He forced the turmoil of emotion from his mind. 'This is not over,' Garro insisted. 'Worse is to come.'

Decius tapped his helmet. 'Sir, a signal from Voyen, on the lower tiers. Something is happening on the gunnery decks.'

IN THE WARP, it was said, all things in the material realm were echoed: the emotions of men, their wishes and their bloodlusts, the yearning for change and the cycle of life from death. Logicians and thinkers throughout the Imperium meditated on the mercurial and unknowable nature of the immaterium, desperately trying to create cages of words for something that could only be experienced, not understood. Some dared to suggest that there might be life, of a sort, within the warp, perhaps even intelligence after a fashion. There were even those, the ones who gathered in secret places and spoke in hushed awe, who were bold enough to venture the idea that these dark powers might possibly be superior to humanity.

If these men could have known the truth, it would have broken them. In the gathering hell-light that thundered around the tiny sliver of starship that was the *Eisenstein*, a vast and hateful intellect gave the ship the smallest portion of its attention. A gossamer touch was all that was needed, spilling the raw power of decay over the frigate's protective sphere. It reached inside through gaps in causality and found corpse-flesh in abundance, pleasing in the ripe putrefaction of the diseased and dead. A diversion was presented here, the opportunity to play a little and experiment with things that might be done on larger scales at later times. Gently, as matters elsewhere drew it away, the power stroked at what it had found and granted a thin conduit to itself.

THE BLAST DOORS sealing in the toxic section of the gunnery deck had yet to be reopened. Issues of greater import had taken the attention of the frigate's crew as they fled from Isstvan, and the clearing of the dead had become of secondary consideration.

The Life-Eater virus was long gone. Powerful and deadly, the microbes were nevertheless short-lived, and Captain Garro's quick actions in purging the bay's atmosphere to the void had stopped the bane from running its full course. The virus could not live without air to carry it, and so it had perished, but the destruction it had wreaked in the meantime remained. Corpses in varying states of decomposition lay scattered about the decking, men and Astartes lying where they had fallen as the germs tore through the defences of their bodies. The vacuum of space had preserved them in their grotesque tableau of death, some frozen with mouths open in endless screams, others little more than a slurry of jellied bones and human effluent.

It was in this state that the touch found them. Riven with rotten flesh, life flensed from them, for something born within the ever-changing rebirth of the warp, it was easy to distort and remould them. With a careful placing of marks, the injection of new, more virulent clades than the human-borne virus. Death became fresh life, although not in a form pleasing to the eye of man.

In the airless silence, fingers frozen to the decking by rimes of ice twitched and moved, shaking off cowls of frost. The essence of decay flowed, rust and age caking the mechanisms of the blast doors, making them brittle. Those who were favoured walked once more, eschewing mortality for a transformed existence.

THE EISENSTEIN HAD two long promenade corridors that ran the length of the frigate's port and starboard flanks, punctuated every few metres by thin observation slits that cast blades of light down across the polished steel decking. It was in this place, on the port side some ten or so strides from the ninety-seventh hull frame, that Death Guard met Death Guard in open conflict.

Garro saw the misshapen things from a distance and thought that the strange, plague-bearing

creatures they encountered at the navis sanctorum
were before them once more, but he realised quickly
that the size was wrong, that these diseased freaks
were the match in height for the Astartes. When they
hove into the light, what he saw sent him skidding to
a halt, his free hand coming to his mouth in shock.

'In the Emperor's name,' choked Hakur, 'what horror is this?'

Garro's blood turned to ice in his veins. The awful
vision that seemed to transmit itself from the dying
adjutant was suddenly here before him, written in
reality over the mutated, swollen parodies of Death
Guard warriors: the same corpse-pallor green of their
battle armour, the same slack faces rippled with
growths of broken tooth and horn, flesh stretched
tight over bodies teeming with colonies of maggots.
Voyen had joined Garro and the others at the
entrance to the corridor and even the Apothecary,
hardened to sights of disease and malady, retched at
the sight of the twisted man-things.

The vision had been a warning, Garro realised, a
glimpse of what he encountered here, and perhaps of
what a failure might engender.

Around the legs of the abnormal Astartes were
things that were once members of *Eisenstein*'s crew,
men caught halfway through the venomous ravages
of the Life-Eater and suspended there, flesh in tatters
and organs awash with ichor. They bayed and scrambled forward to attack Garro's warriors. Decius led the
firing as the Death Guard let fly with bolters and
flamers.

A ragged scarecrow of skin and bone flung itself to
the deck and mewed, fly-blown pustules pocking a face
eaten away by leprous cancers. It spoke, the stink of its
breath reaching them in a reeking wash. 'Master...'

He saw the robes, the skull sigil around its neck. 'Kaleb?' Garro recoiled in recognition, sickened by whatever appalling power had returned his housecarl into this loathsome semblance of life. Without hesitation, Garro turned Libertas in his hand and beheaded the creature. He fervently hoped that death a second time would be enough. Garro hoped fleetingly that his friend could forgive him.

'Watch yourselves,' he shouted, 'this is a feint!'

The tattered crewmen-things were only to draw their fire from the mutant Astartes behind them. The grotesques hammered across the promenade deck towards them, snorting bilious discharges of gas and firing back with mucus-clogged guns. A shambling form advanced on metal-shod hooves among the undead brethren. It was as big as a brother in Terminator armour, and as Garro laid eyes upon it, the thing seemed to be growing larger by the moment. Metal bent and broke as abnormal curves of discoloured bone issued out of popping boils. A distended belly of scarred, pustulent flesh protruded in an atrocious pregnant mockery, studded with triad clusters of tumescent buboes, and atop all this, girning from ravaged ceramite pieces that still resembled Astartes armour, a striated neck ending in a bulbous skull. The bloodshot, rheumy eyes in the grotesque head turned and found Garro. It winked.

'Do you not find my new aspect pleasing, Nathaniel?' bubbled a disgusting voice. 'Do I offend your delicate senses?'

'Grulgor.' Garro hissed the name like a curse. 'What have you become?'

The Grulgor-creature lowed and twitched as a horn, glistening wet with fluids, emerged from the middle of his brow, echoing the shape of Typhon's horned helmet. 'Better, you hidebound fool, better! The first captain was right. The powers are soon to bloom.' He shuddered again, and flesh peeled away across his back to release tarnished tubes of budding bone.

Garro spat on the decking to clear the stink clogging his throat. The air around Grulgor and his diseased horde was thick with contagion, worse than the acrid atmosphere of the xenos bottle-ship, worse than the toxins of a hundred death worlds. 'Whatever force saw fit to reanimate you, it will be in vain! I'll kill you as many times as I must!'

The bloated monster beckoned with a crooked hand. 'You are welcome to make the attempt, Terran.'

The battle-captain waded into the fight, bolter and sword as one in arcs of death, slicing through diseased meat and matter teeming with parasites, cutting towards the monster. In the play of battle, Garro's mind retreated to the familiar paths of war drills, of melee patterns ingrained in muscle and sinew from thousands of hours of combat. In this state, it should have been easy for him to shutter away the chilling horror these warp-spawned terrors represented, to simply fight and concentrate on that alone. The reverse was the reality, however.

Garro had seen the virus savage these men. He had heard their dying screams from the other side of the blast doors only hours earlier, and they stood before him, transformed into some living embodiment of disease, their freakish parody of life sustained by no manner that he could fathom. Was it sorcery? Could such a thing exist in the Emperor's secular cosmos? Garro's carefully constructed world of deeply held truths and hard-edged realities was crumbling with each passing hour, as if the universe had elected to pick apart what he thought to be true and show him the lie of it. With a near-physical effort, the Death Guard forced the inner turmoil into silence, dragging his mind to the single struggle of the fighting.

Close by, Voyen took a glancing blow from a bolt shell that spattered thick fluid across his shoulder pauldron. The Apothecary reeled to dodge a peculiar morning star of knobbed bone. The weapon found purchase instead in the throat of a junior warrior who died clawing at the cancerous wound it left behind. Garro snarled and his bolter echoed him, a burst of fire slamming the killer back and off his feet. The battle-captain cursed as the mutant Astartes shivered, and then pulled itself slowly upward, leaking tainted blood and viscera. The bolter should have ended its life outright. He stormed in and took the traitor's head with his sword, finishing the job.

Still the shambling, filth-encrusted monstrosities came on, the press of their bodies dividing the lines of Garro's warriors, bunching around them as Grulgor moved to and fro, staying beyond close combat range. Perhaps he should not have been surprised to find these mutants hard to kill. Their advance mimicked the battle doctrine of the XIV Legion, the dogged and relentless progress that formed the core of the Death Guard's infantry dogma. They were matched closely, of that there was no doubt, but Garro's men were only Astartes, and as the Emperor was his witness, he had no true understanding of what his enemies were. Garro knew only that an abhorrence had taken root in him, and that these loathsome perversions of his brethren must be destroyed.

SEPARATED FROM THE other Death Guard, Decius found himself besieged by a gaggle of walking dead from the ship's company, the animated corpse-flesh

of the frigate's crewmen pawing at him and beating
on his armour with clubs made from femurs and
skulls. The flamer was spent and he was fighting
hand-to-hand with the good weight of his
chainsword as it rattled in his grip and the crackling
force of his power fist.

The armoured gauntlet pummelled two conjoined
deckhands into a seeping paste of rancid meat and
bone fragments, and he took a torso apart with a
downward sweep of his blade. The spinning
ceramite teeth of the chainsword left a black rent in
the mutant's body, and from the malodorous
wound poured a waterfall of writhing maggots that
pooled around Decius's boots. He turned around
and cut necks with snapping reports like breaking
wood.

The maggot-blown deckhand staggered backward,
and as Decius looked on in fascinated horror the
man-thing coiled the lips of the bloodless cut back
together. Flies and shiny scarab-like insects swarmed
over the wound and chewed at it, knitting the flesh
with livid sutures beneath the repellent, hellish warp
light from the window slits.

What powers propelled these foes, he wondered?
Decius knew of no science that could make dead flesh
animate once again, and yet here was evidence of just
such an occurrence, hissing and clawing at him. The
resurrected men seemed to bask in the glow from the
immaterium beyond the thick armourglass windows
of the promenade. It played over their bloated, pallid
flesh in chaotic patterns. On some deep level, the
Death Guard marvelled at the resilience and the horrific potency of these swarming plague carriers. They
were living vessels for virulent disease, hosts for the
simplest but most deadly of weapons.

Decius paid for his moment of inattention with a typhoon of pain that ripped down the length of his power fist. Too late, he sensed the blow coming from behind him and tried to turn from it. Grulgor's towering bulk moved fast, too fast for something so corpulent and foul. The freakish warrior's battle knife carved a dull arc through the air; like its owner, what had previously been a fine Astartes weapon was now a decayed version of its former self, the fractal-edged knife of bright lunar steel transformed into a blunted dagger of rusty metal.

The attack was aimed at Decius's shoulder, poised to penetrate his armour and cut his primary heart in two, but the Astartes moved. Decius succeeded in avoiding a killing impact, but still his reflexes were not enough to save him from a slash that cut his ceramite armour wide open. He fell down, turning and yelling as he did so. Pain erupted along his nerves as his power fist malfunctioned where the knife had torn into it.

His eyes widened as he saw rust and corrosion worming out across the damaged metals, a time-lapse pict of decay made real. Decius felt agony chewing at his veins and marrow, and sweat burst out all over him as his implanted organs went into overdrive to stem the tide of secondary infections.

Corruption! He could already see his skin distending and blistering where the plague knife had cut him. Decius's gut churned as the invisible phages that swarmed across Grulgor's blade massed inside him. He fought back bile as the twisted Death Guard loomed over him.

'No man can outlive entropy!' spat Grulgor. 'The mark of the Great Destroyer claims everything!'

His joints swelled and became inflamed and painful. With monumental effort, Decius swung up his chainsword and hefted it. The corpulent mutant rocked back, out of range if the young Astartes tried to slash at him with it, but instead Decius brought it down hard across his arm, just below the elbow joint. With a scream of hate, the young Astartes severed his own limb, letting the plague-ravaged flesh and crumbling metal of his gauntlet fall away.

His vision fogged, the youth's body was at its limits fighting infection and injury, and it could not support his consciousness. Decius's eyes fluttered as his body went slack and dormant.

Grulgor snorted and spat out a gobbet of acid phlegm before raising his plague knife again over Decius's unmoving body. Heavy bolt shells tore into his back and ripped away curls of dead flesh, knocking him off-balance before he could deliver the killing blow.

GARRO'S AIM WAS exact, and it sent the Grulgor-thing stumbling, back towards the hull wall and away from Decius. Nathaniel wanted to look to the boy, to be sure that he was still alive, but his old rival was only wounded and from what Garro could see these reanimated men healed as fast as he could hurt them. All around him, Voyen, Hakur and the others were caught in their own small battles. He pushed questions of the *why* from his mind and concentrated on the *how – how can I kill him?*

Grulgor spun around and let loose a gargling roar, emerald-tinted blood trailing from him in a wet arc. Garro's old foe snatched at him, the plague knife and his cancerous fingers slicing through the air and missing. Garro fired again and heard the hollow clack as his bolter ran dry. Without missing a beat, he let the gun drop and took Libertas in a two-handed grip.

'I knew this moment would come,' gurgled the mutant. 'I would not be denied it. My enmity for you is beyond death!'

Garro grimaced in return. 'You have always been a braggart and a fool, Ignatius. On the field of battle you served a purpose, but now, you are an abomination! You are everything the Astartes stand against, the antithesis of the Death Guard.'

Grulgor spat again and made a clumsy, furious pass that Garro parried with quick replies. 'Nathaniel! So blind! I am the harbinger of the future, you pathetic wretch!' He pounded a crooked-fingered fist on the rusted armour over his breast. 'The warp's touch is the way forward. If you were not so blinkered and mawk-ish, you would see it! The powers that exist out there dwarf the might of your Emperor!' Grulgor pointed his knife at the throbbing crimson light beyond the starship. 'We will be deathless and eternal!'

'No,' said Garro, and took the sword to him. Liber-tas swung low and cut into Grulgor's fleshy, fish-belly white gut, and tore. Nathaniel's blade met diseased meat and to his alarm, it sank inwards.

Instead of cutting through pliant skin, the sword became enveloped in a doughy morass that drew on it like quicksand. Flickers of power from the blade sparked and died. Grulgor rumbled with amusement and puffed out his barrel chest, sucking the weapon into his body. 'There is no victory here for you,' he hissed, 'only contagion and lingering agony. I'll make this ship an offering of screaming meat–'

'Enough!' Garro could not draw the sword out. Instead, he ran it through. With all his might, the battle-captain rode the blade down and carved it out across the mutant's abdomen, forcing a full charge through the crystalline matrix steel. He opened

Grulgor with an angry snarl and Libertas at last came free.

Fatty ropes of serpentine intestine writhed and fell from the cut in loops across the wet decking. The former Astartes wailed and struggled to catch them in his hands, stuffing them back into the maw of his belly. Garro rocked back, the putrid gas from inside the bloated body making his eyes stream and throat clog.

The *Eisenstein*'s deck shivered beneath his feet and for a split-second the captain's attention was taken by a rolling flash of chain lightning that surged around the flanks of the frigate.

He heard Hakur shouting. 'The Geller Field! It's failing!'

Garro ignored Grulgor's hooting laughter as glimmering motes of firelight began to form in the heavy air over their heads. He thought of the homunculus plague bearers and the slashing razor-disc predators from the navis sanctorum. If they came to bolster Grulgor and his changed army, the tide would turn against Garro's men. He could sense the engagement slipping away from him, the certain prediction of the battle's play hard in his thoughts just as it had been on the jorgall bottle-world and a hundred times before. He had only moments before the fight was lost to him.

Grulgor saw the expression on his face and laughed. The mutant Astartes spread his hands to the roiling, churning hell-light outside as a willing supplicant, basking in the alien energies. Outside, the membrane of artificial force that separated the frigate from the madness was disintegrating. Already weakened by the incursion of the pestilent touch that made Grulgor live and the breaches of the warp-beasts, the Geller Field unravelled in flares of exotic radiation, layer upon layer peeling back as if it were flesh flensed from bone.

Garro shouted into his vox, a desperate gambit coming to the fore of his thoughts. 'Qruze!' he cried, 'Heed me! Get us out of the warp, crash reversion! *Now*!'

Over the clash of the skirmish and the buzzing interference, he heard raised voices in the background, the bridge crew reacting with shock at his demands. The Luna Wolf was wary. 'Garro, say again?'

'Drop out of the immaterium! These intruders, the warp must be sustaining them somehow! If we stay here we'll lose the ship!'

'We can't revert!' It was Vought, her words laced with panic. 'We have no idea where we are, we could emerge inside a star or—'

'*Do it!*' The order was a thunderous roar.

'Captain, aye,' Qruze did not hesitate. 'Brace yourself!'

'No, no, no!' Grulgor pounded across the deck towards him, raising his blade. 'You will not deny me my satisfaction! I will see you dead, Garro! I will outlive you!'

The battle-captain brought up his sword and batted Grulgor away. 'Be gone, you stinking freak! Back to your hell and choke on it!'

Through the armoured window slits, a flurry of brilliant blue-white discharges signalled the creation of a warp gate, and the frigate dropped through the screaming maw and back into the realm of real space. Grulgor and his freakish kindred bawled a chorus of agony and frenzy, and dissipated.

Garro saw it with his own eyes and still he could not explain it. He witnessed a roaring, shimmering phantom tear itself from the meat sack of a body, drawn up and away as if it were a leaf caught in a hurricane, and for an instant he saw the shapes of both

the mutant and the man that Ignatius Grulgor had
once been before the screaming shade was torn away.
It vanished through the hull of the ship with dozens
of others, the captured energy of all the twisted Death
Guard. *Souls*, he told himself, his mind unable to fur-
nish any other explanation but this most numinous,
unreal of notions. *Their souls have been taken by the
warp.*

TRAILING FIRE AND pieces of itself, shedding waves of
radiation from the brutal emergency reversion and
the collapse of the Geller bubble, the tiny frigate
returned to common existence in a dark and unpop-
ulated quadrant of interstellar space. There were no
stars to sight, no worlds within range, only dust and
airless void.

Directionless and adrift, the *Eisenstein* fell.

TWELVE

The Void
A Church of Men
Lost

'THE FRAGRANCE OF the sick and the wounded,' said Voyen with grim annoyance, 'this ship reeks of it.'

Garro did not meet his gaze, instead ranging about the interior of *Eisenstein*'s infirmary. The frigate's valetudinarium was filled to bursting, temporary partitions made from sheets of metal segregating the areas of the long chamber to stem any chance of cross-infection. At the far end, hidden behind walls of thick, frosted glass and iron seal doors, was the isolation ward. Garro walked steadily towards it, picking his way around medicae servitors and practitioners. The Apothecary kept pace with him.

'The remains were doused in liquid promethium and set to burn for the better part of a day,' Voyen continued. 'Then servitors were used to eject them into space. The helots were then terminated by Hakur, just to be sure.'

Remains. This was the word they were using to describe the diseased flesh-matter that was all that was left of Grulgor and his men. It was easier to depersonalise it that way, to think of the puddles of ichor and bone as just effluent to be disposed of.

To face the reality of what those corpses had once been, what they became, nothing in the lives of Garro's men had prepared them for such sights.

Voyen, in particular, had taken it poorly. As much as he was a warrior like Garro, he was an oath-sworn healer as well, and for him to witness the dead rise to life as crucibles of seething pestilence troubled the Astartes more deeply than he might ever care to admit. Garro saw it in his hooded eyes, and saw the mirror of his own feelings there as well.

Now they were adrift and their flight stalled for the moment with the Navigator's death, the adrenaline of the battle and chase faded. In its place was the reckoning of what had transpired, the realisation of its bleak import. If death was not the end, if what happened to Grulgor was real and not some kind of warp-spawned illusion... then could such a fate be waiting for all of them? That this might be some element of Horus's pact with betrayal chilled Garro's marrow.

Voyen spoke again. 'Has Sendek had any success with the star maps?'

Garro shook his head, seeing no reason to keep the truth from him. 'The woman, Vought, she has been toiling with him, but the results are not favourable. As closely as they can determine the ship reverted to normal space somewhere beyond the edge of the Perseus Null, but even that is nothing more than an educated guess. No traders or scouts have ever ventured into the zone.' He took a deep breath. How long had they been becalmed out here? Days, or was it weeks? Inside the vessel all was a permanent, smoky twilight that made it difficult to gauge the passage of time.

Voyen hesitated as they passed a section of the wall where refrigerated pods hung in clusters around heavy steel stanchions. 'The autopsy on the Navigator Severnaya was completed and I have viewed it.' He indicated one of the frosted pods. Garro could make out the impression of a drawn grey face inside the capsule. 'It is as Master Carya suspected. The Navigator was injured in the engagement, but he died from the psychic shock of the emergency transition from the warp. The apparent bleed-over took the lives of his adjutants and helots. In his already weakened state, it was inevitable.'

'I might as well have placed my bolter to his skull and pulled the trigger,' Garro frowned. 'I should have known. With all the madness running riot through the ship, I should have known he wouldn't survive the journey.' When Voyen didn't respond straight away, Garro shot him a look. 'What choice did I have?' he said flatly. 'The Geller Field was seconds away from collapse. We would have been torn apart in the warp or obliterated in a drive explosion.'

'You did as you thought right,' Voyen replied, unable to keep an element of reproach from his words.

'First it was Decius questioning me, and now you? You would have made a different choice?'

'I am not a battle-captain,' said the Astartes healer. 'I can only observe the aftermath of the choice my commander made. Our ship lies aimless and astray in uncharted space without means for rescue. The astropaths and Navigators are dead, so we cannot cry for help or chance another venture into the warp.' His eyes flared with restrained anger. 'We have escaped the sedition at Isstvan only to die here, our message unheard and the Warmaster free to reach Terra before word of his perfidy. Despair stalks the corridors of this ship, sir, as real as any mutant killer!'

'As always, I appreciate your candour, Meric,' Garro allowed, resisting the urge to chastise him for daring to voice words that bordered on insubordination. They moved on. 'Tell me about the other casualties.'

'Many of the officers and enlisted crew suffered injuries, and there were several deaths from the... the incursions.'

'And our battle-brothers?'

Voyen sighed. 'Every man who fell in combat with those *things* is dead, lord. Every one except Decius, and even he barely clings to the edge of life.' The Apothecary nodded to the sealed section. 'The infections in his body strive to overwhelm him and I have done all I can with the medicines and equipment at my disposal. I confess I am at the limits of my knowledge with his malady.'

'What are his chances of survival? I want no obfuscation or hedging. Will he live?'

'I cannot answer that, lord. He fights hard, but his strength will eventually wane and this disease that has him is like none I have seen or heard of. It changes from moment to moment to mimic different phages, little by little wearing down his resistance.' Voyen gave him a hard look. 'You should consider granting him release.'

Garro's eyes narrowed. 'Events have forced me to end the lives of too many of my kindred already! Now you would ask me to slit the throat of one who lies too weak to defend himself?'

'It would be a mercy.'

'For whom?' Garro demanded. 'For Decius, or for you? I see the disgust you can barely hide, Voyen. You would rather all evidence of the foulness that attacked us be jettisoned, eh? Easier for you to ignore its consequence and whatever connection it might have to your blasted lodges!'

The Apothecary froze, shocked into silence by his commander's outburst.

Garro saw his reaction and immediately regretted his words. He looked away to see the Luna Wolf approaching. 'I am sorry, Meric, I spoke out of turn. My frustration overtook my reason–'

Voyen hid his wounded expression. 'I have duties I must address, lord. By your leave.' He moved away as Qruze came closer.

The old Astartes threw a glance after him. 'We think we have seen it all and yet there always comes a day when the universe shows us the folly of that hubris.'

'Aye,' managed Garro.

Qruze nodded to himself. 'Captain, I took the liberty of compiling an order of battle for your review, following the retreat from Isstvan.' He handed over a data-slate and Garro scanned the names. 'Just over forty line Astartes and half that number of men of veteran ranking, including myself. Five warriors severely injured in the escape but capable of meeting battle, should it come to it. The count does not include you or the Apothecary.'

'Solun Decius is not listed.'

'He's in a coma, is he not? He is an invalid and cannot fight.'

The captain tapped a balled fist on his augmetic leg with a defiant grimace. 'Some dared to say that to me and I made a lie of it! While Decius lives, he's still one of my men,' Garro retorted. 'You'll add him to the roll until I tell you otherwise.'

'As you wish,' said Qruze.

Garro weighed the slate in his hand. 'Seventy men, Iacton. Out of thousands of Astartes at Isstvan, we are all that still live beyond the reach of the Warmaster's treachery.' The words were still difficult for him to say aloud, and he saw that Qruze found it just as hard to hear them.

'There will be others,' insisted the Luna Wolf. 'Tarvitz, Loken, Varren... all of them are good, staunch warriors who won't see such rebellion without opposing it.'

'I do not question that,' replied the Death Guard, 'but when I think of them left behind while we fled for the warp–' He broke off, his voice tightening. The memory of the virus bombing was still painful. 'I wonder how many made it to shelter before the plague and the firestorm. If only we could have saved some of them, rescued a few more of our brethren.' Garro thought of Saul Tarvitz and Ullis Temeter, and hoped that death had come quickly for his friends.

'It is the duty of this vessel to be a messenger, not a lifeboat. For all we can know, other ships may have slipped away, or gone to ground. The fleet is huge and the Warmaster cannot have eyes everywhere.'

'Perhaps,' said Garro, 'but I cannot look upon my brothers hereabouts and not see those we left to face Horus.' He stood, his glove pressed to the thick armourglass of the containment chamber, and studied the papery face of Decius where the youth lay amid a nest of life-support devices and auto-narthecia. 'I feel like I have aged centuries in a day,' he admitted.

Qruze snorted in a dry chuckle. 'Is that all? Live as long as I have and you'll come to understand that it's not the years that count, it's the distance you travel.'

Garro broke away from the sight of his comrade. 'Then by that reckoning, I am older still.'

'With all due respect, you're a stripling, Battle-Captain Garro.'

'You think so, Luna Wolf?' Garro replied. 'You forget the nature of the realm through which we pass. I would warrant that were we to match our days of birth to the Imperial calendar, I would be as old as you, brother, perhaps even your senior.'

'Impossible,' scoffed the other Astartes.

'Is it? Time moves at different rates on Terra and Cthonia. In the warp it becomes malleable and unpredictable. When I think of the years I have spent in passage through that infernal domain or in the little-death of coldsleep on voyages below the speed of light... I may not match you in days, but in chronology the story would be quite different.' He looked back at Decius. 'I see this poor, untempered boy and I wonder if he will ever live to see the glory and the scope of what I have known. Today, I feel more weary than I ever have before. All those days escaped and deaths postponed drag at me. Their weight threatens to pull me under.'

The veil of long-suffering temper that was Qruze's usual mien dropped away for a moment, and the old soldier placed a hand on Garro's shoulder. 'Brother, this is the weight we bear all our living days, the burden of the Astartes as the Emperor gave it to us. We must carry the future of mankind and the Imperium upon our backs, keep it safe and held high for Him. Today that burden weighs more than it ever has, and we have seen that there are those among our number who cannot support it any longer. They chose...' He took a deep breath. '*Horus* chose to throw it aside and become an oath-breaker, so we must bear it without him. You must bear it, Nathaniel. The alarm we hold cannot sound unheard out here in the darkness. You must do whatever must be done in order to warn Terra. All other concerns, our lives and those of our brothers, come a distant second to that mission.'

'Aye,' said Garro, after a few moments. 'You only voice the words I heed inside myself, but it braces me to hear another say them.'

'The Half-heard is heard at last, eh? A pity it has taken such a turn of events to bring that to pass.'

'I accept my lot in this,' the Death Guard noted, fingering the oath paper sealed to the breastplate of his power armour, 'and yet I do not understand it.'

'Understanding is not required,' Qruze quoted the old axiom, 'only obedience.'

'Not true,' reasoned Garro. 'Obedience, *blind obedience*, would have made us follow Horus to his banner and go against the Emperor. What I wish to understand is *why*, Iacton. Why would he do this, to his father of all men?'

'The question that comes again and again.' A shadow passed over the Luna Wolf's face. 'Damn me, Nathaniel. Damn me if I didn't see this coming but had too much pride to accept it.'

'The lodges,'

'And more,' said Qruze. 'In hindsight I see trivial things that meant so little at the time, turns of phrase and looks in the eyes of my kinsmen. Now, under the light of what has transpired, suddenly they show a different aspect.' He mused for a moment. 'The death of Xavyer Jubal on Sixty-Three Nineteen, the burning of the Interex... Davin, it was on Davin that things began to turn, where the momentum came to a head. Horus fell and then he rose, healed by the arcane. I knew then, even if I dared not take the scope of it.

Men took the good and open nature of our brotherhood and turned it slowly to meet their own ends.
Dark shadows grew over the hearts of warriors who
had once been devoted and loyal, Astartes I had seen
grow from whelps to fine, upstanding brothers. When
I finally spoke of these things, they thought me an old
fool with nothing to provide but war stories and a target for their mockery.' The Luna Wolf looked away.
'My crime, brother, my crime was that I let them. I
took the easy road.'

Garro shook his head. 'If that were true, then you
would not be here. If events of recent days have
taught me anything, it is that there comes a moment
for each of us when we are *tested.*' As he said it, once
again Euphrati Keeler came to the surface of his
thoughts. 'What happens in that moment is the true
measure of us, Iacton. We cannot break, old man. If
we do, then we *will* be damned.'

Qruze chuckled softly. 'Strange, is it not, that we
choose that word? A term so loaded with overtones of
religion and holy creed, at polar opposites to the secular truth we are oath-bound to serve.'

'Belief is not always a matter of religion,' said Garro.
'Faith can be a thing of men as well as gods.'

'You think so? Perhaps then you ought to venture
below decks and visit the empty water store on the
forty-ninth tier, and share your viewpoint with those
gathered there.'

Garro's brow furrowed. 'I do not follow you.'

'I have learned there is a church aboard your ship,
captain,' said Iacton, 'and the congregation swells
with each passing day.'

SINDERMANN LOOKED UP as Mersadie tapped him on
the shoulder. He put down the electroquill and slate.

He saw she had a couple of men with her, two junior officers in the uniforms of the engineering division.

The remembrancer hesitated, and one of the men spoke. 'We've come to see the Saint.'

Kyril threw a sideways glance along the length of the makeshift chapel. He saw Euphrati down there, talking and smiling. 'Of course,' he began. 'You may have to wait.'

'That's all right,' said the other. 'We're off-shift. Couldn't make the… the sermon before.'

The iterator smiled slightly. 'It was hardly that, just a few people of like mind, talking.' He nodded to the dark-skinned woman. 'Mersadie, why don't you take these young gentlemen up?' He patted his pockets. 'I think I have a tract I could give you both.'

'Got one already,' said the man who'd spoken first. He showed Sindermann a frayed booklet with the kind of rough printing that came from old and rusted machinery. It wasn't a pamphlet he had seen before, not one of those that had circulated on the *Vengeful Spirit*. It appeared that the *Lectitio Divinitatus* had already made inroads aboard the *Eisenstein* long before his arrival.

Oliton led the men away, and Kyril watched her go. Like all of them, only now was Mersadie coming to understand the path that was laid out before her. Sindermann knew she was holding true to her calling as a remembrancer, but the recollections that she stored in the memory spools of her augmented skull were not tales of the Great Crusade and of Horus's glory. Mersadie had gently moved into the role of documentarist for their nascent credo. It was Euphrati Keeler's stories that she wrote now, storing them and weaving them into a coherent whole. Kyril looked down at the data-slate where he had been attempting to marshal his own thoughts, and reflected. How could he ever have expected to become part of something like this? All around him, a church, a system of belief was accreting, gaining mass and potency beneath the shadow of the Warmaster's rebellion. How could any fate have judged that he, Kyril Sindermann, primary iterator of the Imperial truth, was suited for this new role? And yet here he found himself, shepherding the words of Keeler, moulding them for the ears of the people even as Mersadie stood at his side, blink-clicking still images and recording Euphrati's every deed.

Not for the first time, Sindermann traced the line of events that had brought him here and pondered how things might have played had he spoken differently, thought differently. He had no doubt that he would be dead by now, gunned down in the mass termination of the remembrancers aboard Horus's battle-barge. It was only the intervention of Loken's comrade Qruze that had saved their lives. The echo of the fear he felt at the sight of the bombing of Isstvan III whispered through him again. Death had been only a moment away, and yet Euphrati had shown no apprehension. She had known that they would live, just as she had been able to guide them to this ship and their escape. Once he would have rejected ideas of divine powers and of the so-called saints who communed with them. Euphrati Keeler took that scepticism away from him with her quiet authority, and made him question the secular light of unswerving reason he had lived his life in service to.

They had all been changed after that day at the Whisperhead Mountains, when Jubal had transformed into something that still defied categorisation in Sindermann's thoughts. A *daemon?* In the end,

Kyril was unable to find any other means to explain it away. His light of logic fled from him, his precious Imperial truth was found lacking. Then the horror had come again, this time to destroy them all.

But he lived. *They* lived, thanks to Euphrati. With his own eyes, Sindermann saw her turn the might of a warp-spawned monstrosity with nothing more than a silver aquila and her faith in the Emperor of Mankind. His need for denial perished with the hateful creature that day, and the iterator saw truth, *real truth*. Keeler was an instrument of the Emperor's will. There was no other explanation for it. In His greatness – no, in His *divinity* – the Emperor had granted the imagist some splinter of His might. They had all been changed, yes, but Euphrati Keeler the most of all.

Gone was the defiant but directionless young woman whose picts had caught the history around them. In her stead there was a new creation, a woman both finding and forging the path for all of them. Kyril should have been afraid. He should have been terrified that they would perish fleeing from Horus's perfidy. A single look at Keeler made that all disappear. He watched her talk to the two engineers, smiling and nodding, and a warmth spread through him. *This is faith*, he realised, *and it is such a heady sensation!* It was no wonder that the believers he had encountered during the Crusade resisted so hard, if this was what they felt.

Now, in the *Lectitio Divinitatus*, Kyril Sindermann found the same strength. His loyalty and love for the Imperium had never swayed. Now, if it were possible, he felt an even deeper devotion to the Lord of Man. He was ready to give himself to the Emperor, not just in heart and mind, but in body and soul.

He was not alone in this. The Cult of Terra, as it was sometimes known, was strengthening. The pamphlet in the engineer's hands, the ease with which Mersadie was able to find this disused water reservoir in which to assemble their makeshift chapel, all these things showed that the *Lectitio Divinitatus* existed on this vessel. And if it was here on this small, unremarkable frigate, then perhaps it was elsewhere too, not just concealed in the midst of Horus's fleet but maybe further afield, on worlds and ships spread across the Imperium. This faith was on the cusp of becoming a self-actualised creation, and all it needed was an icon to rally behind, a living saint.

Euphrati made the sign of the aquila and the two engineers followed suit. The hollow, nervous mood he had seen in their eyes upon their arrival was gone, and they walked away with purposeful strides, a new assurance in their spirits.

'The Emperor protects,' said the younger of the two as he passed the iterator, nodding in thanks. Kyril returned the gesture. The girl gave them faith and calmed their fears as she had with dozens of others. The train of men and women finding their way to this rough-hewn chapel had been slow at first, but now they were coming more often, to listen to him speak or merely to be in the presence of the young woman. Sindermann marvelled how word of Keeler had spread.

'Kyril!' He turned to see Mersadie coming towards him in a rush, her perfect face turned in abject fear. 'Someone is coming!' The hushed dread in her words brought back memories of the secret ministry on the *Vengeful Spirit*, and of the men who had come at the Warmaster's behest with bolters and clubs to destroy it. 'A lookout reported in, just one of them: a single Astartes.'

Sindermann stood up. He could hear heavy boot steps ringing off the gantry deck outside the service hatch to the reservoir chamber, coming closer. 'Did the lookout see a weapon? Was he armed?'

'When are they not?' Oliton piped. 'Even without sword or gun, when are they not?'

His answer was lost as the hatch slammed open and the reverberation put every other sound to silence. A towering form in marble-white armour bent to enter the compartment and the iterator saw the glitter of polished brass on an eagle's-head cuirass. Sindermann stepped forward and gave a shallow bow to the Death Guard, fighting down his trepidation. 'Captain Garro, welcome. You are the first Astartes to come here.'

GARRO LOOKED DOWN at the slight man. He was thin and nervous, a cluster of sticks in an iterator's robes, but his gaze was steady and his voice did not waver. 'Sindermann,' noted Garro. He looked around at the inside of the reservoir. It was a large, cylindrical space some two decks tall, with grid-decked gantries on different levels and a network of pipes and vent shafts protruding into the chamber. Tall sheets of metal extended out from the walls to act as baffles when the drum was full of water, but when the chamber stood empty as it did now, they gave the place the look of a chapel knave rendered in old, bare steel. Cargo pallets from the service decks had been arranged as makeshift seating and there was an altar of sorts made from a fuel cell container. 'Are you the architect of all this?'

'I'm only an iterator,' replied the man.

'What are you doing in here?' Garro demanded, a conflict of anger and frustration rising inside him. 'What do you hope to achieve?'

'That would be my question for you, Nathaniel.' The imagist, the woman they were calling the Saint, walked forward into the light of a string of biolumes.

'Keeler,' he said carefully, 'you and I will speak.'

She nodded and beckoned him. 'Of course.'

'You won't hurt her!' The other remembrancer, the one Qruze identified as Mersadie Oliton, snapped at him. Her words were half in threat, half in desperation, and Garro raised an eyebrow at her temerity.

Keeler spoke again, her voice carrying to all the silent congregation in attendance. 'Nathaniel is here because he is no different from any one of us. We all seek a path, and perhaps I can help him to find his.'

And so, saint and soldier found a place in a shaded corner, and sat across from one another at the fringes of the lamplight.

'THERE ARE QUESTIONS,' she began, pouring cups of water for Garro and for herself. 'I'll answer them if I can.'

The captain grimaced and took the tiny tin goblet in his hands. 'This cult goes against the will of the Imperium. You should not have brought your beliefs here.'

'I could no more leave this than you could leave behind your loyalty to your brothers, Nathaniel.'

Garro grunted and drained the cup with a grim sneer. 'And yet I have done exactly that, some would say. I have fled the field of battle, and for what? Horus and my own primarch will name me deserter for doing so. Men I have sworn to honour I have left to an uncertain fate, and even in my fleeing I have executed that poorly.'

'I asked you to save us, and you have.' Keeler watched him kindly. 'And you will. You are the embodiment of your Legion's name. You guard us against death. There is no failure in that.'

He wanted to dismiss her words as insincere and accuse her of speaking empty platitudes, but despite himself, Garro found he was grateful for her praise. He forced the thoughts away and pulled Kaleb's papers from his belt pouch, the brass icon and its chain wrapped around them. 'What meaning do these things have, woman? The Emperor is a force against false deities, and yet your doctrine talks of him as a god. How can this be right?'

'You answer your own question, Nathaniel,' she replied. 'You said "false deities", did you not? The truth, the real Imperial truth, is that the Master of Mankind is no sham divinity. He's the real thing. If we acknowledge that, He will protect us.' Garro snorted, but Keeler kept speaking. 'In the past, a priest would ask you for faith based on nothing but words in a book, a tract.' She gestured to the bundle of papers. 'Does the Emperor do that? Answer my question, Astartes. Have you not felt His spirit upon you?'

It took an effort of will for Garro to speak. 'I have, or so I think... I am not certain.'

Keeler leaned back in her chair, and her beatific, metered manner dropped away. She became challenging and focused, eschewing the saintly serenity he expected from her. 'I don't believe you. I think you *are* certain, but that you are so set in your ways that to voice it frightens you.'

'I am Astartes,' Garro growled. 'I fear nothing.'

'Until today.' She eyed him. 'You are afraid of this truth, because it is of such magnitude that you will forever be remade by it.' Keeler placed her hand on his gauntlet. 'What you do not realise is that you have already been changed. It's only your mind that lags behind your spirit.' She studied him carefully. 'What do you believe in?'

He answered without hesitation, 'My brothers, my Legion, my Emperor, my Imperium, but some of those are being taken from me.'

Euphrati tapped him on the chest. 'Not from here.' She hesitated. 'I know you Astartes have two hearts, but you understand my meaning.'

'What I have seen…' His voice grew soft. 'It pulls at the roots of my reason. I am questioning all that I thought absolute. The xenos psyker child that saw into me, that mocked me with jibes about what was to come… Grulgor, dead and yet returned to life by some gruesome infection… and you, glimpsed in my death-sleep.' He shook his head. 'I am as adrift as this ship. You say I have certainty but I do not sense it. All I see are paths to ruin, a maze of doubt.'

The woman sighed. 'I know how you feel, Nathaniel. Do you think that I wanted this?' She pulled at the robes she wore. 'I was an imagist, and a damned good one. I depicted history as it was made. My art was known on thousands of worlds. Do you think that I wanted to feel the hand of a god upon me, that I dreamed one day of becoming a prophet? What we are is as much where destiny takes us as it is what we do with the journey.' Keeler gave a slight smile. 'I envy you, Captain Garro. You have something I do not.'

'What is that?'

'A duty. You know what it is that you must do. You can find that clarity of vision, a mission that you can grasp and strive to fulfil. But me? Each day of my calling is new, a different challenge, constantly striving to find the right path. All I can be sure of is that I have an aspiration, but I can't yet see its shape.'

'You are of purpose,' murmured the Astartes.

'We both are,' agreed Keeler. 'We *all* are.' Then she reached out and touched his cheek, and the sensation of her fingers against his rough, scarred face sent a tingle through Garro's nerves. 'Since you delivered this ship from the predations of the warp, some of the crew have been praying here for a miracle to save us. They asked me why I did not join them in their calls to the Emperor and I told them there was no need. I told them: "He has already saved us. We only have to wait for His warrior to find the means"'.

'Is that what I am? The Emperor's divine will, made flesh?'

She smiled again, and with it she brought forth again the flutter of powerful emotion that Garro had felt alone in the barracks. 'Dear Nathaniel, when have you ever been anything else?'

'STATUS,' ORDERED QRUZE, catching Sendek's eye at the control console.

The Death Guard nodded at the Luna Wolf with more than a little weariness in his manner. 'Unchanged,' he replied, casting about the bridge to see if any of the officers had anything else to add. Carya met his gaze and silently shook his head. Many of the shipmaster's crew, including the woman Vought, had been granted temporary suspension of their duties in light of the empty void where they found themselves, leaving the ever-wakeful Astartes to man the bridge while the men and women took some small respite. 'Machine-call signals continue to cycle on the short-range vox, although at a generous estimate they will not reach any human ears for at least a millennium.'

The old warrior's brows knitted. 'Do you have anything constructive to add?'

Sendek nodded. 'In the interests of posterity, I have commenced mapping this sector of space. Perhaps if this vessel is recovered at some future date, the data may be of use to those who find it.'

Qruze made a spitting noise. 'Are all you Death Guard this pessimistic? We're not corpses yet.'

'I prefer to think of myself as a realist,' Sendek bristled.

Both men turned as the bridge hatch irised open to admit the Apothecary Voyen. Sendek was still finding it hard to forgive Voyen's association with the lodges and he looked away. The Astartes was aware that Qruze saw the moment between the two battle-brothers, remarking silently upon it with a quizzical look.

'Where is the battle-captain?' asked Voyen.

'Below decks,' replied Qruze. 'I have the conn. You may address yourself to me, son.'

'As you wish, third captain. I have completed a survey of the ship's stores and consumable supplies. If we instigate rationing at subsistence levels, it is my projection that Eisenstein's crew have just over five and one-third months of available resources.'

Carya came forward and ventured a suggestion. 'Could we not put some of the non-essential crew into suspension?'

Voyen nodded. 'That is a possibility, but with the facilities aboard this ship that would only lengthen the duration by another month, perhaps two. I have also examined the option of other emergency measures, such as a cull, but the outcomes are little different.'

The shipmaster grimaced. 'We're not picking any of my men for voluntary execution, if that's what you're thinking!'

'Seven months at sublight in the middle of the void,' said Sendek as the bridge hatch opened once more, 'and Horus out there all the while with Terra unaware of it.'

Garro entered, his stride firm and purposeful. 'Not on my watch. We have come too far to sit back and wait for death to claim us. We have to act.' He nodded to Carya. 'Shipmaster, signal the enginarium crews to charge the warp motors to full power.'

'Captain, unless that saint singing her hymns down below has grown a third eye and plans to guide us home, we cannot hope to travel any interstellar distance!' Voyen's manner became acid and terse. 'We have no Navigator, sir! If we enter the warp, we will be lost forever and those things that attacked us last time will have eternity to pick us apart!'

'I never said we were returning to the warp,' Garro replied coolly. 'Carya, how long until the drive blocks are at maximum potency?'

The officer studied his console. 'A few moments, lord.' He hesitated. 'Sir, your Apothecary is correct. I fail to see the reason for bringing the drives back on line.'

Garro didn't answer the implied question. 'I want sublight thrusters ready for a burn at full military power on my command. Call the ship to general quarters and prepare void shields for activation.'

Voyen gestured around the bridge as the alert siren sounded. 'Thrusters and shields now? Is this some sort of drill, Nathaniel? Some kind of make-work to distract the crew, or did the prophet girl tell you that an attack is coming?'

'Watch your tone,' said Garro. 'My lenience only extends so far.'

'Thrusters at your command,' reported Carya. 'Shields ready to be deployed.'

'Hold,' ordered the battle-captain.

From across the bridge, Qruze rubbed his chin. 'Are we going to learn the point of all this activity, lad? I confess I'm as blind to it as the sawbones there.'

Carya looked up. 'Warp drives registering full energy capacity. Battery arrays are brimming, lord. What do you want me to do with them?'

'Clear the drive block compartments, and arm the release mechanisms on the warp motors. When I give the order, you will deactivate the engine governance controls and jettison the drive block, then raise shields and fire the sublight thrusters.'

Qruze chuckled coldly. 'You're as bold as you are mad!'

'Eject the warp engines?' Sendek gaped. 'With all that energy in them, they'll detonate like a supernova!'

Garro nodded solemnly. 'A warp flare. The blast will echo in the immaterium as well as real space. It will act as a beacon for any ships within a hundred parsecs.'

'No!' Voyen's shout cut across the bridge. 'For Terra's sake, no! This is a step too far, captain! It's a death sentence!'

Garro shot him a hard stare. 'Open your eyes, Meric! Everything we have done since we defied the Warmaster has been a death sentence, and yet we still survive! I will not give up now, not after all this flight has cost us!' He reached out and put a hand on the Apothecary's shoulder. 'Trust me, brother. We will be delivered from this.'

'No,' Voyen repeated, and in a swift blur of movement the Death Guard veteran drew his bolt pistol, bringing it to bear between Garro's eyes. 'I will not let you do this. You'll kill us all, and everything that we

have sacrificed will have been for nothing!' Dread
filled his voice. 'Tell Carya to rescind those orders or I
will shoot you where you stand!'

Sendek and Qruze went for their weapons, but
Garro barked out a command. 'Stay your hands! This
is between Meric and I, and we alone will decide it.'
He met the Apothecary's gaze. 'Shipmaster Carya,'
said the battle-captain, 'you will execute my commands in sixty seconds. *Mark.*'

'Y-yes, sir,' the officer stuttered. Like everyone on the
bridge, he was fully aware of the danger of what Garro
had set in motion. The veteran was right. It could
mean the destruction of the ship if the *Eisenstein*'s
thrusters couldn't push the frigate far enough from
the blast radius of the warp flare.

Voyen thumbed back the hammer on the pistol.
'Captain, please don't test me! I will follow any
orders you give, but not this one! You've let that
woman cloud your thoughts.'

The dark maw of the gun never wavered before
Garro's face. At so close a range, a single shell from the
weapon would turn the Death Guard's unprotected
head into a red mist. 'Meric, it does not matter if you kill
me. It will still happen and the ship will still be rescued,
and our warning will still be carried to the Emperor. I
won't see it, but I'll die content knowing that it will
come to pass. I have faith, brother. What do you have?'

'Thirty seconds,' reported Qruze. 'Release bolts are
armed. The governance circuits are off-line. The overload is building.'

'You've driven me to this,' cried Voyen. 'Death and
death, and more death, brothers ranged against
brothers... how can you be certain we will not be corrupted as Grulgor and his men were? We'll become
like them! Abominations!'

Garro held out his hand. 'We will not. There is no doubt in my mind.'

'How can you know?' shouted the Astartes, the pistol faltering.

Garro carefully reached out and took the gun from him. 'The Emperor protects,' he said simply.

'Zero,' announced the Luna Wolf.

THIRTEEN

Silent Watch
Fearless
Found

HUNDREDS OF EXPLOSIVE charges around the rear ventral hull of the frigate went off in the silence of space, throwing sheets of hull plating away into the void. On rails, the thick cylinders of the starship's interstellar drive motors rolled out and fell into the darkness, conduits snapping and trailing jets of coolant liquid, cables arcing with glints of electricity. Crackling orbs of gathered energy spun and cried inside the discarded warp engines. Power that normally would have been channelled into ripping a doorway to the immaterium had no point of release, and now it churned about itself, faster and faster, spiralling towards critical mass.

The *Eisenstein* leapt away on rods of glittering fusion fire, leaving behind the parts of itself that she had cut loose. As the flexing gravitational output of the warp drives drew the drifting modules together, they sent out whips of brilliant blue-white lightning that lashed blindly, snapping at the frigate's heels. Her void shields glowed but held firm. The true test of them would come in a few seconds.

The engine cores began to melt and deform, the power inside them grown to such capacity that it was a self-fulfilling reaction, drawing potency from the differential states between the dimensions of the warp and the common vacuum of real space. Circular sheets of exotic radiation, visible though the entire spectrum, radiated out of the lumpen cluster of matter and energy. Too soon the warp motors had ripped into the madness of the immaterium, and the rush of force that flooded out was too much, too fast.

The reaction collapsed inward, the jettisoned hull panels, the slagged metals, dust and specks of free-floating hydrogen molecules, the very space around it folding in a final desperate trawl to fuel itself.

If there was an eye that could have seen something so abnormal or glimpsed into a range so far from that of normal sight, an observer might have glimpsed a screaming, clawing beast peering out of the core of the implosion, but then came the detonation.

Across barriers of dimension, the catastrophic destruction of the warp motors produced a sphere of radiation that lit space like a dying sun. In the empyrean, it became a towering shriek, a flash of dead blue, a surge of raw panic and a million other things. In real space it was a wave of crackling discharge that slammed into the fleeing *Eisenstein* and threw her bow over stern with murderous, lethal force.

IN THE DEEP shades of the empyrean, the ragged edge of a shockwave broke upon the preternatural senses of an enhanced mind. The wash of raw input blotted out all other thought-sights in an instant of punishing, agonising overload. It struck the storms of insanity that clung to the mind and tore them away, blasting them apart. The mind was tossed and thrown in the impact, flailing for unending seconds in the turbulent undertow of its passing. Then the flare was gone, fading, leaving only the echo of its creation. Where there had been storms and fog, now there was clarity and lucidity.

The mind turned and peered across the wilderness of the immaterium and found the point of origin. As a flash of night-borne lightning might illuminate a darkened landscape, the shockwave made the molten terrain of the warp visible, gave it solidity when all other means of understanding had failed. Suddenly, paths that had been concealed were clear and discernible. The way was abruptly opened, and across the incredible distance, the epicentre of the effect's creation still burned.

With care, the mind began to compute a route to take it there, curiosity brimming from every contemplation.

GARRO PUT DOWN the electroquill and ran his gaze down the text rendered on the flat, glassy face of the data-slate. He released a deep breath and a cloud of white vapour emerged, fading into the cold, thin air of the observatorium. Everything in the chamber was covered in a thin patina of hoarfrost, the steel stanchions and the wide sweeps of the windows painted with patches of white. In the shockwave of the warp flare, several power mechanisms already stressed by the headlong escape from the Isstvan system failed entirely, and whole decks of the frigate were without life-support. Carya had closed the flying bridge and moved the command crew to a secondary control pulpit, leaving the upper deck to go dead and dark. Moment by moment, the *Eisenstein* was becoming a frozen tomb.

'Captain,' Qruze said coming into view, lit by the dull glow of the starlight through the frosted armour-glass, 'you summoned me?'

Garro showed him the data-slate. 'I want you to witness this.' Nathaniel removed his gauntlet and pressed the commander's signet on his left forefinger to a sensor plate on the slate's case. The device chimed, recognising the unique pattern of the ring and the gene-code of the wearer. He passed it to the Luna Wolf and the old warrior paused for a moment, reading what was written there.

'A chronicle?'

'Perhaps it would be more accurate to think of it as a last will and testament. I have recorded here all the events of note that preceded our escape from the fleet, and all matters since. There should be a testimony for our kinsmen to find, even if we do not live to deliver it ourselves.'

Qruze snorted and mirrored Garro's actions, sealing the contents of the slate with a touch from his signet. 'Planning for the worst. First that boy Sendek and now you? Death Guard by name, dour by nature, is it?'

Garro took the slate back and secured it in an armoured case. 'I only wish to cover every eventuality. This container will survive explosion and vacuum, even the destruction of the ship.'

'So those words on the bridge, then? Your declaration to the Apothecary, all that was just an act, captain? You tell us you know we will survive, but secretly you prepare in case we do not?'

'I did not lie, if that is what you are implying,' snarled Garro. 'Yes, I believe we will see Terra, but there is no harm in being thorough. That is the Death Guard way.'

'Yet you do this thing out of sight of the men, with only a Luna Wolf in attendance? Is that perhaps because you would rather not undermine the faith you have kindled in the others?'

Garro looked away. 'Age has not dulled your insight, Iacton. You are correct.'

'I understand. In times like this, conviction is all a man can cling to. Before... before Isstvan, we might have looked to our faith in our Legions, our primarchs. Now, we must find it where we can.'

'The Emperor is still our constant,' Garro said, looking out at the stars. 'Of that, I have no doubt.'

Qruze nodded. 'Aye, I suppose so. You have made believers of us, Nathaniel. Besides, that chronicle of yours is a wasted effort.'

'How so?'

'The story there is only half-told.'

Garro's scarred face turned in a faint smile. 'Indeed. I wonder how it will end?' He walked away a few steps, thin rimes of ice crunching under his boots.

'Has your saint not told you?' Qruze asked, a note of wry reproof in his words.

'She is not *my* saint,' Garro retorted. 'Keeler is... she has vision.'

'That may be so. Certainly, enough of the crew seem to agree. There are many more attending her sermons on the lower decks. I have it on good authority that the iterator Sindermann has moved their makeshift church to a larger compartment among the armoury decks, to better accommodate them.'

Garro considered this. 'Closer to the inner hull spaces. It will be warmer there, more protected.'

'There have been Astartes seen in attendance, captain. It appears your conference with the woman has given legitimacy to her claims.'

Garro eyed him. 'You don't approve.'

'Idolatry is not the Imperial way.'

'I see no idols, Iacton, only someone who has a purpose in the Emperor's service, just as you and I do.'

'Purpose,' echoed the Luna Wolf. 'That is what this all comes down to, is it not? In the past, we have never had to struggle to find it. Purpose has always been given to us, passed on from Emperor to primarch to Astartes. Now events force us to seek it alone, and we splinter. Horus finds his in sorcery, and we... we seek ours in a divinity.' He chuckled dryly. 'I never thought I would live to see the like.'

'If your wisdom of years allows you to find another path, tell me of it,' Garro said firmly. 'This way is the only one that opens to me.'

Qruze bowed his head. 'I would not dare, battle-captain. I granted you my fealty, and I will follow your commands to the letter.'

'Even if you disagree with them? I saw the reproach in your eyes on the bridge.'

'You allowed the Apothecary to go without him being chastised for his actions.' Qruze shook his head. 'It was a punishable offence towards a senior officer. He drew a weapon on you, Garro, in anger!'

'In *fear*,' Garro corrected. 'He allowed his emotions to overtake him for a moment. He is chastened by his actions. I won't put a man to the whip for that.'

'Your warriors question it,' pressed the other Astartes. 'For now they see it as lenience, but some might think it to be a sign of weakness.'

He looked away. 'Then let them. Brother Voyen is the best Apothecary we have. I need him. Decius needs him.'

'Ah,' the Luna Wolf nodded. 'It becomes clearer to me. You want the youth to survive.'

'What I want is to lose no more of my brothers to this madness!' snapped Garro tersely. 'The rest of my Legion may fall to disloyalty or death, but not these men! Not mine!' His breath came out in clouds around him. 'Mark me, Iacton Qruze. I will not have the Death Guard become a watchword for corruption and betrayal!'

There was a note of genuine pain in the old warrior's words as he looked down at the power armour he wore, still bearing the altered colour scheme of the Sons of Horus. 'Good luck in that, kinsman,' he said quietly. 'For me, I fear that moment has already passed.'

POWER ROUTED TO the valetudinarium from other sections of the *Eisenstein* ensured that the infirmary was kept at a functional level. Garro was aware that Voyen had initiated a move of all but the most badly injured patients to the deeper levels of the ship, in towards the core of the vessel. The battle-captain did not see the Astartes healer as he crossed the chamber, and felt better for it. Despite his words to Qruze, Garro still smarted at Voyen's actions on the bridge and he did not want to encounter him again so soon afterwards. It was better that the Apothecary kept his distance for the moment.

Garro stepped around an injured officer whose only inhalations came from a mechanical breather machine, and stopped at the glass pod of the isolation chamber. With care, Garro took his helmet – the repairs upon it were still visible, unfinished spots where paint had yet to be applied – and sealed it to the neck ring of his armour. Then, after checking the seals on every joint and vent, he locked down the battle suit, preventing any possibility of outside contagions entering his wargear. Garro passed through the chamber's airlock array and entered the sealed room. A medicae servitor tended to Decius with slow, deliberate care. The captain noted that the fleshy components of the machine-helot were already grey with infection. Voyen's reports noted that two servitors had died already from slow exposure to whatever poison Grulgor had poured into the youth's wound. It was a testament to the potency of the Astartes biology that Decius was not dead a dozen times over.

Inside the armour Garro would be safe, and the stringent purification systems of the isolation chamber would stop any contamination following him out. He had no doubts that the chance of infection still existed, but he would risk it. He had to look the lad in the eye.

There on the recovery cradle, Solun Decius lay stripped of his power armour and swaddled in a mesh-like covering of metallic probes and narthecia injectors. The wound where Grulgor's plague knife had cut him was a mess of pustules and livid flesh on the verge between bilious life and necrotic death. It refused to knit closed, bleeding into a catch-bowl beneath the cradle. Portions of Decius's skin were missing where the medicae had plugged feed ducts and mechadendrites directly into the raw nerves. A forest of thin steel needles colonised the thick hide of the black carapace across his torso. Thin, white drool looped from Decius's lips and a pipe forced air into his nostrils with rhythmic mechanical clicks.

The Astartes was an ashen rendition of himself, the colour of a week-old corpse. Had Garro seen such a body on the battlefield, he would have cast it on to the pyre and let it burn. For a moment, Nathaniel found his hand near the hilt of Libertas and Voyen's words echoed in his thoughts. *You should consider granting him release.*

'That would make a lie of what I said to Qruze,' he said aloud. 'The fight is all that we have now. The struggle is what defines us, brother.'

'Brother...'

The voice was so faint that at first Garro thought he had imagined it, but then he looked down and saw a flicker of motion as Decius's eyes opened into slits. 'Solun? Can you hear me, boy?'

'I can... hear you.' His voice was thick with mucus. 'I hear it, captain... inside me... the thunder in my blood.'

Suddenly, Garro's sword seemed to be ten times its weight. 'Solun, what do you want?'

Decius blinked, even this smallest of motions appearing to pain him terribly. 'Answers, lord.' He gasped in a breath of air. 'Why have you saved us?'

Garro pulled back in surprise. 'I had to,' he blurted. 'You are my battle-brothers! I could not let you perish.'

'Is that... the better path?' the wounded warrior whispered. 'Unending war between brothers... We saw it, captain. If that... if that is the future, then perhaps...'

'You would have us embrace death?' Garro shook his head. 'I know your pain is great, brother, but you cannot submit to it! We cannot admit defeat!' He placed his hand on Decius's chest. 'Only in death does duty end, Solun, and only the Emperor can grant us that.'

'Emperor...' The word was a dim echo. 'Forsaken... We have been forsaken, my lord, lost and forgotten. The beast Grulgor did not lie... We are alone.'

'I refuse to accept that!' Garro's words became a shout. 'We will find salvation, brother, we will! You must have faith!'

Decius coughed and the pipes in his mouth gurgled, red-green fluid siphoning away into a disposal tank. 'All I have is pain, pain and loss...' His bloodshot eyes found Garro and bored into him. 'We are lost, my captain. We know not where or when we are... The warp has made sport with us, cast us into the void.'

'We will be found.' Garro's words seemed hollow.

'By what, lord? What if... if the time we were lost in the empyrean was not hours... but millennia? The warning... worthless!' He coughed again, his body tensing. 'We may be ten thousand years too late... and our galaxy burns with chaos...' The effort of speaking drained the Astartes and he sank back into the cradle, the shambling servitor creaking to his side with a fan of outstretched fingers made of syringes and blades.

Garro watched Decius's eyelids flutter closed and the youth's consciousness slipped away once more. After a long moment, the battle-captain turned back to the airlocks and began the arduous process of cleansing his wargear of any lingering taint.

WHEN HE STEPPED out of the isolation chamber's outer hatch, he saw Sendek charging towards him across the infirmary, his face tight with tension.

'Captain! When I could not reach you, I feared something had happened!'

Garro jerked a thumb at the chamber's thick walls. 'The protective field baffles in there are electromagnetically charged. Vox signals won't penetrate inside.' He frowned at the alarm in Sendek's voice. 'What is it that requires my attention so urgently?'

'Sir, the *Eisenstein*'s sensor grids were badly damaged in the shock from the warp flare and the engagement with Typhon, and we have only partial function–'

'Spit it out,' snapped Garro.

Sendek took a breath. 'There are ships, captain. We have detected multiple warp gate reactions less than four light-minutes distant. They appear to be moving to an interception heading.'

He should have felt elation. He should have been thinking of rescue, but instead, Garro's black mood brought him only imagined terrors and predictions of the worst. 'How many craft? Mass and tonnage?'

'The sensors gave me only the vaguest of estimates, but it is a fleet, sir, a large one.'

'Horus?' Garro breathed. 'Could he have followed us?'

'Unknown. The ship's external vox transceiver is inoperable, so we cannot search for any identifier beacons.' Sendek paused. 'They could be anything, anyone, perhaps an ally, perhaps ships on their way to join the Warmaster's insurrection, or even xenos.'

'And here we sit, blind and toothless before them.' Garro fell silent, weighing his options. 'If we cannot know the face of these new arrivals, then we must encourage them to show it to us. They must have been drawn by the flare. Any commander worth the rank will send a boarding party to investigate. We will allow it, and from there take the measure of them.'

'At their rate of closure, there is little time to prepare,' Sendek noted.

'Agreed,' Garro said with a nod. 'These are my orders. Issue weapons to all the crew who know how to use them and get everyone else into the core tiers. Find somewhere they can be protected. I want

Astartes at every entry point, ready to repel boarders, but no one is to engage in hostilities unless it is by my word of command.'

'The armoury chambers would be best,' mused Sendek, 'they are heavily shielded. Many of the crew are there already, with the… the woman.'

Garro's lip curled. 'Sanctuary in the new church. It seems fitting.' He gathered up his bolter. 'Quickly, then. We must be ready to meet our saviours or our assassins with equal vigour.'

THEY CROWDED ABOUT the frigate in the manner of wolves circling a wounded prey animal, observing and considering the condition of the *Eisenstein*. Sensor dishes and listening gear turned to face the drifting warship, and learned minds attempted to discern the chain of events that had led to its circumstances.

Vessels that dwarfed the Imperial frigate placed hordes of armed lance cannons upon the ship's target silhouette, computing firing solutions and warming their guns in preparation for her destruction. Only one volley, and even then not one at full capacity, would be enough to obliterate the *Eisenstein* forever. It would only be a matter of a single word of command, a button pushed, a trigger pulled.

The fleet moved slowly. Some of its number had counselled for the immediate destruction of the derelict, concerned that the flare it had generated to bring them here might only have been a lure. Even a ship the size of a mere frigate, when correctly armed and altered, could become a flying bomb big enough to destroy a battle cruiser. Others were more curious. How had a human vessel come to find itself out here, so far from the rim of known space? What lengths had driven those aboard it to give up their engines in the vain hope of rescue? And what enemies had wrought the damage that scarred the armoured hull?

Finally, the predator ships of the war fleet parted to allow the largest of their number to face the *Eisenstein*. If the frigate was a fox to the wolves of the battleships, then against this craft it became no more than an insect before a colossus. There were moons that massed less than the giant. It was the clenched hand of a god carved from dark asteroid stone, a nickel-iron behemoth pocked with craters and spiked with broad towers that jutted from its surface.

At a great distance, the vessel would have resembled the head of a mace, filigreed with gold and black iron. At close range, a city's worth of spires and gantries reached out, many of them glowing with the light of thousands of windows, others concealing nests of weapons capable of killing a continent. Ships like the *Eisenstein* were carried in fanged docks around the circumference of the colossus, and as it drifted closer the sheer mass of its gravity gently tugged at the frigate, altering her course. Autonomous weapons drones deployed in hornet swarms, staging around the drifting craft. As one, they turned powerful searchlights on the ruined hull and pinned the frigate to the black of the void, drenching her in blinding white beams.

Eisenstein's name, still clearly visible atop the emerald sweep of her bow planes, shone brightly with the reflected glow. Inside, a handful of souls waited for their fate to be decided.

HAKUR STEPPED IN from the corridor, a loaded and cocked combi-bolter looped over his shoulder on a thick strap. 'Outermost decks are all but empty now, captain,' he told Garro, 'Vought has re-routed the atmosphere to storage tanks or down here. Less than a third of the ship has life-support, but we won't lack for breathing.'

'Good.' He accepted the sergeant's report. 'The men on the promenade decks, they have been withdrawn?'

The veteran nodded. 'Aye, lord. I left them there as long as I thought I could, but I've pulled them all back now. I had them spying out through the ports. What with the scrying being out of action and all, I thought that eyeballs were better than no watch at all.'

'Quick thinking. What did they see?'

Hakur shifted uncomfortably, as he always did when he had no concrete answer for his commander. Garro knew this behaviour of old. Andus Hakur prided himself on providing accurate intelligence to his battle-brothers and he disliked having only half the facts about anything. 'Sir, there were a lot of ships and they seemed to be of Imperial lines.'

Nathaniel's lip curled. 'After Isstvan, that information only makes me more wary, not less. What else?'

'The fleet orbits a large construct, easily the size of a star fort, or larger. The brother who laid eyes upon it told me he had never seen such a thing before. He compared it to an ork monstrosity, but not so crude.'

Something pushed at the back of Garro's mind, a half-remembered comment that chimed with the description. 'Anything on the vox?'

Hakur shook his head. 'We are maintaining communications silence, as you ordered. If whatever is out there is close enough to broadcast on our battle frequencies, they are choosing not to.'

Garro dismissed him with a nod. 'Carry on. We'll wait, then.' The battle-captain crossed back into the wide space of the armoury chamber. Partition walls had been hastily opened along the length to allow the ship's complement of survivors to find purchase here, and from where he stood Garro saw a sea of figures huddled in the dim glow of emergency biolume lanterns. Many on the edges of the group were armed, and they had the air of desperation upon them. With deliberate care, Garro went in and walked among them, making eye contact with each of the crewmen just as he would do with his fellow Astartes. Some of the men trembled as he passed them by, others stood a little taller after the nods he gave them.

In all his years of service, Garro had always thought of the ordinary men of the army as warriors in the same cause as the Astartes, but it wasn't until this moment that he felt anything like kinship with them. Today we are all united in our mission, he mused. There were no barriers of rank or Legion here.

He came across Carya, the dark-skinned officer cradling a heavy plasma pistol. 'Lord captain,' he said thickly. The shipmaster's face was swollen with his injuries from the escape.

'Esteemed master,' Garro returned. 'I feel I owe you an apology.'

'Oh?'

Garro gestured at the hull walls around them. 'You presented me with a fine ship, and I have made such a mess of it.'

'You need not comment, my lord,' Carya laughed. 'I have served under your kind in the Great Crusade for decades and still I think I will never understand you. In some ways you are so superior to men like me, and in others...' His voice trailed off.

'Go on,' Garro said. 'Speak your mind, Baryk. I think our experiences together allow us to be candid.'

The shipmaster tapped him on the arm. 'In some ways you are like wanton siblings who yearn for a

place, for fraternity, but also spark against one
another with your rivalries. Like all men, you strive to
escape from the shadow of your father, but also to
seek his pride. Sometimes I wonder what would happen to you brave, noble lads if you had no wars to
fight.' When Garro didn't reply, Carya's face fell. 'I am
sorry, captain. I didn't mean to offend you.'

'You did not,' Garro replied. 'Your insight is…
challenging, that is all.' He thought for a moment.
'As to your question, I do not know the answer. If
there were no wars, what use would weapons be?'
He pointed to Carya's pistol, and then himself.
'Perhaps we would make a new war, or turn upon
each other.'

'As Horus did?'

A chill washed through Garro's soul. 'Perhaps.' The
thought lay heavy upon him, and he turned, forcing
it away.

Garro found Sendek and Hakur scrutinising an auspex unit. With the aid of Vought, Sendek had been
able to connect the device to some of the *Eisenstein's*
external sensory mechanisms. 'Captain! A reading…'

Garro dismissed Carya's words from his mind and
snapped back to battle focus. 'Report.'

'Energy build-up,' said Hakur. 'For a second I
thought it might have been a deep scan of the hull,
but then it changed.'

A complex wave-form writhed across the auspex
screen.

'A scan?' He glanced at Sendek. 'Could we be
detected in here, through this much iron and steel?'

'It is possible,' replied the Astartes. 'A vessel with
enough power behind her sensors could burn
through any amount of shielding.'

'A ship, or something like a star fort,' added Hakur.

Cold realisation seized Garro's chest and he snatched the auspex from Sendek's grip. The pattern; he knew what it was. 'To arms!' he bellowed, his voice echoing around the chamber. 'To arms! They're coming in!'

The auspex forgotten, Hakur and Sendek brought up their weapons and panned them around the compartment. At Garro's words, the crew surged with panic. He saw Carya snap out commands and the men brought their guns to the ready.

'Sir, what is it?' Sendek asked.

'There!' Garro pointed into the centre of the chamber, to an open area just inside the doors where Hakur had arranged a staggered barricade. A low humming, like electric motors deep beneath the earth, was issuing from the air, and static prickled at the battle-captain's skin.

Embers of emerald radiance danced and flickered across the deck, for one moment recalling the strange warp-things that had come to the ship in the depths of the empyrean; but this was something different. This time, Garro knew exactly what to expect. 'No man opens fire until I give the word!' he shouted.

And then they came. With a thundering roar of splitting air molecules, a searing flash of jade lightning exploded across the middle of the armoury chamber floor, the backwash of colour throwing stark, hard-edged shadows over the walls and ceiling. Garro raised his hand to shield his eyes from the brilliance before it could dazzle him into temporary blindness. Then the light and noise were gone with a flat crack of displaced atmosphere, and the teleportation cycle was complete.

Where there had been bare deck and scatterings of discarded equipment, now there was a cohort of stocky, armoured figures in a perfect combat wheel deployment. A ring of eight Astartes, resplendent in battle gear that shimmered in the light of the biolumes, stood with their bolters ranged at their shoulders, with none of the chamber unguarded.

One of them spoke with a voice clear and hard, in the manner of a man used to being obeyed instantly. 'Who is in command here?'

Garro stepped forward, his weapon at his hip and his finger upon the trigger. 'I am.'

He saw the speaker now, his head bare. He picked out a hard face, a humourless aspect, and behind him… What was that behind him?

'You will stand down and identify yourself!'

In spite of the tension inside him, something in Garro rebelled at the superior tone and he sneered in reply. 'No,' he spat, 'this is *my* vessel, and you have boarded it without my authority!' Abruptly, all the strain and anger that he had kept locked away inside him over the past few days roared back to the fore, and he poured every last drop of it into his retort. *'You will stand down, you will identify yourself, and you will answer to me!'*

In the silence that followed, he caught a murmur and as one, the muzzle of every bolter the boarding party held dropped downward to point at the decking. The warrior who had addressed Garro bowed and stepped aside to allow another figure – the shape he had glimpsed at the centre of the group – to step forward.

Garro's throat tightened as a towering shape in yellow-gold armour came into the light. Even in the feeble glow of the lanterns, the raw presence of the new arrival lit the room. A severe and uncompromising gaze surveyed the chamber from a grim face framed by a snow-white shock of hair, a face that seemed as hard and unyielding as the mammoth plates of golden-hued brass that made the man a walking statue; but no, not a man.

'Primarch.' He heard the whisper fall from Hakur's mouth.

Any other words died forming in Garro's throat. He found he could not draw his sight away from the war-lord's armour. Like Garro's, the warrior wore a cuirass detailed with eagles spread over his shoulders and across his chest. Upon his shoulder pauldron was a disc of white gold and layered to that, cut together from sections of blue-black sapphire, was the symbol of a mailed gauntlet clenched in defiant threat. Finally the diamond-hard eyes found Garro and held him.

'Pardon our intrusion, kinsman,' said the demi-god, his words strong and firm but not raised in censure. 'I am Rogal Dorn, Master of the VII Legiones Astartes, Emperor's son and Primarch of the Imperial Fists.'

He found his voice again. 'Garro, lord. I am Battle-Captain Nathaniel Garro of the Death Guard, commanding the starship *Eisenstein*.'

Dorn nodded gently. 'I request permission to come aboard, captain. Perhaps I may be of some assistance.'

PART THREE

UNBROKEN

FOURTEEN

Dorn's Fury
Divinity
To Terra

THE MEN AT the gunnery stations stood in salute as they carried out the orders of the primarch. Heads bowed, they made the sign of the aquila across their chests before the commander of the cannonade island on the prow of the fortress placed his hand on the firing lever. The officer paused for a moment and then pulled the massive trigger.

Four high-yield ship-to-ship torpedoes flashed from their firing tubes, thruster rockets igniting to carry them the short distance from the fortress to the frigate. Each one was tipped with a compact but very powerful atomic warhead. One would have been enough to do the job, but after the catalogue of horrors that had walked the decks of the *Eisenstein*, the overkill was deemed necessary. The ship's duty was concluded, and only in death did duty end.

The *Phalanx* watched the last few seconds of the starship's life unfold. The massive construct, the nomadic home of the Imperial Fists Legion, was more planetoid than it was space vessel. It stood at silent sentinel over the ending of its smaller Sister.

The torpedoes impacted at the bow, the stern and at equidistant points along the frigate's beaten and ravaged hull. The detonations had been programmed flawlessly, all four rippling into one seamless, silent flare of radiation and light. The glow illuminated the surrounding vessels of the Astartes fleet, and cast bright columns of white through the windows of Rogal Dorn's sanctorum atop the highest of the *Phalanx*'s towers.

GARRO TURNED HIS face away from the flash and in doing so felt an odd pang of regret, almost as if he had done the steadfast vessel a disservice in not watching her last moments of obligation to the Imperium. Dorn, some distance away at the largest of the windows, did not move. The nuclear light washed over the primarch and not for one moment did he flinch from it. As the flare died away, the master of the Imperial Fists gave a shallow nod.

'It's done, then.' Behind him, Garro heard Iacton Qruze's remark. 'If any taint of that warp witchery remained, it is ashes now.' The old warrior seemed to stand a little taller now that his power armour had been repainted in the old colours of the Luna Wolf livery. Dorn had raised an eyebrow at the change, but said nothing.

Garro was aware of Baryk Carya at his side. The shipmaster's face was sallow and drawn, and the Astartes felt pity for the man. Commanders like Carya were as much a part of their ship as the steel in the bulkheads, and to give up his vessel like this clearly struck him hard. In his fingers, the man held the brass dedication plate that Garro had seen bolted to the base of *Eisenstein*'s navigation podium. 'The ship died well,' said the Death Guard. 'We owe it our lives, and more.'

Carya looked up at him. 'Lord captain, at this moment I think I understand what you must have felt at Isstvan III. To lose your home, your purpose...'

Garro shook his head. 'Baryk... iron and steel, flesh and bone, these things are transient. Our purpose exists beyond them all, and it will never be destroyed.'

The shipmaster nodded. 'Thank you for your words, captain... Nathaniel.' He looked to the primarch and bowed low. 'If I may take my leave?'

Dorn's adjutant, the Astartes captain from the boarding party, answered the question. 'You are dismissed.'

Carya bowed again to the Astartes and made his way out of the wide, oval chamber. Garro watched him go.

'What is to become of him?' Qruze wondered aloud.

'New roles will be found for the survivors,' replied the captain. His name was Sigismund, and he was a sturdy, thickset man, hair a dark blond with a patrician face that echoed the same austere lines as his liege lord's. 'The Imperial Fists have a large fleet and able crew are always prized. Perhaps the man can be put to use as an instructor.'

Garro frowned. 'An officer like that needs a ship under him. Anything else would be a waste. If only we could have taken the frigate in tow, perhaps–'

'Your recommendation will be noted, battle-captain.' Dorn's voice was a low thunder. 'I am not usually given to explaining myself to subordinate ranks, but as you are of a brother Legion and your disciplines differ from that of my sons, I will make this exception.' He turned and looked at Garro, and the Death Guard did his best not to shrink beneath the steady attention. 'We are not given to waste time with ships that are wounded and unable to keep up with the *Phalanx*. Already during this journey I have lost three of my own vessels to the storms in the warp, and still I am no closer to my destination.'

'Terra,' breathed Garro.

'Indeed. My father bid me to follow him back to Terra in order to lend my arm to the fortification of his palace and the formation of a Praetorian aegis, but with the aftermath of Ullanor and all that came from it... we were waylaid.'

Garro felt rooted to the spot, the same tense awe he had felt before Mortarion and in the Lupercal's Court holding him in a tight embrace. It seemed so strange to hear this mighty figure speaking of the Master of Mankind as any common son would talk of his parent.

Dorn continued. 'We left my brother, Horus, intent on making that voyage at long last, only to once more find the universe conspiring against us.'

Garro failed to keep a glimmer of unease from his face at the mention of the Warmaster's name, and he was aware that Sigismund noticed it. Garro knew from talk aboard the *Endurance* that the Imperial Fists had departed the 63rd Fleet some time before the Death Guard had arrived from the jorgall assault mission. In his years in the Legion, he had never shared the battlefield with the sons of Dorn and knew of them only by their standing with the other Legions.

Fierce warriors and masters of siegecraft, it was said that the Imperial Fists could hold any citadel and make it impregnable beyond the reach of any enemy. Garro had seen their work first-hand, in the design of fortresses built on Helica and Zofor's World. What he had heard of them appeared to be accurate. Dorn and his men seemed as rigid as castle walls.

'The storms,' ventured Nathaniel. 'They almost claimed our lives.'

Sigismund nodded. 'If you will permit me to comment, lord, I have never seen the like. The tempest came upon us the moment we took to the empyrean, and it rendered the careful routes of our Navigators useless. Whatever waypoints we had turned to sand and disintegrated. The finest of the Navis Nobilite, and they were reduced to the level of blind children flailing in a featureless desert.'

Dorn stepped away from the window. 'This is how we came to find you, Garro. The storms ringed us in a disordered region of the warp, put us in the maddening stillness of their eye. The *Phalanx* and her fleet were becalmed. Every ship we attempted to send beyond the storms was torn apart.' A tiny flicker of grim irony crossed the primarch's face. 'The immaterium besieged us.'

'You saw his flare,' said Qruze. 'Across all that distance, and you saw it?'

'A bold risk,' allowed the primarch. 'You could not have known that there would be anyone within range to glimpse it.'

'I had faith,' Garro replied.

Dorn studied him for a long moment, as if he were going to question the captain's words, but instead continued on. 'The shockwave from the detonations of the drives disrupted the patterns of the storm barrier. The energy of the flare allowed our Navigators to get their bearings once more.' He inclined his head. 'We owe you a debt, Death Guard. You may consider it repaid by our rescue of your ship's crew.'

'My thanks, my lord.' Garro felt his gut tighten. 'My only wish is that the events that brought us to this place had not come to pass.'

'You pre-empt my questions, Garro. Now you understand how I came to your aid, it is your turn to illuminate me. I would have you explain why a lone Death Guard warship found itself in the uncharted territories, why signs of battle against Imperial guns lay upon her, and why one of your battle-brothers lies in my infirmary wracked by an illness that confounds the very best of my Legion's Apothecaries.'

Garro threw a look at Qruze for support and the veteran nodded back to him. 'Lord Dorn, what I have to say will not sit well with you, and at the end of the telling you may wish that you had not asked for it.'

'Oh?' The primarch moved to the middle of the sanctorum chamber, bidding them to follow. 'You think you know better than I what will distress me? Perhaps my brother, Mortarion, allows such presumption among the Death Guard, but that is not the manner of the Imperial Fists. You will give me the complete truth and you will excise nothing. Then, before my fleet makes space for Terra, I will decide how to deal with you, and the rest of your seventy errant Astartes.'

Not once did Dorn raise his voice or show even the slightest fraction of aggression behind his orders, yet the commands came with such quiet force that Garro found them impossible to resist. He was aware that Sigismund and a cohort of his men were at the edges of the chamber, watching him and Cruze for any signs of behaviour that might mark them as untrustworthy. 'Very well, my lord,' he replied.

Garro took a deep breath, and began the story at Isstvan and the Lupercal's Court.

ON ANY OTHER occasion, Qruze might have been willing to let his talkative manner come to the fore and lend his own viewpoint to a story told by one of his fellow Astartes, but as the lad Garro began to unfold the events to Dorn and his men, Qruze found himself quieted. He searched inside himself and realised there was nothing he could add to the Death Guard's dry, careful explanations, just a nod now and then when Garro looked to him for confirmation of some minor point.

The Luna Wolf became aware of the silence that had fallen across the rest of the sanctorum chamber. Sigismund and the other Imperial Fists in the black-trimmed armour of the First Company were as still as statues, their faces stoic against the unfolding tale. Rogal Dorn was the only point of motion in the room, the primarch walking back and forth in a slow pattern, lost in thought, occasionally pausing to stop and give Garro his full, unwavering attention. It was not until Garro reached the moment of Eidolon's orders to kill Saul Tarvitz and his refusal to obey that Dorn spoke again.

'You disobeyed a ranking officer's direct command.' It was not a question.

'I did.'

'What evidence did you have at that time that Tarvitz was not, as Eidolon said, a renegade and a turncoat?'

Garro hesitated, shifting uncomfortably on his augmetic leg. 'None, lord, only my faith in my honour brother.'

'That word again,' said the primarch. 'Continue, captain.'

Qruze had heard second-hand from conversations with Sergeant Hakur of the firefight on the *Eisenstein*'s gun deck, but it was only as Garro relayed it that he found a true sense of it. The Death Guard baulked at repeating the seditious declarations of Commander Grulgor, and when Dorn ordered him to, a new tension emerged across the room as he finally gave voice to them. Qruze saw anger pushing at Sigismund's lips and finally the captain spoke.

'I cannot hear this without answer! If this is true, then tell me how the Warmaster allowed Death Guard and Emperor's Children alike to make these plays for power under his very nose? The unsanctioned virus bombardment of an entire world? The execution of civilians? How did he become so blind overnight, Garro?'

'He was not blind,' Garro said grimly. 'Horus sees only too well.' He looked the primarch in the eye. 'Lord, your brother is not ignorant of this duplicity. He is the author of it, and his hands are stained with the blood of men from his own Legion, from mine and from those of the World Eaters and the Emperor's Children as well–'

Dorn moved so quickly that Qruze flinched, but the Master of the Imperial Fists was not coming for him. There was a crack of sound and Garro fell away, skidding back across the bright blue marble of the sanctorum's flooring. Qruze saw Garro hover on the edge of unconsciousness, a livid bruise forming on his face. With care, the Death Guard blinked back to wakefulness and worked at resetting his jawbone.

'For even daring to think of such a thing in my presence, I should have you flogged and then vented to the void,' growled the primarch, every word a razor. 'I will not hear any more of this fantasy.'

'You must,' Qruze blurted, taking a half-step forward. He ignored the ratcheting of slides on the bolters of Sigismund's men. 'You must hear him out!'

'You dare to give me an order?' Dorn faced the old warrior. 'A relic who should have been retired centuries ago, you dare to do so?'

Iacton saw his opening and took it. 'I do, and furthermore I know that you will. If you truly thought that Garro's words had no value then you would have killed him where he stood.' He moved to help Garro to his feet. 'Even in your moment of anger, you pulled a blow that could have broken his neck... because you want to hear everything. That is what you asked for, isn't it? The complete truth.'

For an instant, Qruze saw a flash of titanic rage in the primarch's gaze, and felt his blood run cold. That's it, you old fool, he told himself, that was a word too far. He's going to kill us both for our boldness.

Then Dorn gestured to Sigismund and his Astartes lowered their guns. 'Speak,' he told Garro. 'Tell it all.'

GARRO FOUGHT DOWN the giddiness and pain. Dorn was *so fast*, even in that tonnage of armour, he was lightning. Had he intended real harm against him, Garro knew that he would never have seen it coming. With care, he swallowed and took a painful breath. 'After the bombing, I knew that I had no other choice but to do as Saul Tarvitz and I had discussed, and take a warning to Terra. With Grulgor dead, I ordered my men to secure the *Eisenstein*. In the interim, Captain Qruze had come aboard with the civilians.'

'The remembrancers and the iterator,' said the primarch. 'They had been aboard Horus's flagship.'

'Aye, lord,' added the Luna Wolf. 'My battle-brother, Garviel Loken, entrusted their safety to me. The girl Keeler, she…' He paused, marshalling his thoughts. 'She suggested that Captain Garro could help us.'

'Loken,' said Sigismund. 'My lord, I know him. We met aboard the *Vengeful Spirit*.'

Dorn glanced aside. 'What was your measure of him, first captain?'

'A Cthonian, and all that entails, with a strong spirit if a little naïve. He seemed trustworthy, a man of principles.'

The primarch absorbed this. 'Continue, Garro.'

Nathaniel ignored the tension in his jaw and relayed the details of the signal sent to Typhon and the *Eisenstein*'s pursuit by the *Terminus Est*, then the catastrophic voyage through the warp. There was a moment when one of Sigismund's men made a derisive noise under his breath as Garro described the freakish revivification of Grulgor's dead men, but Dorn silenced that with a hard look.

'There are stranger powers that lurk within the immaterium than we may know,' the warlord said darkly, 'but what you say tests reason even with that qualification. These things you speak of come dangerously close to primitive ideals of sorcery and magic.'

The Death Guard nodded. 'I do not deny it, Lord Dorn, but you asked me to give you the truth as I saw it, and this is what I saw. Something in the warp brought Grulgor back to life, it animated his contaminated flesh through the very disease that had claimed him. Do not ask me for an explanation, sir, as I have none.'

'This is what you come to me with?' The primarch's slow anger filled the room like smoke, heavy and dark. 'A convoluted story of treachery and conspiracy among the Emperor's sons, a collection of ill-informed opinions and rash actions made with base emotion and not cold clarity?' He advanced slowly on Garro, and it took all of Nathaniel's courage not to back away. 'If I were to have my brothers in this room right now, Mortarion, Fulgrim, Angron, Horus... what would they say of your tale? Do you think that you would even be able to draw a breath before you were struck down for such an outright fiction?'

'I know it is difficult to accept–'

'*Difficult?*' Dorn raised his voice for the first time and the room shook with it. 'Difficult is a winding labyrinth, or a complex skein of navigational formulae! This is against our very creed and character as the Emperor's chosen warriors!' He glared at Garro, eyes aflame. 'I do not know what to make of you, Garro! You carry yourself like an honest man, but if you are not a traitor and a deceiver then you can only be possessed by insanity!' He stabbed a finger at Qruze. 'Should I make a concession for some contagious senility perhaps? Did the warp addle your minds and create this hallucination between you?'

Garro heard the sound of his blood rushing in his ears. Everything was going wrong, falling apart around him. In his rush to find a rescuer for the *Eisenstein* and a way to get the message out, it had never occurred to him that he would not be believed. He looked away.

'Look at me when I speak to you, Death Guard!' snapped the primarch. 'These lies you bring into my personal chambers, they sicken and disgust me. That you would dare to say such things about a hero of such matchless character as my brother, Horus, it vexes me beyond my capacity for description!' He placed a massive finger on the sternum of Garro's armour. 'How cheap you must hold your integrity to give it up so easily! I weep for Mortarion if a man of such low honour as you could rise to command a company of the XIV Legion.' Dorn's hand closed into a massive brass fist. 'Know this – the only reason I do not tear you limb from limb for your defamation is that I know my brothers will reserve that pleasure for themselves!'

Garro felt the decking turn to mud beneath his boots and his chest caught in an invisible vice, returning to him the same sickening sensations that he had felt in the corridor outside the navis sanctorum and in the grip of the xenos war beast. As he had there, he reached for and found the strength of will that had carried him this far.

My faith.

'Are you blind?' he whispered.

Dorn was thunder incarnate. 'What did you say to me?'

'I asked if you were blind, lord, because I fear you must be.' The words came from nowhere, even as some part of Garro marvelled at the mad daring of what he was saying. 'Only one struck by such a terrible ailment could be as you are. Yours is the blindness that only a brother might have: that of a keen judgement clouded by admiration and respect, clouded by your love for your kinsman, the Warmaster.'

It was not often that Rogal Dorn's stern mask cracked, but it did so now. The fury of a god made flesh erupted upon his aspect and the primarch drew his powerful chainsword in a flashing golden arc of roaring death. 'I rescind my former statement,' he bellowed, 'get to your knees and accept your death, while you still have the chance to die like an Astartes!'

'Lord Dorn, *no*!' It was a woman's voice and it came from across the room, but it carried with it a wave of such emotion that every man in the sanctorum, even the primarch himself, hesitated.

QRUZE TURNED AND saw the girl Keeler running across the blue marble tiles, her boots clacking against them. Behind her were Sindermann, Mersadie Oliton and a pair of Imperial Fists with their guns at the ready. Iacton felt the echo of Euphrati's voice resonate through him and he remembered the strange warmth he had felt from her hands upon his chest, aboard the *Vengeful Spirit* as things had turned to hell.

'What is this intrusion?' snarled Dorn, his humming blade still hanging at the end of his swing towards Garro's throat.

'They demanded entry,' said the one of the guards. 'She… The woman, she…'

'She can be very persuasive at times,' noted Qruze.

Fearlessly, Euphrati stepped forward to face the primarch. 'Rogal Dorn, Hero of the Gold, Stone Man. You stand upon a turning point in the history of the Imperium, of the galaxy itself. If you strike Nathaniel Garro down for daring to give you his candour, then you truly are as blind as he says.'

'Who are you?' demanded the figure in gold.

'I am Euphrati Keeler, formerly an imagist and remembrancer of the 63rd Expeditionary Fleet. Now I am only a vessel… a vessel for the Emperor's will.'

'Your name means nothing to me,' Dorn retorted. 'Now stand aside or die with him.'

He heard Oliton whimper and bury her face in Sindermann's shoulder. Qruze expected to see fear bloom on Keeler's face, but instead there was sadness and compassion. 'Rogal Dorn,' she said, holding out

a hand to him, 'do not be afraid. You are more than
the stone and steel face that you show the stars. You
can be open. You must not fear the truth.'

'I am the Imperial Fist,' he shouted, and the words
hit like hammers, 'I am fear incarnate!'

'Then see the fidelity of Nathaniel's words. Look
upon the proof of his veracity.' She beckoned Oliton
forward, and with the iterator giving her support, the
documentarist came closer. Qruze smiled a little as
the dark-skinned woman composed herself enough
to show a facade of her more usual elegant manner.

'I am Mersadie Oliton, remembrancer,' she
announced with a curtsey. 'If the lord primarch will
allow, I will provide a recollection of these events to
him.' Oliton pointed to a hololithic projector dais
mounted in the floor.

Dorn brought his sword to his chest, fuming. 'This
will be my last indulgence of you.'

Sigismund stepped up and directed Mersadie to the
hololith. With care, the documentarist drew a fine
cable from among the brocade of her dress and traced
it along the seamless crown of her hairless, elongated
skull. Iacton heard a soft click as a concealed socket
beneath the skin mated to the wire. The other end she
guided to an interface plate on the dais. This done,
Oliton sank into a cross-legged position and bowed
her head. 'I am gifted with many methods in which I
may remember. I will write and I will compose image
streams, and this is aided by a series of mnemonic
implant coils.' She brushed a finger over her head
once more. 'I open these now. What I will show you,
my lord, is as I witnessed it. These images cannot be
fabricated or tampered with. This is…' She faltered,
trembling, her words thick and close to tears. 'This is
what happened.'

'It's all right, my dear,' said Sindermann, taking her hand. 'Be brave.'

'It will be difficult for her,' explained Keeler. 'She will experience an echo of emotions from the events.'

The hololith came to life with an opaque jumble of images and half-formed shapes. In the dreamlike mass, Qruze saw glimpses of faces he knew and some he did not: *Loken, that degenerate poet Karkasy, the astropath Ing Mae Sing, Petronella Vivar and her bloody mute Maggard.* Then the mist shifted and for a moment Oliton looked around the room, the hololith screening what she saw. Her gaze froze on Dorn and he nodded.

THE HAZE OF the hololith changed and Garro found his attention was caught by the dance of motion and replay within it. He had only heard Qruze's second-hand explanation of what had transpired in the *Vengeful Spirit*'s main audience chamber, but here he was seeing it first-hand, through the sight of an eye-witness.

Scenes of battlefield butchery transmitted from the surface of the Choral City on Isstvan III hovered before them and Oliton sobbed a little. Garro, Qruze and the men of the Imperial Fists were no strangers to war, but the obvious, wanton horror of the combat was enough even to give them pause. He saw Sigismund grimace in disgust. Then the recording turned as Mersadie looked to the Warmaster upon a tall podium, his face lit with a cold, hard purpose. 'You remembrancers say you want to see war. Well, here it is.' The relish in his voice was undeniable. This was not a warrior prosecuting a necessary battle, but a man running his hands through tides of blood with open satisfaction.

'Horus?' The name was the ghost of a whisper from Dorn's lips, but Garro heard the question in it, the puzzlement. The primarch saw the wrongness in his brother's manner.

Then, through Mersadie Oliton's eyes, they watched the bombing of Isstvan III and the Choral City. Darts of silver surged from the ships in orbit like diving raptors falling on prey, and as the voices of remembrancers long since gunned down by Astartes bolters gasped and screamed, those darts struck home and coiled into black rings of unstoppable death.

'Emperor's blood,' whispered Sigismund, 'Garro told the truth. He bombed his own men.'

'What… what is it?' asked Oliton, speaking in unison with her own voice on the recording.

Keeler's recorded words answered her. *'You have already seen it. The Emperor showed you, through me. It is death.'*

The recording jumped and unspooled. In fast blinks of recall, they saw Qruze fight the turncoat bodyguard Maggard in the launch bay, the escape from Horus's warship, the attack of the *Terminus Est*, and more.

Finally, Dorn turned away. 'Enough. End this, woman.'

Sindermann gently detached the cable from the hololith and Mersadie jerked like a discarded marionette as the images died.

The cold, clear air inside the sanctorum was rich with tension as the primarch slowly sheathed his chainsword. He ran his fingers over his face, his eyes. 'Perhaps… Did I not see?' Dorn looked to Garro and some measure of his great potency was dimmed. 'Such folly. Is it any wonder I would rebel at the reality of so mad a truth, even to the point of killing the messenger who brought it to me?'

'No, lord,' Garro admitted. 'I had no wish to believe it either, but the truth cares little for what we wish.'

Sigismund looked to his commander. 'Master, what shall we do?' Garro felt a stab of compassion for the first captain. He knew the pain, the shame that the Imperial Fist had to be feeling at that moment.

'Convene the captains and brief them, but see this goes no further,' Dorn said after a moment. 'Garro, Qruze, that order includes you. Keep the *Eisenstein* survivors silent. I will not have this news spread through my fleet uncontrolled. I will choose when to reveal it to the Legion.'

The Astartes nodded. 'Aye, lord.'

Dorn walked away. 'You will leave me now. I must think on this matter.' He threw a last look at Sigismund. 'No one is to enter my chambers until I emerge.'

The first captain saluted. 'If you wish my counsel, lord–'

'I do not.' The primarch left them, and after they left, Garro could not help but see the expression of deep concern on Sigismund's face as he sealed the sanctorum shut behind them.

Garro saw Keeler standing by the door and glimpsed a single tear tracing a line down her cheek. 'Why do you weep?' he asked. 'Is it for us?'

Euphrati shook her head and gestured to the heavy locked hatch. 'For him, Nathaniel, because he can't. Today you and I have broken a brother's heart, and nothing will ever mend it.'

DORN'S FLEET READIED itself for a return to the warp, and the men and women of the *Eisenstein* found themselves left outside the work and progress, isolated in temporary quarters deep inside the stone corridors of the *Phalanx*. Meditation did not come so easily for Garro, and so he prowled the archways and passages of the great star fortress. Once, the *Phalanx* might have been a planetoid or a minor moon of some distant world, but now it was a cathedral dedicated to the business of war and the glories of the VII Legiones Astartes. He saw galleries of battle honours that went on for kilometres and corridors to whole sections of the fortress that duplicated the conditions of different combat environments for training purposes. Garro dallied in a vast chamber that replicated the Inwitian frost dunes where legend said Dorn had grown to manhood. All around him, warriors in golden armour moved with sober intent, without pause or doubt as he stepped carefully, still smoothing out the limp from his battle injury. He felt out of place, the marble and green of his wargear ringing a wrong note among the hornet-yellow and black trim of the Imperial Fists.

Finally, in such a way that he could almost fool himself into thinking it was happenstance, Garro found himself outside the quarters that had been granted to Euphrati Keeler.

She opened the door before he could knock. 'Hello, Nathaniel. I was preparing a little tisane. Would you like some?' Keeler left the door open and vanished back into the chamber. He sighed and followed her in. 'There has been no word from Lord Dorn yet?'

'None,' confirmed Garro, examining the spare space of the quarters. 'He has not left his sanctorum for a day and a night. Captain Sigismund maintains command authority in the meantime.'

'The primarch has a lot to consider. We can only begin to imagine how troubled our news has made him.'

'Aye,' he admitted, taking a cup of the pungent brew from Keeler's delicate hands. He shifted, taking the weight on his augmetic. The machine limb was the least of his concerns these days.

'What of you?' she asked. 'Where has this turn of events brought you?'

'I had hoped that I might find some time to rest, to take sleep. It has been elusive, however.'

'I thought you Astartes never slept.'

'A misconception. Our implants allow us to maintain a semi-dormant state while still being aware of our surroundings.' Garro sipped the infusion and found it to his taste. 'I have tried this past day, but what awaits me there is disquieting.'

'What do you see in your dreams?'

The Death Guard frowned. 'A battle, on a world I do not know. The landscape seems familiar but difficult to place. My brothers are there, Decius and Voyen, and Dorn's warriors as well. We are fighting a creature of some loathsome aspect, a beast of disease and pestilence like the things that boarded the *Eisenstein*. Clouds of carrion flies darken the air, and I feel sickened to my very core.' He looked away, dismissing it. 'It is just a mirage.'

There was a sheaf of Divinitatus tracts on her desk, and a thick candle burning on the mantle. 'I read Kaleb's papers. I think I have a better understanding of what you people believe.'

Euphrati saw where he was looking. 'The flock have been keeping to themselves since the rescue,' she explained. 'There haven't been any more gatherings.' She smiled. 'You said "you people", Nathaniel. Is that because you don't think you're one of us?'

'I am Astartes, servant of the Imperial truth–'

Keeler waved him into silence. 'We've had that conversation before. The two do not have to be mutually exclusive.' She looked into his eyes. 'You are carrying so much weight upon your shoulders, but you're still reluctant to let others bear it with you. This message... the warning, it is not yours alone. All of us who fled the murder at Isstvan, we carry it as well.'

'Perhaps so,' he allowed, 'but that does nothing to lighten my burden. I am in command...' He faltered for a moment. 'I was in command of the *Eisenstein*, and the message remains my duty. Even you told me that it was my mission.'

Keeler shook her head. 'No, Nathaniel, the warning is just an aspect of it. Your duty, as you said just now, is the truth. You have risked your life for it, you have gone against every will in your heart to join your kinsmen to serve it, you even stood in the face of a primarch's fury and did not flinch.'

'Yes, but when I think of all the darkness and destruction that will come of it, I feel as if I am about to be crushed! The import of this, Keeler, the sheer magnitude of Horus's betrayal... It will unleash a civil war that will set the galaxy alight.'

'And because you carry the warning, you feel responsible?'

Garro looked away. 'I'm only a soldier. I *thought* I was, but now...'

The woman drew closer. 'What is it, Nathaniel? Tell me, what do you believe.'

He put down the cup and produced Kaleb's papers and the brass icon. 'Before he died, my housecarl told me I was of purpose. At the time I did not understand what he meant, but now... now I cannot question it. What if Kaleb was right, if you are right? Am I the instrument of the Emperor's will? Your prayers say that the Emperor protects. Did He protect *me* so I could fulfil this duty?' Garro spoke faster and faster, his words racing to match the pace of his thoughts. 'All the things I have seen and heard, the visions that touched my thoughts... Were these to strengthen my resolve? Part of me cries out that this is the highest hubris, but then I look around and see that I have been chosen by Him. If that is so, then what manner of being can the Emperor be but a... divine one?'

Keeler reached out a hand and touched his arm. Giving voice to the words tore the breath from his chest. 'At last you see with clear eyes, Nathaniel.' The woman looked up at him and she was crying, but they were tears of joyous faith.

A SUMMONS WAS waiting for him in the sleeping cell where Garro had been billeted. He followed Sigismund's terse message to a pneu-tram that carried him up through networks of rail tunnels more complex than those of a planet-bound hive metropolis. He arrived at the fortress command centre and a hard-faced Imperial Fists sergeant escorted him to an audience chamber that rivalled the Lupercal's Court for size and grandeur. Garro felt an uncomfortable flash of memory. The last time he had been called to an assembly like this, it set in motion the events of the Warmaster's heresy.

Iacton Qruze was already there, along with the captains from each of many companies of the Imperial Fists. The warriors in yellow barely acknowledged the arrival of the Death Guard, with only Sigismund granting him a terse nod in greeting.

'Ho, lad,' said the Luna Wolf. 'It seems we're to know our fate soon enough.'

Despite it all, Garro felt a new wellspring of vitality deep inside, the words of his conversation with Keeler still fresh in his thoughts. 'I'm ready to meet it,' he told the veteran, 'whatever it is.'

Qruze smiled a little, sensing the change in him. 'That's the spirit. We'll see this through to the end.'

'Aye.' Garro studied the other men in the room. 'This is Dorn's senior cadre? They seem a sombre lot.'

'True enough. Even on the best of days, the Imperial Fists are a stiff breed. I remember battles my lads of the Third fought with Efried, my opposite number.' He indicated a bearded Astartes in the other group. 'Never saw him crack a smile, not once in a year-long campaign. That's Alexis Polux over there, Yonnad, and Tyr from the Sixth... It's not for nothing they call them the Stone Men.' He shook his head. 'And now, they'll be grimmer still.'

'Sigismund told them about Horus?'

Qruze gave him a nod. 'But that's not the sum of it. I've heard rumours that sounds of violence were heard inside Dorn's quarters. One can only imagine the destruction a primarch's temper might wreak when awakened.'

'And Rogal Dorn would never be one to vent his frustration openly.' He studied the other captains again. 'The humour of a primarch sets the manner of his Legion.'

'It's their way,' Qruze noted. 'They bury their rages under rock and steel.'

The tall doors at the end of the chamber yawned open and from the dimness beyond came the master of the Imperial Fists. The battle armour he had worn when Garro had first seen him was gone, and instead Dorn was clad in robes of a simple cut, but the change in dress did nothing to diminish his presence. If anything, the primarch seemed larger still without the trappings of ceramite and flexsteel to confine him. Sigismund and the other captains bowed, with Garro and Qruze following suit.

Given what he knew of the Imperial Fists, Garro expected some sort of ceremony or formal procedure, but instead Dorn strode firmly to the middle of the chamber and cast around, looking at each man in turn.

Garro saw anger set hard in granite behind those eyes, the echo of the rage that he had briefly seen directed at him. His mouth went dry. He had no desire ever to come that close to it again.

'Brothers,' rumbled the primarch, 'something has begun in the Isstvan system that goes against every tenet of our oath to the Lord of Terra. While the full dimensions of it are not yet clear to me, the matter of what must be done about it is.' He took a step towards the Death Guard and the Luna Wolf. 'For good or ill, the statement brought to us by Battle-Captain Garro must be taken onward to its ultimate destination. It must reach the Emperor's ears, as only he can decide how to act upon it. That choice, as much as I regret it, is beyond even me.'

'My liege, if I may speak,' began Captain Tyr. 'If the veracity of this horrifying act is undoubted, then how can we allow it to go unanswered? If treachery is stirring in the Isstvan system, it cannot be given time to gain a foothold.' A chorus of nods came from the other men around him.

'We will answer, of that you may be assured,' replied Dorn, with quiet force. 'Captain Efried, Captain Halbrecht and their veteran companies will form a detachment with my personal guard and remain aboard the *Phalanx* with me. At the conclusion of this audience, I will order our Navigators to set a course for the Sol system. Captain Garro has fulfilled his responsibility in bringing this warning to us, and it is my aim to personally see that task completed. I will go on to Terra, as we originally intended.' He glanced at his first captain. 'Sigismund, my strong right arm, you will take direct command of the rest of our Legion and its war fleet. You will execute a return voyage to the Isstvan system under the auspice of a combat deployment and consider yourself to be entering hostile territory. The journey back will be difficult. Warp storms still rage in that sector and you will find the passage challenging. Go there, first captain, support our kinsmen loyal to the Emperor and learn what is occurring on those worlds.'

'If the Warmaster has turned his back on Terra, what are my orders?' Sigismund asked, ashen-faced.

Dorn's countenance became rigid. 'Tell him his brother Rogal will have him answer for it.'

FIFTEEN

The Fate of the Seventy
Sea of Crises
Rebirth

THE DEATH GUARD captain entered the tiers of the fortress's massive infirmary, and inside he found his way to the ward where Decius was being held. He approached the isolation chamber. Along with the dedication plaque that Carya had taken with him, it remained the only other component of the starship *Eisenstein* that had survived the frigate's destruction. Huge cargo servitors had physically disconnected the module from the vessel's valetudinarium and transplanted it to here, where Dorn's medicae could turn their skills to the warrior's injuries.

The Apothecaries of the Imperial Fists had met with no more success than those of the Death Guard. Through the walls of the glass pod, Decius seemed closer than ever to his end. The livid knife wound was a sink for his colour and complexion, fingers of pallid corpse-flesh reaching out from the injury. Seeping sores collected at the corners of Decius's lips and nostrils, and his eyes were gummed shut with dried runnels of pus. The infection from whatever poison had soaked Grulgor's debased blade was overcoming the defences of the young Astartes, moment by agonising moment.

Garro became aware of someone standing close by. He saw Voyen's face reflected in the glass wall. 'He has spoken once or twice. His words are largely incoherent.' The other man was muted, as if he were afraid to speak to the captain. 'He calls out war cries and battle orders in his delirium.'

Garro nodded. 'He's fighting the disease just as he would any other adversary.'

'There is little we can do,' Voyen admitted. 'The virus has moved to an airborne stage of contagion in recent days, and we cannot enter the chamber to minister to him, even in fully sealed power armour. I have done what I can to ease his pain, but he's on his own.'

'The Emperor will protect him,' murmured Garro.

'We can only hope so. Captain Sigismund has given orders that every aspect of Decius's malady is to be examined and documented by the *Phalanx*'s medicae staff, in case the... the intruders we encountered on the *Eisenstein* return. I have told them everything I witnessed.'

'Good.' Garro turned to leave. 'Carry on.'

'Lord.' Voyen blocked his path, his head bowed. 'We must speak.' He offered the battle-captain his combat blade. 'On the bridge, before you triggered the warp flare, I challenged you and I see now that I was wrong to do so. You promised us rescue and it came. Such defiance as mine cannot go without censure.' He looked up. 'I have betrayed your trust twice. I will accept whatever punishment you will mete out. My life is yours.'

Garro took the knife and held it for a long moment. 'What you have done, Meric, with the lodges and on the *Eisenstein*, did not fall from any malice in your character. These things you did through fear: fear of the unknown.' He handed back the weapon. 'I will not punish you for that. You are my battle-brother, and your challenges are why I have you at my side.' He touched Voyen on the shoulder. 'Never be afraid again, Meric. Look to the Emperor, as I have done. Know Him, and you will know no fear.' On an impulse, he drew out Kaleb's tracts and pressed them into Voyen's palm. 'You may find, as I have, some measure of significance in these.'

CODED ASTROPATHIC SIGNALS had gone before the *Phalanx*, high-level protocols that called to alert the most secure levels of the Imperium's forces in the Sol system. Dorn's authority was enough to set ships in motion and for troops to be put to a higher state of readiness; and there were other forces at work as well, agencies that had sensed the arrival of the star fortress and the precious cargo it carried.

Several light-minutes inside the orbit of Eris, the *Phalanx* exploded from a warp gate with violent concussion, sending sheets of exotic lightning radiating out and away into the void. Delicate sensory devices dotting the surface of the tenth planet registered the new arrival and immediately communicated reports to relay stations on Pluto and Uranus, where in turn they would be sent onward by astropath to Terra and her dominions. The return of the Imperial Fists to humanity's cradle was long overdue. By rights there should have been celebrations and great ceremony on many of the outer colonies of the solar system to mark it. Instead, the *Phalanx* came in with speed and

ruthless purpose, not in a stately cruise about the
solar system's outlying worlds.

The mammoth craft did not fly the pennants and
banners associated with the triumphant arrival of a
heroic vessel. Instead, the colours on her masts and
the laser lamps about the *Phalanx*'s circumference
were lit for urgency. Patrol ships made way, no captain daring to challenge the Master of the Imperial
Fists for his haste. Drives flaring like captured stars,
the fortress-vessel passed in through the ragged edges
of the Oort Cloud at three-quarters the speed of light,
down into the plane of the ecliptic, crossing the orbit
of Neptune in a flicker of dazzling radiation.

ONCE AGAIN, GARRO was summoned to Dorn's chambers. At the rear of the great hall, massive iron panels
folded away into the ornate walls, revealing a glass
bowl that looked down to the command nexus of the
fortress below. It was like the bridge of any starship,
but magnified a hundredfold in size and scope. Garro
was reminded of a stadium, with concentric rings of
operator consoles raised in staggered tiers over an
arena in the middle. The central portion of the command deck was a gallery of hololithic displays, some
of them four storeys tall, forever glittering and shifting. Statues of armour-clad Astartes in the wargear of
the Imperial Fists were ranged along the sides of the
nexus, arms out as if they held Dorn's observation
bowl at their fingertips.

On this level, repeater consoles were arranged so
that the primarch and his officers could draw
information from any post in the nexus with a single
word of instruction. Garro realised that from this
high vantage point, a single general would be able to
direct an entire war of millions of men and

thousands of starships. He acknowledged Qruze where the Luna Wolf stood in conversation with Captain Efried and bowed before Dorn.

'You sent for me, lord?'

'I have something for you to see.' The primarch nodded to Halbrecht, a tall Imperial Fist with a sharp face and a shaved skull. 'Show the battle-captain our new escort.'

Halbrecht touched a control and a pict screen emerged from the broad console. Garro saw an image of void outside the *Phalanx*'s hull and of a large, dark silhouette that moved in echelon with it. The structure of the other vessel was only defined by the places where it blotted out the stars: a Black Ship.

'The *Aeria Gloris*.' It was unmistakable, and the instant Garro seized on the configuration his mind filled in the empty spaces. He had no doubt it was the same craft that had appeared near Iota Horologii.

'Correct,' said Dorn. 'This phantom joined us as we cleared the shadow of Neptune and fell in to match us in course and speed. They brought with them orders from the Council of Terra itself and directions to harbour. Specific reference was made to you, captain, and the woman Keeler. You will tell me why.'

Garro hesitated, unsure of how to proceed. 'I have had dealings with Amendera Kendel, a senior Oblivion Knight among the Silent Sisterhood,' he began.

Dorn shook his head once, a curt gesture of command. 'Your dealings with these Untouchables do not concern me, Garro. What troubles me is that they know Keeler is aboard my ship, and they have bid me to have her isolated.'

Garro felt a surge of concern. 'Euphrati Keeler is no threat to the *Phalanx*, sir. She is… a gifted individual.'

'Gifted.' Dorn made the word a growl. 'I know the kinds of "gifts" that the Sisterhood come seeking. Have you brought a mind-witch aboard my fortress, Death Guard? Does this remembrancer bear the mark of the psyker?' He grimaced. 'I was there at Nikaea when the Emperor himself censured the use of these warp-spawned powers for the good of the Imperium! I will not allow such forces to run unchecked among my warriors!'

'She is no witch, lord,' Garro retorted. 'If anything, her gift is that she has felt the Emperor's touch more keenly than any one of us!' The tremor in his voice drew Qruze's attention and the Luna Wolf came closer.

'We shall see. Sister Amendera has requested that Keeler be kept under lock and key, and Halbrecht's men have placed a guard upon her. The woman and her cohorts will be turned over to the Sisters of Silence once we make orbit at Luna.'

'Sir, I cannot permit that.' The words streamed from him before he could stop himself. 'They are under my protection.'

'And mine!' broke in Qruze. 'Loken entrusted their safety to me personally!'

'What you wish and what you will permit are of no interest to the Imperial Fists!' snapped Halbrecht, stepping up to face Garro. 'You are guests of the VII Legion and you will conduct yourselves as such.'

'You labour under a misapprehension, both of you,' said Dorn, moving to the windows. 'Have you forgotten what you said to me? The Death Guard and the Sons of Horus have turned against the Emperor, and if so then their Legions are soon to be declared renegade, as will all their warriors, protectorates and crews in service.'

'We risked everything to bring the warning!' Garro's words were brittle ice. 'And now you all but name us traitor?'

'I say only what some already have, what others will. Why do you think we travel to make port at the Luna base instead of taking orbit about Terra? I will not risk the lives of the Council and the Emperor on a whim!'

Qruze spat angrily, the old warrior's normally reticent manner melting away. 'Forgive me, Lord Dorn, but did you not see the Lady Oliton's mnemonic recording? Are not the sworn words of seventy Astartes proof enough for you?'

'Seventy Astartes whose Legions have turned their backs on Terra,' said Efried grimly.

The primarch nodded. 'Understand my position. Despite all the evidence you bring me, I cannot be certain of this until I see it through the eyes of an Imperial Fist. I do not call you liars, brothers, but I must see all sides of this, consider every possibility.'

'What if *you* are the traitors here?' demanded Halbrecht. 'Suppose Horus has been laid low by some conspiracy among his own men, and you have been sent to assassinate the Emperor?'

Garro's hand fell to the hilt of Libertas. 'I have killed men for lesser insults, Imperial Fist! Pray tell, how could we do such an impossible thing?'

'Perhaps by bringing a witch-psyker to Terra in secret,' said Efried, 'or a man wracked with a plague that no medicine can defeat?'

Ice formed in Garro's chest and the anger left him in a cold rush. 'No... no.' He turned to Dorn. 'Lord, if what I have told you and shown you is not enough to convince you, then I beg to know what it will take! Must I fall upon my own blade before you believe me?'

'I have this hour spoken to the Imperial Regent, Malcador the Sigillite, via machine-call vox,' said the primarch. 'It was my affirmation to him that, despite the dedication you have shown to the Emperor in braving the gauntlet to carry forth your warning, the Council of Terra cannot be fully certain where the loyalties of such men ultimately lie.' There was a hard edge to Dorn's voice, but for the first time Garro sensed the tension in him. It was not easy for the primarch to utter such words to fellow Astartes. 'My orders were to return to Terra to bulwark the planet's defences and it seems that I may have to do that in order to resist my own brothers.' He glanced at Garro. 'I will attend the Imperial Palace and brief the Emperor on this grave news. You, the refugees from the *Vengeful Spirit* and all the Astartes from the *Eisenstein*, will remain in secure holding at the Somnus Citadel on Luna until our master decides what your fate will be.'

Slowly and carefully, Garro drew his sword and turned it in his grip, offering the weapon to Dorn just as Voyen had offered his combat knife to Garro. 'Take my sword and end me with it if I am a deceiver, lord, I implore you, for I grow weary of each test that is heaped upon us! With all the lies and distrust that have bombarded me, I cannot face the same from those I call kinsmen!' With his free hand, Garro reached up to his chest and touched the eagle cuirass. He nodded to the primarch's armour and the similar aegis there, both echoes of the wargear worn by the Master of Mankind. 'We both carry the mark of the Emperor's aquila. Does that count for so little?'

'In these dark times, nothing can be certain.' Dorn's face turned to stone once again. 'Put away your weapon and be silent, Battle-Captain Garro. Know this: if you resist the edict of the Sigillite in any way, then the full and unfettered wrath of the Imperial Fists will be set upon you and your cohorts.'

'We will not resist,' Garro said, defeated. 'If this is what must be done, then so be it.' Libertas returned to its sheath in silence.

The primarch turned away. 'We will arrive in a few hours. Assemble your men and be ready to disembark.'

The distance across the marble floor to the chamber's doors seemed to expand as Garro's injured leg tensed with ghostly pain on every step he took.

THE PHALANX APPROACHED Luna through the hanging ornaments of orbital defence stations and commerce platforms, her path an open corridor through the darkness towards Terra's natural satellite. As the fortress of the Imperial Fists found harbour at the gravity-null La Grange point beyond the moon, the *Phalanx* mimicked the orbit of Luna around its parent world.

Once, the satellite had been a mottled stone wasteland where humans had ventured in their first infantile steps away from their birth world. They had built colonies there, testing their mettle in the pitiless cold of the void in preparation for future voyages to other planets, but as Terra's people had advanced, Luna had become little more than a way station, a place to pass by on the journey to the interplanetary – and later, interstellar – deeps.

For a time, in the Age of Strife when Terra was engulfed in war and blood, the moon had become desolate and empty once again, but after the rise of the Emperor, Luna had known a rebirth. Waxing and waning, the satellite came full circle as the Age of Imperium brought it new life.

Bisecting the grey stone sphere across its equator lay a man-made valley many kilometres wide. This was the Circuit, an artificial canyon that laid open the rock and stone beneath the dusty lunar surface. All along the length of the chasm lay gateways into the moon's interior, vast doors to the honeycomb of spaces carved by mankind in the heart of Luna. The ancient, dead boulder of the moon became the largest military complex ever built by humans. A vast shipyard for the armada of the Imperium, thousands of starships from the smallest shuttle to the largest battle barge were built and maintained there, and across the face of the far side there were complex stations for observation of the great void beyond. Port Luna was the cold, stone heart of humankind's great fleets.

The satellite was as much a weapon as it was a safe harbour. Much of the metals mined from the moon's heart and the rock from the Circuit's excavation had been employed by the Emperor's most skilled engineers, fashioned into a synthetic ring that girdled the planetoid. The vast grey hoop held batteries of lance cannons and docking bays for more warships. Wherever the light from Luna fell, those who saw it could sleep soundly knowing the ceaseless guardian stood to their defence.

And beyond it, Terra.

The cradle of humanity was in darkness. The light of the sun glimmered around the curvature of the planet, a brilliant arc of golden colour. Terra's night side showed its face towards Luna, the features of her continents and towering hive city constructs largely hidden beneath thick storm fronts and haze. In the places where the cloud formations were thin enough, the pulsing spark of lights from the great metropolis arcologies made necklaces of stark white and bright blue, some clustered in haloes, others extending out along coastlines for hundreds of kilometres. Dark patches where the oceans lay shimmered like spilled ink.

On the yellow-hued Stormbird that carried the first group of the *Eisenstein* seventy, Nathaniel Garro detached himself from his acceleration cradle and made his way to a viewport, ignoring the neutral stares from Captain Halbrecht and his men. He pressed his head close to the hemisphere of armour-glass and looked with naked eyes upon the planet of his birth. How long had it been? Time seemed to weigh so much more upon him than it had before. Garro estimated that it had been several decades since he had last seen Imperial Terra's majesty.

There was a pang of sadness. In the dark of night, he could not hope to pick out the terrain formations and landmarks that he had learned so readily as a youth. Would there be men down there looking up as he stared out on them, Garro wondered? Perhaps a boy, no more than fifteen summers, out in the wild agri-parks of Albia for the first time in his life, would be staring up into the night sky and marvelling at the impossible magnitude of the stars.

Turning there below, somewhere beneath him was the place where he had been born, and all the other landscapes of his childhood. Down there was the heart of the Imperium, great complexes of infinite majesty and achievement like the Red Mountain, the Libraria Ultima, the Petitioner's City and the Imperial Palace itself, where even now the Emperor resided. It was so close, Garro felt like he could reach out and take it in his armoured fingers. He pressed his gauntlet to the window and his palm covered the planet completely.

'If only it were that simple to keep it safe,' said Hakur. The sergeant joined him at the viewport.

In spite of everything, Garro felt strangely cheered by the sight of his home world, even as his emotions pulled him towards melancholy. 'As long as one Astartes still draws breath, old friend, Terra will never fall.'

'I would prefer not to be that one Astartes,' replied Hakur. 'With each passing day we are isolated further still.'

'Aye.' The Death Guard reflected. Time indeed was passing more swiftly than he had anticipated. While the *Eisenstein*'s escape, becalming and rescue had seemed like little more than a matter of weeks for those on board, Garro soon discovered that their subjective period did not marry with the passing of days elsewhere. According to the central chronometer broadcast from the Imperial capital, more than twice as much time had passed since the attack on Isstvan III. Once more, Garro spared a thought for the loyalists left behind to face the guns of Horus.

The Stormbird turned and dipped its nose towards Luna, filling the viewport with spans of hard white stone the same shade as Garro's marble-hued armour. They were falling towards the Rhetia Valley and beyond it the Mare Crisium – the Sea of Crises where the Silent Sisterhood kept their secure lunar citadel.

Garro caught movement from the corner of his eye, the yellow of an Imperial Fist going forward from the aft compartment. Hakur saw him notice. 'I dislike being treated like a noviciate on my first mission off-world,' he said quietly. 'We don't need escorts, not from these humourless dullards.'

'It is by Dorn's orders,' Garro replied, although he said it with little conviction.

'Are we prisoners now, captain? Have we come so far only to be clapped in irons and stowed away in some lunar dungeon?'

Garro eyed him. 'We are not prisoners, Sergeant Hakur. Our wargear and weapons still remain in our possession.'

The veteran snorted. 'Only because Dorn's men think we are no threat to them. Look there, sir.' He nodded at the warriors at the far end of the compartment. 'They pretend to be at ease but they are too stiff to carry it off. I see the patterns of their movements through the ship. They walk as if they are on guard duty, and we are their charges.'

'Perhaps so,' admitted Garro, 'but I believe it is more that Captain Halbrecht fears what we represent than who we are. I saw his face when Dorn revealed the truth of the Warmaster's deceit. He could not comprehend it.'

'That may be, lord, but the tension grinds like blades upon me!' He looked around. 'It's an insult to us. They separated us, placed the Luna Wolf with Voyen and the boy Decius's capsule on another shuttle, and I never saw what happened to the iterator and the women.'

Garro pointed at something through the viewport. 'We're all going to the same place, Andus. Look there.'

Outside, the sheer brass tower of the Somnus Citadel turned to meet the descending drop ship. As they came closer, Garro saw that the building was made from hundreds of gates, one atop the other, arrayed like the faceplates of the golden helmets of the Silent Sisters. The Stormbird fell into a spiralling turn, orbiting around the tower. A dome became visible in the floor of the vast crater beyond, and slowly it opened, triangular segments drawing back to present a concealed landing field.

'We are on final approach to the citadel,' said Halbrecht. 'Take your seats.'

'What if I wish to stand?' replied Hakur, open defiance in his tone.

'Sergeant,' warned Garro, and waved him to his place.

'Are all your subordinates so obstreperous?' grumbled the other captain.

'Of course,' said Garro, returning to his acceleration couch, 'we are Death Guard. It's our nature.'

THE STORMBIRD'S HATCH yawned open and Garro strode out down the drop-ramp, catching Halbrecht unaware. Protocol meant that as it was an Imperial Fists ship, an Imperial Fist should have been first down the ramp, but Garro was finding less and less use for such pointless etiquette.

A cadre of Silent Sisters was waiting for them in a careful formation on the landing apron. Garro glanced around, up over the folding wings of the Stormbird to the open hatch far above. The soap-bubble shimmer of a porous aura field was visible, holding the atmosphere inside the chamber but allowing objects of high mass like the ships to pass through unencumbered. A second Stormbird was dropping in behind on jets of retro thrust, and out in the void a third ship was approaching, twinkling with indicator lights but too distant to see in any detail.

The Astartes came to a halt and bowed to the Sisters. 'Nathaniel Garro, Battle-Captain of the Death Guard. By order of the primarch Rogal Dorn, I am here.'

Halbrecht and his guards came down heavily after him, and Garro felt the annoyance radiating off them. He kept his eyes on the Sisters. Their squad markings varied among the group and he searched for some that matched those of the Storm Dagger cadre.

Garro saw the same kinds of warriors as he had on the jorgalli world-ship, but with stylistic differences upon their armour in the same fashion as those of the various Legiones Astartes. One group wore armour detailed in wintry silver, the lower halves of their faces hidden behind spiked guards that resembled a barrier fence. Another woman, standing to the edge of the group, had no armour at all. Rather, she was clad in a thick, buckle-studded coat of blood-red leather, with matching gauntlets and a high collar ranged around her neck. The woman had no eyes. In their place were two augmetics, heavy lenses of ruby-coloured glass fixed to the skin of her brow and cheeks with hair-fine wires. She studied Garro with all the warmth of a chirurgeon observing a cancer beneath a microscope.

With an abrupt sensation, Garro felt a chill range deep through his bones. It was the same odd feeling he had encountered when he saw Sister Amendera in the *Endurance*'s assembly chamber, the same peculiar *absence* of something indefinable, only now he felt surrounded by it, the disquiet pressing in on him from every side.

'Battle-Captain Garro, well met,' said a familiar voice. A slight figure in robes dropped back her hood and he recognised the novice girl he had spoken to before. 'And to you as well, Halbrecht of the Imperial Fists. The Silent Sisterhood welcomes you to the Somnus Citadel. It saddens us that your arrival must come under such difficult circumstances.'

Garro hesitated. He wasn't sure how much the Sisters knew of the Isstvan situation, or what Dorn and the Sigillite had communicated to them. He covered

with a salute. 'Sister, I thank you for granting us a
haven while these matters are addressed.'

It was a lie, of course. Garro did not wish to be here
and neither did his men, but the Sisterhood had
proven themselves worthy of his respect and he saw
no need to begin this meeting on an adversarial note.
He had taken his fill of such behaviour with the
Imperial Fists. 'Where is your mistress?'

The novice girl's neutral expression faltered for a
moment and Garro saw her give the woman in the
red coat a sideways glance. 'She will attend us
momentarily.'

The rest of Garro's men from the first Stormbird
had fallen in behind him and under Hakur's command, presented a parade ground formation.
Halbrecht stood at Garro's shoulder and eyed him.
'Captain,' he said with formality, 'a word.'

'Yes?'

The Imperial Fist's eyes narrowed, but not in annoyance as Garro expected. Halbrecht showed what might
have passed for compassion. 'I know what you must
think of us. I can only begin to comprehend what you
have experienced.' *If it is true.* Garro could almost hear
the silent addendum. 'Do not think ill of my primarch.
These orders he has given ar to preserve the security of
the Imperium. If the price of that is a wound to your
honour, then I hope you will see it is a small one to pay.'

Garro met his gaze. 'My kinsmen have betrayed me.
My master has turned traitor. My honour brothers are
dead, and my Legion is on the path to corruption. My
honour, Captain Halbrecht, is all I have left.' He
turned away as the second Stormbird settled into
place with jets of spent thruster gas.

The other transport opened along its flanks and
servitors scurried out with the isolation capsule in

their grip. Voyen walked in lockstep with them. As Garro watched, a contingent of Silent Sisters, all of them armed with powerful inferno guns, formed a guard around the module as it was carried past them.

'Where are you taking him?' he asked.

'The Somnus Citadel has many functions, and our hospitallers are highly skilled,' said the novice. 'Perhaps they may have success where the medicae of the Astartes did not.'

'Decius is not a xenos corpse to be poked and dissected,' Garro replied tersely, his thoughts returning to the alien psyker-child. 'You will treat him with the respect a Death Guard is due!'

Sendek and Qruze approached, joining Hakur's formation with the last of the men. 'Be still, lad,' said the Luna Wolf. 'Your boy is not dead yet. Still he clings on to bloody life, even now. I've rarely seen a fighting spirit of the like.'

Garro grunted, his mood darkening. At last, the final vessel dropped down into the chamber and turned, landing struts extending from the spread wings and fuselage. He recognised the shuttle, the black and gold livery identical to the ship from the *Aeria Gloris* he had spied on the landing deck of the *Endurance*. The swan-like ship settled gently on the apron and fell silent. Garro knew instinctively who he would see aboard before the egress hatch opened. A ramp extruded from the ventral hull and a handful of figures disembarked. Leading them was Amendera Kendel, her proud and noble bearing somewhat muted. She seemed distracted and wary. Two more of Kendel's Storm Dagger Witchseekers marshalled the other passengers from behind: Kyril Sindermann, Mersadie Oliton and at their head, Euphrati Keeler.

Keeler's gaze crossed the chamber and found Garro. She gave him a nod of greeting that seemed almost regal. He had expected her to appear afraid, as nervous as Oliton and the old iterator obviously were, but Keeler stepped down into the citadel as if she were fated to be there, as if she were the mistress of the place.

Sister Amendera did something in sign-language and the unblinking woman in the red coat and her cohorts moved with sudden, graceful swiftness.

'An Excrutiatus,' said Halbrecht of the woman. 'It is said that each one of them must personally burn a hundred witches before they can take the rank.'

Keeler stood, unruffled, as the prosecutor squad approached her. With exaggerated caution, the Sister Excrutiatus gave Euphrati a cold and clinical once-over, looking her up and down. Then she signed to Kendel and gestured sharply to her warriors, who surrounded the refugees.

Both Garro and Qruze came forward at the same moment, ready to step to battle if events fell that way. 'These people are under my aegis!' barked the Death Guard. 'Those who harm them will face me–'

Sister Amendera and her witchseekers stepped in to block the Astartes's path, but it was Keeler who gave them pause.

'Nathaniel, Iacton, please, don't interfere. I will go with them. It is necessary.'

The woman in the red coat signed and the novice translated. 'This one demonstrates traits that are of issue to the Sisterhood. By the Emperor's edicts and the Decree of Nikaea, we have the authority to do with her as we wish. You have no right of claim in this place, Astartes.'

'And the civilians, a documentarist and an iterator?' snapped Qruze. 'Are you free to take them as well?'

'Wherever Euphrati goes, we will accompany her!' Mersadie managed a defiant interjection and Garro saw Sindermann nod in agreement.

Keeler began to walk. 'Don't be afraid for us,' she called. 'Have faith. The Emperor will protect.'

Garro watched the procession of figures disappear down a ramp and through a thick iris of steel leaves that slammed closed behind them. He could not shake the sudden, icy certainty that he would never see them again.

Amendera Kendel was still in front of him, still studying him with iron eyes. She signed again. 'Captain Garro, and the men under your stewardship, know this,' the novice translated in a clear, crisp voice, 'we grant you sanctuary here until such time as the Master of Mankind makes ruling on what shall be done with you. Quarters have been prepared.' The Silent Sister never once broke eye contact with him. 'You are our guests and you will be treated as such. In return we ask that you behave only as the warriors of the Legiones Astartes should, with honour and respect.' The novice paused. 'Captain, she asks you for your word.'

It seemed like an eternity before Nathaniel answered. 'She has it.'

IT WAS A PRISON, in any real sense of the word.

There were no bars upon the windows, no locked doors on the spartan tier of the citadel where the Sisters gave them quarters in which to wait, but outside was barren rock and airless void, and for kilometres in all directions there were autonomous sensor units and gun-drones. If they left the spire, where could they go? Steal a ship from the launch bay? And then what?

Garro sat in his small chamber in silence and listened to the men of the seventy as they talked among themselves. All of them gave voice to the things that churned inside their minds, thoughts of what futures lay before them, fears borne of desperation and plans that went nowhere and did nothing.

Sister Amendera was no fool. He saw the look in her eyes. He knew as well as she did that if the Astartes of the *Eisenstein* decided that their confinement was at an end, there would be little the Sisters of Silence could do to stop them from leaving. Garro was certain that Kendel's warriors would make it a costly path for them, but he estimated he would lose no more than ten of his men, and probably only the ones who had been slowed by injury during the escape from Isstvan.

He knew the *Phalanx* was still nearby, and Dorn with it. Perhaps if they did try to leave, the primarch would send Halbrecht and Efried to convince them otherwise. Garro frowned. Yes, that was a sensible tactic and Dorn was nothing if not the master of level-headed strategy. Stepping back for a moment to examine the situation, Garro had to give the lord of the Imperial Fists his due for handling the *Eisenstein* men in the manner he had. If Garro and the others had remained on the star fortress, eventually friction would have flared and blood would have been shed. By placing them here, under the roof of the Sisterhood – and the very same women who had fought alongside them only months ago – Dorn forced Garro to give pause to any thoughts of unfettered combat.

Even if they fought through the Sisters and the Imperial Fists, and got themselves a ship, what would it earn them? It was madness to think they might approach Terra and demand an audience with the Emperor to vindicate themselves. Any atmosphere-capable ship would be ripped from the sky before it came within sight of the Imperial Palace, and if they fled for deep space there were hundreds of battleships between Luna and a navigable jump locus.

Of all the things he feared would happen to the seventy, Nathaniel Garro had not expected this. To come so far, in measures of both his soul and of distance, only to be held at bay here, within sight of his goal… It was torture, in its own way.

Time passed and no word came for them. Sendek wondered aloud if they might be left here to live out their lives while the matter of Horus was settled on the other side of the galaxy, the seventy an inconvenient footnote forgotten amid the fighting. Andus Hakur made a joke to him about it, but Garro saw the real concern beneath the forced humour. Barring death in battle or fatal accident, an Astartes was functionally immortal and he had heard it said that one of his kind might live a thousand years or more. Garro tried to imagine that, being trapped in the citadel while the future unfolded around them, unable to intervene.

The Death Guard had attempted to rest for the first few days, but as it was aboard the frigate, sleep came infrequently to him and when it did, it was brimming with images of darkness and horror dredged from the madness of the flight. The corrupted, diseased things he had seen masquerading as Grulgor and his men lurked in the shadows of his mind, tearing at his will. Had those things truly been real? The warp was after all, a reflection of human emotion and psychic turbulence. Perhaps the Grulgor-daemon was that, a freakish mirror of the black, diseased heart that beat

beneath Ignatius's chest made real, a fate that other
unwary men could also fall to. At the opposite end of
the spectrum, he felt the golden glow of something –
someone – impossibly ancient and knowing. It wasn't
Keeler, although he sensed her as well. It was a light
that dwarfed hers, that reached into every corner of
his spirit.

Finally, he awoke and decided to give up his efforts
at sleep. There was a war being fought, he realised, and
not just the one out in the Isstvan system, the one
between those who stood by Horus and those who
stood by his father. There was another war, a silent and
insidious conflict that only a few were aware of, people
like the girl Keeler, like Kaleb and now Nathaniel himself: a war not for territory or material gain, but a war
for souls and spirits, for hearts and minds.

Two paths lay open before him and his kindred.
The Astartes understood that they had always been
there, but his vision had been clouded and he had
not seen them clearly. Along one, the route that
Horus had taken, that way lay the monstrous horrors.
The other led here, to Terra, to the truth and to this
new war. It was on that battlefield that Garro stood,
the battle looming ever closer like thunder at the
horizon.

'A storm is coming,' said the captain to the air, holding Kaleb's brass icon of the Emperor before him.

THERE WERE ALWAYS two paths. The first was wet with
blood and he had already stumbled a good way down
it. At the end point, always visible but forever out of
reach, there was release, painlessness and the sweet
nectar of rebirth.

The other route was made of knives and it was
agony and torture and grief without respite, with only

greater suffering heaped upon those that already wracked his mind and body. There was no conclusion to this route, no oblivion, only an endless loop, a Mobius strip cut from hell.

Solun Decius was Astartes, and against an unrefined man among the billions of the Imperium, his kind were the sons of war-gods; but even a being of such strength has its limits.

The wound grew to become a fanged maw that chewed upon him, biting and drawing his essence from the Death Guard's body. Where Grulgor's plague knife had sunk through his armour and into his flesh, Decius was invaded by a virus that was all viruses, a malady that was every disease that man had encountered and more that it had yet to face. There was no cure, how could there be? The germs were made from the living distillate of corruption in its rawest form, a writhing pattern of tri-fold and eight-pointed microbes that disintegrated everything they came into contact with. These invisible weapons were the foot soldiers of the Great Destroyer, each of them stamped with the indelible mark of the Lord of Decay.

'Help me!' He would have screamed those words if only he could have opened his rictus-locked jaws, if he could have parted his dry, gummed lips, if his throat could have channelled anything but a thick paste of blood-darkened mucus. Decius writhed on the support cradle, livid bruises forming about his body where flesh went dull with infection. He clawed at the glass walls around him, arms like brittle sticks in bags of stringy muscle and pallid flesh. Things that looked like maggots with three black eyes bored through the meat of his torso, raking him with tiny whips of poisonous cilia. There was so much pain, and every time Decius imagined he had reached the peaks of each new agony, a fresh one was brought to him.

He so wanted death. Nothing else mattered to him. Decius wanted death so much he prayed for it, Imperial truth be damned and burned! He had no other recourse. If peace would not be granted by any source in this world, what entreaty did he have left but to beg the realms beyond the real?

From the agony, came laughter, mocking at first, then gradually softening, becoming gentle. An intelligence measured him, considering, finally seeing something in the youth, a chance to refine an art only recently discovered: the art of remaking men.

Sorrow flowed over him. *How terribly sad it was that the men Decius had called brother and lord ignored his pain, how cruel of them to let him suffer and suffer while the malaise burrowed deeper into his heart.* He had given so much to them, had he not? *Fought in battle at their sides.* Saved their lives with no thought for his own. *Become the very best Death Guard he could be… and for what?* So they could seal him inside a glass jar and watch him slowly choke on the fumes of his own decay? *Did he deserve this?* What wrong had he committed? *None!* Nothing! *They had forsaken him!* He hated them for that! *Hated them!*

They had made him weak. Yes, that was the answer. In all this vacillation over Horus and his machinations, Decius had let himself become weak and indecisive! He never would have suffered Grulgor's blow if his mind had been clear and focused.

Yes, through the burning pain it became clear. His error traced its roots to one place, to a single point. He had bowed to Garro's orders. Despite the way in which it chafed upon him, Solun had let himself believe he was still raw and untested, let himself think that Garro's way was best. But the truth? That was not the truth. Garro was irresolute. His mentor had lost his killer instinct. Horus... Horus! There was a warrior who knew the nature of strength. He was mighty. He had turned primarchs to his banner, Mortarion included! Decius thought he could stand against that? What madness must have possessed him?

Do you want death? The question echoed in him, the agony suddenly abating. *Or will you grasp new life? A new strength that cannot be made vulnerable?* The voice that was no voice whispered, dank and rancid in his thoughts.

'Yes!' Decius spat bile and black ichor. 'Yes, damn them all! I will never be weak again! I choose life! Give me life!'

The dark laughter returned. *And so I will.*

WHAT RIPPED ITSELF from the medicae cradle was no longer Solun Decius, naked and close to the ragged edge of torment. It was alike to an Astartes, but only in the ways that it was a brutal parody of their noble form. Across rotten bones and raw, pustulant skin grew chitinous planes of greenish-black armour, gleaming like spilled oil beneath the light of the biolumes. Eyes that had shrivelled to knots of dead jelly erupted into gelid sapphires, multi-faceted orbs that massed across a wrecked face and set into the bone. Mandibles joined brown, cracked teeth in the mouth. A stump reached up and batted away the glass rigs of potion bottles, growing and malforming as it did into a clawed limb with too many joints. The serrated fingers inflated and hardened into solid knives of bony carapace the colour of sword beetles. What was no longer Solun Decius opened its mouth and roared, and from bleeding, suppurating lips spewed a cloud of insects that raced around the shivering body in a living shroud, a cape of beating, swarming wings.

On newly clawed feet, the Lord of the Flies raised himself up and shattered the armourglass walls of his confinement, and began a search for something to kill.

SIXTEEN

Lord of the Flies
Silence
In His Name

TOLLEN SENDEK STEPPED off the gravity disc as the floating platform reached the infirmary level. The oval plate hovered for a second after he departed, then drew silently away, up one of the many vertical shafts that cut through the interior spaces of the Somnus Citadel. His lip curled. The tower had a peculiar array of scents to it that the Death Guard found off-putting. Different levels had different odours, cast out from censers and odd mechanical devices that resembled steel flowers. It was some element of the Silent Sisterhood's discipline, a way of patterning the women used to mark out quadrants of the building. Similar methods were used for the blind astropaths on some starships and orbital platforms. Perhaps it was this unwelcome similarity that made Sendek uncomfortable. He disliked all things about the psyker arts, and all things that connected to them. Such realms were at odds with his rational, reductionist view of the universe. Sendek believed in the cold, hard light of science and the Imperial truth. The freakish facilities that verged on the edges of sorcery were disquieting to him. Such things were for the Emperor to understand, not for those with minds of lesser breadth.

But the smell... today it was different. Before it had been like roses, collecting at the edge of his senses. Now it was strange, sweeter than before, but with a sour metal taste beneath it. He kept walking.

Without making an order of it, or with anything approaching official sanction, the men of the seventy started a watch. They had nothing to do inside the citadel but drill and spar in the cramped quarters a few levels up the length of the tower, and the waiting, the inaction, chafed at them. So they took it in turns to keep the watch on their fallen comrade. Iacton Qruze was not expected to participate – Decius was a Death Guard and Qruze was not – but all the other men under Garro's command automatically accepted and understood what was required of them. Quietly, they made sure that there was never a moment that passed when a warrior of the XIV Legion was not attending the sick bed of Solun Decius. That the young warrior was destined to die was not questioned by any one of them, but it became an unspoken imperative that he would not die alone.

Not for the first time, Sendek found himself wondering what would happen when the end came for the youth. In a way, Decius had become something of a symbol for them all, an embodiment of the resilient endurance of their Legion. He thought of the two of them matched over a regicide board on the *Endurance* and felt a pang of sorrow. For all of Solun's brashness and arrogance, the cocksure warrior did not deserve a death of such ignominy. Decius should have perished in glorious battle instead of being reduced to fighting a war with his own body.

The smell was becoming stronger. Sendek's frown deepened. Iago, one of Hakur's squad and a deft hand with a plasma gun, took the watch before Tollen's, but he was overdue. It wasn't like Iago to be so thoughtless. Sergeant Hakur's hard training and battle drills burned that out of his men.

Then the unmistakable aroma of blood finally raised itself from the mix of scents and Sendek tensed. There was no movement anywhere along the infirmary corridor, and where the corner turned to the isolation ward the biolumes in the walls and ceiling had been doused. Only a faint red light showed him the vaguest outline of the corridor. He broke into a run, his senses taking in everything. For a moment, the Astartes thought that there had been some kind of accident, like the spillage of some great casket of oil across the floors and wall, but the charnel house stink overwhelmed him with the raw bouquet of fresh blood and rotted meat. Sendek realised abruptly that the biolumes had not been deactivated after all. It was only that there was so much blood, in thick, sticky layers, that it damped down the glow from them. His ceramite boots crunched on a paste of broken bone fragments and melted teeth. He made out a shape in the rancid gloom: a forearm ending in rags of torn meat, still partly sheathed in the marble armour of a Death Guard. Glittering black motes moved all across the severed limb.

Sendek went for the bolt pistol on his belt as the sound began. Around him the blackened walls flickered and hummed with the sharp, piercing scrapes of insect wings. The swarms grazing upon the effluent stirred, sensing the presence of the Astartes.

He saw into the isolation ward and felt his throat tighten. There was Decius's capsule, now little more than a broken glass egg torn open from within. Organs and fleshy objects were scattered about the tiled floor where servitors and other living things had been ripped apart. Sendek's hand went to the neck ring on his armour, as the buzzing grew louder, instinctively keying the battlefield vox channel that would tie him to his squad leader. 'Andus,' he began, 'alert the–'

The claw took him by the leg and yanked him savagely from his feet. Sendek cried out and lost the pistol at once, as his attacker threw him bodily into a glass cabinet filled with vials and bottles. He clattered through the storage compartment and rolled to the floor, hands and knees falling into puddles of thick fluid. The Death Guard tried to recover, but a hooked foot swung up and hit him in the face, spinning him over and down.

Sendek slid away, knocking aside remnants of what had once been the torso of Brother Iago, and gasped. The shrieking, roaring storm of flies hammered around the room like a cyclone, the beating of their wings sharp in his ears. He groped for something to use as a weapon and found a large bone saw among a tray of discarded chirurgeon's tools. The Death Guard launched himself forward, turning the bright rod of surgical steel in his grip. He would make this intruder pay for killing his kinsmen.

He had only fleeting impressions of the black figure. He saw the strange wiry hairs festooning the surface of the oily armour, he felt himself gagging at the monstrous stench of death that enveloped it. A head with too many eyes and a chattering spider mouth came at him, but beneath the corrupted, fly-blown flesh there was a shape that seemed familiar to him. A terrible moment of recognition struck Sendek like a bullet.

'Solun?' He hesitated, the arc of the bone saw halted in his shock.

'Not any more.' The mouth moved but the voice came from the flies, rippling their wings and scraping their carapaces to create a droning facsimile of human speech. The claw came out of the dimness and punctured the meat and bone of Sendek's head, splitting the Death Guard's skull. The pink-grey contents gushed out across his armour, and the swarm dived upon the richness to feed.

'NATHANIEL!'

THE WOMAN'S cry tore through Garro's body in a shuddering wave that set his nerves alight. He gasped and the steel mug in his hand fell away from nerveless fingers, a tongue of dark tea spilling across the floor of the exercise chamber. Voyen saw his reaction and reached out to steady him. 'Captain? Are you all right?'

'Did you hear that?' Garro said, tension running through him. He cast about. 'I heard her call out.'

Voyen blinked. 'Sir, there was no sound. You reacted as if you had been struck–'

Garro pushed him away. 'I heard her, as clear as you speak to me now! It was…' The import of it came all at once, the powerful, unfiltered jolt of fear projected into him. 'Keeler! Something is amiss, it was a… a warning…'

The chamber's hatch slid into the wall and Hakur was there, his expression one of deep concern. Immediately, Garro knew something was very wrong. 'Speak!' he snapped.

Hakur tapped the vox module built into the collar of his power armour. 'Lord, I fear Sendek may be in trouble. He started to send me an alert call, but his words were suddenly cut off.'

'Where is he?'

'He went to relieve Iago,' said Voyen, 'at the boy's side.'

Garro tapped him on the chest. 'Voyen, remain here and be ready for anything.' The battle-captain strode into the corridor. 'Sergeant, get the Luna Wolf and a couple of warriors to meet us at the drop-shaft.'

'Sir, what is going on?' asked Hakur. 'Have these women turned against us?'

Nathaniel closed his eyes and felt the echo of the cry still swimming through his spirit, a dark tide of emotion following with it. 'I don't know, old friend,' he replied, taking up his helmet and locking it in place. 'We'll know soon enough.'

THE RESONANCE OF gunfire climbed up the shaft to them as Garro and the other Astartes rode the gravity disc down. Qruze shot him a look. 'This damn war's followed us here.'

'Aye,' replied the battle-captain. 'Our warning may have come too late.'

Hakur cursed under his breath. 'No signals from Sendek or Iago, not even a carrier wave. At this distance, there is no way I could not reach them. I could yell and they would hear it!'

The disc slowed as it approached the infirmary level. The stink of new death wafted up to the platform and every one of the Astartes tensed. 'Weapons,' ordered Garro, unsheathing his sword.

He led them off the elevator and through the corridors, crossing through the dank, blood-slick passage.

They entered the infirmary proper and Qruze made a spitting noise. 'Sendek is here,' he said, leaning over a dark shape in the gloom, 'what remains of him.'

Even through his helmet filters, the odour of decay assaulted Garro's nostrils as he came closer. The spongy slurry of meat resembled a body exposed to months of putrefaction. It was undeniably Tollen Sendek, even though the remains of the dead man's skull were a ruined, bloated mass. He recognised the honour pennants and oaths of moment affixed to the armour. These too were discoloured with age and mould, and fingers of orange rust looped around the joints of the limbs.

One of Hakur's men choked back a gasp of disgust. 'He looks like he's been dead for weeks... but I spoke to him only this morning.'

The Luna Wolf leaned closer to the body. 'Iacton, keep your distance–'

Garro's words came too late. Thick white pustules on Sendek's body trembled as they sensed the closeness of Qruze's blood-warmth and burst, throwing out streams of tiny iridescent beetles. The veteran rocked back and batted the things away, pulping great masses of them with his armoured palm. 'Agh! Filthy vermin!'

The captain nudged a severed limb with his boot. There were too many torn hanks of meat and bone strewn about the room to be the component parts of just one human body, and he knew with bleak certainty that Iago was as dead as poor Tollen.

From across the chamber, Hakur peered cautiously into the broken isolation pod. 'Empty...' He snagged something with his combat blade from inside the glass container and held it up for the others to see. 'In all the days of Terra, what is this?' It resembled a thin scrap of torn muslin, slick with black liquids. As it turned in the air, Garro made out holes in the material that corresponded to eyes, nostrils and a mouth.

Qruze gave the rag a grim examination. 'It is human flesh, sergeant, sloughed off, as species of snakes and insects shed their skins.'

The flat bangs of bolter fire echoed down the corridors leading to the other compartments of the infirmary and Garro gestured sharply. 'Leave that. We move, now.'

QRUZE'S FACE WAS locked in a permanent scowl of harsh, cold anger. At every turn, just as he thought he had weathered each new sinister twist of fate, a fresh horror was heaped upon the others. Qruze imagined a vice turning about his spirit, gradually tightening, the pressure upon his mind and his will growing ever more intense. He felt as if he were on the verge of shutting down, as if the goodness and light inside him were in danger of guttering out. Each new sight repulsed and shocked the old soldier in ways he thought he could never be touched.

The Astartes passed quickly through a series of seal doors that lay off their hinges, ripped apart by something of great strength and violence. Past that, they came upon a curative ward with rows of medicae cradles and sickbeds, one of the Silent Sisterhood's hospices for those of their number injured in action, he decided. The ward resembled a slaughterhouse more than a place of healing. Like the isolation chamber, the room was thick with death-stink: blood and excrement, the fetor of disease and rich organic decomposition. In each bed, the patients were dead or near to it, each beneath the smothering hands of a different malady. Qruze saw a pallid, skeletal witchseeker shaking and foaming at the mouth from some sort of palsy. Next to her was a bloated body wreathed in gaseous vapours. Then a victim killed by bone-rot, a weeping novice wracked by bubonic plague, and a naked girl bleeding from her eyes and ears.

It was not just living flesh that was polluted. Corrosion covered the steel frames of the medicae cradles, and glasses and plastics were cracked and broken. The decay touched everything. He looked away.

'They have been left to die,' said Hakur, 'infected and left to fester like discarded cuts of meat.'

'A test,' said Garro. 'The hand that did this was toying with them.'

'We ought to burn them,' said Qruze, 'put these poor fools out of their misery.'

'There's no time for that kind of mercy,' Garro retorted. 'Every moment we tarry, the cause of this horror walks free to spread more corruption.'

At the far end of the ward, they came across more dead, this time the bodies of Silent Sisters in the armoured garb of vigilators. Spent, broken bolt pistols lay near them, barrels clogged with gobs of acidic mucus. Thousands of tiny scratches covered the places where their skin was bare. They had died from puncture wounds in the chest, from what seemed like a cluster of five daggers stabbed into their torsos. 'Too narrow for a short sword,' Qruze noted.

Garro nodded and held up his hand, flexing the fingers in a gesture of explanation. 'Talons,' he explained.

Hakur and his men were already working the rusted wheel of a large airtight hatch that would give them access to the next section of the tier. The gummed metal shrieked as they forced it open.

'What kind of creature has claws like that?' Qruze asked aloud.

The hatch crashed open off its broken hinges with a roaring displacement of air, and there before them was the answer.

THE ADJOINING CHAMBER was an open space criss-crossed by gantries and walkways, suspended in a steel web far above the open platform of a hangar bay several tiers below. Situated halfway up the side of the Somnus Citadel, the hangar was one of many tertiary landing ports designed for the shuttles deployed aboard the Black Ships. This landing port served the infirmary, allowing injured Sisters to be taken directly to the medicae centre in the event of a critical emergency. Normally it would be busy with servitors performing maintenance tasks on the landing grids, the ships or the airlock doors, but now it was the site of a pitched battle.

Garro saw the gold and silver of a dozen Silent Sisters engaged in close combat with a whirling, screaming mass of claws and green-black armour. It was difficult to get a good eye on what was happening. A foggy mass of smoke wreathed all the combatants; but no, not smoke. The cloud hummed and writhed with a will of its own, and he saw one witchseeker pitched over the lip of a gantry and sent falling to her death as the swarming mass of flies blinded her. The form barely visible in the midst of the insects, tall and shimmering, continued to send out savage attacks into the lines of the Sisters.

Hakur raised his bolter, but Garro waved him back. 'Careful! There are oxygen lines and fuel conduits in the walls. A stray round could set off an inferno! Blades only until I order otherwise!'

The catwalks were narrow and they forced the Astartes into single file movement. Garro saw Qruze split off with one of Hakur's squad and make an approach along a different gantry. He nodded and ran forward. The metal decking clanged and shook beneath the heavy boots of the Death Guard. It was hardly built for the weight of men in ceramite and flexsteel.

The swarm's motion was that of a single living, thinking creature. As the Astartes came close, it cut off portions of itself and sent them screeching through the air, separate and distinct clumps of dense, poisonous forms clawing at the eyes and skin of the warriors. Bolter fire would not harm this enemy. The tiny bodies resisted their attack, and the men were reduced to snatching at the air, pulping the serrated insects into messes of cracked chitin.

Blue light gathered along his blade. Swinging Libertas over his head, Garro cut a swathe through the thickening edges of the swarm and reacted swiftly as a figure in gold cannoned into him, propelled backwards by a vicious blow. He caught the Sister in a vice-like grip and arrested her fall towards a broken guide rail. She hissed loudly and the captain realised too late that the woman's arm was scored with hundreds of slash wounds where razored insect wings had cut her flesh. Garro reeled her back in and found himself looking into the eyes of Amendera Kendel. She was flushed with effort from the fight.

To Garro's surprise, she made a quick string of word gestures in Astartes battle-sign. *Nature of enemy unknown.*

'Aye,' agreed Garro. 'You know this tower better than we do, Sister. Block the escape routes and let my men deal with this mutant.' He had to raise his voice so it

would carry over the chattering squeals of the swarming bugs.

Kendel signed again, getting to her feet. *Proceed with
caution.*

'That time has passed,' he replied and threw himself
into the rippling mass of the swarm, the sword's
power field crisping great clumps of black flies from
the air around him.

THE SISTERS DREW back and followed Garro's command. There had been a moment, just the smallest of
instants, when Nathaniel Garro had heard Keeler's cry
and feared that the women had turned against them.
His own battle-brothers had already raised weapons
against him, and it was sad and damning that his first
reaction was to assume it had happened once more,
this time with Kendel's witchseekers out to murder
them. He felt a measure of relief to learn he was
wrong. To be confronted by another betrayal added
to those of Horus, Mortarion and Grulgor... Was fate
so cruel to curse him again?

Yes.

In his heart, in his soul he knew who it was he
would find at the heart of the swarm even before he
laid eyes upon him. The clawed, reeking monster
spread the too-long fingers of his distended left hand
in a grotesque greeting as Nathaniel fell into the eye
of the swarm storm. The hexagonal steel decking
beneath him squealed and moaned, shifting.

'Captain.' The word was a mocking chorus of rattling echoes, humming into his ears from all
around. 'Look, I am healed.' For all the gruesome
malformations of his flesh and bone, the aspect of
the man beneath the changed body was clear to
Garro's eyes.

He teetered on the brink of despair for one long second, the revulsion at what stood before him threatening to knock the last pillars of reason from his mind. A flash of memory unfolded. Garro remembered the first time he had seen Solun Decius, on the muddy plateau of the black plains on Barbarus. The aspirant was covered in shallow cuts, streaks of blood and a patina of dirt. He was pale from exertion and ingested poisons, but there was no weakness of any kind lurking behind those wild eyes. The boy had the way of an untamed animal about him, brilliantly fierce and cunning. Garro had known in that moment that Decius was raw steel, ready to be tempered into a keen blade for the Emperor's service. Now all that potential was wasted, twisted and destroyed. He felt a terrible sense of failure settle upon him.

'Solun, why?' he shouted, furious at the youth's folly, his voice resonating inside his helmet. 'What have you done to yourself?'

'Solun Decius died aboard the *Eisenstein*!' thundered the rasping voice. 'His existence is at an end! I live now! I am the pestilent champion… I am the Lord of the Flies!'

Garro spat. 'Traitor! You followed Grulgor into his grotesque transformation. Look what you have become! A freak, a monster, a–'

'A *daemon*? Is that what you were going to say, you hidebound old fool?' Callous laughter echoed around him. 'Is it sorcery that has renewed me? All that matters is that I have cheated death, like a true son of Mortarion!'

'Why?' Garro screamed, the injustice hammering at him. 'In Terra's name, why did you give yourself to this abomination?'

'Because it is the future!' The voice buzzed and chattered. 'Look at me, captain. I am what the Death Guard is to become, what Grulgor and his men are already! Undying, living avatars of decay, waiting to reap the darkness!'

Garro's senses were heavy with the stench of corruption. 'I should have let you perish.' He coughed, faltering for a moment.

'But you did not!' came the scream. 'Poor Decius, trapped at the edge of mortality, wracked with such pain it would grind down a mountain. You could have released him, Garro! But you let him live in agony, tortured him with every passing moment, and for what? Because of your ludicrous belief that he would be saved by your master…' The creature took heavy steps towards him, the claw reaching out. 'He begged you! Begged you to end him, but you did not listen! He prayed to your precious gaudy Emperor for deliverance, and again he was ignored! Forsaken! Forsaken!' A slashing blow clipped Garro and he dodged away, falling through a haze of flies. The breathing slits on his armour locked shut, holding out the scrabbling, biting mandibles of the insects.

Garro had the brass icon and its chain wound around the fingers of his gauntlet. 'No,' he insisted, 'you should have survived. If you had held on, if you could give your spirit in the God-Emperor's service–'

'God?' The swarm bellowed the word back at him. 'I know god! The power that remade Decius, that is god! The intellect that answered him when he lay praying for the bliss of decease, that is god! Not your hollow golden idol!'

'Blasphemy!' Garro snarled. 'You are a blasphemy, and I will not suffer you to live. Your heresy, that of Grulgor, Mortarion, *Horus himself*, will be crushed!'

The battle-captain launched a brutal flurry of counterstrokes, chopping at the discoloured armour.

Each blow was parried. 'Fool. The Death Guard are already dead. It is ordained.'

Garro's answer was a vicious downward slash that cut a wide gouge through the rigid planes of chitinous shell. The thing that had been Solun Decius staggered with the pain of the blow and jets of thin yellow mucus streamed from the cut. Instantly, flies from the hurricane swarm around them hurtled inward and buried themselves in the wound. In seconds, the pulpy mass of writhing insect bodies was bloating and distending, staunching the injury, the flies feasting on themselves to seal it closed.

'You cannot kill decay,' hissed the voice. 'Corruption comes to all things. Men die, the stars burn cold–'

'Be silent,' commanded Garro. One of Solun's character flaws was that he had never known when to shut up.

Libertas gleamed as it arced through the air, this time cutting horned chunks of the insect armour off the monstrous foe. The distended claw, huge and heavy, swung around and slammed into the Death Guard's chest, denting the eagle cuirass and cracking the ceramite.

The knife-sharp fingers scraped across his arm, trying and failing to gain purchase. Garro brought the sword around and attacked again, forcing his enemy to push back along a gantry. Neither of them had room to manoeuvre, but corralling his enemy would only make the fight more difficult.

Blade and claw met over and over, the crystalline blue steel sparking off the chitinous talons. The speed and power behind the blows was stunning. Even at his very best, Decius had never been this deadly. It was taking every iota of Garro's skill to stay toe-to-toe with his former pupil, and where he felt the edges of tension and fatigue in his muscles, his adversary clearly did not. *I must end this, and swiftly, before more people die.*

He recalled the fight with Grulgor on the promenade deck, but there it had been the warp sustaining the diseased foes. Here, there was only the rage and anger of Solun Decius, convinced that his kinsmen had abandoned him. Garro knew one thing for certain: only he was the match for this Lord of the Flies. None of his battle-brothers had been able to beat Decius before, and in this mutated form, he would certainly kill them.

The gantry they fought upon complained and listed as Garro jumped to avoid a low, sweeping strike. The sound brought a cold smile to the battle-captain's face, and he threw out a powerful downward blow that his enemy evaded with ease.

'Too slow, teacher!' the grating snarl pulled at him.

'Too quick, apprentice,' he retorted. The strike was a feint, never intended to hit his opponent. Instead, the sparking blade sliced though the guard rail and hex-grid of the catwalk, severing cables and leaving red glowing edges where the sword cut molecules in two. The gantry moaned, twisted beneath their weight; and then it snapped, bending along its length to throw the two combatants into the air. Garro and the mutant fell, still clawing and slashing at one another, until they impacted on the wide open deck of the hangar level. The swarm buzzed angrily and came coiling down after them, as if it were furious at being left behind.

Garro got to his feet, ignoring the pain of the fall, and drew his augmetic limb forward just as the

Decius-thing struck out with a sadistic side-kick. Garro took the blow full force on the mechanical leg, the steel bones creaking, flares of hard pain clutching at his abdomen. He backhanded the mutant with the heavy pommel on his sword, smashing the hilt into a face of arthropod eyes and black mandibles. As the swarm came on them, Garro spun the blade and slashed at pallid, fly-blown skin. The cut opened the corpse flesh and spilt powdery blood. The insects reacted, howling and smothering Garro from head to foot in a thick, shifting mass.

He brought Libertas up to his chest and ran the blade at full discharge, the crackling aura dancing about his armour in coils of lightning. The winged mites puffed into dots of flame and perished, black ash smearing his wargear. Garro drew a glove across the lenses of his helmet in time to see the Lord of the Flies filling his vision. His enemy slammed into him, throwing the Astartes off the flank of a cargo pallet. Garro resisted and turned the fight back to the foe, blocking the wicked claw and sending a storm of punches into the damaged muscle and bone of the face. The flies hummed around him, trying to mend the smashed meat even as Garro broke more shards of carapace and gristle. He took a hard blow, a desperate blow, and disengaged. The mutant Astartes stumbled back a step, over the lip of an inert landing scaffold.

Garro saw the opportunity that presented itself. Beyond the Lord of the Flies and his chattering, shrieking swarm, there was a wide iris hatch that opened directly out to space. He looked up at the figures on the service gantry overhead and shouted into his vox pickup. 'Kendel!' He pointed forward. 'Open the hatch! Do it now!'

The Decius-thing couldn't hear his words, but the creature wasn't slow on the uptake. 'You think you can stop me? I carry the Lord of Decay's mark!'

Alert klaxons sounded and garish orange lumes blinked in wild strobing patterns over the steel and brass walls. Garro heard the clanking of metal gates parting on the other side of the hatch. The Lord of the Files bayed, his swarm carrying the humming, rattling voice through the air, over the chorus of sirens. 'I was right, Garro! I see the future! In ten thousand years, the galaxy will burn–'

The words vanished into a screaming tornado of sound as the iris slammed open.

With an explosive jolt the air and the loose contents of the hangar bay were torn away into the lunar night. Small objects, strips of printout and data-slates, tools and strings of dust raced away, and with them went the swarm. Garro's adversary flailed, reaching out to snag his claw on Nathaniel's boot. He fell and rolled as the vacuum dragged them both towards the roaring black mouth of the airlock. Garro felt the jagged digits score the ceramite of his greaves. He tried to strike with Libertas, but the decompression was stronger than either of them, the breath of a god carrying the two combatants away.

A cargo pod slammed into his back and the Astartes tumbled, rolled and came off his feet, buoyed by the tempest. Garro saw the walls of the landing bay flash past him and glimpsed the shimmer of his foe falling with him. Then they were in the freezing blackness, thrown from the face of the Somnus Citadel, tumbling down towards the brilliant white sands of the moon amid a cloud of ice crystals. For a brief second, he saw the brass disc of the iris hatch cycling shut

behind him. He spun lazily, end over end, the wasteland racing up to meet them.

HE NEVER FELT the impact. Time blinked and Garro
was in a cauldron of pain, agony tight around every
joint in his body. The only sounds were the gruff
pulse of his breathing and the hisses of atmosphere
inside his armour. Warning runes danced on his visor.
There was a puncture somewhere in his wargear, a
slow leak issuing air out into the dark. The regulators
inside the armour's fusion power pack were flashing
alerts. Garro ignored them all, and pushed himself up
from the pit of moon dust where he had landed.
Spears of hot pain ripped through his shoulder. The
joint was dislocated. He tabbed a restorative pill from
the auto-narthecia dispenser in his neck ring and
gripped his wrist. With a hard yank, Garro snapped
the limb back into place with a bark of agony.

He took stock of his surroundings, a small crater,
thick with dust and dotted by small porous boulders,
with steep walls. The brass tower of the citadel dominated the black sky beyond. A man-shaped imprint
showed where he had landed, and close by there was
Libertas lying flat on the dust. Garro moved quickly
towards it in a loping motion, half running, half skip-
ping. The gravity out on the lunar surface was much
lower than that inside the citadel, where artificial field
generators kept it to a Terran one-gee standard, and he
had to be careful not to stumble. In full armour, he was
suddenly unwieldy, and it took long seconds to adjust.

There was no sign of his opponent, and for a brief
moment Garro wondered if the Decius-thing had
landed somewhere else, perhaps outside the crater.

Something shattered under his boot as his foot
touched the soil and interrupted his train of thought.

Small, glistening objects were scattered all around him, shining like tiny jewels. As he bent down to recover his sword, Garro realised what they were: the frozen corpses of thousands of insects, flies and beetles.

Nathaniel!

The forewarning brushed the edges of his thoughts, a faint breath of wind upon the ocean of his mind, but it was not enough.

The moon dust exploded upward in a storm of grey, Libertas tumbling away as the creature lurking beneath the powder burst out, talons reaching for his throat. Garro grappled with the Lord of the Flies and went off his feet into a slow motion tumble. He grunted with effort as he punched his adversary hard in the sternum, and felt chitin give with the impact.

The Death Guard had known a thousand battles, and in every one the constant clatter of weapons had been the music that accompanied them; the hue and cry of fighting men locked in struggles for their lives. Now, out on the airless sun-blinding whiteness of Luna, there was no sound at all. The silence was broken only by the rush of blood in his veins, the rhythm of his exhalations. There was an absence of scents too: the foetid stink of the creature that wreathed it inside the citadel was gone. In its place Garro could only smell the tang of his own blood and the acrid traces of burning plastics from his armour's damaged servos.

They fought unarmed, hand-to-hand, every battle skill they could draw upon pushed to the fore. Using the low gravity to his advantage, Garro pushed off a rock outcropping and let his momentum flip him up and around. He turned a boot to meet his enemy's face and saw a compound eye burst into a cloud of polluted blood. The droplets froze instantly into hard black jewels that scattered over the moon dust. Some questioning, analytical portion of the battle-captain's mind wondered how it was that this freak could even exist in the vacuum. It had no suit seals, as Garro's did, no airtight layer of atmosphere to sustain it. There were patches of dark frost on the limbs of the pestilent champion where the cold of space had iced over spilt fluids, but still it lived on, defiant by its very existence.

He took a blow that knocked the breath from him, ignoring the new alert runes that haloed his vision. Streams of white vapour – precious air – issued out from points of damage beneath the eagle cuirass. Eventually suffocation would come, even to an Astartes. 'You must die, abomination,' Garro said aloud, 'even if it be my last victory!'

The Lord of the Flies pressed upon him, and Garro's back slammed into the wall of the crater, into the inky shadows cast by the rock formation. The ruined insect face leered over him and the great claw tore the cuirass from him, tossing it away. He fought back, but the Decius-thing was faster. Burning pain lanced into him as the warped Astartes bored the serrated talons through layers of ceramite and flexsteel. The thing was going to rip his armour open and expose the meat inside to the killing vacuum.

'Is this my duty?' Garro asked. 'I am Death Guard… I am dead…' A sudden sorrow engulfed him, the weight of all his darkest, most morose moments returning as one. Perhaps it was fitting that he perished here, in this lifeless stone arena. His Legion was already destroyed. What was he now? No more than a relic, an embarrassment, his warning delivered and his purpose ended. The cold was filling him, leeching

out the life from his bones. Perhaps it was for the
best, to accept death. What else was there for him?
What did he have left? His vision blurred, the pressure pushing him down.

Faith.

The word exploded inside him. 'Who?' he gasped.
'Keeler?'

Have faith, Nathaniel. You are of purpose.

'I… I am…' Garro choked, blood in his mouth sti-
fling his voice. 'I am…' His fingers touched loose rock
and closed around a fist-sized stone. '*I am!*'

With a bellow of exertion, he swung the piece of
moon rock and slammed it hard into the Lord of the
Flies. The impact echoed up his arm and the mutant
fell back, a great curl of dead skin flapping back to
reveal a distorted jawbone and a forest of teeth. Garro
threw himself forward and clasped at his fallen
sword. The chain of Kaleb's icon was snagged around
the hilt and he caught the brass links in his fingers,
dragging the weapon into his grip. Then Libertas was
in his hands and he felt a surge of power from the
mere act of holding it once more. He felt complete, he
felt *right*. Garro had told Kaleb of the weapon's origin,
and now as the globe of Terra became visible at the
lunar horizon, the blade made all his doubts and
pains vanish.

With a sword in his hand and the God-Emperor at
his back, the Death Guard realised that his duty was
far from over. He would not die today. Nathaniel
Garro was of purpose.

The creature that he had once called brother was on
its knees, trying to gather up the pieces of its face and
press them back together. He had blinded it. Garro
loped to the mutant's side and drew back the sword.
His breath came in shallow gasps and he brought the

weapon to bear. For a moment, there was pity in Nathaniel's eyes. Shame and compassion warred for a brief instant across his expression. Poor, foolish Decius. He was right. He had been forsaken, but only by his own spirit.

The Lord of the Flies looked up to meet the edge of the blade. Garro beheaded the monstrous Astartes with a single strike of the sword, taking his enemy through the neck. The corpse tumbled away and burst silently into a cloud of blackened fragments. The papery twists turned in the darkness and disintegrated, into ash, into motes of black and then nothing. The head dropped to lie in the moon dust and twitched with unheard laughter. It melted even as Garro watched, curls of skin and flensed bone becoming cinders, as if burning from the inside out. Finally, a shimmering twist of smoky energy burst free and shot away, up into the sky, trailing sense echoes of mocking amusement.

You cannot kill decay. The words repeated in his thoughts, and with care Garro sheathed his weapon. 'We will see,' he said, tipping back his head so that he could take in the sight of the Earthrise.

The sphere of Terra shone in the darkness, the eye of a god turned to face a universe ranged against it. Garro placed his hands to his chest, palms open, thumbs raised, in the sign of the Imperial aquila. He bowed. 'I am ready, lord,' he told the sky. 'No doubts, no fears, only faith. Tell me Your will, and Thy will be done.'

SEVENTEEN

The Sigillite Speaks
The Oncoming Storm

WHEN THE SILENT Sisters came for him, he was on one knee in the meditation cell, his sword drawn and the brass icon in his hands. The words of the *Lectitio Divinitatus* were on his lips, embedded in his thoughts after so many repetitions, and the women exchanged quizzical looks with each other to hear him murmur them beneath his breath. They summoned him with brisk gestures and he did as they demanded. His duty robes gathered in close around him, the feel of the roughly woven material on his skin still chafing on the new scars from his injuries and the vacuum burns. He left his power armour in the chamber, but the sword came with him. Libertas had not left his side since the duel in the Sea of Crises.

They led him up the length of the Somnus Citadel, to the glass needle at the very tip. It wasn't until he entered and they closed the doors behind him that he laid eyes on another Astartes. It seemed like weeks since he had last seen a kinsman.

The figure came closer. The chamber was a cone made of glass triangles and thick coils of black metal, and the architecture cast strange shadows with sharp edges from the reflected earthlight. 'Nathaniel. Ah, lad. We feared the worst.'

He nodded. 'Iacton. I live still, with the grace of Terra.'

The Luna Wolf raised an eyebrow. 'Indeed.' Unlike him, Qruze wore his battle armour, proudly sporting the colours of his old Legion.

There were other figures at the edge of the shadow and Garro studied them. The Oblivion Knight came forward with her novice behind her. 'Sister Amendera,' he said with a shallow bow. 'Why have you summoned us here?' He tried and failed to keep an edge of annoyance from his words. 'What trial must we answer to now?'

Garro glanced at the novice, expecting the girl to provide an answer, but her face was flushed with tension and fear. At once, the Death Guard's hands tensed around the scabbard of his weapon.

'Others…' Qruze warned, nodding into the shadows.

'You are here, Astartes, because I have ordered it.' The voice came from the dark. It was firm but quiet, not in the manner of a military commander, but that of an educator, a counsellor. A puff of flame flickered into being in the shadows and Garro saw the shape of a golden eagle sculpted with wings spread as if to take flight. A brazier burned underneath the raptor, tricking the eye with the dance of light and heat.

Footsteps approached, and with them came the heavy tapping march of a staff against the stone-tiled floor. Garro's throat tightened as he flashed back to the assembly hall aboard the *Endurance* and the arrival of his primarch, but it was not Mortarion who emerged from the shadows this time.

There were two men, but they were much more than that. Even barefoot, the taller of the two would easily have been a match for Iacton Qruze in his full armour. The watchful, hard lines of his face emerged from a suit of golden armour that was cut like that of a Terminator, but worn like that of a normal Astartes. Even at a distance, Garro could see an infinity of worked tooling in the etching that covered the glinting metal, the repeated shapes of eagles and lightning bolts. A cloak of rich red material hung around his shoulders and a towering gold helmet with a plume of crimson atop it was held in the crook of one arm. In the other, at an angle that betrayed the ease with which the warrior held it, rested a weapon that was half lance, half cannon: a guardian spear, the signature wargear of the Emperor's personal guard, the Legiones Custodes. Garro had often heard it said that the Custodians were to the Emperor as an Astartes was to his primarch, and looking upon this man, he believed it. The warrior studied Garro and Qruze with a level, emotionless gaze.

The guardian's presence alone was enough to indicate the lofty status of the man he accompanied, and they bowed to the hooded figure in his simple administrator's robes. The man in the voluminous mantle would blend seamlessly into the masses of any Imperial hive city were it not for the staff he carried, atop it, the golden eagle in its basket of flames, with steel chains looping down the length, each inscribed with axioms. This was the Rod, and it could only be held by one man: the Regent of Terra himself,

First of Council, Overseer of the Tithe and confidant of the Emperor.

'Lord Malcador,' said Garro. 'What do you wish of us?'

He dared to raise his gaze. The Sigillite's hooded glance came to rest upon him and although Nathaniel could not see his eyes, he was immediately aware that he was under intense scrutiny, in ways that he could only guess at. Malcador, so the stories said, was second only in psychic might to the Emperor. So unassuming in aspect, but here in the chamber with them the man exuded a serene kind of power, quite at odds with the brash energy of a warlord primarch, but no less potent.

At the corner of his vision, he saw the witchseeker back away a few steps, as if she were afraid to be too close to him. The Regent's vision fixed Garro like a spotlight, sifting through his spirit like sand. He tasted a greasy, electric taint in the air. The Death Guard met it and did not resist. He had not come this far to keep secrets.

'The Emperor protects,' said the Sigillite slowly, as if he were reading the words from the page of a book. 'He does indeed, Astartes, in ways that you cannot begin to comprehend.' Malcador paused, musing. 'I have heard the words of Rogal Dorn, examined the evidence of your testimony and the mnemonic records of the Lady Oliton, and thus I will be direct. Garro, you came home in hopes of seeking an audience with the Master of Mankind so that this warning could come to his ears. This will not be.'

Garro felt a flash of disappointment. Even after all that had happened, he still kept the light of hope alive. 'But he will hear the warning, Lord Regent?'

'You cannot come to Terra, so Terra comes to you.' Malcador nodded at the staff. 'I have heard the warning and that is enough for the moment. The Emperor is indisposed as he engages in his great works within the Imperial Palace.'

Garro blinked in surprise. 'Indisposed?' he repeated. 'His sons turn against him and he is too busy to learn of it? I do not understand–'

'No,' said the Regent, 'you do not. In time, these matters will become clear to all of us, but until that moment, we must trust in our master. The message has been delivered. Your obligation has been completed.'

Garro saw Qruze tense. 'Is that why he is here, Lord Regent?' The Luna Wolf nodded to the Custodian Guard. 'Are we to be dealt with, to be removed from the field of play?'

Malcador was very still. 'There are many on the Council of Terra who suggested that just such a resolution should take place. Matters of men's loyalties once thought to be solid are now in flux.'

Garro took a step forward. 'I will say to you, lord, what I said to the primarch Dorn. Are not our deeds enough to convince you of our fealty? I know you can see into the truth of a man's heart. Look into mine, and tell me what is there!'

A hand emerged from the folds of the robes. 'There is no need, captain. You have no call to prove yourselves to me. After your ordeal, I felt that you were owed the truth. I came here to give it to you in person, so that there would be no misunderstanding.'

'And now?' asked Qruze. 'What of us, Lord Regent?'

'Aye,' said Garro, clutching the icon in his grip. 'We cannot stay here, watching the stars and waiting for the day that Horus comes seeking battle. I request…' He fixed the Regent with a hard glare. 'No, I *demand* that we be given a purpose!' Garro's voice began to rise. 'I am an Astartes, but now I am a brother without a Legion. Alone, I stand unbroken amid all the oaths that lie shattered around me. I am the Emperor's will, but I am nothing if He will not task me!'

The Death Guard's words echoed around the glass tower and Kendel's novice shrank visibly to hear them. Malcador gestured with the eagle-head staff. 'Only in death does duty end, Astartes,' he said, with a hint of satisfaction, 'and you are not dead yet. As we speak, the Lord Dorn assembles his plans to oppose Horus and the primarchs he has turned to his banner. Lines of battle are being drawn across the galaxy, arrangements for a war of such magnitude that mankind has never known.'

'What will our place be in it?'

Malcador inclined his head in a tiny gesture. 'There is a matter to which you will be set, not today, perhaps not for many months, but eventually. The Warmaster's disposition has made it clear that the Imperium requires men and women of inquisitive nature, hunters who might seek the witch, the traitor, the mutant, the xenos... Warriors like you, Nathaniel Garro, Iacton Qruze, Amendera Kendel, who could root out the taint of any future treachery: a duty to vigilance.'

'We are ready,' said Garro with a nod. 'I am ready.'

'Yes,' replied the Sigillite, 'you are.'

HE FOUND VOYEN in one of the meditation cells, carefully ministering to his wargear. The Apothecary bowed slightly to him. Garro noted immediately that Voyen's robes were the plain, unadorned clothes of a citizen petitioner, not the duty mantle of an Astartes. The sewn patterns of the two-headed aquila and the skull and star of the Death Guard were absent.

'Meric?' he asked. 'We prepare to leave and yet you have kept yourself isolated from us. What's wrong?'

Voyen halted and glance at his commander. Garro saw something new there, a kind of defeat, a melancholy that was etching into the lines of his face. 'Nathaniel,' he began, 'I have read the tracts you gave me, and I feel as if my eyes have been opened.'

Garro smiled. 'That's good, brother. We can draw strength from them.'

'Hear me out. You might disagree.'

The battle-captain hesitated. 'Go on.'

'I have kept this from you, from all of the others. What happened at Isstvan, what Horus and Mortarion did, and then Grulgor and Decius...' He took a shuddering breath. 'To my very core, brother, these things shook me.' Voyen looked at his hands. 'I found myself frozen, my weapons useless.' His eyes met Garro's and there was fear there, true terror. 'It broke me, Nathaniel. These things, I fear I may be a part of them, responsible...'

'Meric, no.'

'Yes, brother, yes!' he insisted. Voyen pressed something into his palm and Garro studied it: a bronze disc embossed with a star and skull symbol, crushed and twisted. 'I must atone for my dalliance with the lodges, Nathaniel. The *Lectitio Divinitatus* has shown me that. You had me promise that if the lodge ever compelled me to turn from the Emperor, I would reject them, and so I do! The lodges were part of all this, you were right to shun them!' He looked away. 'And I... I was so very wrong to join them.'

The leaden certainty in his voice told Garro that no argument would shift his brother from this path. 'What will you do?'

Voyen indicated his wargear. 'I relinquish my honour as an Astartes and warrior of the XIV Legion. I have had my fill of death and treachery. My service from this point on will be to the Apothecaria Majoris of Terra. I have decided to dedicate the rest of my life to search for a cure for the malady that claimed Decius and the others. If Grulgor did not lie, then that horror may already be spreading among our kinsmen, and I must hold true to my oath as a healer above and beyond my oath as a Death Guard.'

Garro studied his friend for a long moment, then extended a hand to him. 'Very well, Meric. I hope you will find victory in this new battle.'

Voyen shook his hand. 'And I hope you will find victory in yours.'

'NATHANIEL,'

HE TURNED from the window of the observation gallery and gasped. The woman stepped out from between the two Silent Sisters and touched him on the arm. 'Keeler? I thought you had been taken.' She smiled a little, and he studied her. She seemed fatigued, but otherwise unharmed. 'They have not hurt you?'

'Is there ever a day when you don't concern yourself with the welfare of others?' she asked lightly. 'I have been allowed a moment of respite. How are you, Nathaniel?'

He threw a look back at the curve of Terra beyond the armourglass. 'I am... uneasy. I feel as if I am a different man, as if everything that led up to the flight from Isstvan was just a prologue. I am changed, Euphrati.'

They were quiet for a moment before he spoke again. 'Was that you? In the citadel, when Decius broke free, and then again out on the surface? Did you warn me?'

'What do you believe?'

He frowned. 'I believe I would like a straight answer.'

'There is a bond,' said Keeler quietly. 'I'm only just starting to see the edges of it myself: between you and me, between the past and the future.' She nodded at the planet. 'Between the Emperor and his sons. All things, but like all bonds, it must be tested to keep it strong. That moment is upon us now, Nathaniel. The storm is coming.'

'I am ready.' Garro's hand found hers and enveloped it. 'I was there when Horus betrayed his brothers. By the Emperor's grace, I will be there when he is called to account for his heresy.'

Beneath the light of Terra, the two of them, soldier and saint together, looked to the birth world of their species; and as one, they began to pray.

TIMELINE

Millennia	Age	Notes
1-15	Age of Terra	Humanity dominates Earth. Civilisations come and go. The Solar system is colonised. Mankind lives on Mars and the moons of Jupiter, Saturn and Neptune.
15-18	Age of Technology	Mankind begins to colonise the stars using sub-light spacecraft. At first only nearby systems can be reached and the colonies established on them must survive as independent states since they are separated from Earth by up to ten generations of travel.
18-22	Age of Technology	Invention of the warp-drive accelerates the colonising of the galaxy. Federations and empires are founded. First aliens encountered and first Alien Wars are fought. First human psykers scientifically proved to exist. Psykers begin to appear throughout human worlds.
22-25	Age of Technology	First Navigators are born allowing human spaceships to make even longer, quicker warp-jumps. Mankind enters a golden age of enlightenment as scientific and technological

progress accelerates. Human worlds unite and non-aggression pacts are secured with dozens of alien races.

25-26	Age of Strife	Terrible warp-storms interrupt interstellar travel. Sporadic at first, the storms eventually prevent any warp-jumps being made. The incidence of human mutation increases rapidly. Mankind enters a dark period of anarchy and despair.
26-30	Age of Strife	Human worlds ripped apart by civil wars, revolts, alien predation and invasion. Human psykers and other mutants dominate some worlds and these rapidly fall prey to warp-creatures. Humanity is on the brink of destruction.
30-present	Age of Imperium	Earth is conquered by the Emperor and enters an alliance with the Mechanicum of Mars. Finally the warp-storms abate and interstellar travel is possible again. The Emperor builds the Astronomican and creates the Space Marine Legions. Human worlds reunited by the Emperor in a Great Crusade that lasts for two hundred years.

About the Author

James Swallow's stories from the dark worlds of *Warhammer 40,000* include *Faith & Fire*, the *Blood Angels* books *Deus Encarmine* and *Deus Sanguinius*, as well as short fiction for *Inferno!* and *What Price Victory*. Black Flame novels to his credit include *Jade Dragon*, the Judge Dredd novels *Eclipse* and *Whiteout*, *Rogue Trooper: Blood Relative*, and the movie adaptation *The Butterfly Effect*.

James's other credits include writing for *Star Trek Voyager*, scripts for videogames and audio dramas. He lives in London and his website is

hometown.aol.co.uk/Redwingproject/main.htm